Purest Blood

by

Cheyanne Murray

First Printing, 2015
Website: www.cmurrayauthor.wordpress.com
ISBN: 1492725218

« CHAPTER 1 »

Steady rain fell through the canopy, sliding down the thick of her tensed bow and onto the wet soil below. The droplets also gathered on the brim of her hood and fell past her eyes, but now she was too focused to notice.

As she looked past her arrow, she no longer smelt the fresh pine nor rotting wood, nor felt the chill of the wind or the wet of the rain. There was only her bow, her working muscles, and the satisfying stretch of her bowstring. The arrow drew back - sliding across the shaft- and instinctively, she aimed.

Slowly, she let out a breath. Tension released from within her, and she drew the breath back in. Driven by her beating heart, her fingers itched to release.

Her first target lay just ahead, his back facing her as he looted from the woman he just killed.

Three soldiers in total. Child's play.

She let the breath out half way then sharply made it stop.

The arrow released with a snap.

Before she could even duck behind her tree, she heard the man fall with the rain. As he hit, mud and water splashed from the force, and only then did the other two notice something was wrong.

Quickly, they scrambled from their stolen treasures and into action.

She calmly let the breath out.

Two left now.

Again the archer readied her breath as she knocked an arrow. Like no more than a branch swaying in the wind, she slowly leaned out from the tree and took aim.

The two had their shields out and were spinning in some sort of crouched defensive strategy against an ambush of arrows. Round and round they spun with their backs to each other, seeming to hope to defect the oncoming assault. Their eyes squinted to see past the falling rain.

They would not see her in the thick of the woods. The archer was too still, and clothed too natural colored.

The next arrow flew and hit the man deep in the side.

'Ashes! A miss and a hit all the same!'

This time she did not hide. Her hand swept for another arrow.

Just as the man turned, following the line of fire and onto her, the arrow flew and hit home. The man's head flung backwards, and he smashed into the mud next to those he helped slaughter.

The last man was struggling to stand, the arrow in his side causing too much trauma.

He abandoned his shield to crawl towards the brush.

As he did, she came for him. She glided over to the fallen before the man could escape, and with the same dignity she would show a hunted deer, she knocked one last arrow. For a moment, she could see herself in the puddles of the road; a hooded archer distorted by ripples.

He kept crawling, making desperate glances back at her then to his fellow soldiers as if to will them back to life. When this failed, he flipped over onto his back so he could face her.

"Please." He begged suddenly. "Please don't kill me! I am worth far more to you alive."

Her lips drew up into a taunting smile at that, though she doubted how much he could see from the black of her hood. "Sir, you are worth the same to me dead."

The arrow flew, and the man slid backwards, and then was still.

For a long moment she just stood there; steadying her breath and heart while watching the rain mix the blood into earth. Then, she turned from the man and carefully put her bow safely away and out of the rain. She had risked it enough in the wet already.

Once done, she drew her hood up farther against the rain, and examined the fallen, this time without pity.

One woman, two men-five counting the soldiers-all laying with the earth.

The victims of the soldiers looked to be nothing but farmers on the way to town to sell some goods, but the soldiers cared not of innocence. In fact; they were paid not to.

With the coming war, the soldiers of the White Gryphon were a common sight and fear in the woods these days; and to make it worse, their numbers seemed endless. No matter how many were killed, more would simply spring forward to continue the business of stopping any sort of supplies from spreading throughout the kingdom; be that by killing farmers and burning farms, or taking supplies for their own such as with travelers as these.

Starve the people, win the war.

Luckily, this was neither her war nor her worry. The woods hid her from such dangers.

Her bow safe, she walked to the men and started scavenging. After all, the men would need them no longer, and nights were cold this far into the woods.

Fingers sorted through candles, flints, her own arrows, and various foods, but her hand stilled when it came across something cool and round from within a bag. With her occupation, she was more than used to finding things in the dark, but this was something even her skilled fingers could not pinpoint.

Clasping it, she hesitantly withdrew the mystery item from the bag. It was a metal orb, about the size of her palm, with the oddest markings she had ever seen. The markings covered the surface in lines and sparkled even in the dim light. She let her fingertips brush the surface, and a metal band spun upon the orb. She jerked her hand back in surprise.

"What...?" Her question trailed off, as the single word seemed as sufficient as any.

Five lines of markings for three spinning bands. Just what was this orb? Some sort of witchcraft from the eastern side of the mountains?

Just when the archer was about to investigate further something again caught her attention, and she reluctantly dropped her eyes from her find.

Inches from her boot was a strand of rope. It was long -frayed as if cut- and judging by the lack of mud, it was freshly done so.

Interest peeked and her eyes widened as she followed the muddy trail that lead from the ropes, and into the forest.

Whoever these men were, they lost a prisoner during the havoc.

Before she could investigate, a horse nickered, and her head snapped up the road.

More soldiers crested the hill, but this time with the sign of a sparrow. They called out in surprise at the bodies and urged the horses forward, but by then the archer was already gone.

Silently as a cat, she padded through the trees and into the thick, leaving the shouts long behind her.

The forest was her territory and like any home should, it hid her well.

* * *

"Oh, and Sellclie, make sure you tell him that if it's not done right away, I'll skin him myself!"

The assistant nodded, and hurriedly left the room, her long, silky, black hair swaying along her curves as she went.

Askyel Lochsell watched her with a smirk, his eyes trailing slim figure until his office door slammed shut, a little more roughly than normal, and with a grin he once more went back to writing.

Being notes of very specific details for very specific people, they had to be written perfectly. Some, heading to his favorites, were carefully encrypted in his own personal language, while others, heading to areas where most could not read anyways, did not have to be.

These things of his could only be done in places like this; with one door directly across from his desk, and thick wood and stone walls to hide his words to anyone that may be listening. The only light came in from the windows to his side, but those let in more than enough for the time being.

His quill carefully scratched away at note after note; stopping only to put one paper off to dry, and to grab another new piece.

Then, something made his quill still. It was no more than a slight breeze upon his skin, but none the less, his left hand ever so carefully reached under the table for his knife.

It was too late. Just as his fingers grazed the cool metal, something pricked at his neck. Breath catching, the criminal leader sat stiff in his chair.

"I would not do that, if I were you." A highly amused voice whispered in his ear, and he relaxed, but only slightly.

"Ah," He breathed, his neck convulsing in a hard swallow. "The princess of the king of thieves; Valerlanta. To what do I owe the pleasure of this unexpected visit?"

The knife removed from this throat.

"I need to know what a certain thing I found is." She said, as she rounded the corner and sat on the edge of his desk. She was partially turned away, but her eyes were only for him; they watched from the corner of her eye, and his own blue-green eyes watched right back.

Slight irritation was pressing his brows downward on his handsome, almond hair framed, face that most women loved to whisper cheek-reddening stories about. However, his irritation faltered as his eyes settled on her hands. Within them was a parcel wrapped in worn cloth, and she was holding it cupped in her palms as if it was a precious wounded bird.

A mystery item.

Leaning his head on his hand, Askyel tried to give a smile that she was sure charmed most women into giving all he wanted. "I am intrigued." He said, his tone more flirtatious then she preferred. "Not just anything can make you leave the woods."

Valerlanta shrugged it off. "I heard you were in town. Thought you might want a visit from an old friend."

"Friend?" Askyel took the item as she handed it. The round ball fell in his hand, and instantly she could see him calculating it's value simply from the weight. He did not even know what it was yet, and he was already thinking of selling. "Now that's an interesting word to use."

Carefully he removed the fabric, and a metal ball fell into his hands. His brows shot upwards in surprise as he spun it around.

A brass ball with five lines of lettering's, and three movable rings. It clicked with each ring he turned; seeming to line up the strange markings. They were not any letters she knew-not that she could read them even if they were - but he might have a chance.

Just like when she tried it for herself, a single ring he turned made lighter sounding click then the rest when two similar symbols lined up, but also like when she tried it, nothing happened from it. Could be nothing, sure, but on the other hand, it could mean that it lined up with the symbols above.

He kept spinning, hungrily soaking up each lettering.

Click, click, click, it sang one by one.

"What does it say?" She asked impatiently.

Askyel took a moment longer looking it over, then set it casually on the table before him and looked on at his trespasser. "Just who did you steal this one from, may I ask? It looks very valuable."

"What does it say?" She asked again, avoiding the question.

His brow rose up in a why-should-I-tell-you fashion, and a mischievous smirk broke onto his lips. She smiled back, though her eyes grew a little darker, daring him to play this game.

He seemed tempted, the corner of his mouth curling his smirk up a little wider, but he did not bite her bait.

Any other person he would, but never with her. Without a weapon, they were too evenly matched for his personal tastes, and he had too much to lose, so instead he sighed and pushed the ball away.

It rolled across the desk, and she caught it up into her hands to quickly put it away.

Valerlanta watched the greed wash over him as it disappeared beneath her cloak; hidden once more. She responded only with a calm motion of brushing her loose strands of dark blond hair behind her ear, her fingers felt the outline of leather on her face as she did.

"Well?" She urged.

He cleared his throat as if to also clear his disappointment.

"It is an old item, you have there, and I am sorry to say that it is much older than I have the pleasure of knowing to read. I can, however, tell you this; that is not human made lettering's. It is Elf-script."

At his words, the heavy weight came over her, than was suddenly lifted with a small realization. Her eyes lit up, and for no longer then a second, her eyes darted over to where she knew the forest was beyond the walls.

The thief knew exactly where to start looking. There was only one place in the mountains she know of left with elf history, though it was not one easy to get at, she knew where in her forest it was hidden.

She could do it. There was nothing holding her back, so why not?

She could search for treasure; just like one of those adventurers in the exciting stories told by the campfire.

"Val..." Askyel said a little darkly, his eyes looking on at her as if she were one of his crime ridden messages to be read. "There has been a lot of movement in the woods these days; movement from both sides of the mountains. They are searching for something, or someone, very important. If you happen to know what this could be, I suggest you heed this as a warning and avoid that mountain."

She laughed so he would know trying to convince her was a pointless attempt. The more danger there was, the more she would want to go through with this, and yet he tried? "I'm flattered, Askyel. I had no idea you cared."

He snorted. "Care? Perhaps not, but it would be a deep inconvenience to my spare time." He folded his hands on the table before him. "I do enjoy our games."

She gave him one final flash of a smile, and then jumped up as she heard the tell-tale steps of someone approaching the door.

As the assistance's hand no more than grazed the handle, Valerlanta was back through the window as silently as any cat. The door to the office swung open and the assistant stepped in moments later.

Sellclie saw the gang leaders gaze, and followed it to the open window, then back to the warn fabric still on his desk. "Was someone here?" She asked, her voice as silky beautiful as the rest of her.

"Yes, but thankfully this time it was not me she was looking to steal from." He mused, though mostly to himself.

This answer only seemed to make her all the more confused, but he was too busy tapping the end of his quill to his lips in thought to notice.

The thief Valerlanta gave one final smile from her perch then climbed back down to the dirt road below with ease. Once safely on the ground and out of sight in case her *"friend"* decided to send his men after her again, her hand dug deep into her bag and drew out a leather bound book wrapped in a cloth for protection.

It was from so very long ago, and was one of her first steals; and perhaps for some sort of sentimental value or something else, she had held on to it all this time. It was a children's book with tales from all over the land...or so she had been told. Not being raised with wealth, Valerlanta could not read the writings herself, but her father once read them to her by the light of their fire, and one story in particular stood out to her from that night.

Carefully she leafed to the page she wanted, and looked down at the familiar markings. Only one single letter at the top told her she was on the right page. The letter was surrounded with the peak of a fierce mountain with a tip of gold, and a crown to top it.

This was the place she would seek.

A place from fairy tales.

As Valerelanta sunk back towards the forests with the book in hand, she could not help but wonder if Askyel would miss the extra quills she lifted from his desk. She surely would not after she got a chance to sell them.

The thief put the quills in her bag, and soon after she left the black-market leader far behind, she was back. Back into her sanctuary, back into her home, back into the only place that kept her safe.

The forest.

Leaving it always made her feel uncomfortably naked, and the only way to fixed it would be to return. Somehow, the varied shades of leaves, the smell of bark and dirt, and the sound of light hearted song birds, all made her feel whole again. The forest changed that naked feeling to as if she were clothed in the warmest of blankets.

As the weight of having left the forest finally lifted, Valerlanta stopped at her camp only long enough to take it down enough so that only the trained eye would ever notice it was even there. It did not take long, after all, it only consisted of a forest made lean-to and a fire pit, but every step was important none the less.

The hardest to get rid of was always the pine boughs. She could bury the fire and sweep it over, she could scatter the dead fall she used as polls to hold her shelter up, but the pine boughs she used as a roof were cut from a tree. Anything cut was a sign of humans, a sign of her; so she carefully positioned them around a tree, far enough up to be out of sight, and in enough to look like any other branches.

By the time they started to whither, she would be long gone, so she only had to hope a trained eye was not on her trail. Any other soul would simply walk on oblivious of her visit here.

Once done, she did one final look over, then grabbed her bow and was gone for yet another part of the forest, and a new place to sleep. Like always.

As she went, she gathered various plant life along the way, some for meal, some for medicine, but this time something was clouding her mind, preventing her from the peek consideration she needed. It was the weight, not overly heavy but noticeably there all the same.

The metal ball, still there and safe.

The excitement of it made her check often to insure it's safety, even though it was a constant pressure on her hip, and whenever the trees would open like a curtain and allow a teasing view, the feeling made her eyes dart constantly upwards. Up and up her eyes went, until they stilled on the Illfain mountain; her destination.

The peek was always there, taunting her along the way and bidding her closer.

Valerlanta found the tracks she was looking for easy enough; they lead along the valley, and to the river where she found them. After confirming they were the same tracks from before, she followed them for a time to learn her prey.

From what she could tell from his prints, he was a normal sized man who knew little of the mountains. Last night when Valerlanta was sitting comfortably in her shelter next to the fire, this man spent it curled up under the branches of a tree with a stack of gathered berries that he very wisely chose not to eat. Good thing too, considering they were very poisonous. If he had eaten just one, she would have already come across his body.

He seemed healthy enough, from his walking stance, and moved with brisk determination.

And what was more, he was heading right where she thought they would, though in a round-about lost fashion to say the least.

It seemed Valerlanta was not the only one chasing fairy tales, this man too was heading to the very mountain mentioned in the story. Mt. Illfain; the harsh mountain hiding away the lost elf kingdom of one of the richest men this land has ever known, who simply disappeared during the purging of magic. Or so the stories said. They also said the castle was a gift from the dwarves, but if either creature ever existed was questionable.

Knowing she was heading the right way made her heart flutter with excitement, and it would have lasted too, if it were not for the next tracks she found.

Horse hooves pressed the soil, and Valerlanta knew just the shape. This was not a farmers horse shoe nailed on, it was directly from the castle itself; a soldiers horse. No two blacksmith created the same shoe, and these were the work of Hernthorn.

They did not quite follow the same path as the mystery man, veering off in random places as their tracker lost the prisoners trail, but was heading in the same direction.

This should have disheartened her, should have sent her away, but instead it simply made her want it more. Whatever this treasure was, the thief wanted it first.

And she knew an advantage; she knew a short cut.

* * *

After leaving the trees that stood lonely with their fire-blackened trunks, and entering parts where the trees again grew old and larger than she could even think of putting her arms around, the mountain she hoped for loomed high above her with its peeks high out of sight, as if caressing the golden rays of the sun. It looked like she was an ant at the foot of a giant.

Only just about to start her long path up, the thief heard the low mummer of voices.

Quickly, she ducked behind some leafy coverage, and ever so slowly, peaked out.

What she saw made her utter a soundless curse.

Soldiers -a whole lot of them from what she could tell- were hiding at the base of the mountains waiting to pounce on who ever came near; and being careless, she was nearly one of those pounced upon.

Thankfully, the thick brush and her unprecedented way of entry saved her.

Valerlanta could see a few of them, and heard the rest. Those closer were huddled in some bushes, and she could just barely make out the markings of the swallow upon one of their backs.

Alecaven soldiers waiting to ambush at the base of Illfain?

And just like that, her pouch felt all the more heavy. These were not the same soldiers she saw the hoof tracks off down the valley, these were a separate branch within the same army, but a very different branch all the same. This could only mean one thing; the king himself was involved. Only his word could control both men.

As she carefully slipped away, a sly grin grew across her face.

Yes. This would be a fun game.

The men knew their duties and only left their posts to relieve themselves. Otherwise, they lay where they were told; whispering quietly to whoever they were closest to.

She should go around; after all, there were not enough men in the entire army to circle the whole mountain, but this was the only part that one could climb, and she was impatient with excitement.

They never saw her climb the largest tree she was closet to, nor did they see her balance across a high branch, and right onto another one. With well-practiced ease, Valerlanta ignored the men directly below, and walked upon swaying barked limbs. Her steps caused the branch to creak gently like an old man, but luckily her slow steps made it sound like nothing more than the wind pushing them to groan. This skill -while mixed with her earthy toned clothing- made her nothing to notice.

When she ran out of branches and her feet finally hit the soil, her body knelt low, knowing a human shape would be first to be spotted. Then, carefully, she made her way forward.

The thief could hear the men rustle then relax as they changed positions and stretched their stiff limbs, but even though her ears strained for any more unpleasant surprises she heard nothing else to cause worry.

Best she tried, Valerlanta heard not a soul but those now behind her, and saw none either. There were only the men at her back that were risking her chances of reaching the mountain.

She carefully brushed branches away, and assisted their swing to stop them from snapping backwards as she went. It was like an odd dance, hand in hand with nature as leafy arms lead her onward.

A solider mocked a bird call from behind, startling her.

There was movement directly beside her.

Her eyes jumped in that direction, only to find a squirrel nestled comfortably on a swaying branch.

Another mock call and...

Valerlanta was back behind the safety of the brush, and starting her climb. As she went she could hear the soldiers starting a ruckus behind her, finally catching a fly in their nets but not even knowing that one already slipped through.

And so, she started to climb, leaving the soldiers, and whoever was unfortunate enough to be caught, far behind. At first it was manageable; a steep upward slant that she was more then used to from her life in the wilds, but then the higher she went, the more troublesome it became.

After sleeping under the deadfall of a fallen tree, by the following mid-day, she was working her way up on all fours due to the steep slant of the terrain, grabbing onto plant life as leverage as she went to keep from sliding back, then the plant life all but disappeared and only rock remained.

Her hands and feet worked in sync, one holding on while another looked for a new place to grab.

Soon she wished she had packed a little less as the bag seemed intent on pulling her backwards in a way that made her stomach lurch. But it was too late now. Now the only way was up.

No more handholds on her side.

Carefully, her eyes looked rightward, and saw what she was looking for. There more than enough a few steps away, but to get there she would have to go without the use of her hands at all. Between was only a small ledge, just barely big enough for her toes.

Reading her breath and trying to calm her scrambling heart, she counted down from three.

Three.

Her muscles strained as she sifted ever so slightly.

Two.

Her breath quickened with anticipation.

One.

She slid her way sideways and felt her hands come free. Quickly she stepped onto the ledge. Her hands slid along the rock, and for a second all she could notice was that same stomach lurching sensation as her pack willed her backwards.

Without a moment to lose, her hand snatched the handhold, and she scrambled to safety.

Pressed against the rock, she fought to breathe and just focused on holding on even though her limbs shook with adrenaline.

She waited for her limbs and breath to calm, and then continued to climb, and as she went, the rock got colder and colder under her fingers. Soon, as her limbs began to ache, she saw why. As she climbed, she saw a little ledge of white; the first of snow and ice.

A frown overtook her smile. Valerlanta did not like the cold, and she liked the snow even less; she spent too many cold winters to have fond memories, but still she climbed.

It seemed like every time she reached a ledge she thought was the top, she was only to find out there was another towering above her. Tired, the thief reached one of these places that tricked her and stopped to pull on her warmer clothes, and to toss anything unnecessary from the bag. Once done, she started the climb again.

When she neared what she thought was the top for sure this time, Valerlanta found herself in a world of white as clouds clung around her. Like fog, it misted her clothes and chilled her to the bone.

Then finally she reached it and pulled herself over. Snow greeted her face as she simply stayed there, fighting to breathe. Lying until she could bare the cold no longer, she gathered the courage to look around.

The thief was at the top of a crumbling staircase, and in front of her was a castle stilled for eternity in ice and snow.

A long white stream of white breath escaped her mouth as she viewed upon the most marvelous architecture she had ever had the privilege of seeing.

It started with a set of doors that could have only be built with giants in mind, as it towered as high as any tree she had known, and continued inward into the mountain. Planes of glass every so often emerged from the rock, making the castle seem all but hidden until the gaze continued upward and towers upon towers reached skyward.

Squinting, she tried to follow them with her eyes upward, but they disappeared behind white; as if being swallowed up by the sky.

Never before had Valerlanta felt so small, so fragile, and for a moment all she could do was simply stand and stare out at the wonders before her.

This was the work of the past, and it was beautiful.

A part in her heart wanted her to stay longer, to take in every detail, but the cold was not willing to compromise, and already she was starting to feel the effects of being still on her hands and feet. Then, as if the chill was not enough motivation, as her eyes glanced downwards, they caught the most unsettling sight.

Prints marked the snow and ice, and they were not human.

"Dragon." She breathed out in a white stream, and her heart began to race. Instantly her eyes searched the skies for any movement, then the surrounding rocks. Just like a mountain lion, a dragon adored to catch prey by surprise; especially from behind.

Valerlanta saw nothing. The dragon was either hunting, or already inside.

Excitement washed over her like a cool wave, and sent chill down her spine and her hairs on end. This was perfect; this was exactly what she was craving.

"Stealing treasure from a dragon now, Val? What a story you are creating!" She breathed to herself.

As she got up while rubbing her hands together, Valerlanta was suddenly glad for the warmth of her leather mask. It blocked some of the bite that came from the cold wind swirling off the ice.

"Right then." She breathed. "Time to go."

And so she went, into the doorway a giant would gladly fit through, and into a frozen world.

Inside the architecture was just as stunning as it was out, and sparkled like diamonds from the layers of ice. Icicles hung from the roof and chandeliers, and some even hung from a golden large statue of a forgotten king. He was elf kind, that was apparent, and had mean, piercing eyes that looked out from the visor of his armour. Though it was not the eyes that made a shiver rush down her spine, it was the fact that all the gold jewels decorating him lay still intact, as if he were still protecting them.

Valerlanta fought back the urge to risk taking some, and continued on.

Her feet slipped every so often as she went, forcing her to walk against the wall, but sometimes all the snow and ice would disappear altogether, making it seem like a servant or two would simply walk down the hall at any time.

Down the hall was sky reaching windows, some broken and left with piles of snow, others casting a glow of colors all around. They depicted a tale of some sort involving a knight and an evil tree monster, but the last of the story was lost in broken glass.

A door was slightly open off to the side, so Valerlanta tried to push it open, but it hardly budged. Putting her shoulder into it, it finally scraped open across the icy stone, and the thief slid herself in. Inside was bedroom like none other she had ever seen. Frost crept in from the window and door, but if it melted, it would look as if the room was still being used. A slightly aged canopy elegantly draped over a bed, and a rug crunched with ice under her feet. Stepping forward, Valerlanta neared the bed and pressed into it. It was cold, but still soft enough to dip in under her touch. Where the thick quilt skimmed the ground, she saw a little white strain of fluff upon the floor.

A feather? In here?

Lifting the thick quilt, she found another one peeking under the ties of the mattress.

A feather; the bed was stuffed with feathers. She did not think even she had ever hunted enough for that many feathers.

Turning away, the thief found a tiny crystal tree with twisting roots and a delicate canopy sitting on a table. Tapping it with a light finger, the canopy spun slightly with the chiming of leaves. Valerlanta had never seen anything like it, but it was not what she had come here for, and something told her that taking more than what she set out for would end badly.

Reluctantly leaving the room, her soft steps continued down the hall.

The path lead deeper into the mountain, and while it should have been growing colder, it was not. At first she thought it was just a trick from being out of the wind, but then she realized she could almost take her gloves off.

Soon the thief turned to a hallway too dark to see down. For a long moment she stood hovering between the light and darkness, hesitant to enter. Least she would want is to run into the dragon without knowing it was there, but at the same time, if she lit a torch she might alert the dragon all the same.

Then as her eyes adjusted, Valerlanta saw it. Down the hall, a light flickered.

Instinctively she wanted to look away, thinking it was a will-o-the-wisp trying to lead her astray like in the stories, then she reminded herself that she was no longer in the forest and they could not work their magic here. So, sucking in a breath, she stepped into the darkness.

The thief tried to make her steps as delicate as possible.

When she finally made it to the other side, startled by a wind gust but all in one piece, she pressed herself against the cold stone wall, and peeked around the corner. Inside was the most beautiful room she had ever seen. Large pillars circled the room, meeting at the top where there was a complete ring of windows that were shaped like none other than she had seen. Somehow they looked...bent, and directed the light specifically onto parts of the floor.

The floor itself was tiles of white and gold swirls, but what was left of them was covered in large piles of goods. Some riches that could easily buy a herd of horses while others nothing more than shiny metal. All of this lead up to two thrones; grand and elaborate.

Was the dragon somewhere inside? She could not help but wonder.

Valerlanta was only just about to test this theory, when she felt something press against her spine.

The thief felt her heart skip a beat and her muscles tensed all over.

"Do not move." A voice whispered fiercely. "Not one step."

« Chapter 2 »

Valerlanta felt the prick of the sword as it pressed into her back, and realization of danger came crashing down upon her with throat-clenching fear.

Behind, she heard his breaths, laboured and angry as if he had ran the whole day trying to get away from something.

"Who are you?" The voice urged. "Why are you here?"

Ever so slowly, Valerlanta turned her head to glance over her shoulder, but the sword poked at her hood and forced her head forward again.

"Do not move. I will not repeat myself again." Something in his voice put her on edge; it was a sort of angry desperation. A dangerous mix. "Who are you?"

And for a moment, the thief did what she was told. She did not move, she simply stood there, hands up in surrender, and an aggravated sigh escaping her lips.

She was pinned between two dangers, and neither were in her favour. However; the only way to see how far one could go is to poke a sleeping bear, so again she turned her head, and luckily, he did not chop her in half for it.

It was indeed a man, a well-toned youth with broad shoulders, a worn expression, and a little above average height. His almond hair was cut shorter than most court men; not nearly long enough to put back, but enough to have wavy almond strands brush past his piercing eyes.

Upon him was the leather armour of a knight. Of course the metal battle armour would have done him better up here, though she could understand why he failed to carry it all this way.

Unless, that is, he never had the metal to start.

Even in the dim lighting, she could see the dark circles under his bloodshot eyes. His whole body shook with either determination or fatigue.

Suddenly the thief had little doubt that if she checked his wrists, there would be red markings upon them.

"And what, sir knight, do you plan on doing if I fail to provide such an answer?"

The knight seemed confused either by her reluctance to answer, or the femininity of her voice. "Lower your hood." He snarled at a whisper. "Do it now, and tell me your purpose here."

She thought about it. She considered doing as he ordered; lowering her hood, showing her all too female features and watching his expression change from ruthless to heroic as he jumped to save the obvious damsel in distress, but there would be neither fun nor gold in that. So instead, she reached to her hip, her movements masked by the shadows and her cloak, brought out the metal ball, and watched as his expression changed from confusion, to downright horror.

His hand reached out to snatch it away, but she spun about and held it out of his grasp.

"Give it back!" He wagged the sword between them threateningly, but it only made her smile. She knew who had real control now.

"Give it back?" She said, mocking his strict tone.

Her feet were right at the corner now; teetering between light and darkness.

"Yes!" The sword dug into the folds of her elk skin jacket. "Give it to me! Give it now."

She gave another smirk, and stepped backwards. Light shone upon her, and the knight cringed accordingly.

"Come back here! Right this instant!" He said, though his words were all the more quiet now, as if it were easier for the dragon to hear voices whispered into light. His hands waved her wildly towards him, back into what he thought was safety.

Instead, she simply shrugged and shook her head; as if to tell him she had no idea what he was saying at all. In doing so, her hood fell back a little from the shake, and the knight's eyes widened.

He only waved at her all the more ferociously, his hands moving back and forth like a fish out of water.

Content her little knight was too afraid to follow; she gave him a wave with the hand holding the metal ball, and sprang away, into the dragon's lair. Though, she would have liked to have stayed to watch his face.

Valerlanta had no way of knowing if the dragon was in or away, only that she could not see it. She did not particularly take time to study them; unless you count hiding under a tree huddled like a rabbit avoiding a dinner plate while one flew over head "studying," so she had no grasp on the habits of such creatures.

Well, no matter. It was too late for that now.

The room arched high, and the room wide, but still, she saw no dragon.

Unless it knew she was here and it was smart enough to hide...

Without warning, her feet rooted to the ground unmoving with a moment of fear at that thought. Then, after a few deep breaths, she was able to shake it off and continue; though her steps had grown much more hesitant, as if Valerlanta was stepping into icy waters and each step froze her a little further.

Her exploring ventured opposite of the throne, edging around the various items in the pile of shiny things. Armour, weapons, even silverware, all seemed to be a treasure worth more than gold to this creature, even though they were only mildly expensive to humans; but they were not what she was hunting for. No, she craved for her item like a wolf craves flesh. The urge to find it burned within her, and she knew without a doubt that her greed would lead her to it. Although; as much as she hated to admit it, Valerlanta knew she had to plan something, otherwise she might end up as a tasty snack after a meal of cattle.

The thief had the bronze ball, she found where it came from, and, well, that was pretty much where her plans lead to. So quickly as she dared, she skirted around a pillar, and stayed for a moment hidden behind it's cold stone as she peeked around for clues.

The center of the room held the thrones sitting upon a round platform, then was the pillars rounding that, then the walls, then the reaching windows above.

The thief was looking for something of value; something elfish- which was stating the obvious in an elf castle- the hard part was trying to figure out what thing of value she needed.

It would have to be old, and maybe a matching pair with the ball. It would be valuable; perhaps something the king would have wanted to show off to his subjects; somewhere for everyone to see. Naturally this would be the best room for that; as anything beyond that was too private for lower ranking folk to venture, so not nearly good enough for gloating. Theoretically, something such as that needed to be somewhere most everyone would look when in the room.

Carefully Valerlanta tried to picture it. Entering the throne room, bowing before entering, taking some steps -eyes cast downwards of course- then you kneel at the king wanting to look anywhere but him. Even a glance at the feet would seem to risky, so you look at the ground in front of you, but that makes you feel too small, so you look to the side and...

No, not there.

Business done and plenty insulted, you bow -walking backwards of course- bow again, then turn and give your eyes the freedom they deserve. You look upwards...and there! On the wall above the doorway!

Carefully Valerlanta snatched a quick glance around her hiding spot to investigate.

Beautiful stonework arched up the door way in delicate vine-like swirls that would match the clouds outside in detail. Up and up they went until meeting at the top, and drawing your eyes directly to a glimmering sword.

It was a weapon matched only in dreams. The blade-although it should be aged- was shined to perfection; its surface reflecting like a pool of still waters only to be disrupted by the odd ripple of letterings making their way halfway down its length. She could not tell for sure from the floor, but on first glance, it indeed looked like the same lettering that circled the puzzle-ball.

Where sword met guard, a cascade of layered metal, just like dragon scales, made it all connect seamlessly. The guard emerged from the scales like wings, and the handle was clothed in some sort of silvery white fabric. The pommel topped it all off with the elegant grace of a metal tear drop shape.

It was a sword like none other, and she wanted it; which is why it only made sense that it would be locked. A thin chain wrapped it like a dragon's tale, keeping it safely on its stand against the wall. To add to the heart break, a lock hung from the chain as if to taunt any on lookers with what they could not have. Valerlanta, on the other hand, simply took this barrier as an amusing challenge.

Nothing could tell her what she could not have, and if they did, well, she would just have to steal it from them and have them pay to get it back.

But was this worth the risk of both knight and dragon?

Glancing away for a brief time, the thief tried to consider it, but somehow the sword was able to drag her eyes back in several small greedy glances. As she tried to avoid it, her hands itched out of desperation just to touch the cool metal in a way that no rubbing would stop.

She needed it to be hers.

It seemed exasperating after her long climb here, but none the less she wrapped her hands around the pillar, thankful for its fancy designs giving her something to grab, and pulled herself upwards. It was easy enough from there, just like climbing a tree.

Once she reached the top, she simply had to grab hold then swing hand over hand across the stony rafters with her feet dangling, with all the while the strange sword coming closer.

At her best attempt, she tried not to notice how the temperature near the ceiling was uncomfortably warm, and despite how she willed it not to, sweat began to gather on her hands. Somehow the rock dust seemed to help with that, but only a little. She had not thought it would be too much of a problem, but then she ran out of roof designs, and the only thing between her and the door way was empty air.

"Perhaps you should have planned all the way to the sword, Val." She said under her breath, then, with her hands side by side, she started to sway forwards and back upon her already slippery hands.

Swing after swing, grip came more and more off the stone until she was hanging by only her fingertips.

One last swing and her fingers came free. Her arm and legs swung through the air as she was catapulted forwards.

Her breath caught, her stomach leaped, then pain, and the feel of her fingers as they frantically wrapped around the door frame and held her there. Abruptly, it hurt to breath, and she made a mental note to not jump into a wall again.

Pulling herself up onto the frame, Valerlanta found it just wide enough for her feet to stand on. Her fingers found a hand hold in the brick, and she paused to catch her breath.

The sword was beside her, so tantalizingly close that it took every inch of her will power to not touch it. Somehow, it was even better up close; never had the thief ever seen a metal that reflective.

Just when she was about to reach out and gain her reward, she found herself startled by a shuffling movement, and her hand stilled as her eyes shot downward.

The dragon was still seemingly still away, but the knight had made an appearance below. It was such a graceful entrance that he was struggling to stop a spear from being knocked off the wall it was leaning on and onto the pile of treasure. Thankfully, he saved them both from the loud clang that it would make, and set it silently on the ground instead.

Valerlanta let out the breath she was holding, and allowed her eyes fall back onto the lock. It looked to be well made, the best a king could buy, but she was a thief; and what kind of thief would she be if she could not pick a lock as old as this?

As she reached into her pouch for what she needed, the knight had worked up the courage to look for her again. He was trying his best to step silently as he walked, and he was doing a fantastic job at it for someone not used to the sort of thing, but his body waved back and forth as he walked just like a bird. He bobbed his way along the room, and it took everything for Valerlanta not to snort.

It was like watching a chicken trying to sneak up on a bear.

Shaking her head, the thief started picking the lock. It was very careful work; part knowing the lock, part using the ears, and mostly having careful fingers that could feel the slightest change in texture.

A little bit farther, a little more of a twist, and it clicked open. A new record for her, she thought.

There was a little bit more of shuffling as she figured the knight had scoped out where she was, but by that time she was pulling the chain off, stuffing it in her pack to keep it from making a sound, then taking the sword from its stand.

It was far heavier then she expected with its dainty designs, but somehow weight felt expensive as it lay in her hand. She saw her own eyes reflect in its silver, and instantly, Valerlanta was struck with an overwhelming desire to examine it more, but she had a dragon to avoid, so instead she swiftly-though reluctantly- belted it around her hips with the sheath, and looked for a way to the ground.

She found one quickly, as the bricks were inset enough for her to climb just far enough down to drop without injuring herself. As her feet touched the ground, she gave the knight on the other side of the room a victorious smile. He accordingly gapped at her from the pillar he was just about to climb, and again waved at her like a flopping fish to stay where she stood.

Naturally, she turned around to leave, to escape with the treasure long before the chicken-walking knight could even make it out of the room, when her foot banged a goblet and it clattered across the floor. Valerlanta winced as the loud noise of metal-on-stone echoed throughout the castle, but where it went was much worse.

It rolled into the dark of the hall, and to the claws of the dragon as it took the last stalking step out of the hallway towards her.

The monstrous creature stared down at her with its cat like eyes.

Its throat started to rumble and its breath grew hot on her face.

Valerlanta instinctively dove to the side before the teeth could come down upon her.

The thief could feel the wind of the beast as it went over, and as it whipped back towards her with the speed of any snake, she dove behind the nearest pillar and again just missed its teeth.

Her back pressed the cold stone and fear clenched at her chest while the dragon snapped its jaws at her again and again, biting away chunks from the protection she had no choice but to keep ducking behind. The ground rumbled with its strength and stone flew.

She was trapped, and soon she would have now where to hide. The pillar would not last much longer.

Panicked, her fingers felt for her arrows. When she finally grabbed hold of one, she was forced to duck around the pillar again to escape the snapping jaws filled with unnaturally sharp teeth, and the arrow fell from her fingers and clattered across the stone floor.

Gasping, she reached down to snatch it up, but she was too slow. The dragons head rounded the pillar, and went for a meal.

With the speed like none she had ever seen before, a blade shot forward and sliced the beast across the jaw. In one startled moment, it recoiled, and that was all the time Valerlanta needed to knock an arrow and fire.

The arrow sped through the air, and landed deep within the first weak spot she saw, the eye.

An ear piercing screech rang out, and while the dragon whipped its head back and forth in pain, both knight and thief ran.

She felt the ground rumble beneath her feet. The dragon was chasing a meal.

Abruptly, as they bolted down the halls, there was a crash enough to shake the stone walls and a tail shot far over top of her and shattered the last of the intact glass story. Like some sort of tragic ending, the glass knight fell with the monster he fought in a shattering rain of colored glass.

As the dragon recovered from skidding into the wall, the glass came down upon them.

Her hood blocked most of it, and the rest was thwarted by her hands shielding her face protectively.

The glass hit the floor, and the chase continued.

In no time, both knight and thief darted out of the castle as fast as their legs would carry them.

The knight was now a fair distance ahead, and her just after. Her feet slipped upon the ice as she went, but she did not fall.

Without warning the knight stopped, and Valerlanta smashed into him, nearly toppling them both over the cliff. On the tip of his toes and glancing to the far drop below, the knight swung his arms managed to catch his balance.

The cliff; she had forgotten about that.

It was then they both turned back in time to see an ancient monster burst outside.

As instant as it shot out, it stopped, staring them down as they stared right back. Its head sunk low, letting out a threatening grumble in a challenge. It was not used to taking on prey face-to-face, so it appeared to be judging them.

The knight raised his sword in response, and Valerlanta took the moment to duck behind him. A human shield was better than no shield, after all. She hoped at least this way it would give her time to knock an arrow.

Her hand slid back, reaching the comforting feel of her bow, and as she moved, the dragon watched her with a lowering head and a hiss. It started walking, pacing in a half circle in front of them, it's one good eye was fixed only onto the thief.

That's when she realized it; this dragon knew her secret; it could smell it, that's why it was hesitating.

It watched her as it would to another dragon; it was judging a threat.

When they failed to move, failed to impress, its head raised in confidence and its mouth curled back in a large toothy smile. As it did, smoke slithered out from between its teeth.

"Ashes." Valerlanta muttered in her odd little swear, and from behind the knights back, her hand moved from her bow, and onto her glove. Her arrows would do no good here, not if the dragon did what it was hinting to. Even if she shot it dead, it might just topple them both over the cliff in the process. She needed something it would not expect, something to still it.

She removed her glove.

The knight shot her a look, but it only lasted a second as the dragon once more demanded attention. With ease, the monsters claws grinded into the ice and as its muscles tense to burst the flames in its belly as it prepared to lunge, Valerlanta called on the magic.

Her hand glowed a faint blue, and an unsettling cold started to fill her, as if a bucket of icy water was slowly being poured within her.

She would not have much time.

The cat like eye narrowed with understanding and the dragon charged and before the shocked knight could stop her, so did she.

It roared, opening its mouth wide to swallow her whole.

Monstrous jaws came down upon her.

At the last minute, Valerlanta dove and let the ice take control. She slid across the slippery surface, feeling the thunder of jaws come down inches behind her.

Her hand trailed after her as she went, leaving the same blue glow behind her that lit up her hand as it touched the cold ice.

Unfortunately sliding to a stop under the dragon's belly, a clawed hand swiped her way. Without a moment to lose, she rolled out from underneath, and with one final burst of magic, she slammed her glowing hand into the ice.

The reaction was instant. Ice waved to life all along the blue line, and with no warning it pushed upwards in the form of spikes.

The dragon howled a horrible ear piercing screech that forced Valerlanta to cover her ears as she tried to stand up and get away.

Although the magic was now released, the cold effect remained. It made her stumble for her first few steps until she was able to get her footing again. As she did, the dragon recovered and moved violently, shaking the ice away as if it were merely a little dust. The ice was not strong enough to penetrate its scaly armor.

Just as it took a threatening step towards her, the ice groaned.

"Oh." Valerlanta said as the knight joined her. He opened his mouth to ask what was wrong, when the ice popped and answered for her.

It started with simple sounds like an aching old man, then cracks began to appear. They snaked their way along the ice, and as they did, the cracking became much deeper sounding, much hollower.

Valerlanta and the knight exchanged worried looks, then instantaneously ran. Their feet skidded across the ice as they went, but as the ground started to tilt, they had no time to worry about slipping.

The dragon pounded after them, and as its heavy weight moved, that's when the ice began cascading back like a waterfall.

The thief saw this over her shoulder and swore. Faster and faster she pushed herself; her legs begging her to slow as the ground pulled backwards.

The world slanted skyward, but she did not stop. Her feet pounded into the ice, and at that moment, she found herself suspended in air. Her jump took her off the ground, and her arms reached for land.

Ice fell behind, taking the dragon with it. The ice spikes had not been strong enough to puncture scaled armour, but were more than enough to pierce wing.

Valerlanta hit the cliff. Her hands scrambled to hold something as she fought off the blackness invading her vision from the wind being slammed out of her lungs. She was suddenly torn between willing herself to breathe again, and the certain doom she was sliding back towards.

Her fingers finally caught hold of a chunk of rock, just a small thing half in ice, and her breath returned with a gasp. As her eyes refocused, it was there again; the silver gleaming tip digging into her neck, and preventing her from climbing upward.

Slowly she looked up, and saw the knight glaring right back at her.

"Give them to me." He ordered, his voice telling he was serious, but his eyes even more so. They pierced into hers as sharp as the ice she just wielded.

Muscles starting to shake with the effort, she knew she would not be able to hold much longer.

"Why?" She dared to ask, but it came out strained. "There is plenty of treasure left in that pile for you, knight."

"No treasure like what you have. Give them to me now, witch, or I shall let you fall."

"And chance wreaking what you fought so hard for?" She smirked, and her fingers slid back the smallest amount. "You will not risk it."

He looked her over for a moment, and that moment was all it took for her fingers to lose their hold and start sliding backwards. Valerlanta let out a gasp, her one hand moving for a knife to hold her in, while the other tried hard to hold on to nothing but ice.

Her eyes swept downwards, looking past her feet to the impossible lengths below. Rubble was still falling into the clouds below.

Something grabbed her forearm and stopped her fall.

His hand held her tightly, and his brows pressed together with the effort. Brown eyes stared into hers, and with her own eyes wide, the thief was roughly pulled half back up, and the sword once again pricked her neck.

Those eyes stared into hers with anger much worse than the dragons, as if for this knight, this was all just one problem after another.

"You know the forest, yes?" He hissed.

Valerlanta tried to ignore how her feet still dangled precariously, and nodded. "Yes."

"All the way through?"

Again she nodded.

Without warning she was yanked over the edge and tossed to the side much rougher than a man who just climbed a mountain should be able to muster, and he stood over her, his head held as high as any knight should hold it.

"You will lead me through the forest. Understand? And if you so much as go to utter a spell, or tip-toe the slightest bit away, I will have your head."

She could not help but hate that cold metal as it licked at her chin. She hated everything about it, and him. Knights, or even fake knights.

"What would be in it for me?" The sword batted her face in a threaten, but she snorted. "Knight, I am a female thief living in the forest, if you think that a man threatening me to do things will make me comply, well, you shall have to think a little harder."

He looked down at her, his face a mask void of emotion. Then, he smiled right back at her in a way that sent a chill up her spine.

"You will do it." He said with up most certainty. "You will do it because you want to."

She raised a brow in disbelief, and went to say more, but he leaned in and continued.

"You will do it because you want to know what those pieces you hold are for, and without me, the only person you have left to ask is the king. You will do it because you cannot help but wonder why so many want to have them. You will do it, because more than anything, you crave the danger and what riches might a wait you after. " His gloved hand grabbed her by the shirt, and pulled her so close, she could feel the warm breath of his smile upon her face. "If not, give me the sword, give me the orb, and simply walk away to prove me wrong. I will honestly allow it, just this once; though know you might not find me after."

He let her up then, pushing her away and allowing her to get to her tired shaky feet.

Her eyes darted back, looking to the forest far below, her home, that was calling her for a much needed sleep, then ever so slowly, no matter how she fought it, they slid back to the knight that could easily chop her in two.

He stood there, watching her with such certainty in his eyes that she wanted to punch it right out of him. However, as much as she wanted to prove him wrong, she could not fight the dark warmth of curiosity. And he knew it.

"You say there could be riches?" The words reluctantly came out, and as they did, his smile grew.

« Chapter 3 »

It was after a short rest and a reckless climb down that both knight and thief were back in the forest, and as entering it, Valerlanta was more tired than she could remember being for a very long time.

There, in a the thick of brush at the base of the mountain with not so much as a shelter, they lay down to sleep, though it did little good, as there was not only soldiers in the area to be weary of, but they also had each other to fear.

As the sun crept over the mountains and they were off again, carefully leaving the ice castle-and the soldiers at the base of the mountain- in the distance.

The thief reluctantly lead the way, and the knight followed behind her like a hunter would a dog; a hunter which insisted on telling her no more than "north" for a direction to lead him in. She thought this was a very vague description for someone looking to escape death, though maybe one did not need a plan to do so. Either way, not knowing did not seem to bother him in the least. In fact, despite everything, nothing-not even his many nights without sleep- seemed to even slow him down. He still allowed no breaks, and his hand flinched instantly for his sword whenever she tested how far away he would let her go. Somehow, he still had his wits about him even in his near dead state, and that alone kept her a prisoner to her mountain-top decision.

The knight forced her forward at a brisk pace, and she went grudgingly, but not without casting back a wealthy supply of glares. He seemed not to care, and simply kept her moving towards wherever it was he was expecting her to go. In truth, just for lack of a better idea, she had been leading him in circles for about a half day now. That, at least, she knew he did not notice, for her head was still nicely intact upon her shoulders.

Valerlanta simply could not decide if she made the right choice or not; or even if the wiser path would be to abandon all her things and disappear. She could survive without them till she managed to find one of her hide-a-ways where more supplies were hidden, but somehow the thought of leaving what she had now behind pained her like losing a friend; she had simply had them for too long. What was most important was the thief had no way of knowing if the reward of staying was worth the risk it would bring.

'I am supposed to be a thief, yet here I am, leading a man who has everything I own except for the clothes I wear.' Her thoughts told her. *'I have to get them back.'*

Even when they stopped for more water and she splashed the cold water on her face, her thoughts still lingered.

She did not understand it; why was he trusting her to lead him? It completely baffled her, and yet she did not want to question luck when it came her way, so she held back her confusion.

After drinking, the knight sat on a rock with a sigh, his hands finding the dragon-scaled sword on his hip and adjusting it from his spot beside him. His eyes flickered to it, then to his own sword as if comparing the two. True to her thought, he removed both from their sheaths, and with one in each hand, he compared the weight of them both.

His own sword was rather plain, but the sword from the castle was pure beauty. The white leather and mirror like metals seemed out of place in this dirty forest.

Looking casually at her boots the thief picked some burrs off the leather while pretending doing so was a very important task. "Are they similar?" Valerlanta asked in as uncaring a tone as she could make.

Even though she tried her best, he glared a warning shot, somehow sensing the curiosity bubbling within her. Still, he answered. "Mine is heavier, but they are made similar." He set down his own sword, and examined the blade of the new sword with his gloved hand. Lightly, he shook the sword, and the blade held firm. Next, he took a leaf and slid it across the blade. The leaf easily cut in half and floated down to the forest floor. "It's well made and still sharp. I have never seen a sword forged like this; it is like art. The leather on the hilt is something I know, though. It is stretched and polished leather from a rare type of seal; it is something only the royals are allowed to own and has been that way for as long as people know."

"The sword of a king?" She suggested.

"Yes, the sword of *a* king. That is the most likely case." He confirmed. "One that put up his sword for a reason; probably as a symbol for times of peace."

"Why a sword?" She asked. "What does it have to do with the other treasure?"

Much to her disappointment, he put the sword back in its sheath, then carefully wrapped it in his cloak to protect it, and tied it to the bag; her bag. "We need one more piece to find that out."

"One more?" She asked, feeling herself rise up with interest.

Pulling on the pack, and adjusting his sword, he turned and started towards the direction they had been heading. "Yes, one more piece for the final puzzle."

He looked at her carefully as she walked around him to lead; and she noticed his hand was carefully on his sword as she moved past.

"Although, the ball is not the real puzzle here. *You* are." He said, and Valerlanta stopped, only just ahead of him, and looked back at him. There was a challenge in his eyes that made her wonder which of the weapons she could grab first if he tried anything. "Not that I do not appreciate the help, the more I think, the more I worry. You see, you could very well have been casting some sort of spell on me for a while now, but that is what confuses me the most. You see, I thought for certain all the witches were driven over the mountains, but yet I saw magic with my own two eyes only just yesterday. How did you manage to escape their gaze? Is that why you wear a mask?"

'Witch.'

At the mention of that word Valerlanta looked at him like she would with any pesky fly that was buzzing around her ears; with the exception that she doubted swatting the knight would make him any more inclined to leave her alone. Irritation fluttered in her chest like a trapped bird.

"I am no witch." She told flatly, and saw the obvious disbelief on his face. "I speak the truth."

"Is that so? Now, it just might be me thinking this," His smile was so confident that she wanted to hit it right off him, "but personally, glowing blue hands just does not quite seem normal to me."

She frowned, but it was not at him, it was at the fact that *her* puzzle ball, was in his hand; and if that were not enough, he also had her bow, new sword, and everything else rightfully her own. He immediately noticed her discontent, and waved the ball tauntingly, and in a tad too familiar way.

Her fingers curled into fists and her glare became deadly.

The knight only snorted in amusement at her attempts at intimidation. "Well?"

"I am not a witch." She continued in a rather grumpy tone, perhaps a little too much like a child denied a tasty cake. “I am Valerlanta; daughter of the greatest thieves in the kingdom.”

He gave no reaction and she felt her mouth fall open. “I steal from your kind all the time! You really have not heard of me?”

The almond-haired man shook his head and she felt her heart sink.

Bubbling with disappointment, the thief continued. "Witches, for as far as I know, use dark spirits to craft their magic. I -on the other hand- use nothing of the sort. And besides; there have been no witches on this side of the mountains for hundreds of years, maybe more. I am not even nearly half than old enough to be from those days."

"And I am supposed to be inclined to believe this story?"

"You should know more than most. Your king must have gloated about it more then enough times."

"*Our* king." He corrected. "And yes, it is a widely mentioned fact that only the royals can wield magic, and yet, here *you* are; a mystery of magic hiding in the woods. If you are not a witch, then what could you be to allow such a power?"

She waved him off casually as she led them steeply upwards for about the third time; maybe more. "It's none of your concern. You are much too small minded to understand such things."

This time he laughed. It was a pleasant and natural sound that could only come from a man used to happiness. The laugh of a noble. "Oh am I?"

Now it was her time to feel in control let the corners of her mouth curl up mischievously, even though she knew very well she might soon regret it. "Well one can only assume such, as you are following a guide who you have yet to even tell where to go."

He stopped; his face paling. "So you *have* been leading us in circles?"

She rolled her eyes. "Ah, and he catches on. As you can see, sir knight, I am even less of a mind reader than I am a witch. Now I will admit, I am a fantastic guide -you really will not find one better- but even I am incapable of guiding someone without a destination."

With a flash of metal his sword was out, the shining metal between them once more. Valerlanta stared down at it with mild interest, feeling much more confident with it there while knowing that she could easily outrun the tired knight here in the forest if she so chose to.

The thief could see it now, the pale in his face and the face and the dark circles under his eyes of a man who had not eaten in days. If he wore rags, she might mistake him for a poor man like this, if not for the face of a nobleman. As he was, he lacked the long tangling beard or sore marked skin. Instead he had the stubble of a man who shaved recently, maybe three or four days ago, a strong chin, and apart from the odd visable scar, he had near perfect and tanned skin. Valerlanta supposed he would be fairly handsome, if he were not a knight.

Of course the sword between them was not what she would call attractive either.

'Perhaps, just maybe, telling him was not the smartest of ideas I have ever come up with.' She thought to herself as she eyed the blade.

"Do you know what danger we are in?" He snarled. "Do you realize these games could have gotten us both killed?"

She shrugged him off. "I am not so stupid to walk in the path of soldiers. I have been skirting them with ease; no thanks to your deep stomping prints."

"But you admit you came close! You risk me when a single question could have saved solved this?" He stepped closer, and she forced herself not to flinch. "Do you know how much you are risking with my life? Do you know the danger of all this? The lives of many rest on my survival and the success of my goal. Without me, they all die. All of them!"

Her lack of understanding only seemed to anger him more, and he screamed in frustration, swinging his sword at nothing at all before pacing back and forth. He continued this, and Valerlanta almost enjoyed it, if not for the watching of her things pacing with him. The thief looked on at her pack and her bow with the greedy wish to simply hold them again.

Her eyes trailed down to where she knew the prefect soft-spot in his armour would be. One stab there with his back turned, and he would bleed out without help

All she needed was a knife.

When he finally stopped pacing, the sword once more came up between them. "Lead me out of the forest."

"I need more specifics." She said, ignoring the fact that the tip scratched her across the chin as he brought it up. "The forest here leads to many destinations with a single direction."

He pressed a little closer so he looked down at her, and his normally warm almond eyes suddenly seemed as cold and dark as a raging storm. The stare sent a chill down her spine. "Lead us on trails they won't expect, somewhere safe. Head north; *really* north, this time. Head towards the Flantane Mountain so I know this time you really are leading us true."

"North?" She asked, realizing then that she was correct in her thought before. This knight had no plans for escape just yet. He was simply using her as a way to gain time over the soldiers.

His sword-tip nicked at her chin, and as it did, she winced to hide the moving of her hand, reaching to his belt. The knight made no reaction as she slid the knife away from his care, and up into her sleeve.

"North." He repeated. "And no more games; otherwise you might just find your head lost from your body."

The thief glared a little longer at the knight staring down at her, daring him a little further, then wordlessly spun on her heal and started to lead the way. She went a path of her own choosing, but north she went, for real this time.

Just as she hoped, she had at least discovered a little more about what she had gotten herself into, and had managed to steal a knife at the same time. Now she only had to decide how she would use them.

This game they were playing, the game of forest-folk, was a hard one. Every detail mattered; right down to the smallest print in mud or the slightest bend of grass. The thief knew she could not go without a trace with the inexperienced city-raised knight, but this was still a game she could win if played carefully. She lead him across the rock, and away from the fresh greenery or branches in their path, and ever so slowly, their rocky path lead them upwards. It was risky, going this way where a slide had cleared away all trees, but it was also a path with many means of escape.

Mountains loomed on either side of them, and before long, the fierce looking peak they just recently climbed started fading into the distance. Now they were following an old rocky mountain goat trail along the side of a steep fall, and an even sharper climb. The path itself was more than wide enough, but the way kicked rocks were smashed about among the boulders as they fell of the side of the path was more than daunting.

Her eyes shot towards movement in the trees below, but for the moment they saw nothing. Valerlanta told herself that it must have been a deer or a bird. Least she wanted to admit it, the desperate tone of the knight following behind her was making her more jumpy than necessary.

Why was he so nervous? What could possibly be so important about that sword? Was it really worth that much?

"Are all forest-walkers like you?" The knight asked abruptly, as if the question had been bothering him for some time.

Taking her time before answering, she first gave the forest below and behind them one last scan. She could see nothing in the thick canopy, but she knew there was something there; the forest always had a way of hiding things; be it animals or human. When she finally looked over her shoulder to the knight, she gave him a quick look over. He was against the rock beside him, his whole weight against it as an pitiful attempt to rest, and by expression, she knew he would soon need sleep. "Like what?"

"Alone, dressed in clothes close to rags. And where are your men?"

Now Valerlanta turned fully back to him and bit back a laugh. "My men?"

"Yes, your men." He said as if it should be blatantly obvious. "Your father, your brothers, your husband; your men. Do you have none?"

Now she did laugh, though not at his words, but at the way he blurted it out. "I have one man; a father."

"Then where is he?" He asked, clearly more than used to the lifestyle where it was a man's job to protect the women of his family, and not at all the place of a woman to wander about without anyone at all.

"In the woods, I would think, or maybe not."

"You do not know?" He raised a dark brow, the curiosity plain on his face. Clearly, she realized, he must not only be tired, but also bored to no end to want to ask meaningless questions like this.

"No, my father is not the type to follow me as I go. He would much rather leave me to my own skills to make me learn to manage on my own then with his aid."

"Sounds cruel." The knight breathed before taking a long swing of water from the spring she had found them just a little before starting this climb. She smirked at this, but would not be offended by the truth of his words, after all, harsh was her father's way. It made her stronger; it made her the way she was today.

"Without my father, I would have never had managed to survive this long. I might be without him, but I am stronger because of it."

Besides, his ways were never without kindness. She could still remember the times when he first left her alone in the woods. She was terrified by every sound, every whisper of the wind, every scrape of a branch, and would have spent her entire night crying in a small ball if not for catching sight, though no more than a flash of a man watching over her carefully the whole time without her knowing. He did this many more times after, and she pretended not to notice he was there as she tried hard to survive on her own to make him proud, and eventually he left for real, but he always came back.

He cared, just differently.

Looking back at the knight, she found him watching her closely with some sort of understanding in his eyes as if he had read her every thought. Startled, she quickly turned back to the path, about to start when once more, movement caught her eye and this time it sent her stiff.

Down in the forest, mostly shielded from the trees, she caught sight of a man, a solider, hurrying on the back of a horse through a break in the canopy. Like rats, where there was one solider, there was always more.

Instinctively she reached for her bow, but of course it was not there. Her fingers only met empty air, suddenly making her as if she were naked, and every leaf around her was a watching eye.

"What is it?" The knight asked.

"We need to take another path." She murmured, and took to rushing up the rock beside them. It was hard, with the sore muscles from the climbing they had endured recently, but she ignored it and made it to a ledge.

"Why? What did you see?" The knight asked, unmoving. He looked between her and the forest; his face a cross between worry and doubt.

"I saw a solider. There," She pointed to the break. "In the trees below. They are trying rush on horseback to meet us at the bottom. I know another way, but we must move very fast."

The knight hesitated, clearly dreading on trusting the thief on going any higher. Valerlanta could only imagine what he was thinking of, and most probably ended with her pushing him off the cliff. Which she would gladly do, if it would not lead the soldiers to her.

Not to forget that he would also have all her things with him as he fell.

"There will be treasure." He told, looking up at her on the ledge. "There will be riches beyond your dreams if you help me get to where I need."

He held her gaze for a long time, waiting for what he said to sink in. She knew he was silently letting her know that if anything should happen to him, she would miss out on a much superior prize.

"Come quickly," She urged, "You can tell me how rich I will be later. I will not be caught dragging about some stupid knight. It would make me the joke of the entire kingdom."

He hesitated a while longer, then scrambled with her up the rock.

It was a hard climb of loose and shaking footings, but thankfully it lessened in steepness as they went.

Reaching the top, she quickly led him down the other side where a log gracefully awaited them like a bridge. Actually, it was a bridge.

Smugglers walked this very path often, and used the bark covered bridge across the far drop to make a quick get away from any soldiers. Ropes held it still, but could easily be cut to ward off pursuers. After, it was simply down the rocky path -good for losing bad trackers- and back into the woods.

Valerlanta scrambled across it with ease and not so much as a glance below, but much to her amusement, the knight was not so swift.

"Across this?" He blurted, his dark brows rising at the log as moss shaken from her steps drifted down to the creek far below. "Are you mad?"

"Do you know another way?" She asked, and without one to suggest, he reluctantly stepped onto the log with a shaky leg.

"It's easier if you hurry." She sang back to the slow stepping knight. "Otherwise you will just hesitate and make yourself fall."

He shot her a glare, but regretted it as he nearly lost his balance. He caught it quickly enough though, and continued his slow foot over foot way across. Clearly, the weight of all his things and her own was putting him off balance.

His eyes looked down at the drop, and she saw his neck work a hard swallow.

As he went, Valerlanta scanned the area behind him, but so far saw no one. It would not be long, though, before those soldiers realized that they caught on to the trap and hurried to stop them.

"Quickly now." She urged, her amusement starting to leave her voice.

He grumbled something under his breath, and that's when they heard the shouts. The sound was not close enough to understand, but knowing it was human was more than enough to cause her to worry.

"Quick!" She hissed. "We have no time!"

His face paled, but he did quicken. His arms flailed about, and at the last minute he jumped the rest of the way. Instantly, Valerlanta cut the rope that was holding the log down, and then pushed hard upon it's bark.

The log creaked, but did not move. The recent rains had sunk it deep into mud.

"Come on!" She told the log as the shouts grew louder. "Move. Move!"

Suddenly there were extra arms beside her, and with his help they were able to push the heavy log over the edge. It fell with a clatter, and it was not until she turned, not until she heard the trees, the lack of birds, and the tracks at her feet, that she realized something was very wrong.

"Stop!" She screamed at the knight who was already a few steps ahead of her, but it was too late.

That was when the whole world went white, and everything hurt.

***

The first thing she noticed as the world started coming back into place around her was the fact she could hear nothing but a high pitched ringing. Although Valerlanta knew she should be hearing the soft tweet of distant birds, the rustle of wind caressed branches, and the shuffle of nearing footsteps, she heard nothing; nothing but that piercing ringing.

The thief found the strength to lift her heavy head, and what she saw filled her with a dull sense of panic.

The dust and dirt had started to settle, and from its depths came solders. They were not normal soldiers; she could tell that from first glance.

These were the hired kind. The kind only a selected few could afford.

Worst still, they were men she knew the faces of.

Askyel Lochsell. They were his men.

The knight lay only a few steps away from her with his head down in the dirt, seemingly unconscious or dead. No movement came from his limp body even as the men slowly started their approach.

The men neared, and her eyes focused on something almost within reach. Her bow was among a scatter of arrows.

Reaching out her fingers, they stretched and stretched towards it only to find it just beyond the tips.

She tried to ignore the coming men and pulled across the dirt as best she could, her fingers reaching and reaching, until her fingers grazed the cool wood.

Finally. Her bow was back where it belonged.

Men noticed her even through the falling clouds of dust, and called out.

Their forces ran towards her.

But they were too slow.

Finding sudden surge of strength, the thief clumsily burst up, knocking an arrow simultaneously as she went.

The bow raised, the men neared, and an arrow flew.

The first hit the closest man right between the eyes, giving her the time she needed to reach down for another. As the comforting shaft came between her fingers, another man neared with his sword held high, but once again he lacked the speed to strike.

The arrow shot from her bow and had him deep in the throat. That man to fell too, only to have more approach in his wake.

Again her fingers found an arrow and again she fired having another man fall, but there were too many getting closer, and she was running out of arrows. These men...where most would have ran for cover, these men were sacrificing each other just to strike her down. It was a terrifyingly inhuman reaction...and it was working.

Frantically she reached for another one to knock her bow with, and shot a man no more than a step away.

But the other one came up too fast.

With one swipe of steel, he knocked the bow from her hands leaving her with nothing.

The sword came up once more, this time with intent of finding her flesh.

Valerlanta dove to the side, the blade streaming overtop and only just missing her.

Rolling back to her feet, the thief tripped on root and tumbled backwards again. The blast was still affecting her balance.

The soldiers were mere steps away now, their faces contorted with anger at their fallen friends.

Panicked, she reached for something, anything, to protect herself but found only her knife.

The closest man raised his blade, the metal shimmering above her.

The blade came down.

With a ferocious clang, another sword was abruptly there, pushing the other away. They parted then met again as the knight stood over her and forced the men backwards. The knight was smaller and had blood dripping down his forehead, but was faster, and was able to keep the attackers a fair distance away so she could right herself.

Using this distraction to her advantage, Valerlanta stole the last remaining arrows from the quiver on his back then raced for her bow.

True to his title, the knight fought with astounding swordsmanship. His speed seemed like something of a dream as somehow he managed to ward off four men on his own.

His blade came up, and all other attacks were batted away with ease. He was not just good, but he was better than all the men he was facing.

However, despite how valiantly he kept them off, he could not just as easily bring them down. No matter how he attacked, another solider always seem to be there to block his advances. It was a game he could not win; he was the more skilled, but they had the more blades.

Without a moment to lose, she snatched up her bow. Thankfully, it was still in one piece.

The thief knocked an arrow only to notice someone on the out skirts of the battle she never saw before.

An archer.

As she brought tension bow, as did he with an odd sort of smirk on his lips. It was game to see who the better shot was.

Suddenly the knight was catapulted backwards by a miss-step, and his momentum was lost. As he tried to recover, the men came in as one just as the other archer aimed his bow.

She had little choice now.

At the last minute she rolled to the side, and the enemy arrow dug deep into the dirt beside her.

No time to spare, she aimed and brought the solider closest to the knight down. The knight gave her a startled look as the solider hit the ground hard. One enemy attacking the knight turned to look at her, and it was the last decision he ever made. The knight made sure he joined the other solider in the dirt.

Her bow spun back to the enemy archer, ready to fire, when abruptly there was pain. Her eyes fluttered wide in shock and her clothes grew alarmingly warm and wet.

The world swayed, the archer grinned in victory, and thief started to fall.

Her knee hit the ground, the world started to tilt, and in one final attempt, she steadied her breath, relaxed her grip, and fired her bow.

Both archers hit the ground.

Only one still moved.

Faintly she heard the battle rage on, but she ignored it as her hand gingerly trailed down to where fingers met warm blood and arrow.

It lay deep into the right side of her belly, somewhere between where her hip met torso. It was not good, but not immediately lethal. Luckily, it hit mostly bone, and she hoped nothing else.

Eased by that thought, she sat, readied herself, then shakily stood after two tries. Her leg begged to buckle, but she would not let it. If she still had time, then she refused to spend it laying in the dirt.

The world swayed as she put pressure on the wound, and then even once it steadied everything seemed slower, dream like even. Somehow, her legs now held strong, and though the thief did not know how much she had to thank to adrenaline, she did not want to wait to find out.

The knight was still fighting amazingly well, his back to her as he fiercely held the men off and took some to the ground, but like water through a broken dam they just kept on coming. Within seconds, they were surrounded by ten new and ready men.

Valerlanta and the knight found themselves back to back, both searching for a way out, but soon there was none. They were far from any sort of trees, and were on just a cliff of rock, so they had no good cover to shield them even if they did break from the circle of men. There were just rocks and more rocks.

Nowhere to go, very outnumbered, and she had only a matter of time before she bled out.

Valerlanta frowned deeply and called on the magic. Instantly she felt the tingle in her fingers and the chest tightening pleasure begging to be released.

She would need to call on the right magic, something not too strong, and even then it had the possibility of killing her at this stage. She was too weak and only getting weaker. Already her knees were slightly shaking even though she fought to hide it.

One of the men, perhaps the leader, was saying something, but she could not hear him. His head was raised high and proud, and she had no doubt he had power in his voice, but eerie silence of magic saw to overpowering that. It was like being stuck in a black cave, with no light, no sound, just the gentle caresses of magic as it told you over and over again that releasing it would feel great.

Since this was unfortunately not her first time in such a situation, the thief had little doubt the leader was going on about their many crimes to the crown and what their punishment would be.

The leader stepped back into line, finished his grand speech, and readied his men for a final attack.

Valerlanta felt the knights back press closer against hers as the archers bows raised.

Arrows slid along the shafts, aims were made, and while they waited for their leaders command, Valerlanta directed her magic.

However, she soon found she did not need to.

Just as both her and the men readied to release, a sudden downpour of air knocked many off their feet. All turned their heads skyward in time to see a great beast make a sloppy landing that shook the ground and toppled trees.

It lashed its tongue, raised its head, and stretched its tattered wings.

As it did, havoc broke loose.

Men scrambled in all directions, all but ignoring their leader's orders. Some men simply turned and ran, leaving their own behind, while others raced for a closer or farther position to strike from.

The dragons eyes narrowed on to Valerlanta, and she let the magic reluctantly melt away.

"Ashes." She murmured, feeling the blood drain from her face. It seemed she had made a rather large enemy.

Then it lunged.

Unexpectedly Valerlanta found herself being catapulted sideways, and the snake like jaws of the dragon sailed overhead and snapped up a misfortunate soldier behind her. Tilting its head upwards, the dragon swallowed the man whole with ease.

"Come!" The knight called; back on his feet from tackling her. "Now is our chance!"

He pulled her upwards, and with his help they both pushed through the tangled mess of soldiers who scarcely even seemed to see them.

The two dove behind rocks and slid across the ground to avoid the thick of the fight.

Arrows, and occasionally even men, were flying about all over.

The soldiers were fighting fiercely, but the dragon was cutting through them and smashing them down with a swipe of a tail or slice of a claw.

The men had a bigger thing to notice then two escapees.

"Now!" The knight called, pulling her from out behind the safety of a boulder and down the rocky cliff.

The way was clear, and the tree line nearing.

They could make it!

Without warning, a man stepped out in front of them from behind a rock. He had a blood streaming from his hairline, and a nasty wound darkening his side. The leader; probably carried to safety until the fight was over.

"I shall not let you pass." He said, though his whole body shook with the effort. "By the name of the king, I will not let you escape!"

Valerlanta could almost admire his determination, were he on their side. As was, he simply looked pitiful.

He neared closer, a blood drenched sword in hand, and the knight raised his own sword.

The leader bought his blade down with fierce determination, and the knight deflected it as if it were no more than a fly. The leader went to strike again, but the dark haired youth side-stepped away and sliced. The older man looked on at them, with wide glassy eyes, then crumpled to the ground with a final sigh of defeat.

The knight was just about to turn back, to tell her to get moving, when another man rounded the rock.

He was about to take the knight out.

Without time to think, a knife flew from her hand and hit home.

The knight looked behind him, startled, then back at her.

"How did you get that knife?" Was all he said, clearly forgetting that it was her who cut the ties on the log.

Valerlanta just gave him her innocent smile, however shaky it might be, and he sighed before snatching it back. "No matter, we must go."

And they did. With the battle clanging on behind them, they scrambled down the gravel and into the thick of the trees

« Chapter 4 »

As Valerlanta watched the sun streaming gracefully through the leaves above, she wondered if this was how she would die.

With the smell of fresh earth below her, and the feel of sun warmth upon her skin, it was all she could do but gaze at the wind tussle with the branches, sending the light upon them dancing in gentle beams...but then she remembered it could not be now. She still had things she needed to finish.

But the thief would not mind going in a place like this...

Warmth, smells of nature, and a beautiful view....

A new sort of warmth brought her from the darkness; the feel of hands on her shoulders. A cool shadow now blocked the sun's rays, and when her eyes fluttered open, the knight was there; watching down at her with a cold look that did not suit him.

Why was she here? For a moment it took her time to remember, but then his eyes made it all come back. Even the pain.

Valerlanta found she was sitting now, causing herself to have a kinked neck, but she was still breathing, so she could not complain.

The mental fog finally dissipated, and she slowly remembered. With her help, they were able to find a safe place to hide for a while, and sometime after that, she must have passed out.

She could feel the tightness of new bandages around her, but also the chill of fresh blood meeting air. The arrow, best she hoped it not to be, was still there.

As she tried to sort everything out, the knight sat not far from her, his sword flipping about in his hands as he examined all ends of it.

"How did you find the location of this sword?" He asked coldly without looking up, and the chill in his voice was enough to make that beautiful sword look heavy with danger once more.

This was an interrogation.

His eyes then left the sword and fell on to hers in a gaze that was more frightening then any blade. His desperation and anger was flaring brightly, and she did not like it.

She heard his leather gloved hand tighten upon the sword with impatience.

"I took a chance, a risk really." She found herself blurting out.

"A chance?" Then he was up, stalking closer, and she had nowhere to go nor the energy to try. "You expect me to believe you found the castle on a guess?!"

The blade found her neck, and she discovered how sharp it was. He was leaning in close, his icy eyes baring down on her as he pressed the blade against her skin and drew blood.

"Not a guess, a risk." She corrected in a gasp. "It was a risk of chasing fairy tales."

"Is that so?" He said with a tone of disbelief, and the blade pressed harder.

"It is." Her words came out in a gasp as her fingers reached and failed to grasp his boot knife. It was only just out of reach, taunting her.

"What tales might that have been? It is not one I have heard." He asked.

The thieves searching hand paused, but kept her face blank. "The story of the Brideless king?"

He gave no reaction.

"The king who would find no suitor worthy no matter what damsel was placed before him? The king who got lost in an enchanted forest on a hunt?"

Again he gave no inclination of knowing, and her suspicion deepened. "It's a common tale from Hernthorn, your neighboring kingdom."

"Our kingdom is now one kingdom." He lectured in a snarl. "There is now no kingdom of Hernthorn as they no longer have their king, but that does not give me need to learn children stories from wives and elderly."

"No, I suppose it does not." She said, flinching as the blade shifted upon her neck. Her breath shook slightly as she breathed out a long breath, knowing she had no choice but to give in now. "I think I have the tale in a book; in the bag just there."

"You think?" His words were daring dangerously for her to try lying.

"Yes, well I had someone read it to me a long time ago."

"You cannot read letters?"

"Only nobles are taught to read. However, as there are no letters on trees, up until this point, I have not needed the skill."

He tilted his head, almost questioningly. "So tell me, witch-thief, do you think your magic would save you if I slit your throat now?"

She tried to shake her head, but found that to be a bad idea at the bite of the blade deepened, so she answered and it came out shaky as her chin quivered. "N-No."

"No? It sure did a nasty job on me at the cliff."

"That was not me! That was Askyell and his men! They have something, a powder, it explodes! It is why no criminals can touch him. Just some of that powder, and no more than a lick of flame, and the whole area is lit up. I have not the energy, and even if I did, it does not quite work that way. I-I can ask something to help me, but it does not always answer. I'm not strong enough to fully control it. More often than not, it does the controlling if I am not careful and nearly kills me. It is why I try not to even touch it."

He scanned her face for any hint of lies, but seemed satisfied as he continued. "And the mask? Witch-thief, should I not just cut it from your face right now and see who you try to hide? Why would I not?"

"Because," She spat, majority of her fear melting away into anger. "I am not who is under the mask."

He raised a brow questioningly, and his eyes scanned the leather upon her face temptingly. But then, just when she thought he would reach up, remove it, and see what none ever saw, he stood up and the blade left her neck.

Gasping, she relaxed and gingerly touched the cut. It was not worrisome, but it was more than deep enough to hurt slightly and bleed only a little. As she tried to rub the sting out, she watched the knight as he strode over to her bag of things and started digging. This time, Valerlanta just barely was able to bite away the anger growing in her chest as she watched someone snoop through the only possessions she owned.

Soon after, his hand emerged again, revealing the simple leather bound book. Her first steal. It was nothing pretty, to say the least, just tattered leather and printed words, but even now her eyes lit up at the sight of it.

For a moment, she heard that father reading from it again as he did all those years ago. His children listening close, and Valerlanta too from her hiding spot. First, being no more than a child herself, she had thought it was some sort of magic that people were able to read out stories from its squiggles, but after she stole it and realized it had no powers-or at least none that she possessed-to make it tell her stories; and it was then the delicately drawn pictures at the start of each story that fascinated her. Compared to the sloppy slanting scribbles, they seemed unreal.

She got her own father to read from the stories once, as they sat near the light of the fire, but that seemed like a long time ago now.

The swordsman cleared his throat; startling from her thoughts and making her realize she was staring. He wanted something.

"What is it?" She asked.

"The page?" He asked, probably for the second time. All the anger in his voice had faded now, leaving only the faint tone of desperation.

She reached out her hand, and he gave it to her and she quickly, yet gently, flipped through the pages until she came to the crown-topped mountain. Reluctantly she gave it back, and watched as his eyes narrowed at her once more-carefully warning her not to try something that would prove stupid-then took to reading the page.

He did not read it out-loud, but she still remembered it well enough to know what he read.

It was a story of a brideless king who was deep in troubles. The kingdom mourned because no matter what fair damsel was placed before him, he refused them all, wishing to think only of the problems of his land.

You see, although he was a strong and wealthy solider, he was born into a world chaos. Magic ran rapid through the kingdom, and in those times it was much too easy for one to kill another. Everyone was at war.

Then one day, on a grand hunting trip with his men, he became lost in the woods while chasing a boar. He called for his men, but they seemed to be nowhere in sight, and then, while he waited there a hopeless mess, the boar he wounded turned into a beautiful elf.

Instantly he fell in love with her.

The king cared for her wounds in order to make up for the injury he caused, and as he did, she asked him what two things he wanted most. He told her he wanted to be rid of all magic in his land, and for her to be his queen.

The rest is mostly details, but in the end she fulfills his wish, all magic is removed from the land, and the king lives the rest of his days in peace until old age, when he is invited to live in the mountain top castle of the elves and live in bliss till his death.

When the knight finished, he closed the book and looked at her.

He was thinking there had to be more to the story to make her guess the castle, and he was right.

She knew what was left untold, and he could not. No one could.

He opened his mouth to say more when she gingerly brought her hand up from her side, and it came up red.

At the sight or realization of it, a soft warmth tried to fight its way over her eyes. She tried to fight it, but everything swayed. Eventually she pushed it off, and when her vision came to once more, he was standing watching her closely.

"The arrow needs to be removed." He said quietly, and she saw on his face it was true.

They could wrap around it, and cover it in yarrow to slow blood loss, but that would not fix the damage, only prolong her life...but on the other hand, if they pulled it out, she could bleed to death completely.

"Will you help me?" She whispered, as much as is pained her to say the words. This was not an average wound from the woods, and she was not alone. Here, she had a chance of removing the arrow while doing less damage upon bringing it out.

Without him she might die, with him she would have to swallow her pride.

He looked down at her for a long while, perhaps thinking of her stubborn choice that almost killed them both, or perhaps -even worse to her- he was thinking she would only be a burden as she was now.

"I will not slow you down." She hissed.

He hesitated, letting out a long sigh and running a hand through his almond air. Clearly he was unsure about the safety of this situation, but he still needed a guide. She clung to that hope tightly.

"And if I refuse?" He asked coldly.

Then she would die; bleed out maybe, or be found by soldiers and be killed in search of information anyway. She could try to do it herself; to fix her wound, but her chances of staying awake throughout it were slim.

He was her best chance.

"Then you lose your only chance of getting through the forest alive." She answered.

He looked her over a while longer, hesitating, then as if shaking his head in disapproval of what he was about to do, he agreed. "Fine. Lead us out. No more games."

She nodded, ignoring the pride screaming her to say 'no.'

He started setting out everything he would need. It was somewhat unsettling to hear his shuffling around her, so she tried to instead focus on her own breathing like she often did while shooting.

Breathe in and breath out. Breathe in, and breathe out.

"This is good?" He asked, holding up the needle and gut from her bag. She nodded and he went to readying it.

Breath in, breath out.

Suddenly his hand was there, with a stick in hand and urging her to put it between her teeth.

"I do not need it." She said, and he sighed and pushed it closer to her lips. "It is not needed!"

Reluctantly, he threw it away then positioned himself closer and looked her in the eye. "Ready?"

She nodded and flinched slightly as his hands touched the shaft. He looked at her again but she shook her head. "Take it out. Take it out now."

His grip readied, and hers tightened into fists holding nothing.

His muscles flexed, his breath sucked in, and that's when she panicked as she watched her life in the hands of a stranger.

"W-wait! Leave it in! Leave it in!" She called, but it was too late. Within an instant it came free, and she looked skyward as she clenched her jaw in a hiss of a scream.

As her vision blurred, then returned, the knight was setting to work to sealing it closed the best he could.

Carefully she tried to steady her breath and spinning head.

'No, Val, do not think of the pain.' She told herself. *'Thinking of pain will not calm the mind.'*

She had to think of something else, so she instead thought of the betrayal of a man she never trusted, but thought they had come to an understanding.

Askyell.

The thief let out a painful shuttering breath, realizing how thick this game had become, and it was at that time that the swordsman's gaze fell onto her face instead of the wound. He watched her carefully, as if deciding how long she had.

"Help me wrap it." The thief whispered, hoping he would not refuse. After all, if this situation were switched, she would.

He looked at her for a moment, and then nodded.

They had little time to make it perfect, so instead while she held the wound, he cut steady lines from her prized hand-made winter coat. Then, with hands as steady as any healer, he wrapped it tight. She gasped in pain, her hand finding his shoulder for support, but she tried hard to think of other things. To think of her goals.

When he finished, again he looked her in the eyes, judgingly.

"I will not slow you down." She said again, confidently; though she was sure her face was telling of her pain. "I will lead us away through the fastest paths I know."

His eyes seemed to show it all; his lack of trust in her, his contemplating on his own ability to make it through the woods, and his fear of what was chasing them. He saved her life, but that did not mean he wanted her to go with him. He could leave her injured here, taking all of her things and risking the wilds on his own. It was not something she would put past a knight, or herself.

"Will you at least leave my bow?" She said desperately.

Upon that, his expression changed, his brows relaxing and his eyes softening, but before she could read it further, he turned away causing her heart to pound with panic.

"You will do no more tricks, and you will lead me through the forest with the speed of someone uninjured, or believe me, you will be left behind and all your things will be with me. I will not kill someone I just fought beside, but that will not stop me from tying you to a tree to starve. Understand, witch-thief?"

"I understand." She murmured.

Without warning he stomped over and pulled her arm across his shoulders, taking some of her weight. They locked eyes for a moment, his showing a silent warning, and hers a glimmer of hope.

Then they started to walk.

"My name is not witch-thief, by the way." She lectured daringly as they went. "It is Valerlanta."

He took her in for a long moment, as if not believing even this smallest of facts. "Is that so? Well in that case, you may call me Venic. Just that. I am afraid I have dishonoured my family name too deeply to share the rest.

"I must say, Valerlanta, you have quite the shot."

"A bad shot is a starved winter." She said with a hiss as they stepped over a tangle of roots.

"I suppose it is." He replied.

"And you, Venic- for a new knight- have sword talent."

"The new within me shows that much?"

"It does. Many knights are taught to have at least a glimmer of direction sense."

"Well, I have something to work on then..."

* * *

The thief felt like she was but a spirit being pulled along the way as her body got away from her. Every path she should know felt new, and every moment seemed merged with the next. Days were passing, but the exhausting moments of travel seemed hard to remember; each time she thought of it, it felt like to her that the trap had happened only that day.

Valerlanta pushed as hard as she could- feebly leading the way while using any sort of shortcuts she knew in an attempt to gain distance from the men behind- but sometimes she found she had collapsed onto all fours, out of breath during a climb she would normally find easy.

As she went Valerlanta carefully pointed out edible plants for him to grab, and every time he would ask a few small questions of the plants use, then store it away for later. The thief told herself it was for food that she was teaching him since she was unable to collect it all herself, but she knew it was also a pathetic attempt to still try and appear useful to the knight even though blood loss was limiting her speed as a guide.

When they stopped for the night-or when she passed out and would awake to find it night- she would start the fire, and the knight would handle the rest. He threw what dried meat she had left into the pot, then would also throw in the plants she recommended. He always had her take the first taste, perhaps in fear of poison, and although humiliating as that was, what was worse was the caring for her wound.

Come nightfall, more often than not, she lost the strength to even lift an arm, so he changed her bandages, and even gathered the plant she told him about, which warded off infection. He did it all wordlessly without her even asking for it, and she allowed it, sitting still as he worked with her eyes staring off into the forest.

On the third night, he was tying off what was nearly the last of the bandages made from her jacket, and she tried again to ignore the brush of his fingers as he wrapped around her waist. When he finished, and she forced back a wince as he tied it off, she croaked a small "Thank you."

Grunting in reply, the knight lay back against a tree, took off his boots, and put his feet near the heat of the fire with a tired sigh.

They were near the top of a cliff, and a cool breeze came down the valley, causing a shiver to creep up her spine. Edging closer to the flames, she eagerly soaking in the warmth, her eyes staring at the flames as if hypnotized by the orange dancing.

From the pot hanging above, the smell of soup came onto the air, and Valerlanta frowned as her stomach grumbled in demand of a taste.

"We are still heading north, then?" The knight asked, breaking the silence. When she looked at him, his eyes were still closed, the firelight flickering across his features.

"Yes." Valerlanta answered. "We are still heading north."

"Good." He replied, and it appeared that the two of them were going to again fall into another still of silence, until the words bubbled out of her.

"Why does all this matter to you?" Valerlanta asked before she could stop herself. It might have been the injury making her drunk on pain, but she suddenly did not care what the knight did.

She had do know; she had to know why he was here. "You do not strike me as a money loving man. No, what you are seeking is something else entirely. Why are you doing this? What is in it for you?"

The knight regarded her carefully, his expression an emotionless mask. His eyes looked on at hers, then finally he sat up a little straighter and turned himself towards her. "Fine then; fair enough. I suppose you deserve to know who you travel with. Your guess was well thought; I was indeed a knight, and trained by the very king himself. Though, I'm not anymore." His own words caused him to wince. "Stealing this ball saw sure to that ending, and now I am being hunted for it.

Before all this happened, I was the king's favorite. Or so I thought.

According to the other knights, everyone was surprised with my talent of the sword. It is because of that I was knighted, despite being so inexperienced...which you were kind enough to point out to my pride that you noticed. Well,-" He paused and watched as she leaned over to stir the soup, perhaps to gather his thoughts. "-one night I overheard the king talking about magic, and curiosity got the better of me. Once they left, I snuck into his study and found the puzzle ball inside a box with glass windows, along with his notes on what it was and where the next prize was. I have never seen glass so clear, not once. I guess that was what showed me the true value of it."

He stopped to frown at her, and she raised her brows in a 'what-did-I-do-now?' fashion.

"You really found the next location on a guess?" He asked. She nodded and he shook his head before continuing. "No one from the cities knows that place exists. The king had to hunt down and force the answer out of your kind; or so the notes told."

"It is no secret among my folk." Valerlanta said. "We just don't help soldiers."

At her own words, she felt similar pang of regret at what she was doing, who she was helping, but brushed the feeling away as she pushed a strand of blonde behind her ear.

Venic continued as she readied their meals, his eyes watching her hands closely as usual, though if she wanted to poison him, he should know she would have put it on the spoon or something even cleverer.

"The notes had a book translated, and it said that these objects hold the key to unlocking an ancient magic surrounded by wondrous treasures. That magic, gives more power than anything; enough to destroy kingdoms; enough to raise forests. For one man, he could become the most powerful man ever in existence."

"Where?" Valerlanta asked, frozen with curiosity. He smiled, and she knew he would not tell. He could not tell her everything; otherwise she might as well slit his throat and go on herself...just as she could not teach him how to travel through the woods for the same risk.

He continued as if she said nothing. "When I found out the power the king was trying to gain, I hurried to get to the mountain before him; to save others from what he could get. I care for my king, I do, but he is tainted with greed for power. I am simply keeping him away from his sickness. What I do is helping him- and helping his kingdom as well- he just has yet to realize it. He does not know he is powerful enough in his subject's eyes already."

"Then why not destroy it?" Valerlanta cooed, sensing there was more to the story. "Why not find a smiths fire and melt them both, if you worry so?"

He frowned, and she knew she caught his gap in his story. Clearly, he did not think she would have been clever enough to notice, but she knew there was a reason he kept on the quest, and she doubted it was reason he gave. He might be many things, but he did not strike her as someone that noble and self-sacrificing.

"What of you?" Venic asked, ignoring her question yet again. "I have told many of my own secrets, what of yours?" His eyes scanned up her leather mask and Valerlanta flinched and fought the urge to raise her hood further over her head.

"What is there to tell?" She said, wishing the subject to change.

Venic shrugged his mind fishing for a question as her eyes warned him to be careful with his choice.

When he thought of one, he motioned to his surroundings. "How about this, then? Why live in the mountains?"

Her eyes went wide in surprise at the question.

'Why?'

Valerlanta had never thought as to why before; it was simply always her home. Where else would she live? Cities and towns were too crowded and boring for her tastes, and much harder to slip away when in danger. No, there was nowhere else for her.

"It's where I like best." She answered finally. "It is where I was raised, and where I plan to stay."

He stared, as if that just confused him, and he looked around as if to wonder what there was to like. Then, giving up, he looked back to her and asked another question. "What is it that you find so attracting about the woods? I do not see it."

Now that stumped her. Could one really choose a few things to like about the forest?

"It gives me all I need." She answered finally. "If I am poisoned, the forest gives me a counter. If I am hungry, the forest always has food on hand. If I fall ill, well, I can always find the right plant to sooth it. It has everything."

"Not people." Venic mentioned, and Valerlanta raised her chin and crossed her arms.

"There are enough for me."

"But why though? Do you not wish to be around others? To make friends? Have some fun? With your past as a forest walker, you could surly get a job as an herbal healer, or with your skills, you could probably even convince someone to let you be their tracker despite your gender, so why don't you even want to try?"

Valerlanta smiled, the thought of her being sought after for help rather than to catch was somehow amusing. "I am a female who can fire a bow better than most men; I would probably be burnt alive at the stake as a witch. I will not change myself to fit in when I already have a world out here that I fit in just fine to."

"Do you not get lonely?"

She paused to think. "Sometimes, but it just makes the company of those I care for seem all the more better."

Venic breathed out an exasperated sigh, giving up in trying to understand. "Well I have to tell you, I could never live out here. The flies eating at you, the beasts to kill you, the roots to trip over, and the branches to scratch you; this place is no paradise, that is for certain."

"It will grow on you." She smiled, though mostly to herself. "The air is fresher here, and the food and the views are better. In a few days' time, I'll take you on a path; one that goes right over the valley and looks over it all. You will look on at the mountains golden with the morning glow and see it spread like waves over the forest one tree at a time, and you will understand. It's enough to even make the old and the dying feel alive; I guarantee it."

"We shall see." Was all he said, but even in the firelight she saw an amusing amount of curiosity glittering there in his brown eyes. He lay back again, and his eyes closed.

The soup was simmering quietly over the fire, and the air was still.

It was as the thief watched as his face relaxed and his breathing slowed, that she quietly but carefully got up and crept from the camp.

Away from by the fire, the night air sent her hairs on end with goose-bumps and her feet stumbled with weariness, but there was something she needed to do.

A light damp wind blew by, whistling through the trees and seeming to sing to the night dwellers and herself.

Gingerly lowering herself down by the cliff side, Valerlanta sat and brushed a wind tussled stray hair behind her ear.

The thief knew she did not have long, after all, if that man woke, he would assume that she just was stepping out for a moment to relieve herself, but she found she needed this, and as a cricket song lulled her shoulders into relaxation, she found her eyes closing and her ears drifting along with the sound.

Trees rustled, birds finished final songs, and somewhere in the valley, a stream clapped to it all.

Her lips lifted into a gentle smile and she found her wound now hardly hurt.

This, all this, was her most favourite lullaby.

A sound came across the forest. The sound was light as a feather, and then swept low as if it was singing of the setting sun itself.

Instantly she found her eyes fluttering open and her head tilting towards the sound with interest.

This was what she was waiting for.

It came again-the bird song- crisp and clear as it echoed throughout the valley- though close as it sounded, it was probably over a day's travel away, and only carried by the valley and quiet air.

Her lips parted, and her eyes widened, and she found herself leaning in.

This was forest speech, and it varied group to group. This language in particular was of her father's guild. It was fairly complicated-with the raises in sound and durations leading to different meanings or words-but she knew it perfectly.

The message was for her; from her father, and was being carried on by the many men carefully positioned throughout the forest.

'Little bird, are you well?' The fake bird asked. *'Rumours carry, rumours vary.'*

Almost desperately her fingers found her lips, and she burst out a reply.

'I am well.' She called. *'What rumors spread?'*

Then there was silence, and her heart dropped and her eyes scanned the nothingness around her eagerly. When no response came, she fought the tightness growing in her throat and itchy eyes, and was only just about to repeat-afraid she went unheard-when it came.

'This news is good, I will spread word shortly.' The bird call answered. *'Rumours are many. Is it true you run with a knight?'*

She found her throat tensing, so she swallowed hard.

'I chase the king's worth of riches. A...-' she paused, for there was not a word in bird song for what she was about to say. *'-..."freed" knight from our kingdom travels with me until he can be lost.'*

Again there was a pause as the message carried upon the winds.

'You pursue dangerous prey. Hunt with eyes open wide. Be warned, the man you hunt with may not be who he says.'

"May not be who he says." She whispered under her breath to herself. What did that mean?

She felt her eyes narrow. Were her first suspicions correct?

Abruptly her head was filled with images of a knight on top of the mountain with a tired and desperate expression, then the tattered rope from the soldiers she killed.

A knight, and a prisoner, but why would both sides be chasing him? What could one man do to provoke the chase of two kingdoms?

Instead of asking that, she had another thought bothering her. *'There are wolves at my heels, but I am uncertain to how close their nips are. What rumors spread of them?'*

'Last word said that a pack of wolves passed by the canyon hermit a little after noon.' Was all the stranger said. *'The guild wishes you a good hunt and should be in touch soon.'*

Then it stopped, and the messenger was surly on his way to spread the word to those also waiting for bird echoes in the woods. If all went well, it would be within her father's range by morning.

The canyon hermit was no more than a half day away from her, which meant that somehow the men were keeping up with her. Although her methods had been legging with her wound, her pathways she chose should have left little to no prints, which meant that whoever was leading them knew the paths she was taking; knew the forest.

She had to step up her game, and not to mention figure out what to do about that following kn-

"Thief? I mean..."- A voice asked, startling her from her thoughts. The very man of her thoughts paused to correct himself as she stood. "Valerlanta?"

"I am here." She said, reluctantly making her way towards him.

He watched her approach, she could tell that much, but his face was hidden in the shadows of night and his expressions therefore unreadable.

"You took a long while." He said, his arms crossing.

She grinned innocently, knowing she had been caught doing something suspicious. "What can I say? It was nice to get away for a while. You snore, you know."

"I do not snore."

"If you are sleeping, how would you know?"

He paused, clearly trying to figure out a way to combat her lie, then clearly gave up and waved her back towards the fire. "Just get back to camp."

She did as she asked, and slowly sat down at the fire just in time for the soup to be done.

"Do you know what I miss while being here in this forest?" Venic asked as he passed her the first bowl; if you could call it a bowl. She carved them herself, which was why they were slightly lopsided, but normally it was her father sharing the second. Giving it to a stranger felt odd.

Valerlanta raised a brow at the small talk, but took the bait. "Making people feel lower than you as you eat a feast and they eat bread?"

His jaw tensed, but instead of getting angry, he sat back against his tree. "I miss my bed. More than anything, even though I have to swat these bloody mosquitoes away and eat this food that seems to have no taste other than 'bitter," what I miss is my bed. Laying back on the soft instead of on rocks."

Valerlanta paused, her spoon hovering near her lips. "You miss....your bed?"

"You are saying that you never do? You never once want to sleep somewhere soft?"

"I would not know." Valerlanta took in the spoonful and swallowed. Like the knight said, it was indeed bitter with all the herbs she helped Venic collect, but she was used to it. Nutrition is always more important than taste. "I have never slept in a bed before."

He made a choking sound as he nearly spat out his soup. "Never? You have never slept in a bed? Not even once?"

Valerlanta shook her head, looking at the curves and swirls of the wood of her carved spoon. "Not once. Why?"

His eyes stared at her and did not seem to know how to answer, as if she had just told him that she did not breathe all the time.

Before he could come up with anything to say, she shrugged and finished off what was in her soup. "If I want somewhere soft to lay, I will find some moss."

“That is really not the same.”

“How is that?”

“Well,-” He paused in thought. “-there is no pillow for one. Or walls.”

“Do you need those things for a place to be considered a bed?”

“Well, no, I suppose you do not.” He frowned deeply. “It is still not the same, though.”

She smiled. “I will have to take your word for that, then.”

He stared at her, seeming totally baffled.

“You have never?”

"....Is that not what I said?"

"Not even once?"

"Now I know I will be repeating myself; I have never slept in a bed. Not once, not ever. Never in my entire life."

"Huh." He said, his brows pressing together as he thought it over, as if she was more of a puzzle to figure out than any one they carried with them.

Laughing at his confusion, she set the bowl aside and gingerly lay with her back to him so she would not have to see his perplexed gaze.

"You can take first watch." She said over her shoulder.

"Goodnight." He murmured, and then only the fire was left talking in its words of snaps and crackles.

* * *

Smoke was snaking its way up into the morning air.

It was only just down the valley from where Valerlanta stood, and as she looked out over the landscape, her eyes narrowed in on the clearest sign of human life she knew; fire.

Someone had lit a fire for their breakfast, and, by how it was turning white, Valerlanta had only to guess that it was only just put out by that same person.

Whoever it was, they were getting on the move again.

Whoever it was; they were following Valerlanta.

How? How did they know where she was planning on going? How were they noticing the tracks that she was being extra careful to hide?

'How?'

Hurrying back to camp, she quickly threw items at the knight and hurried to make the camp invisible. "Get ready to leave. Move as fast as you can!"

"What is the hurry?" The knight asked; clear worry now vivid on his face.

"There is smoke just down the valley." She moved dirt over the ashes of their fire from the night before. "They are still a days behind, but are far too close even just there. If we keep up this pace and run into something unexpected, they might catch us. We need to gain ground on them."

"How can we?" Venic asked, quickly pulling their gear over his shoulders. "How are they keeping up? How are they gaining so much ground?"

Valerlanta frowned at him. "The only possibility I know is that they have a tracker, and horses."

Cursing, the knight rushed to help her hide the camp, then they were off at a brisk pace that caused enough pain in Valerlanta's wound that it was hard to breath.

Still, she kept moving.

Horses, the hateful creatures, had a faster pace than a human.

She altered their route; changing to steeper inclines and slightly thicker brush to slow the horses, and when it came time to stop for a break of food and drink, Valerlanta was already beyond tired. It was barely mid-day, and she was already leaning against a tree with closed eyes and unable to catch her breath.

"You should drink." Venic said, and Valerlanta opened an eye to look at him. His eyes were serious, so she nodded and took a long swing of water. It cooled her throat, but did nothing to dull the pain.

As she was bringing down the water-skin, she saw it, and her hand slowed.

"Finally, some luck!" She breathed, and before Venic could reply, she was scurrying across the river; hopping rock to rock, and right to a willow tree. Quickly, she picked several leaves and, after stuffing some in her bag, she put one in her mouth. It tasted awful, but it would make it so she could continue.

Relief filled her, and when she looked back, the knight gave her a small smile. He clearly knew at least this plant; though there were few who did not. The leaves of this plant would help with her pain, and so they could keep up their pace and perhaps even be able to use her bow.

Relaxed by that thought, they continued, and as they did, Valerlanta thought it was time to test something.

It was as they were making their way down a rather steep drop that the sounds came through her lips. In streams of air came the whistled tune of a song called "My lady, so round a and fair." She whistled it as she used the trunks of trees to slow her trip down, and continued when loose rocks made her feet slip and slide towards their destination. By the time they reached the bottom, the song was done, finishing the tale of a man's love for a larger woman, who- in his eyes- was the most beautiful woman in town.

Venic watched her the whole time out of the corner of his eye, and though he did not make her stop despite the extra noise she was making, he also made no indication to comment on the song.

Annoyed he failed to take the bait, she frowned at him.

He did not appear to be someone of worry; true he was handsome, but not overly so. His hair was cut ordinarily, and his clothes were simply the basic uniform of his kingdom. Everything about him seemed to be trying to convince her that he was simply a normal man; but a force so great did not chase ordinary people. For whatever reason, two kingdoms were after one man, and she wanted to know why.

The knight, who was trying his luck on the puzzle-ball as they walked, noticed her unsatisfied gaze.

Valerlanta looked away sharply and avoided his eye as he quickened his pace to catch up with her.

His arm suddenly blocked her path as he pressed his hand against a tree and forced her to look at him.

"Is there something you want to ask? Or are you just going to stare like that all day until the question eats you alive?"

Clearly, though he did not show it, she was annoying him.

"Who are you?" She asked to get it over with. "Who are you really?"

He looked at her, his face void of emotion. "What do you mean? I already told you-"

"You understand what I mean!" Her arms folded, and her hand clutched a hidden piece of shale she grabbed when they were traversing the loose rock. It was a pathetic but sharp weapon for just in case this conversation went badly. "You know I am a tracker, so you should also know that part of the reason I knew I was heading to the right mountain is that I found your tracks. I found the ropes of the prisoner being held by Buragen soldiers, and I also found that he got away when Alecaven men attacked. The prisoner was heading to the mountain, so I took a shortcut to get ahead, and because of that, I beat you there just barely.

“There are two kingdoms after you, and I want to know why. What makes you so important? Why are they chasing us with horses so hard that it is as if their very lives depend on it?"

Much to her surprise, the knight did not attack her, or even rush to threaten her, he looked at her, taking her words in. Somehow, his lack of reaction was almost worse. It caused a chill to rush down her spine, and she barely managed to escape a shiver.

"I do not see why this is your worry." He answered coldly. "I am just the client you are leading through the forest."

"You very well know that this goes beyond simple curiosity. Depending on who is chasing us changes everything. It makes certain areas unsafe to pass through, and causes otherwise trusted people to become enemies. Besides, you have said it once before; I deserve to know who it is that I am traveling with. You do not know it, but you already know more about me than anyone but my father does. You know what I do, you know who I am, and most importantly, you know I can do magic; which is more than enough to have the whole kingdom want me dead, so at least give me something to even the odds against that."

The knight took in a deep breath while holding his hands out above the heat of the tiny flames. He rubbed them for a moment, and she caught a glance at his strong and well-worn fingers. Unlike the royals she saw with hands white and smooth as milk, his hands were well used. Working hands.

"I underestimated you yet again, but surly you understand that I had a need to lie." He paused to sigh, his hand running through his almond strands of hair, then returning to his face again to run his temples, as if what he was about to say was causing stress to build up like a flood of water against a dam. "I am not from the land of your king. I am-or rather *was*-a spy."

"Was?" She asked with surprise, but at that moment her mind flickered back to the rope she found long ago. His home kingdom was chasing because Venic must have betrayed them.

'You switched sides.' Valerlanta realized silently; though was somehow not at all intimidated by learning his occupation. Perhaps it was because she was a thief and a killer, and a spy did not seem much more of a climb up the criminal ladder from that.

"Yes, *was.* That place...to be honest Buragen was never a home to me, not really. I was a prisoner my whole life to the ways of money, then-due to bad choices-I became a prisoner in the literal sense to the military. I was trained to come here and give information on the limits of the kings magic, and at first I did, but then I realized what I was feeling around me was freedom." His expression darkened and his frown deepened. "I came under the guise of a captured solider being released back for ransom, but the king knew who I was even then, and yet he took me under his wing and had his best train me. He called me talented. It was great, you know. I had mead come with but a raise of my hand, and everyone would simply give me items I wanted in order to gain my trust. Suddenly, everyone was looking up at me, not like in my own kingdom where I was nothing but a criminal. It was-by far-the best time in my life."

Valerlanta nodded, trying to find more holes in his story; though something in her was telling her that she was hearing some form of the truth. "So why leave, then? Why betray the king that has treated you best?"

His eyes locked with hers, and for once Valerlanta did not feel danger from him. His hazel eyes looked on at her through strands of straggly hair, and in their depths, she saw something there. Confusion? Pain? She could not put her finger on it, but it bewitched her as strong as any spell.

They both wore masks, but his was made of skin and hardened eyes made only to hide that underneath he was lost, but still fighting.

"Val-" He started, but his words fell apart as both of them tore their gazes apart at the sound of voices. Among the rustle of leaves was the soft sound of a human voice from in the valley.

When her eyes came back to the knight, he mask was back.

"That business is my own." He answered in a more hushed tone.

She bit back her words that she wanted to say, and also got up to leave for the day. She did not want to leave it at that,-she did not want to continue this air of mystery-but something told her he was done talking and would say no more even if she asked it.

Of all things, this was a feeling she understood most.

Without thinking, her hand clutched around her side to graze where she knew a scar started, that extended far up to her shoulder.

Yes, she knew there were something's that were hardest of all to talk about.

Venic moved to more cover, but it was not necessary yet. Through the mountain air, noise travels farther than it would in a city; so the group they were hearing could be further away than expected.

Shifting the pack on her back, she resisted the urge to hide it in a tree and come back for it. Today, Venic had decided to give her some of the weight and gave her back her pack as well as her bow, but he kept the arrows and weapons. Unfortunately, because of that, the pack was currently pulling uncomfortably at her wound.

Making up her mind for the sake of stealth, she decided to come back for it and pressed it into a thick of bushes.

Motioning for him to wait in the spot, she crept forward, and Venic followed. She shot him a look, but started darting from cover to cover as she neared the voices, and he followed her every movement with a steady hand on his sword.

'I cannot be alone even a little?' She wondered, holding back her annoyance as he scurried to follow her under the green bows of a tree.

Under the long-hanging skirts of green needles, Valerlanta saw a group of five soldiers upon the road the two needed to cross. The thief and knight were both still a far distance away, but she could still make out the mark on their armour.

Alecaven men.

Their horses were loosely tied up at the men ate a meal, so more than likely they were on some other mission rather than tracking the treasures, and were simply taking a break.

By the relaxed pace they were eating at, the thief doubted anyone was expecting them any time soon, so her eyes locked on the closest of the men. He was patting the nose of his horse with a smile on his young face as the horse nudged his armour.

Luckily, the canopy was high enough for a shot. If she could get them all fast enough and left one alive, she could get the information she needed.

Grabbing her bow, she snatched an arrow from the quiver on the swordsman's back, and took aim.

The boy was running a hand through his tightly curled hair, as if he were hot under all his gear.

Valerlanta took in a slow breath and slowed her heart-rate.

Everything else blurred away except for her target.

Her hand tensed then relaxed, her fingers itching to release as pain rippled from her wound in her side.

"No!"

She was tackled to the ground. Her arrow shot off somewhere high into the canopy, missing its target and merely startling a few birds.

Struggling to keep her bow from being snatched away, the thief kicked the larger man in the stomach, giving her the space she needed to roll out from under him and grab another arrow as she went. As she backed into the forest, branches scraping her skin as she went, she knocked an arrow at Venic.

He stood, and reacted by placing a ready hand on his sword. His eyes were cold and hard,

"What was that?" She hissed as loud as she dared. "I thought we were on the same side? Why did you protect them?"

"You cannot just kill anyone you please!"

"They should not be here anyways; the only people on this road are merchants taking the longest path they can because they want to avoid trouble."

"And the road tax."

She opened her mouth to reply, but stopped when she noticed the strange tone in his voice. "Wait, those men have the markings of Alecaven; *please* tell me this is not just because you were part of the same army?"

He did not answer.

"It is?!" The bow shook under her tight grip, and her healing wound protested greatly. "I don't know if you realize this, but they are now your enemy!"

"I could have fought side-by-side with some of the men in that army." He answered. "I could have talked with their families, played games with their kids, and ate with them at banquets."

"And now they will kill you if they see you; even those you know best. They might be fine as an ally, but as an enemy, you will see a side of those soldiers that you never knew! The kind that kills kids and bullies supplies from people."

"They would never-"

"They *would*, and they *have*." She snapped. "Now choose quickly whose side you are on, because if you do not, I will disappear and you will be left to find your way out of this forest on your own."

Whirling around, she released the tension on her bow and stomped away. As she went, she stole one last look back in time to see the swordsman's grip tighten on his sword and his muscles tense. Turning on a tree, his fist slammed against the bark.

Then he disappeared behind leafy greens as she left.

Back at the place they had left, Valerlanta slumped on a log. She frowned, glancing at the fading sunlight.

'What are you still doing here, Val?' She wondered, and it was not the first time.

Shaking the thoughts away, she started checking on the food and found they only had enough for one more day, if that. Valerlanta was starting to wonder if this day could get worse.

After some time, Venic returned. His hand was bloody from where it hit the bark, and his eyes were downcast; his hair making his expression invisible.

Looking away bitterly, she finished closing the straps on her pack. She was only just about to swing it on when the knight stopped where she knelt and held his open hand out towards her. She could see blood on his fingers from where his knuckles had been cut, but none of the bones appeared broken.

Hesitantly, her eyes followed the hand up to his face, and saw two drained almond eyes looking back. His jaw was tightly clenched and his shoulders tensed, as if just being here was suddenly a fight for him.

She willing lifted her bag into his waiting hand, and he took it up and pulled it onto his shoulders. "Come." He started walking, carrying all her things again as if it were his way of an apology, though he also took back the arrow she nearly used.

Valerlanta ignored apology and followed the knight.

The knight had made his choice, and with the look on his face-the confusion and regret- she almost found herself believing his story; almost. However, she was not completely heartless, so she held her words in for at least that one night.

She let the men go -though habit was telling her she should do otherwise- and simply lead the swordsman onward until she came to a spot that could lead in two different directions.

The sun was bursting its final display of brightness from the highest point in the sky, when Valerlanta faltered, looking between the two directions. One way she knew where a good shelter was sure to be, but the other way was the view.

When asked by Venic, she told him this, and he simply pointed in the way of the view. "I want to see it. I want to see the view that you say will make a woodsman out of me."

She smiled at that, trying to picture him as anything close to one, and so the thief continued on, and was followed by the man she had recently discovered to be a spy.

The sun was just about to start its steady escape for the night, leaving the forest glazed with gold and shadows stretching long.

For not the first time that day, Valerlanta stole a glance back at him, but as with all the times before, she could see no sign that he was still angry from their talk that morning.

"Is it far?" Venic asked tiredly as they made their way through a thick of ferns.

"No, it is just over there." She pointed to where the light was brightest through the trees. "Just watch your step as you get close. We are much higher than you would think."

Reaching closer to the edge, they found themselves amongst crumbling ruins much older then she could place. Vines crept up their smooth rock, leaving what she could only assume to be a temple now a place for nature.

As they walked under a large arch, Venic frowned uncomfortably at a large statue staring on at them.

The stone man was long since toppled on its side, and its cheek lay half deep into the soil, but it was still larger than the both of them, and watched with an almost sad expression. It lay covered in a blanket of emerald moss, and standing it would clearly be larger than any tree in this forest.

"What is this place?" Venic asked.

The thief simply shrugged as she climbed the stairs to a balcony free of roof and walls except for the odd rubble or half-left pillar. “There are many ruins like this in the woods; forgotten places. Though, there are more on this path then any others I know. We will see more tomorrow as well. My father said some of them, like this here, are left over remains from when magic ruled the land, but who is to say?" She got to the edge and felt herself smile as she looked on at the view. "Only the past knows now."

The knight did not seem happy with that answer, and hesitated to follow her to the edge, but when he did his eyes widened.

The sun was sliding behind the mountains, but as if to ensure no one would forget its beauty, the sun painted the world in gold and the sky with pink.

Gold kissed the tops of trees far below, and Valerlanta felt her heart beat faster as she held onto a crumbling pillar and leaned over as far as she could. Cold wind caressed her face, pushing her hair to tickle her nose as it waved, and for a moment she almost forgot everything in a flood of intoxicating taste of freedom.

Venic leaned over too, though far less, and his wide eyes took in it all, including following a flock of birds as they flew by below. A flicker of a smile came across his face before he stepped back to view at a safer location.

"It is even better in the morning." She said excitedly, watching the birds till they were no more than distant specks. "There are other places like this too, some even higher than this if you can imagine. I swear to you that there is one place where the waterfalls run hot no matter the weather, and they fall upon each other in many, upon many, different pools. Or there is a cave, hidden and dark, but when you go inside, the rocks glow like stars! Or there is-" Valerlanta froze as she saw Venic listening, brows raised, and suddenly her cheeks flooded with heat of a blush. Instantly she looked away, to hide it.

"I got carried away. I apologise." She murmured, not knowing what else to say.

Venic laughed, startling her, and when she stole a glance back, he was smiling. "It's fine. I do the same when it comes to talking about this." He wiggled his sword on his hip. "Apparently I have been known to go on about it like a lover when I drink too much."

"About a sword?" She laughed, and was still concentrated on ridding her cheeks of their fire as the swordsman sat down. His feet hung over the edge, and for a moment he saw a sparkle of amusement in his eyes, but then as swiftly as she saw it, it was gone again and the shadows came back over their surface.

"Yes, about a sword. I was told long ago that every sword you own has to be to you better than any friend you have ever had, and that really stuck with me, though maybe a little too much. I have been told that I have even made it a song."

"Now that I would like to hear." Hesitantly she sat too.

"Not a chance."

"Not even a little?"

"You will not hear a single line."

"Pity."

There was a moment of silence between them as they both sat together content with the fading head on their faces, then Venic again spoke up. "I still do not understand it."

"Understand what?" She asked, glancing at him quickly as he ran a hand through his almond hair, then away again as if observing something she best not.

"What I do not understand." He began, turning to her. "-is why you are still here. You have had plenty of chances to escape, and you and I both know it. You could have left many times now, and it worries me- it has worried me from the start although I dared not admit it-and yet, here you are. Still here, sitting with a man who threatened to kill you."

Valerlanta listened, then let out a irritated breath; her eyes trailing up, past the forests that had been her home for as long as she had known, and then up to the world birds and dragon kind only knew. She could still feel the swordsman eyes on her as he waited for an answer, but it was an answer to a question she had been trying to figure out as well.

Why was she here with the swordsman she barely knew? Why had she not tried to kill him yet?

Then, as she watched a large flock of birds fade into the skies beyond the mountains, she got the answer.

"Well," she said. "Perhaps I found I am not much better than a raven. Steal, then hide, steal, then hide. There is comfort to always staying in the same nest; but peace always dulls to boredom after time. Sometimes you have to fly off to somewhere new to find what you need."

He looked at her for a while, and then laughed. She looked at him in shock that he could be insulting what she just said, but instead he only had a genuine smile waiting for her.

"What? What is it?" She demanded. "What did I say that is so funny?"

'It was the bird talk.' She thought, wondering what embarrassment her lack of socialization practise had thrown her into this time. *'It had to be the bird talk.'*

"No, no, nothing like that!" He corrected, putting his hands up between them as if in surrender. "I was just wondering what kind of girl is sitting beside me. Who gets bored of risking their lives daily?"

Valerlanta pinched her brows in confusion. "Everyone gets bored of doing the same thing every day."

"Not everyone climbs mountains and fights dragons in search of treasure; and if they do, most certainly do not do so willing. Most men in half the situations you put yourself in would wet themselves, so I cannot help but wonder about someone who has grown to find such situations dull."

Valerlanta grinned. "Now, when have I ever said I was sane?"

He smiled back. "Are you afraid of anything? I have seen you traverse heights, face dragons, and take on soldiers double your size. Is there anything that daunts you?"

At that her smile faltered slightly. "There is, but I refuse to tell you what it is until I hear your sword-song."

He winced, perhaps considering the lyrics such as song he wrote could have. "I guess it shall forever remain a mystery."

The thief smiled at the spy, and the spy smiled right back; both easily forgetting what chased them at least for a moment.

* * *

In the grasses still fresh with morning dew, Venic sat; his face bright with a golden glow as the sun slowly peeked over the huge mountains. Fog that was hovering below in the many valleys started burning off in the heat of the day, and the birds of the forest called out a greeting.

Unnoticed; the thief smirked.

The knight no doubt thought she was still asleep, so slipped out to enjoy the views as if he was stealing away to meet a secret lover.

Valerlanta noticed this escape, and at first thought the man could be planning something dangerous, but when she followed him, she found that he simply sat and enjoyed.

Before he could notice she was being his shadow, she snuck back to camp, leaving him to enjoy.

When he returned and pretended to be coming back from relieving himself, they left again and Valerlanta lead them down the valley and onto the waves of rocks that smoothly flowed along the river.

"This is too open." The knight said as he followed her along the rocks, his hand holding onto branches for balance as he walked. "An archer could easily get us from here."

"We do not have a choice, we need the advantage. Sometimes, to get ahead, you must take risks. Besides, no horses can follow us here." She looked over her shoulder at the man. "And do stop that, you are not a child so learn some balance. By holding those branches you are leaving a clear trail."

Venic glared, but did release he branch he was holding, letting it snap back to the forest behind him, as if to make a point. She rolled her eyes in response.

When they came across a sweet smelling meadow, kissing the edge of the rocks, Valerlanta stopped in the shadows of the forest, and carefully looked over the expanse of grasses and flowers before continuing.

She was on the lookout for bears as this was their favorite type of area, but she also kept a keen eye out for men or worse creatures, but the area seemed clear, for now. So, she stepped in, eyeing the ground for edible food, while Venic went off somewhere. He did not say where, just simply told her he would be back before she could blink, but she figured she had a pretty good idea as to what it was he was up to. The human body could only hold in fluid for so long, after all.

Kneeling down, saw what she was looking for and carefully picked off what she needed from the meadow-sweet. This particular plant was not for eating, but it was instead used as a treatment for pain by many herbalists and forest walkers alike. All she had to do is make it into a tea, and drink it down. It was a simple enough remedy that would hopefully put off the pain long enough for her to get a good night's sleep.

Just as she gathered the last amount into her arms and was about to get up, her hand hesitated over something; a simple white mushroom. She was frozen there for a long while, her hand hovering over it temptingly. Just even the smallest of pieces would be enough, then all the information she needed would be hers and he would be...

With a whirl of her blonde hair, she broke away and left the poison behind.

After carefully walking backwards in her prints, the thief met Venic back at the river, to where a stream fed into it. The stream itself was a completely different view to her from last time she visited this place. After the flooding last spring, many of the rivers changed course, which included the small stream they filled their drinks from.

What was once a human's castle was now part of nature once more as a waterfall flowed from what appeared to be the two doors of the ruins; making it almost seem like the whole thing was crying at the loss of its owner.

The castle tears gently swept down the rocky ridge, and into the rivers.

As she knelt there, a single leaf floated by like a little boat, sailing down the turning waters before crashing into dipping hands. It stuck there for a moment, until Venic picked his hands back up out of the water, and the little boat was able set sail once more.

Water was being splashed onto the knight's face and strong neck in an attempt to wash, and then he came up a dripping mess while feeling the stubble on his chin as if it were something strange to him. Had he never let it grow before? If not, why not shave it again if it was making him uncomfortable? Strange.

Valerlanta paused, watching him, then wrinkled her nose as she decided she did not care enough to ask, and turned away.

"We need to keep moving." She said reluctantly, dreading more climbing.

"Does your father have any other kids?" The man following behind her asked.

"No." She answered.

"*Hmm*. That is strange, do you not agree? Most families have at least four, and that is considered small. Even I have several siblings."

"It is different out here. Most people become forest walkers because they want to be alone; and they are able to remain invisible by being just that; alone. By having a family, you put all of you at a higher risk of getting caught. the more people, the more signs of life to be followed; so, majority do not have a family at all."

"So they never miss the company of women?" Venic said, his tone implying that he was starting to wonder if the forest walkers could possibly be sane.

Valerlanta smirked, looking back at him with a raised brow. "I cannot say I have ever asked."

"No I would imagine not. It is a slightly personal question, I suppose." Venic realized with a faint smile of his own. "Do you think there is a town ahead? I am sure if there is, I could persuade someone into giving us horses."

“No. In fact, I am very certain there is not. Even if there was, no horses. Horse shoes leave too defined of a print; they are far too easy to follow.”

“Hmm." He said with obvious disappointment. "Well, what is this print here? A mountain lion?”

“No. It was a wolf.”

“So I was close this time?”

“No, not at all.”

And that was when she thought of something. Stooping low, she picked two near identical blue berries from two different plants, grabbed his wrist, and slapped them into his hand.

"Which one is the poisonous one? I think I have taught you enough to figure this out.” She said, and then continued on, leaving him to figure it out as they went.

She glanced back occasionally, and saw him poking at the two berries with a puzzled look on his face; clearly wondering how he could figure it out without actually eating one. He rubbed some on his skin, smelt them both carefully, and looked at them so close that she thought he might poke himself in the eye with one.

Then, as time went on, she saw him gradually bring them closer to his mouth until -much to her surprise- one of the berries popped into his mouth

He chewed only once.

Spitting the berry out, the swordsman panicked.

"Bah! I ate the poison one!" He shouted; his eyes wide. He swished the water they had only just collected into his mouth, and then spat it out as if to wash the poison all away.

Even though she tried to hold it back, Valerlanta smiled mischievously. "Oh, did you? Now that really is unfortunate."

He barely looked at her as he swished water about in his mouth again. "What is the cure?!" He asked. "Do I need one? I only ate a little."

"No, you do not need a cure." She mused, her lips curling up into a larger smile. "Although a juniper berry tastes awful, it is edible. In fact, so is the blueberry I gave you."

He looked at her for a moment, and then rage slowly settled in on his face. "You tricked me."

"Yes, and it was easy to do too." She said with a laugh. "I guess something's really never change."

He dove for her to whack her across the back of the head, but with a laugh she ducked out of the way only to have pain steal her balance away, and have her land butt first in the dirt.

Despite the hot pain in her side, she still could not help but laugh, and received a bitter glare from the knight.

"That was not amusing even in the slightest amount." He said, though she could have sworn she saw the corners of his mouth twitching. He crossed his arms and attempted to look intimidating, but this time it was having no effect on her.

"I disagree." She answered with a laugh. "The look on your face made it more than worth it!"

The swordsman made a rather unimpressed sounding grunt, and then motioned her with his head to continue up the trail. He did not say anything for a long while, making her plan all the more worth it.

The thief smiled to herself much of the way, but as with all good things, her happy moment did not last.

As she lead them through a thick patch of branches, and she was holding a bent one forward to keep it from wiping back and whacking the knight, she saw a strip of red on a tree ahead. Startled, Valerlanta shot forward to the tree, completely forgetting about the branch which flew back and hit Venic in face with a hard 'smack.'

"Hey!" Venic shouted angrily as he rubbed his nose.

"Oh, sorry." Valerlanta said blandly, as she picked the red from the tree. A strip of cloth, softer then a commoner could afford, but without a nobles silky light touch. It was a little fringed at the edges, and when she brought it to her nose, she smelt nothing recognisable; the fresh air had swept all such smells away.

Her eyes finally found the ground, but saw no prints. This was an old trail; perhaps months old. She let out a relieved breath.

"What is that?" Venic asked.

Valerlanta scrunched it up in her hand then threw it away. "Nothing important. Just an old trial."

It was strange for a noble to be this far into the forest, but then people did sometimes get lost on hunts. Normally she would follow the path for days; curious to find where they ended up and loving the thrill of wondering if she could catch up, but now it was just a forgotten strip of cloth found on a tree that she saw on her way to greater adventures.

Venic looked at the disregarded cloth with clear discomfort. Valerlanta tried to ignore his expression and went to continue, but there was something in his pressed brows that made her curiosity spark, so her feet remained glued.

"What is it?" She asked.

"I must be wrong, but it looks like the cloth of a uniform. The color is almost just right for Buragen; though a little faded." He said as he knelt to pick it up and examine it closer. He rubbed it in between his fingers; testing the texture. "How old would you wager the trail was?"

"A few months, maybe two, maybe more, maybe less. There has been so much rain that it is hard to say at this point. Why?"

Venic stood up and looked at her with a serious glint in his eye. "There has been soldiers in the forest disrupting trade routes for a while now, do you know of that?"

"Of course." Valerlanta scuffed, somewhat offended. "No one enters my territory without my knowledge."

"And how long have they been showing up in the forest?"

Valerlanta thought about it. "It has been happening much of the year; just after the first big melt."

"Valerlanta, I know you said the trail is old, but is there any way of you knowing at all his direction?" His eyes looked at her with enough hope that it was nearly drowning her. Those brown eyes...it was just like seeing a lost puppy in the rain ending up on your doorstep.

Running a hand through her hair, she let out a long sigh. "Fine."

Kneeling down so that she could see the shine of the sun on the forest floor, she looked hard. Every branch, every blade of grass, it was all evidence.

First she started at where they found the strip of cloth, and she pictured the angle she found it in. Then she followed the possible path with her eyes, while also picturing his path with her imagination. If her experience was right, hopefully her guesses could lead her to a good clue in a limited amount of time.

"Are there any prints?" Venic asked, and she could feel his gaze hot on her back.

"No." She answered. "However, they are not what I am looking for. See here?" She pointed at a small bush, and indicated to a bent branch. "This was broken by a force hitting it. The rain might take away the prints, but there are other ways of finding a person. Here too," She moved to where the end small log was pinched between two trees and pointed to the one of the trees. "You see here, where the bark has been shaved of? Someone stepped on that log, and the pressure caused it to slide down against this tree." Standing she turned back to him and shrugged. "I would need to find more hints to be sure, so for now this is just a guess, but if you asked me now, I would have to say he is heading in a north-westerly direction."

The knight raised his brows, and for a moment Valerlanta thought he might actually be impressed, but then he brought his hand up to his chin to think, and the expression quickly was gone. "One man?"

"From what I can see, yes. A group would have left more damage for us to see. There could have been two of them, though, walking in similar steps. Why? What are you thinking?"

"I am thinking a scout from our enemy kingdom Buragen went through here."

Valerlanta tilted her head slightly, and despite her best interest, her interest was sparked. "A scout? Why through here? There is nothing here for a long time; even the nearest decent road is a few days away."

"That, I do not know." Venic sighed, but even though he said that, she could have sworn she saw something in his serious tone.

Was he afraid?

What did he know?

"Well, fear not. A scout, or whatever he is, will not get far. One of the men in my territory will find his trail soon enough, and they know what to do." Valerlanta smirked at him before continuing on.

He did not even flinch, just rolled his eyes and followed her.

The two were making up great ground as she was hoping, and Valerlanta was scarcely noticing her wound now. The thief figured pretty soon it would simply feel like a bruise, and at that time the stitches would need to be removed. Still, just to be sure, she was keeping it clean as she could, and checking often for any hints of the red inflamed skin of infection.

What was more pressing than that was that they needed food. They still had a small amount of her dried meats from her bag, and the plants she foraged, but now that she was feeling well enough to hunt, it just did not seem like enough.

It even almost seemed like a sign, as out of all the people, it was the swordsman who pointed out the tracks of a deer the next day.

She checked it several times to be sure, but for once somehow, he had noticed something that she had not. As they were walking, he stopped and pointed it out.

They were so fresh it gave her goose bumps.

They needed to find it.

However; Venic did not agree with her plan.

"Listen, just let me have my bow, and before the sun sets, I will have us a meal." Valerlanta begged, and not for the first time.

"Let you run off with a weapon to kill me with?" Venic scuffed at the obscenity of her request. "I think not! You'll not be leaving my sight. Can you not just pick us some plants to hold us off?"

"Well yes, of course I could, but do you not think that even the most inexperience tracker will notice our pickings along the way? No, we do not yet know the skills of those tracking us, and killing the young deer would be food for a week! Perhaps even longer! By the time they come across the carcass, we will be long gone and have no need to pick a trail!"

"You would kill the kings game!? Are you mad?"

"What kind of dried meat do you think you have been eating? I am no rabbit, and foraging for plants is much harder in the winter!"

"Killing the king's game is a criminal offence!"

She mocked surprise. "Is that so? Well in that case, I will most definitely think twice before eating his meat. I mean really, out of all the things in my bag, can you imagine if they found meat?!"

He looked at her blankly, not at all seeming to find entertainment in her words. "...Amusing." He said dryly.

"I thought it so." She replied.

His arms crossed, and his jaw tightened with anger, but she could see that she was getting to him.

Even he must be craving a good meal by now.

His eyes drifted off to a mountain; the one that he asked them to head to in order to prove their destination was true. Flantane mountain was there, just a half day ahead, just as promised. Did he really have a reason to not trust her now? "Even if I did let you leave, how would I know you would not simply run off? Or shoot me from behind?"

"I had plenty of perfect moments to shoot you at both the cliff, and with the soldiers, do you not you think? If I wanted you dead, you would be dead." He rolled his eyes at that, but she continued. "And even if I run, I am in this now.

Yes I could hide in the woods well enough, but if I'm going to go through the effort of running away from them, I might as well have something to run to. Besides, if there truly is treasure, I want a go at it as much as the rest of you."

He looked her over for a moment, seeming to try and read her thoughts from expressions, but when that failed he shook his head and sighed. "Can you even fire a bow as you are?"

That made her frown. It was true, even if she was feeling better, overdoing it could just rip her wound open again and put her back where she started for healing, but no matter what way she looked at it, however, without food they would not make it to Palenwood alive. With how much they were walking each day, she knew they did not just want something better, they needed it.

"I can shoot." She answered confidently. "It will not stop me."

He hesitated. "I could hunt."

"That is very chivalrous of you, but I can myself."

"Are you looking down on me? High class men are told to shoot daily from the days of a boy, you know."

"I do not doubt it, but the fact still remains that I am a better tracker. Listen, I know you and your lot might have gone out on a few good hunting bouts with horses, dogs, and endless game a few times a year, but here on foot in the woods things are different. How do think you would even start to know?"

"I know most my prints well enough to follow one deer." He defended in a snarl, then sighed and ran a hand through his almond hair. He paused;

hand still in hair, and his brown eyes looking into the distance; again eyeing Flantane mountain for some reason. "But I do understand your point..."

At that, Valerlanta looked at him pleadingly; offering to him her very best innocent smile, and it worked. He looked away with an aggravated sigh and waved her off. "Fine, but you better come back or I swear I'll burn the whole forest to ashes till I find you."

"Yes, yes, point taken. Now my bow, if you please?" She said, her hand out and waiting.

Then he gave it to her, and watched as her shoulders visibly released their tension as it came into her hands.

Her bow. Her partner.

Her hand slid across the wood tenderly.

"Here." He grunted, handing her the quiver..

Then the knight was snapping his fingers to get her attention again. "Are you listening? Sundown. No later."

"Aye, sir!" She said in her best solider voice, but ruined it with a smirk as he glared. "Don't you fret; I will track you down by then."

She knew she was pushing it, but having her bow back was like regaining a very part of herself, so needless to say it put her in a wonderful mood. Besides, it had to be said. He had to know he could not hide from her.

"Do not dare let yourself forget." He warned once more, and she waved him off dismissively and turned to leave.

"Sundown. Easy enough to remember. Just do what I told you; head for that peek straight ahead and wait for me when you come across the falls.

Watch that peek; it will keep you from losing your way."

He said nothing else, but as the thief went, she felt his glare hot on her back the whole way.

Walking up hill, it almost felt like the arrow head was still in there, pressing on and piercing her insides. He was right about one thing, if she had any sort of smarts, she would never even think about pushing so far. Luckily, she never once told herself that she had any smarts to start.

Once out of sight, Valerlanta fully regarded the print at her boot. It was only about the length of between her thumbs, to the tip of her finger, and was new enough to feel soft under touch. So it was a yearling or so, judging by the hoof size, probably just old enough to leave its mother.

If it kept up its current direction and was not disturbed by anything, it would head right into the valley ahead; perhaps making its way downhill to a water source to reach at sunset.

As the thief followed it, the thief found that the deer was not making a straight path, and was zigzagging towards different food sources as prey animals always do, so if she cut right to the valley, could she meet it there?

It was worth a try; after all, it was the only likely chance she had of catching up.

Valerlanta turned her route, and tried to not hiss in pain at her own fast pace. As she went, she could not help but think of the stories her father would tell her when she was a child; stories of knights and heroes who would get five arrows in them, maybe more, and still keep fighting. Valerlanta wondered what made her weaker than them, why five arrows felt like nothing to them, but one was enough to bring her down, and in front of that knight to top it off!

How pathetic. She had to do better.

Her uneasy steps had lost their usual silence, but she knew they would still be quiet enough. Luckily, the earth was soft moss, bad for leaving tracks, but perfect for masking sound.

By the time she reached the start of a valley, she found it.

It was nestled within the leaves, eating with careful ears rotating for any unusual sounds, and having no idea that it was walking into a trap. With fur of brown with splashes of white, it blended into the forest until it was nearly invisible, and only its own movement pointed it out. Small, hand like, antlers were only just starting to up from its head.

Upon seeing it for the first time, she carefully had kept her distance, skirting a fair ways around until she came to a spot down-wind where she knew the deer was sure to go.

Normally the thief would not bother with a deer so small -after all, father always told her in order to give a forest a chance, you have to let the young ones grow-but she had neither the time nor the strength. Besides, she might not have a chance like this again, and a deer his size would not live long alone.

So, as she knelt by the cover of branches, she knocked an arrow, and slowly pulled to aim.

It still ate, its gentle face carelessly deep in the grasses, with not a care in the world. Occasionally it would lift its head to look at a branch rustled by wind, but was otherwise still.

Valerlanta leaned out slightly, took careful aim right for the place right near where the front leg ended and the heart waited.

At that same moment, the deer stiffened, spooked by something.

It froze, and its limbs readied.

Before it could bounce away, she fired.

As the tension left her bow, Valerlanta collapsed to her knees with a small scream and tried to get control of the pain threatening to make her black out. Once it calmed, she pulled up her clothes and took a quick peek. No new blood, but the pain still seared.

Valerlanta wiped her mouth, and glanced up at her kill.

The arrow hit true, and the deer fell fast and still; this one felt no suffering.

However, the fact still remained that the deer had been spooked by something near; something she was sure was not her. The wind was not right for it to smell her, so it had to be something upwind.

She was not alone. Chances were high that it could be anything from a wolf to a wildcat, but she should still hurry. Even the creatures of the forest could prove dangerous if not careful.

Forcing herself to her feet, she staggered over, withdrew the knife the knight failed to notice sewn hidden in her quiver, and took to work. There was a time, long ago, when she had refused to skin animals, but now she hardly thought about it. It was second nature. Soon, with several piles of meat and no choice but to leave the rest, she wrapped it all in a cloth and put it in her pack.

She would have to cook it later; it was time to leave.

However, just when she was leaving, she heard a branch snap. Without thinking, Valerlanta turned and simultaneously knocked an arrow, and in doing so she locked eyes with a cougar.

The wild cat was quite a distance away, just stalking away from the tree it climbed down, when it froze and they took each other in.

Valerlanta tilted her head and lowered her bow, relived but still on edge. She slowly backed away, showing her respect to the beast, and it waited until she was farther off before continuing on to its meal. Valerlanta backed even farther away, and then hesitantly turned her back on the fierce creature. It was true that wild animals rarely, if ever, hunted people that treated them fairly, but she would hate to turn her back on the one that does.

Smiling to herself, she made her way through the woods until she found the prints she recognized, and followed them. She found the knight soon enough. He was looking towards the mountain she pointed out, with a hand on his sword and his eyes scanning all around him. He did not see the road just a fair way away from him, or if he did, he did not have enough time to hide from it.

She was just about catch up to greet him, when someone else did it first.

A horse and its rider tiredly made its way down the road. Venic stared at the rider suspiciously, and then before she could stop him, the knight hurried forwards to greet the stranger.

Valerlanta rushed forward, waving frantically for him to stop, but the knight did not notice.

He darted from the trees, startling the horse. The rider hurried to calm the huge tossing head, and then smiled in wide-eyed amazement at the person before him. "By a stroke of great luck- Venic! Venic, it is you, is it not? Ah, thank goodness! It is you!" The man screamed as jumped off the horse and rushed to greet the other male.

He was clothed in the same garb as Venic, but had long tied back dusty-blond hair that was quite tossed around and full of leaves. Unlike Venic's more lean build, the stranger was heavier with muscle and carried more upon him. Most importantly, he was huge. He was almost a full head taller than Venic, making even Venic look tiny in comparison.

Another knight. She did not like this.

Venic reached for his sword and glanced around for more attackers. "You made it, but are you alone?"

"Now, now, Venic." The stranger yelped, jumping back and putting up his hands up in surrender. "We have not come to that, have we? Listen, I did not come here to fight, I came here to help you, just as you asked! Just look at me! Do I look like I came here by anything other than the most hurried speed?"

It was in that moment, Valerlanta realized she knew this voice, knew his expressions. In fact, although it had been a very long time, she knew him quite well. He was a long-time friend of hers.

Instantly her hand grabbed the same arrow that its use just moments ago, dropped the bag of meat, and took aim. As she did, Venic lowered his blade, and looked on suspiciously at the other knight.

"You brought what I asked?" Venic pressed cautiously. "While making sure no one followed?"

"Of course, and more! They were all so concerned about you that I was able to sneak out with more than we were hoping for." The blond called as she silently stepped from the trees and into the clearing. The arrow aimed carefully for the man's head.

Venic saw her, and waved his hands to stop her. "Wait, do not shoot! Drostan is a good friend!"

"Alstred Cothhaven is no friend of yours." Valerlanta said and watched as the far larger blonde turned, and paled as white as any cloud could go. He swallowed hard, and forced a shaky smile.

"Hey there, Val." He said with a small wave, but flinched when she glared. "You would not shoot an old friend, would you?"

"In case you have forgotten, no friend of mine wears the clothes of a knight. You have some nerve entering my territory again." She answered. "Talk fast, snake, before I lose my hold."

The blonde haired knight looked between them, but got no aid from either side. Even Venic had partially removed his blade, wanting answers.

Upon seeing this, Alstred snickered. "Ah, it seems I have been caught. I must say though, Val, I never expected you to team up with someone like him, or anyone for that matter. You really ruined my plans. What are you doing with him, might I ask?"

"It's Valerlanta, not Val." She snarled. "Why are you here?"

"You know, with most friends I would call their bluff, but you would actually do it, wouldn't you? You would shoot me."He said, and she gave him no reason to think otherwise, and watched him squirm under her gaze. "Well I suppose there is no use fibbing about it now, is there? You ruined that chance." He looked at Venic. "I am no lord, and I am certainly no knight. All I am is a thief after king's gold who knows how to pay people off well. So well, in fact, I was only just about to steal from his royal library when you offered me to join you on your little quest." He motioned to her. "When you told me you would meet me here, you said nothing about her."

So this is where he went when she was trying to hunt him down for revenge? This was how he disappeared? Under the disguise of a knight?

Her blood boiled.

"Why her, may I ask?" Alstred continued. "You do know she is a thief, right? Do not get me wrong, I know those pretty eyes might tell you otherwise, but trust me; she is trouble. She will rob you blind the moment you so much as think of leaving her."

Venic shot a glance at her, but did not need to say anything.

"You already know?" Again the fake-knight sighed. "Then I am at a loss. So what is it then? What do I have to do to join your little party of misfits here? After all, I did bring you all these lovely things, so this is the least you can do."

Both knight and thief exchanged looks, and the huge man looked hopefully between them.

"I will not kill him without cause." Venic said. "Lies or no lies, he was a good friend, and did save my life once, and him being here may very well have done it again. He risked his life stealing those goods for me, and I cannot let that be."

Hope was welling up in the blonde's eyes, but Valerlanta would not let it stay there long.

"I could do it." Valerlanta said. "He cannot be trusted. He could simply be here to slit our throats in the night. I might be a thief, but he is something even worse than that."

Alstred winced at that, clearly offended. "You know as well as I do that no thief with so much as a little brain would dare touch a hair on your head, princess. Love, you are frightening and all, but there is no hiding from you-know-who, and frankly there is no gold enough to make me want to live through what the king of thieves would do to me. Besides, I, unlike you, am good at making friends, and tempting as it might sometimes be, I will not kill one."

Valerlanta narrowed her eyes at that final insult, knowing very well what event he was referring to, and he returned the look with challenging eyes.

They were building up each other's anger like two dogs ready to fight over a meal.

To prevent the battle, Venic stepped between them and put his sword away.

"He lives." He said pointedly to her, and put up a hand to silence her before she could even open her mouth. "I trusted you, did I not? And I knew you far less. He might be a liar and a cheat, but he was always was good to me. He lives."

She did not like this, not the slightest. She was out-numbered, and now had to work with someone as greedy for gold as herself to top it, but what could she do?

Valerlanta lowered her bow but did not yet resist the tension. “You said that you told him to be here, what did you mean by that?”

Venic looked at her carefully, as if worried by how she would take the news. “I might not be able to navigate through a forest, but I can read a map. Before I was forced to leave, I told Alstred to meet me at this road, knowing that if I headed directly north, I would have to cross this road. I told Alstred to cross up and down this road until we met, and that is what he did. He is here because I told him to be here, and he wants to travel with us for the same reason you do.”

Valerlanta was hesitating, feeling her heart pound and her lips press together into a slight grimace, and then she relaxed her arrow with only a minor wince of pain. "Fine, but he sleeps nearest to you."

"Terrific!" Alstred clapped his hands together. "Now Val, since you are here, I have something to tell you too..."

« Chapter 5 »

Trust is a very delicate thing. Just like a spider's web, it will bend and flex under a breeze, but if the wind batters it too much, it will break, and a smart spider would rebuild elsewhere, never to be bothered by that same breeze again.

And yet her she was, standing with the one who broke her web but unable to relocate again.

"What information could you possibly have for me?" Valerlanta asked in disbelief that the thief-knight could possibly know anything that would be any aid to her.

Just as Venic ordered, her arrow was free and her bow downcast, but she was comfortable with the knowledge that it could easily be ready again. Her relaxed arms were her warning to him, and the dangerous look in his eye said he understood.

"Oh, this and that..." He replied, waving her question off before giving her bow a very serious glance. Instantly her hand flinched, itching to rise to meet his arrogant gaze. "You know, princess, there are better weapons out there now. Those are not used anymore, they just are not. The newer versions are far more superior in every way."

Valerlanta raised a brow, glancing momentarily at the crossbow on his back, and then returning again to his face. "I will stick with what I have, thank you."

Alstred was only just about to counter her, when Venic broke in first.

"Enough picking fights." He shot hotly, then rummaged through his things until he found a large map. "Like it or not, Alstred, I need her as a guide."

Right away curiosity flared in the thief-guide.

Maps were curiously hard to come by, only the rich or military could find the funds to have one made, and even then they were mostly wrong. However, when she was only just about to edge over and peek over the knight's shoulder, he turned and took to pacing swiftly between them; muttering to himself as he went.

Valerlanta stiffened, knowing this was a reaction of anger from not knowing what to do next.

Alstred mirrored her stillness, and both of the thieves dared not say a word or so much as move a finger as the knight thought.

Back and forth he went, his hand pressing at his temple as he tried to think. Then he stopped, sighed, and turned to Valerlanta, causing the thief to flinch. Despite her obvious discomfort, Venic simply frowned, staring for a movement longer, then sighed again while glancing back at the map and turning away. "Alright, time to go. We can talk more as we walk."

"What?" Valerlanta asked, looking between the two. "That is it? That is all you are going to ask?"

"I told you-" Venic answered without even turning to look at her. "-He is my friend, and I trust him as one."

"You did not even know his name!" Valerlanta sputtered, but the knight simply started and kept on walking.

Reluctantly, Valerlanta turned too, but hesitated mid-step momentarily to give the huge blonde a good glare.

With the knights back turned and feeling much braver now, Alstred grinned victoriously.

In response, Valerlanta held up her bow for him to see, and made a mock motion of shooting him. Then, satisfied he got the message, she nodded him forward, and with angry eyes he went with the horse right behind him.

They continued like this-with her at the back ready to pounce, and the other two ahead- until Valerlanta realized that Venic was about to get them hopelessly lost again, and she took the lead. Wordlessly Venic took the rear.

The thief did not like having the Alstred-and the horse for that matter-directly behind her, but she would just have to trust the swordsman to have her back. However, trusting as little as she did, she glanced back often just to be sure, and each time he would smirk at her tauntingly.

She led them carefully, taking into account the new man behind her and planning accordingly. Thanks to his path directly on the road, she had to trust on tricking those following him into thinking she was planning on following it for a while.

The thief hoped it was working, though if the army was only a half day behind before, she had little doubt that they would soon catch up if she was not careful.

Unfortunately, she could not also take into account her wound, which made her eyes fog with tears whenever they started steep climbs or drops. It hurt, and she knew she should tread carefully, but she would not allow herself. No matter the outcome, she did not want the snake behind her to know how injured she was. Tough as it might be, she scarcely allowed herself even so much as a hiss of pain in fear that he might notice.

Then, as they walked up the rocky riverside and behind a waterfall she stopped. As if catching her idea, Venic finally started to talk; as if the thunderous roar made him feel safe to do so.

Mist sprinkled her face with cool water, and - not knowing if it was the fact that she was drunk off pain or just simply wishing for a distraction- but for a small moment she found herself admiring the view and nearly missing what the knight was saying. Light danced in through the falling water, sending a sort of tranquil feeling throughout the small cave, even though the water cascaded in a wall of powerful force.

"So, out with it then." Venic said from behind her-having to raise his voice over the roar-and she tried to shake the daze out of her head to listen. "What do you need to tell us?"

There was a pause, and she found herself glancing back and saw Alstred Cothhaven standing comfortably as if they were all just friends out for a stroll. Venic actually also had a light shimmer of relaxation in his eyes, which was the first she had ever seen on him. He trusted his friend fully, felt safer with Alstred here, and she did not understand it. As the horse nickered in dislike at the sound of falling water, Venic even went up and patted the horse on the nose to calm it from beside Alstred; a man who could very well stab Venic in the back at any time.

The only one she was ever like that with was her father, but that was natural; these two might as well be strangers. Seeing them standing so calmly next to each other, she almost felt like she was made of something different entirely.

'How can the knight be so stupid?' Sighing angrily, Valerlanta turned back away and opened her bag to start mentally splitting up the meat of her hunt into meals. They would need more now, if the snake was to be joining them. Was it even worth the attempt to preserve it? Now it seemed it would not last long...

"I was sent out with some men to track you all, and guess who was in charge?" Alstred started as the thief only half listened.

Perhaps she should hunt some rabbit? How much do men eat anyhow? Her father ate a lot, but was every man like that?

"Fealdeer?" Venic asked, as if it should be obvious.

"No, Efailden was chosen." Alstred said, and Valerlanta nearly tipped over. Swiftly she breathed carefully to steady herself, and fought a swore.

"Efailden? Jerstain Elfailden? But that crazed soul is obsessed with thieves. He never bothers with anything but. He is mad." Venic countered.

"Exactly." Alstred said, and suddenly she could feel his eyes on her. "But there is one thief in particular he is most obsessed about catching. So much as a whisper of a rumour, and he is off in the direction it spread from." He paused to yawn, though somehow the sound seemed acted, as if he wanted to appear disinterested. "I do not know all about it myself, but he always mumbles something about regaining his honour. Frankly, I just think his mum had slippery fingers and dropped him a few too many time. Whatever the reason, though, he is completely set on catching her."

She pictured it for a moment; the reason. The glass in her hand, the blood spraying, then the screams.

"Her?" Venic echoed, and she felt his eyes also fell upon her back.

The thief knew she should not be surprised, after all, the man followed her like a crow does a dying deer, but somehow she still was. It had been a long time since he last attempted to catch her in the woods, so she assumed he had given up that far.

Apparently not.

It was not like he was particularly dangerous, after all, he was very predictable, and she often had fun at taunting him over his failed attempts, but Alstred was right about one thing. Efailden was obsessed. Even if all his men died one by one of winter cold, he would not stop if he thought he was close.

"Is there anyone in this forest who does not know each other?" Venic sighed, and Alstred chuckled, his age over them suddenly seeming apparent by his father-like laugh; though in no more than a moment that feeling was gone.

"Think of it, Venic, there are not all that many forest dwellers, so the forest is kind of like a town.

Everyone either knows each other, or at least can point you to someone who does; or so someone once told me."

She could still feel the eyes of both men on her as she considered things, but she ignored them and instead glared on at the falling water.

Commander Efailden.

If it was true, then this was perfect. She was in the game again! If she could just be sure to skirt the men until she was strong enough to fight, she could win this!

It was true, Askyel was harder game, but Efailden? She had outsmarted him more than enough times to know how he thinks, and knowing Askyel, he would just sit back, wait to see how the other men failed, then wait to play his own pieces till the battle field was to his advantage.

Askyel had simply challenged her in that first fight and she just accepted it.

Once her wound was healed, she would be in for the thrill of her life; she was sure of it.

Her hands clenched in anticipation, and realizing it, she quickly shook it off and started looking on at the meat again before the men behind her would take notice. However, her small hidden grin remained.

Oh the stories she would soon be able to tell! And a dragon was to be only the start. By the end of this she would be a legend with all the riches she would ever need.

"Is he someone to worry over?" Venic asked finally. "I have scarcely even seen the man at the castle."

"Hmm." Was all Astrid replied, and she knew they were relying on her to answer.

"No." Valerlanta replied curtly, and then stomped out of the cave, not waiting for them to follow.

"My, she even talks less then when I knew her." Astrid said as she went with a small, almost sad, laugh. What was that? A hint of regret in his voice?

Perhaps, but not enough. He did not nearly regret what he did enough; not yet.

That night, while they were getting ready by gathering firewood and readying a shelter to protect against the sounds of thunder clouds nearing. Alstred had left to go gather firewood after Valerlanta refused to let him help her, so instead Venic stayed behind and held the ridge-pole against the tree as she tied it on.

"He is not so bad, you know." Venic said as she finished off the first knot.

She paused to glare at him before moving over to the other side of the pole. Not caring of her hint, Venic continued. "He smells sometimes, I will give you that, but he is not a bad man."

"It is unfortunate that the smell is only the small of the problem. I do not know why you can stand even being near the man." She shot.

The last knot tied, he let go, and she went to pass him to go get another pole. He grabbed her arm as she went by, and stopped her. "Listen, I do not know what man you knew, but I promise he is not that man now. Now, I do not know what he did, so I cannot say the price of shame it brought upon you, but I can tell you this, he saved my life once." Venic said. "I was ambushed on one of the king's errands, one of the first I had been on, and was very outnumbered-by thieves none the less. All my men were killed, and I was soon to be as well, but then like a wisp he was there, and took down a man with just a swipe of an axe. We fought then, side by side, and any on lookers would have sworn it was theatre with how easily the men fell. We have been friends ever since. I trust him."

Valerlanta was just about to stop him, to make him stop trying to piece trust between her and them, when she caught notice of something odd with his final words.

They came out normal enough, but with a different sound then the rest of his speech. It was a slight tone, hardly there, but it was enough to send a down her spine. She could not quite describe it, but it was like a greed, a *need*, for her to like the other man, yet totally different then wanting a friend to want a friend.

"Turning hate into friendship is not that simple."

"I understand that," He said, picking up a long pole and putting it over his shoulder, "but I stand by the argument that he is not the man you knew. Not long before meeting me, he lost someone very close to him, and that changes a man."

Valerlanta paused, thinking of when her trail for finding Alstred once went cold. After some time, she found out it was because the tall man had fallen in love, only to have the father of the wife-to-be displeased by their plans of a secret marriage, and murdered his own daughter in front of Alstred out of revenge. Valerlanta did not want to admit it, but she gave up chasing him when she heard about that.

Valerlanta had visited the grave to be sure it was true, and found a grand stone carving of a woman walking into a forest. The thief found out soon after that Alstred had done nothing but drink and work until he had finished it. "You think losing his wife was punishment enough?"

He looked surprised that she knew who it was Alstred lost, but then nodded. "I do."

"Hmm." Was all she said, and went back to just setting up the shelter, with her leading the way, and him mimicking her actions in a way to learn.

As they finished leaning all the poles against the one tied to the tree and was about to start on the evergreen shingles, Alstred returned, an arm load of firewood and smiling at them as innocently as a child.

"Food?" He asked, true to her thought, and Valerlanta glared at his rude way of asking for the food 'she' hunted for, but could not deny her own hunger.

And it was only moments after that when she soon learnt something very important; men eat a lot.

That was a simple fact she found out quick enough as the men ate just as fast as Alstred could cook, and would have continued eating all the rations for tomorrows breakfast had she not swept it directly behind her and gave death-glares to both the hungry men.

Somehow watching them eat reminded her of two starving coyotes after the same meal. True, they had the stiff backs and high heads of one used to castle affairs, but there was no hesitation when she told them they would have to eat without a plate. It was positively horrifying. Were all men like this? If so, how? How was it possible to fit so much food into two men?

'I'll need to go hunting again.' She thought to herself as she looked on at them while she simply held onto hers. 'Maybe twice.'

Perhaps if she walked them less they would eat smaller amounts? She would have to try that tomorrow, for today they seemed their stomachs were bottomless pits.

Once both the men had picked clean every last bone, they sat back, feet close to the small fire, and watched on at it with sleepy eyes and content expressions.

"Somehow, that tasted much better than any of peacocks the king fed us." Venic said, and the man beside him laughed, but then Venic tilted his head considering. "Although, it was the first real meat I have had since I left the bloody castle...that could very well be part of it."

Valerlanta raised a brow at that. Granted, even she preferred this over the soup, but he was in no way starving. "Excuse me?"

"Listen, Valerlanta, you have no ability to taste what you are eating." He took another bite of his deer, and made an expression of pure joy. "I honestly have no idea how you can eat that every day! Even you must admit Alstred is a far better cook."

Pressing her lips tightly together, she held back any grumbles she had in response.

The blonde man beside Venic laughed. "Perhaps now you will gain some of your thickness back! As you are now, you look like a half-starved woman." Suddenly Alstred motioned to the air with an idea. "Ah! Val, I do not suppose you have a dress somewhere on you, do you? It might be a good disci-"

Suddenly the blonde was cut short as the swordsman smacked the back of his head. "Me? You are the fool with hair past your shoulders."

The blond touched his ponytail tenderly. "This? I thought it made me look more manly? Like a barbarian from over the ocean."

Venic snorted with laughter and smiled at his much larger friend. "Maybe that is part of their plan, to hide among their women. Although, I heard their women are ugly as mules, perhaps you are doing your hair like a woman? What if we have been fighting women this whole time?!"

Both laughed.

Suddenly feeling uncomfortable, Valerlanta stood, bringing her food with her. "I will take first watch." She said and both men stopped to notice her. "Unless either of you...women...would rather for me?"

"Ah, I am more than fine here thank you." Alstred said, wiggling bare toes near the hot flames of the fire, so she looked to Venic and he nodded her off in approval.

"Wait," Alstred said before she could get away, and tossed something towards her. Raising a brow, she opened the cloth wrappings and found perfect crust inside. "I know you have not ate muck bread before, right? In my mind, it is only fair that you are the one to have it."

Valerlanta regarded him with a blank face, and then let it drop from her hands. It landed on the forest floor, and she turned to leave without a second glance.

"I do not need anything from you." She said over her shoulder.

When she entered the much colder air, she shuddered and carefully moved her collar up further against the chill. It did little good though, after being so close to a fire moments ago.

Even her eyes took long to adjust, so she tread slowly until she found herself a low-lying tree and pulled herself up the lower branches; though it made her blink with pain and nearly fall. Once upon her perch with her bowl of food, and satisfied she could easily see both the men and the surrounding area, she leaned back to relax.

Taking a tentative nibble of her own deer meet, she was dissatisfied to find it actually was better than anything of hers. It was cooked with a small amount of salts, spices, and vegetables Alstred was able to sneak with him, and the meat melted in her mouth.

'Even the food is against me.' She thought bitterly to herself as she took another bite, and then ate the rest.

She was more than reluctant to sleep next to the blonde, she stayed up most the night. However, even from her location she could hear the other man snore, who was clearly not as nervous as her.

When she finally grew too tired to watch, the moon was far passed the highest point in the sky, and so she dragged herself over to the dimming fire, threw some more wood upon it, then kicked Venic's feet to wake him.

He grumbled as he woke, but rose willingly, so she reluctantly lay outside the shelter by the fire facing the sleeping face of the man she so badly wanted to hunt down only seasons ago, then slowly closed her eyes and hesitantly welcomed sleep.

* * *

The following day she led them through a path known by locals as only "the path of whispers." It was said to be haunted, even though many parts this far north were, this path in particular was infested by a certain type of ghost. This kind sparkled like stars in dark nights, and led travellers to their deaths, and such travellers rarely risked this road, and when they did, night travel was a risk for fools.

Here giants of stone kings and kings of old lay crumbling, and various houses, some in better states than others, were left to be housed by only nature.

Venic did not seem to mind, but Alstred shivered visibly. "I do not like this road; not even in the least of amounts. Can we not take another? What is this place?"

"This one?" Valerlanta looked around and saw many of the houses around her. These were much more new than others they had past; in fact, fires black paint still stained many of their stone walls. "This place is known as the path of whispers. It is said that a man can hear the calls of the dead and see the river run red with the hundreds of years this place has of blood. According to locals, this place is cursed, and any that stays here dies brutally. The last that tried to live here was killed by your king. This place is a graveyard of the murdered."

She looked back at them, content to see the blond as pale as snow, so she quickly decided to keep going. "Do not step slowly here; we do not want to stay here longer than needed."

Alstred babbled something she could not understand, but Venic pushed the frozen man aside so he and the horse could be second in lead.

"The king is a great man, he has murdered no one." He said. "I have heard the story of this place; these people led a raid against the king, and were suspected in aiding the rebals that assasinated the royals. Their deaths were their own cause."

Alstred whimpered as if the ghost would get offended, but Valerlanta just shrugged, thinking of the day it happened. She was far away with her father, but even at that distance, they could still see the smoke and glow of the flames upon the mountain.

"You know less than you could ever imagine." Valerlanta said calmly, then shot one last look around then continued on. "Have you not ever wondered why everyone in your court of nobles is so young? Why would those that attacked the castle be so careful to only kill the old? It is suspicious enough for even you to admit it as so."

"We should speak carefully! This place is haunted." She heard Alstred whisper from behind her, much to her amusement.

"There are no such thing as ghosts." Venic replied sharply. "You are worse than an old lady, did you know that?"

"You will not be saying that after they get you, and you have none of my charms to protect you."

"You got those charms from a street leach! And every time you pass, they have a new one for you. You waste your money."

Alstred had said something else, but Valerlanta smirked and ignored it, realizing she should be paying more attention to tracking and less to them, when she nearly over stepped a bear print unnoticed.

It was old, more than a day in fact, but it annoyed her none-the-less.

They traveled long and hard after that, stopping only for water and what food, but suddenly she found the blonde moving with much more haste, as if something was chasing him and him alone.

She knew she should have told him they had left the valley well before noon, but she was enjoying his silence far too much. In fact, he had scarcely said a word since they last stopped, but just in case, she still flicked her head sideways every once in a while, and she heard him whimper, thinking she had heard a voice.

Along the way they found a cave, a shallow little thing surrounded thick by brush, and the men insisted on staying for the night. She still did not like it and tried to argue against sleeping in a cave, but she could find no sign of life inside to make them decide otherwise. Despite that, Valerlanta lingered outside; making excuses of finding firewood until they had an enormous pile and Venic told her to stay.

"We have enough firewood." He told her.

"Enough for days." Alstred laughed.

Valerlanta opened her mouth to argue, and quickly rounded a tree with her bundle of wood to do so, and came face to face with the horse. Squeaking in surprise, Valerlanta stepped back away and fell. All the firewood shattered around and upon her, and she rushed to pick it up, but not before one more careful step away from the snorting horse.

Uncaring of her dramatic reaction, the horse went back to eating the grasses at its feet. Both men, who were about to enter the cave, turned and stared blankly, as if they could not believe what they were seeing.

"You do not like horses." Venic said blandly, as if such a thought was insane to him.

Firewood back in hand Valerlanta fought the fire coming to her cheeks and glared at all three of them; even the horse. "Horses are nothing but a deathtrap. The moment you let your guard down, they strike like a snake!"

"Not Bluebell!" Alstred exclaimed, rushing forward to nuzzle his cheek with the horses. The horse nuzzled back, and Valerlanta rolled her eyes. "I was wondering why you were keeping so far away from something this adorable! Bluebell would not hurt a soul, would you, girl? No, you would not! Come on, Val, you are just being an idiot. This horse would not hurt a soul! Just give her a pet, right here above the nose. We do not want the sweetie to get offended, do we? One pet, and I promise I will not talk to you all night. Deal?"

Reluctantly, her hand outstretched, and as it came in near, the horse recoiled and snapped it's teeth. Valerlanta only just pulled back her hand in time and glared.

"Bluebell!" Alstred exclaimed, wagging his finger at the horse. "Strange, she normally likes everyone."

"Do not worry." Valerlanta ensured. "The feeling between the two of us is very much the same."

As she was walking past Venic to find the stream they had located earlier, she noticed him trying to hide a laugh in an unconvincing cough into his hand.

"Not a word!" She warned him, and he nodded, though his eyes were watering at the effort.

Once alone near the gentle trickle she let her eyes glance at the cave she had no excuse not to sleep in. Venic and Alstred walked inside the opening, disappearing inside as if being swallowed into the darkness of a huge mouth.

The thought made her stomach want to turn, so she quickly ripped her eyes away.

Cold water seeped into her boots, but she did nothing to stop it.

'Do not be weak.' Her brain told her over and over again. *'Do not show weakness; especially in front of Alstred. Do not be weak.'*

How could she do it, though? How could she sleep in a place that was so much like that place?

"Gah!" Shaking it off, the thief stretched her arms then slapped her cheeks lightly as if to shock away the growing fear within her. When that did not work, Valerlanta removed her mask and set it on the rocks beside her as she leaned down and cupped icy water against her face.

The chill of the glacier-fed water was nearly enough to make her gasp, but she welcomed the cold that came as the droplets slid down the nape of her neck. It seemed to energize her with the shock of it, so she did it several more times after.

When she finally stopped, and simply sat there, face dripping wet as she looked between her hands and at the water between them, she saw the water still to show a dark reflection of herself.

Blonde hair framed her face; and she could only just recognize cold and empty eyes staring back at her.

"I am not you anymore." She whispered softly to the reflection. Dipping hand in, she shook waves and disturbed the image until she was satisfied that the person she hated was no longer mirrored there. As the water waved and threatened to settle again, worked on her hair. Brushing the blonde strands with her fingers back into place, Valerlanta worked it back up until she could pin it back and it would no longer be in the way of her mask ties.

Done, thief grabbed her worn mask. The holes in the soft and worn leather seemed to stare back at her as it came into her fingers, but she ignored it.

"So you do take it off." A voice said, and Valerlanta quickly stumbled with the leather cordage to put the mask back on her face. It was only once it was safely back where it belonged that she was willing to turn back.

Venic was there, his arms crossed over his chest and an almost curious looking expression of a raised brow. His head was tilted slightly, as if he had been leaning to get a better look at her naked face before she hid it.

She flushed, as if shamed that she had accidentally showed him something private.

"Of course I do!" Valerlanta shot. "I am not some filthy creature who never bathes."

"Yes, I suppose you would." Venic said carefully, his eyes trailing over the mask slowly. “When I first met, I thought you were hiding your identity from everyone, and then I thought it again when I saw your magic, but that is not the case, is it? No one would know your face even if they saw it." When she refused to respond, he continued. "I know I should not have looked, but I did, and just now, when I caught a glimpse of what you hide, I saw nothing worth being ashamed of, so now that I have seen it, I cannot help but be curious."

"I have told you before, have I not?" She shot. "I will not say it again."

"Yes, you have." His eyes went wide with memory, and he nodded in understanding. "We all have something to hide, and it is normally something that cannot be seen."

She frowned at him deeply and her mind drifted to the night she first put it on.

Smoke was heavy on the air as the huge fires cackled, seeming to want to join in with the excitement of the surrounding people. Everyone was laughing and cheering; their glee seeming to be a great contrast to their terrifying faces.

Masks were on every one. Some were made of leather or old sacks for holding farm goods, and others were made from strips of bark or wood, making it seem like the trees themselves had come alive for that night.

'Why?' Valerlanta had croaked, her voice still strange to her ears as she was still not used to using it. *'Why are they wearing masks?'*

Her father neared from behind her and wrapped his cloak around her so that both of them were in its warmth.

Leaning back, she felt safe as a caterpillar in a cocoon. Safe; this feeling too, was still something strange to her.

'People wear masks to become someone or something else.' Her father explained. *'On this particular night, it makes the dead mistake us for one of their own. It is protection.'*

As Valerlanta slowly lowered her hand, she found herself looking at the grasses at the base of the fence.

She knew the mask had no use now that she was old enough to know that her father was just explaining a town's superstition, and yet she could not be parted from the mask, as if it was only the thin piece of leather that was preventing her from reverting back to the scared child she once was.

Venic frowned at her, as if perplexed by her reply, or rather her lack of one. Then, after one last careful look into her eyes, he too walked over to the river and filled up her pot with water. He knelt directly beside her, waiting for the pot to fill.

There was plenty of room elsewhere, but for whatever reason, he chose to be near enough that just by raising her elbow would surely put him off balance. Here, she could easily find a way to fight him, but chose to trust her; to be near her.

"You confuse me." She said bluntly.

He smiled. "I feel the same about you."

She wrinkled her nose at him, looking into his amused almond eyes, then turned and stomped away.

The thief sat at the fire they placed at the back of the cave, trying to keep her mind on the flames to ignore how the darkness of the cave was clinging around the light tightly.

It seemed like within the time of a blink, they ate, they readied their beds, and then it came time to sleep.

"I will take first watch." Valerlanta suggested, but the two boys shook their heads.

"They will not look at night." Alstred said. "They would not risk their carts."

"He is right." Venic confirmed. "As long as we move as soon as the sun comes up, we will be fine."

Unable to argue otherwise, the thief watched as the two boys were swift to slumber, and even though she was not cold, she lay as close to the fire-and the light it put off- as she could.

Valerlanta did fall into a light sleep; however, as the night went on, the fire started to dwindle, and as the heat slowly crept away from the cave, she realized the feeling of the cold stone was familiar, too familiar.

The realization woke her up with a gasp.

'But not the same.' She tried to remind herself. *'This is not the same.'*

She knew that she was curling into a tiny ball, but did not feel any warmer.

Her breath felt fast but she could not still it. Her palms were near bleeding, but she could not unclench her tightly curled fingers.

'It is not the same!' She willed over and over again, but something told her that was a lie. It was very much the same. Same cold stone, same blinding dark.

She would be trapped, trapped again.

Then, there was a shifting sound that sounded oddly to her ears, the sound of logs being added to the fire and suddenly a warmth on her back. It was a faint feeling, and yet just enough to bring her back and release the caves chilly clench upon her neck.

She was back, her nightmare was fading.

Abruptly, she could again hear the soft rumble of snores from Alstred, and smell the damp of the cave.

Venic.

He had shifted over so they were back-to-back so that they were touching just below the shoulder blades, and did not say a word. The pride she still had wanted her to wiggle away, to push away such help, and yet as her breathing calmed and her heart rate returned to normal, she stayed exactly where she was.

Light was once again filling the cave, and the tiny amount of warmth against her back calmed her breath.

"Thank you." She murmured, possibly too low for him to hear, and he said nothing in return.

* * *

Banging. There was some sort of banging. Scratching; there was that too.

But what was causing it?

Groggily Valerlanta opened her eyes, and was momentarily panicked by the amount of darkness, but then her eyes focused and she saw that she was in a shallow cave, not in a shelter under the stars, and she was not alone.

Sighing heavily, she sat up and looked around. The fire was nearly out, and that snake of a man was curled tightly around it for the heat. Venic was asleep with his back to her; directly beside where she now looked around from.

The scratching sound came again, and her hand clumsily found her knife. But she saw nothing. From nowhere in the cave did she see so much as a chipmunk, yet when she was holding her breath and her ears strained for sound, she heard it again to the far right, hidden behind a set of large rocks.

Reluctantly, -though silent as a mouse- she slid to her feet and into a crouching position. Once there, she opted for her bow, and waited.

The sound came again, like rock dragging on rock, then again. Still nothing reviled itself.

'Too loud for a snake.' She thought, tilting her head at the noise. *'Not enough room behind that rock to be a bear or wildcat...what are you?'*

Hesitantly she glanced around the cave to be sure the blonde still slept and nothing else was around, then curiosity got the better of her and she found herself stalking forward.

Her arrow slid back on her bow, and rose to aim.

Her feet stepped forward one by one without so much as a crunch.

Then, as the thrill started making her breath short and her heart race, she reached the rocks and looked over.

And there was only darkness there.

Barely enough room for a chipmunk and definitely no room for anything but.

The sound stopped, leaving her all the more puzzled.

"What is it?" A voice asked, and Valerlanta turned back to see the knight sitting up.

Shrugging she turned her head back to inspect, and was attacked.

Out of the cracks and holes came thousands of little winged creatures, swarming the cave like a hive of angry bees.

They came on them at once, pulling hair, biting skin, and tearing at clothing and items.

Alstred was awoken with a scream as a particularly nasty bunch pulled his beard and startled him right into the hot embers of the fire. As he got up screaming and swearing, Valerlanta and Venic swatted in a panic as they tried to make it through the thick of the angry crowd.

The pixies -clearly territorial and angry- swarmed them in circles to keep them from running, and did their deadly work. Some took what torn patches of clothes to stock their nest, but others, mystified by the sparkle of metals, started digging in their packs for treasures.

Squawking as her final arrow was almost lifted away, Valerlanta swatted them with her bow like an old lady would a broom and only just managed to keep the arrow from being captured.

Her face was now very scratched, though could have been much worse had it not been for her mask, and her bare skin was bleeding in small little cuts. Yet they just kept coming, and while they tried to make it to the exit of the cave, it was a slow process of swatting and defending what they could.

"Not. My. Hair!" Alstred screamed as he brandished a flaming stick above his head, aiming for some nest driven pixy. Just as the blond man swung another time, Venic-while fighting over his own bag-was forced to duck under the heated weapon and fell hard to the ground and his items scattered.

One of the items was a little metal orb.

Gasping in horror as she saw many pixie turn and look in awe, Valerlanta rushed for it.

The pixies tried to stop her; scratching at her skin and pulling hard at her head.

The monstrous creatures reached the orb; their tiny hands working together to lift it into the air, so, bitter and tired, Valerlanta called for the magic.

Echoing her emotions, the fire rose and burned a hot bright white, spreading out through the cave and startling the swarm. The pixie squeaked in surprise and horror, giving Valerlanta the time to reach the orb and snatching safely back into her hands, but she soon wished she never tried.

Just as the ball touched her skin, pain over took her and collapsed her to her knees.

Screaming in pain, Valerlanta crumpled forward, but she could not drop the ball as it burned and seared into her hand.

Then, as she thought she could take no more, the white flame vanished into darkness as if swallowed up, and then was replaced with a fierce red glowing from ruins on the orb.

Hungrily it soaked in her energy as she screamed, and as it drank its fill, images flashed before her.

'A giant tree.'

'A proud king.'

'A nation at war.'

'A man forging a sword.'

Then nothing, and she was back, leaving her stunned and unmoving. Her whole body shook, and everything seemed dull and slow.

Valerlanta no longer screamed, but she found she did not even have the strength to close her mouth.

Everything was cold. Everything was numb.

She heard someone calling her, and she started to lift her head to see who, when suddenly she was pulled up by strong arms, and she was helped towards the exit as the swarm squeaked around them and was ready to re-attack.

But then, as both her and her helper burst into the bright outside, she saw Venic rush forward and pull her other arm around his shoulders.

So if it was not Venic, then who was it she was clinging to?

The swarm and the cave with it got farther and farther behind, and soon they found themselves back at the cliff-side ruins, where Valerlanta was dropped onto the mossy staircase, and both her saviours were able to stand up and tend to themselves.

Alstred, red with anger and a mess of scattered blond hair stepped away from her and lost it. "What was that? What just happened?!" He motioned between both thief and knight with a raised posture and clenched muscles. "What happened in that cave? What did I just see?"

Venic, composed and head high, looked on at the other man with a daring expression. "It is nothing of worry." He said, and Alstred sputtered.

"N-Nothing of worry? Nothing of worry?!" Alstred grabbed the other man by the shirt and pulled him close. "How dare you say that to me! We were attacked by pixies, the bloody fire turned hotter than a blacksmiths, the stupid ball of yours lit up on its own, and you call 'that' nothing of worry? You are going to tell me what is going on, or I can promise you, you will regret it."

"Sorry." Valerlanta mumbled, finally getting her breath back, and both men turned to her. Too tired to feel anything but ashamed, she let her head lull. "I should never have...I never thought...I panicked and....-" She trailed off to silence. Her mind too foggy to think the right words. She was just too cold.

She expected screams, she expected pain, but what she did not expect was for gentle fingers to grab her hand and pull it forward.

"There is nothing to forgive." Venic said with eyes locked onto hers as he knelt before her as he slowly and carefully uncurled her shivering fingers from the metal ball.

She winced and gasped at the pain as her fingers came off, but Venic kept talking to distract her from seeing. "We could not get out as we were, you saved us. On top of that, you even unlocked me a little clue of the orb." He smiled small. "Do not worry for him over there. He will catch on soon enough."

And at that point, the blonde's eye grew wide, and his mouth babbled un-heard words as he gaped at Valerlanta.

Thinking of all the times Alstred looked down on her in the past for being weaker, Valerlanta wondered if he was regretting that now.

"See?" Venic smirked, following her gaze and glancing back. "And besides-" he lifted and showed her the ball that was now free from her grasp. Her hand was red, raw, and blistering, but luckily no skin went with the ball. "-I just learned something else important. My dear king thinks that only he could bring our friend here to life. You know what that means?" He leaned forward, his grip on the wrist of her sore red hand tightening. "I have the advantage."

Valerlanta blinked in surprise, and opened her mouth to voice her confusion, but as she raised her head, she found herself tipping backwards against the stairs. Venic reached forward to help her, and her back then head gently touched the cool stone.

Her eyes rolled back and found warmth.

« Chapter 6 »

Flexing her bandaged hand, Valerlanta winced as the wound there burned as if still hot. When the stinging stopped, she could not help but frown. This, mixed with her painful headache and shaky limbs was the worst kind of news to her.

'Can I shoot like this?' She wondered, fear causing cold to spread deep in her chest.

She had woken just before the sun had started to greet the world, and struggled to remember the night before. The two men were nearby, with Venic laying down with his back to her, and Alstred in a sitting position to keep watch, but also fast asleep. Their clothes were torn and their hair was wild, and Valerlanta wondered if she looked just as pathetic as they did.

She sure felt it.

Slowly, she touched her bow, her fingers gliding across the familiar surface. Then, grabbing it up completely, she staggered to her feet, and walked away from the group while using the stone of the ruins for support.

Once she was far enough away, she found a target quick enough. As her eyes drifted up the tree with empty seed shells at the base, there at the top she found a chattering squirrel. It regarded her from its high branch with curiosity, but also with territorial anger.

It was small, but this should be easy game.

Taking up her bow, she knocked her last arrow, and took aim while ignoring the searing pain.

The squirrel, not used to humans, stayed where it was, observing her carefully while chattering at her.

The thief clenched her teeth tight to keep from gasping from the pain as the squirrel swayed in and out of view. Then, when it aimed up close enough, she fired. The arrow shot and only just missed, but left Valerlanta collapsing to her knees and hissed in pain while squeezing her wrist, as if doing so would suffocate the pain away. Blood showed through the bandages on her fingers.

"Ashes." She hissed.

She could shoot, but it felt like she was ripping her skin away when she did so, which it probably was.

Frustrated tears swam in her vision.

When she had finally gotten control of her pain again, Valerlanta stood and went to find the arrow and her catch. She found it soon enough, but discovered her little act had nearly shaved off one side of feather fletching. Her only arrow would not fly straight anymore.

Cursing twice, then several more times, she got to her feet and kicked a rock. Then, when it did not move, she kicked it several more times until it came free of the soil, and rolled away. At that time, with no more rock, she gave one final kick to a tree. The kick shook the leaves, but the tree did not move, so Valerlanta let out a shaky breath and leaned forward to let her brow touch the rough white bark.

"Useless." She breathed at the tree, and her anger swiftly dissipated at her own words.

What was she going to do if she could not shoot? Of course her wound would heal, but that could take many days!

There was other ways to hunt, but her bow was her best protection; and the one thing she knew that snake Alstred could not beat her at.

Images flooded her mind of Alstred helping to carry her out of the cave the night before.

Why do that? Why leave someone for dead one time, but save them the next?

And what did Venic mean by when he said that he now had the advantage? What did he know that she did not?

Her anger flooded back at her own confusion, but she ignored it as she flipped around so her back would be against the tree, then slid down to sit. Her head relaxed back against the tree, and her eyes drifted up to the green leaves, then the sky beyond that.

It was going to rain soon.

"Just perfect." Valerlanta said sarcastically.

"What is?" A voice asked, and the thief looked up in time to see Venic emerging from the ruins, and up to where she sat. His expression was slightly concerned.

Somehow disgusted, Valerlanta turned away. "Nothing."

"Hmm." Was all he replied as he knelt down near her, clearly not catching the hint that she wanted to be alone, or he was just ignoring it. "How is your hand?"

"It is fine enough." She hissed, jumping back up to her feet, though the fast action almost made her fall over.

Venic reached forward to help her, but she staggered away and instead grabbed onto a tree.

"I do not need your help." The thief snarled. She did not need him pretending to like her.

His expression stoned over at that, but he did withdraw his help, and so she stomped back to the camp.

Once there, she paced several times, then nudged Alstred on the feet.

"Wake up!" She shot.

He did, his snoring coming to a swift halt as he sprang to his feet and looked around for danger with groggy eyes. He rose his axe up, but she only rolled her eyes. "What is it? What is wrong?"

"Nothing, but you have slept enough." She replied coldly. "Get your things, we are leaving."

Alstred looked at her with a look of tired confusion, but when she kept glaring, he shrugged and got ready.

By the time the blonde was done, Valerlanta had already snuck back into the cave to grab what else she could of their things, then stuffed it all back into her pack and returned to camp. As if to put salt on the wound, one of her favorite daggers, and her best pot, had been swallowed into the pixy nest.

Then it started to rain.

Grumbling to herself, Valerlanta covered her bow under her cloak, brought up her hood, and started leading her way through the woods in a stomping fashion.

"I see that our brave forest guide is pleasant on this fine morning." She overheard Alstred say from behind her, though she suspected she was meant to.

Venic only grunted in reply.

When the rain continuously got worse until the point where the trees were bending back under the force of the wind, they had no choice but to stop. Valerlanta found them a somewhat sheltered area between where two trees had fallen on top of the other, and then she added to it by quickly adding a roof. Then, all three huddled inside.

Valerlanta normally avoided dead-fall shelters when possible due to the bugs that hid in the logs, but with this rain, the critters would probably also wait until the rain let up, so this would have to do, for now.

The rain pounded the forest outside their shelter, and although they were sheltered inside, Valerlanta shivered from the dampness of her clothing.

While Venic was staring somewhere off into the distance, Alstred, however, had his eyes directly on her bandaged hand. Although she was trying her very best to ignore the heat of his stare, it kept making her shift with discomfort. Then finally, after a blast of lightning lit up the forest, he spoke what was on his mind.

"So you are- so then, you can...?" Alstred trailed off, and Valerlanta sighed with annoyance.

"Yes, Alstred, I can wield magic." She shot back, hopefully to end the conversation. It was confusing enough for her just to be around

Alstred he had saved her, but now he wanted to talk too.

"But you-how? I thought only royalty can do magic?" He mumbled, completely confused. "Does this mean there are more like you?"

Valerlanta paused before talking to think about it, though it was a question she had often thought of hundreds of times on her own. "No, it should just be him and I, I would think. At least I have never come across another."

"Then how?! Are you royalty?" The blonde blurted out, and then she looked back from where she knelt and caused him to flinch with her stare.

"No. I am not royalty. I was raised here, by my father." She leaned and whacked the back of the blonds head. "You know that, you met me as a child! You used to pull my hair when we visited until I kicked you between the legs, remember?"

He calmed slightly, his shoulders relaxing only the slightest, but concern still remained in his scrunched brows. "How then?" He asked flatly.

Slumping in defeat, she looked to Venic for help, but the almond-haired man was also watching out of the corner of his eye with interest.

"Listen carefully; I cannot use it often; I do not have the control to. More often than not, it is the one that does the controling, so I only use it if I feel I have no other choice. You should know this better than most, though. Do you remember when father and I would go to see you and your sister when we were young? Sometimes while he talked to your sister, you and I would play hiding games, but other times I would not be there and my father would say I ate a bad plant or something along those lines? Well he lied. He is always lying to protect me. The truth was that he had me hidden away somewhere close so he could protect me as I delt with a fever worse than any I have ever felt from sickness."

His eyes finally flashed with at least a small understanding, so she continued.

"As I have gotten older, the effects of magic are not as bad, but I still cannot turn you into anything, nor can I make something that is not there; such as making a tree grow when there is no seed, or making fire in water. I cannot curse you, or call on the dead, and I can barely do much at all. It is like...whispering for someone in a dark tunnel full of people; sometimes the right magic hears you, but othertimes it is something totally different that comes out of the darkness.

After that that, when the magic does come, the rules apply just as normal as you could imagine. Just as with you how lifting a heavy rock for a long time would make you tired, the same would happen doing the same through magic." However, at that moment she let her eyes narrow and her grip tighten on the hem of her cloak. "But listen very carefully Alstred, you cannot tell anyone of what you saw. Even if you did, they would probably think you mad, but if you try, I swear I'll find you and kill you. No one can know; no one."

Alstred shifted uncomfortably at her threat, and a moment of hurt glimmered in his eyes, but he did not move away. "How can you use it?" He asked again. He was being very brave for such a superstitious man, she thought.

"I do not know!" She lied, trying to choose between looking at him and the rain. "I do not know. I do not know why I can use it; I just know that I can and that others should never see it. I am no witch, I am just a freak. Now stop asking questions."

"Your father..." Alstred dared.

"Does not know why either. Or if he does, he has never told me." That was also a lie. Her father knew her past as well as she did, but Alstred could not know everything.

It was too dangerous for anyone to know the truth.

"Oh." Was all he replied and all three of their gazes returned to the road.

When the rain let up and she had successfully hid any sign they had been there, the three traveled further. Valerlanta tried to hide how weak she felt as they went, but then when Valerlanta could hardly stand, Venic took notice of her shaky stance, and told them to stop for the night.

She took advantage of this by quickly setting up camp, then hurrying to gather herbs she knew helped with the symptoms followed by using magic to calm her shaking limbs. Magic was strange to her still, even though it has been with her for her whole life. She did not yet understand why making a fire burn hotter took more energy than shifting ice, but then, there were still a lot of things she did not know. She did notice, however, that this was not nearly as bad as it once was; as if magic were simply a muscle that would become stronger with use.

After gathering more plants to create a stew of the last of the meat, and hurried back.

Both men were looking at her expectantly, waiting for their next meal. Despite her previous anger, she shook her head and suppressed a small smile.

Once they were done, and the men were hopefully full for a while again, Venic got up and stretched, sighing contently before heading off into the forest.

"I will be back in a small while." He said as he went and neither questioned it.

Him gone, Valerlanta hesitantly looked back to the man across the fire from her who had recently saved her life. He sat with an odd sort of smile on his face and his toes wiggling free again by the fire, but when he felt her stare he looked up with a glimmer of curiosity. There was no fear in the surface of his eyes now, simply a dull acknowledgement, and perhaps it was that which made her work up the courage to speak, or maybe it was just the threat of the knight's return, but either way, the words burst out of her before she could stop herself.

"Why did you do it?" She asked, and a dark sort of mood settled over the man's face as he realized the subject of her question. However, it only seemed justified after he asked her so many questions of his own today. "Why did you leave me to die once, but save me another time?"

Alstred shifted uncomfortably, glancing to make sure Venic was still gone.

"Alstred!" She urged, needing to know. It was never what happened that bothered her the most, but why. Why her? Why did no one help? What made her not valued enough to keep? What did she do to deserve so much pain?

"That event involving the Jerstain was not my idea." The blonde picked at something on his pant leg, easily avoiding her eye contact.

"You went along with it, and that is the same guilt as being the first to think it. By doing nothing to stop it, you agreed that it should happen too. You could have warned me, but you did not even try! One word-a single word-could have saved me, but you just watched me go!"

"Well..." He started, trying to find the right words, then continued. "I was scared. I admit it; I was scared out of my wits. They might have done the same to me if I warned you before, but if I tried to help after...how could I face an entire army?" He shook his head. "I regret it Val, and I would have even more if you died. I told myself we were friends, but I did nothing. After it happened, I did not sleep for nights." He paused, clearly hesitating to say his next words. When he did, they were careful, as if dancing near the edge of a knife. "I have always wondered; how did you get away? How did you do what I could not and take on a whole army?"

The thief felt a cold weight on her chest as she pictured that night; the night the first and only guild she joined sent her to fetch something forgotten after their steal, when in actuality it was a trap directed at using her to be a distraction to get away.

As she snuck into the tent, the flaps were throw up and she was surrounded, while her companions- who tipped to the men that she would be there- got away.

They never wanted her on their guild, they just used her that night as an easy way out, and she would never forget it.

"I fought." She said quietly. "I fought, I ran, and almost died."

The thief could not say the full story out loud.

She could not talk about how hard she was beat and thrown around after he caught her. She could not talk about how he broke her bones and nearly bled her out. She could not talk about the man's screams as the glass in her hand took his eye.

No, she could not talk about that.

Shivering with the memory, she looked up to see Alstred frowning at her deeply.

"I regret it." He said, and she almost believed it.

"Thank you for saving me earlier." Was her only reply.

He shrugged, as if that was nothing in the scheme of things. "It was nothing."

They sat the rest of the time in silence, simply enjoying the heat of the fire until Venic returned.

The knight strode back and smiled as he sat down next to his friend. "Much better." He sighed, causing Alstred to snort about 'not needing to know that', but Valerlanta would not join in. She simply watched the knight, wondering if maybe he had been listening in the whole time.

* * *

It was as bright and warm as it always was this time of year, so when Valerlanta opened her eyes and looked at the golden lit grasses and flowers, she could not help but sigh out all her tension.

The dew of the morning still had yet to burn off, so its wetness still dampened the world and left little mirrors on every blade of grass and petal of flower.

Reaching out, she brushed a purple flower, and watched as the little drops fell. A few drops landed on her fingertips, and as much as she wanted to sit there and marvel at nature in its best lighting a little longer, the real world was calling, so instead she reluctantly sat up.

The camp was strangely empty, and the fire long since out, but she could still see the bends in the grasses where her two companions had been sleeping under the shelter.

Where they had gone was still a mystery, but she could at least tell it was not long ago; perhaps just after daybreak. With a panic, she thought for a moment that maybe they had left without her, but then she noticed that all of the things were still waiting by the fire.

Valerlanta frowned.

She did not remember falling asleep when after her watch, nor did she-a normally light sleeper-have any memory of hearing them leave. For a moment, even with the evidence proving otherwise right in front of her, her mind suddenly wondered everything that had occurred after finding the ball and starting on her adventure was simply a dream. But then she flexed her hand,

and the pain under her bandages reminded her of the truth.

Everything had all happened so fast since meeting Venic.

While she waited for them to return, and bit back the fear that there was a chance they might not at all, she cleaned up best she could to hide they were ever there, and made sure all the items were packed correctly. It was during this packing that she grabbed out a rough woollen cloak, and something suddenly rolled out onto the forest floor.

Surprised, Valerlanta was quick to snatch it back up before it could roll away, and as such she discovered the very thing she did not want to see right now; the metal ball.

Venic must had decided it would be safer to split up the items, especially if she did not even know if she was carrying it.

Looking on at its old metallic surface, she no longer felt the same lust to own it like she once did; not after what happened. She could still feel it humming with some sort of life on her fingers, as if it had been woken up.

Even though part of her told her she should drop the pain-causing puzzle where she found it, curiosity spurred within her, and although some strange thought whispered she should throw it away, instead she lifted a hesitant finger, and flicked one of the rings.

It clicked as normal.

She was only just about to continue when she abruptly heard a branch snap and so she quickly rolled it back in the cloak and stuffed it in the bag just in time to see the large blond emerging from the trees.

"Well hello there!" A booming voice called, and Alstred came stomping from the woods, proudly swinging two rabbits around in front of him as he smiled ear to ear. "Sleep well, princess?"

Valerlanta glared and he laughed.

"Well, while you were sleeping like wee babe, us men were out testing our own skills with game. And look what I found from it! A real meal, I would say."

He set them at her feet, and then sat crossed legged across from them, staring expectantly. Unable to hold out under those eager child-like eyes, Valerlanta finally forced a smile and took notice. "A fine hunt, Alstred." She said, and the bigger man lit up with excitement.

"I caught them by a creek. It was quite by accident, actually, but thankfully good old Alstred is still as fast with his crossbow as he was as a lad. Got them both, and not a moment too soon!" He said proudly.

Valerlanta nodded. "They were both good shots. No meat was wasted."

"I know! And good thing too, last thing we would want is to keep having relying on you. We never know when your luck will run out."

Now her smile did falter as Valerlanta nearly gasped. "Luck? I need no luck!"

"No, but then if it helps you hunt, then why not bring it along, right?" Amusement glittered in his eyed as Valerlanta glared.

"I have the better shot, and we both know it."

"Yes but it does not matter because I have the better weapon." He hoisted the small crossbow onto his shoulder. "This here is far more precise."

"It depends who is shooting it."

"My bow fires at a heavier weight than yours; it can easily pierce armour."

"It might, but it takes you ages to load it! By the time you pull that string back, I will have already loosened five arrows!"

"It makes up for its speed in power! I can knock a man straight back with one bolt!"

"So can mine, when close enough; but it does not matter how badly you kill someone, because after that one kill, a long-bower will have already shot you dead; even after having four attempts to fail!"

And that was when Venic returned, and stepped in just in time to stop Valerlanta from leaping forward to punch the smug smile from the taller mans face.

"I swear," He said as he pushed Alstred over with a kick of his boot. "It is like you two are siblings!"

Her brows rose, and she jumped to her feet. "We are nothing like siblings!"

"Thankfully." Alstred murmured playfully, and received a hard smack on the head by Valerlanta when the other knight's back was turned. When the knight turned back, Valerlanta pretended she was picking at something on her sleeve, as if nothing had just happened.

"Hmm." Venic said, eyeing her suspiciously, and then let out a long sigh that seemed to say I-am-too-tired for this-today, and nodded for her to lead the way. "Go on then; you first. Alstred, behind me."

They did as were told, and were separated like children.

Valerlanta lead through the forest, suddenly realizing how naked she felt without being able to use her bow. Every sound made her jump in surprise. She still had her knives, but it just did not feel the same. She thought of what would happen if a wild animal came across their paths. It was true, bears were lazy opportunists who would rather eat berries rather than fight for a meal, but what if one was hungry enough? She did not think a knife would to any good in that situation.

It was at this time when her keen eyes noticed something shiny ahead. Instantly cautious, Valerlanta glanced around while motioning for the others behind her to be still before proceeding forward. There, in the grasses, lay a single arrow.

Quickly, Valerlanta motioned them all to get low and be quiet. They listened, their hands going for their weapons.

Valerlanta picked it up and inspected the weld, and frowned. She handed it to Venic, and he turned it over in his hands with Alstred peeking over his shoulder before both men exchanged glances, then nodded to her.

This was their kingdoms arrow.

Just beside where the arrow was found, she spotted a print. It was fresh, too fresh.

But how? Was this by chance? Or...

Valerlanta paled.

Or was Askyel and the kings army now working together?

Men this far into the forest, it was not normal. Mentally in her brain she mapped everything out. Askyel was bringing up the rear, pushing them forward as they slowly tracked after them, and last she heard from Alstred, they were somewhere west, but what if they split the army and was moving back, towards Askyel? It was a enormous forest, so there was no way for the army to cover the whole expanse, but if Hernthorn was coming from the east...

They were using Hernthorn to essentially herd the three of them into a trap!

"What is it?" Venic whispered.

Valerlanta quickly told the two men her thoughts, and they both also visibly paled.

"It only makes sense; it is exactly something Askyel would do." Valerlanta explained. "He is going to pretend to go along with the king's army until the last minute, and then take everything for himself."

"How far are we from the nearest town?" Venic asked seriously.

Valerlanta thought on it. "There is a mining village about two days north-east, but that is where the kings watch is. The whole area will be swarming with soldiers to protect the gold. The only other place is to the north, about three days; but that's a castle. We will never get into it."

Venic hesitated on speaking a plan, his eyes staring at the arrow carefully. Then, "I think we should split up."

"What?" Alstred and Valerlanta said as one.

"If we split up, they will not know what tracks to follow. It will cut down on their numbers as they split to follow us, and mess up their plans as they scramble to catch all three of us. It is the best plan we have!"

So he was trying to get rid of her already?

"No, absolutely not." Alstred said.

"Fine." Valerlanta said, crossing her arms. Both men looked at her in surprise for agreeing so fast, but she was not done yet. "However, I'll have to take the sword, and Alstred will be having the puzzle-ball."

The dark haired knight's jaw dropped. "What?"

"You heard me." Valerlanta said. "Otherwise how will I know you are not just trying to keep all the riches to yourself?"

"That is not it at all-"

"Then hand them over." She put a hand in a waiting gesture. Even the normally carefree expression on Alstred had gone cold stone as he realized that he too might be getting the bad end of a deal.

"Fine, we forget the plan." Venic sighed. "I cannot let those items out of my sight, so we go together."

It was at that moment that a branch snapped, the blonde haired man's head perked up, and he was pushing Venic over in time to avoid an arrow. It hit the ground with a solid 'thump.'

"Move!" Venic shouted, running with his body crouched, and Valerlanta and Alstred followed suit.

There were shouts from deep in the forest as men became apparent, charging towards the three.

Alstred yelped as several more arrows snarled deep into the trucks of trees as they ran.

"Do not stop!" Valerlanta shouted, knowing a moving target was near impossible to hit here.

But she did not need to tell Venic and Alstred. Their battle trained minds already had them heading for the thickest parts of the woods.

Branches whipped by, and their boots bounded over roots.

Then, when Valerlanta looked at the ground just in time to see an ankle height snare, she burst forward to bang into Venic, pushing him out of the way. Startled by her sudden movement, the horse thrashed; breaking free and slammed its side into her and over the edge of the cliff. The horse ran, and she slipped backwards.

She gasped, and reached out to grab something, but it was too late. Her feet slid across the loose shale.

Venic reached out towards her and was only just too slow. His fingertips grazed the fabric of her clothes as she continued backwards.

Alstred and Venic disappeared from view, and she kept falling.

Rolling down the hill, she tried to find something to grasp, but only resulted in her getting scrapes and cuts from the sharp rock.

Her body rolled out of control, rocks bashing her skin, and plants yanking at her clothes.

When she finally stopped on her back, and gingerly turned her head to look back up the ridge, she knew she was not getting back up it, not here. It was far too steep.

She could see the two hesitating at the top of the ridge, but both men were not getting down it unless they wanted to risk breaking bones.

"Go!" She heard Alstred shout, and saw him pushing the hesitating Venic along. "She will find us again!"

Hearing that, she stumbled to her feet, shook the pain out her limbs, and looked at for her bow. She found it not far from where she had come to a stop, and it appeared to still be in one piece.

Satisfied with that, she started moving in a hurried limp. Soon she found herself in the trees again, trying to make it back to her two companions, while also trying to avoid an advancing army.

Abruptly she jumped at a sharp sound and found her hand reaching for her arrow, but stopped when she saw the source. A crow sat on a branch above and looked down at her with a curious cock of the head.

Far beyond the forest canopy came the deep sound of thunder rolling along the valley, and Valerlanta found herself pausing, and then picking up her speed faster than before. Another rainstorm was coming this way; and it was not just the thunder telling her, she could also smell the moisture rising in the air. She would not have much time to find them now.

As the ground beneath her levelled out and she was kneeling to examine a print, the rain slowly began. It trickled lightly from the sky, sliding down leaves and into the print she examined, where it was soaked into the thirsty soil.

Venic had gone this way, and the other looked to be Alstred; however, there was another. This was not their prints; it was only slightly wider, and pressed harder on the heel. Worst was that it was following the two with unnerving accuracy; it was a tracker.

Instantly her bow came into hand and an arrow to knock it.

Then -moving much more quietly- she continued on.

However, her feet treading lightly upon the soil suddenly came to a stop as she heard a voice croak. No wait, not a voice, another crow.

She kept going.

Above, lightning lit up the sky in short bursts, and then was gone again, only to be followed by harsh drums. It started raining harder, blinding her vision with the heavy droplets and erasing many of the prints.

Harder and harder she rushed herself until suddenly her feet slid backwards in the mud, and came out from under her. She landed hard onto the dirt, and cringed as her sore hand dug into a branch. It felt hot, and she knew without looking that the tender skin had been cut without even looking at it.

Valerlanta was only just about to get up when she spotted something just head; small pine tree with pine-bows arching down all around like a ladies skirts, and all around was thick willow brush.

It would not be a perfect shelter-she would be leaked on-but it would do for now, and those bushes would help to break the wind.

Valerlanta took one last look back through the falling drops and saw no one, so she made her way into the shelter and settled down as close to the trunk as she could. Leaning her head back against the bark, she looked up at the leafy roof and closed her eyes as water dripped down her face.

'You were bested by a horse, Val.' She thought to herself.

The lightning had stopped by then; at least from what she could tell. She could still hear the drums of the sky, however, as they made their way down the valley.

"Stupid." Valerlanta whispered to herself bitterly starting to quickly wrap her badly bleeding hand. "Stupid, horse, stupid cliff, stupid thief."

After her bandage was wrapped tightly around her wound, she flexed her fingers to test her work. The palm ached with the movement, but the bandages held properly.

Frowning at the wound, she thought of the ball that caused it.

It was still in her bag; she could leave now with it.

Instead, she got up, and returned to the last prints she had seen.

As she went, she passed near a cliff with a near deadly incline. She hesitated there, in the shadows of the trees, looking down at the rumbling creek below hoping for any signs of the men, when the tweeting came.

They were just barely audible over the rain. Normally she listened to bird-song messages with only mild interest of knowing the happenings of the world beyond the forest, but ever since the last message, she found herself willing her ears to catch every sound.

From what she could tell, the first messages were intended for someone else, though it was hard to tell since the words came broken over the sound of the thunder. They were telling of a force of some kind attempting to cross the forest. It warned to be careful.

A force...an army, perhaps? Was the Hernthorn army actually planning on attacking?!

She felt her throat clench.

It had been months, maybe well over a year now, since the eastern king started sending the men to kill farmers, and staging it best they could to make it look like the work of thieves, but if the army truly was coming, things would certainly get much worse.

A shutter came over her as she thought about all the blood that would be carelessly spilt and farms burnt or lay with salt for the sake of a royal's war. Then, realizing the message was continuing, she listened back in.

This time she realized this message again was specifically for her.

'Little bird, little bird, are you well?' It repeated multiple times, and then paused, waiting for a reply.

Valerlanta replied as quickly as she could, putting as much force as possible into her little tweets.

'Please carry far enough.' She begged of her message.

The pause made her tap her fingers impatiently.

She had so many questions she wanted to ask! Was her father well? Was the force far behind them? How soon until war would break? So many questions!

Still no reply. Did her message not carry?

Valerlanta had readied herself to repeat when the message finally came; this time it was clearer.

'They moved to be better heard.' She realized.

'Father worries.' The message started. *'Getting too water into trouble. He wants to see you.'*

'Too water?' Valerlanta wrinkled her nose in thought, going through the words that would match the sound, and then realized it. *'Too deep! Too deep into trouble.'*

She felt frustration boil in her chest at herself for not instantly catching a word so obvious. Why was she so off from her normal today?

'I am fine.' She whistled. *'I travel to a good catch.'*

Again a pause, and again her throat clenched.

Waiting. She hated waiting.

'King has eye on you.' The stranger sang in bird-song. *'More eyes too, and one pack of the king closing in. Very deep into danger.'*

So he did know about the men following them.

'Now he tells me.' She herself rolling her eyes at the warnings, but the message continued.

'The man you are traveling with is not who you think. Official reward said for knight. Word says he will be hung under charges of being a spy'

She said nothing; after all, it was a fact she already knew.

'Are you returning to thief guild camp?' The whistler continued.

Valerlanta leaned back onto her and hesitated.

Thoughts of Venic wanting to split up was circling in her mind, then she remembered; the ball was in her bag.

If she were to leave now, Venic and Alstred would look for her at first, and then they would have to give up and continue on without her. Alstred was not as long-lived in the woods as her, but he should be able to lead them in a straight enough path.

They could not continue without the ball, from what she could tell, so she could have the upper hand. Besides, she was injured, tired, near out of arrows, and still feeling some of the sickly effects of using magic, so it only made sense that she should go...right?

She bit her lower lip in thought.

'Venic...he did want to split up anyways, so it was better if leave now on my own terms, right?' She thought.

The forest was still, seeming frozen in apprehension of her answer.

But what was her answer?

The ball abruptly felt heavy in her bag, and her hand stung at the thought of it.

Her father; he would hang back into the shadows and wait for a meal like a spider on a web. She had the chance; she should do the same.

'I will come.' She replied in bird-song, and the stranger said he would carry on this message too, and then all went silent. The message carriers were all those who saw themselves better in the woods then with man. "Hermits," as some would call them, so Valerlanta pictured him walking to carry the message down the mountain range, and then heading home. He would sit by the fire, content with just his memories for company, and feeling free of all the troubles those outside his world has to face.

That was her, once. Maybe it could be again.

She was turning away; away from the arrows, away from all her responsibilities, when a sound came, then kept on coming. It was a sound unmistakeable to any of those who had heard it; the sound of metal hitting metal.

Her feet hesitated, and then started again.

It was not her problem. It was not.

***

Venic hit the oncoming force with his entire strength.

There were too many men to run from, and more than too many to fight, but the swordsman refused to give up. He let out a furious war cry as he bashed his sword at man's shield again and again until another enemy came to his aid, and Venic was forced to face them both.

They circled him like starving dogs drooling over a meal.

Venic raised his weapon, and took them head on. He flicked both their swords away with seemingly ease, then, as he bashed one off balance, a bolt pierced the armour and the man fell dead.

Alstred reloaded his crossbow as more men swarmed down, but his next shot missed and instead dug deep into the soil behind the solider. Growling with anger, he threw the crossbow down, grabbed his axe, and faced the nearing men with it high over his head. He could not deflect the oncoming blows like Venic, but instead jumped back away from them as they came, then sprang back in with just enough time to bring down his blade upon them. Every blow lacked grace but made up for it in precise aim.

They were trying to lead the men to a path that lead in between two rock faces that were too narrow for the horses to fit down, and also where the soldiers would have to funnel in to fight mostly one-on-on with the two companions; but the opponents refused to allow it. There were simply too many men to move.

As Venic fell yet another man, he took the time to look up in hopelessness at the oncoming forces. Just as he did, a man crested the ridge on horseback and stared on at them arrogantly.

The leader. Jerstain Elfailden.

Beside his steed standing on the ground was a man dressed in earthy colors, and probably had more bruises than normal skin on his body. He looked on dazed, as if this were only a dream to him. He was a forest walker; and now a tracker for the king.

The men were overpowering the two companions now; using their sheer numbers to force them back. What was worse was that there were some rounding the fight; racing to block any chance of escape by surrounding them completely.

That was when her arrow sprang from her bow.

It fell the first man in line rushing past the men, and those following stumbled, looking for where it came from. Ducking low, the thief pressed herself against the stone before any could pinpoint where the arrow had flown from.

Her hand was pulsing with a pain that made stars dance in front of her eyes.

She was nearly out of arrows.

After following the sounds of battle, the thief found herself standing on a large boulder overtop of a deep crevasse. It was fairly rounded, so if she risked standing again, those below would surely see her.

'Think Val, think!' She thought to herself. *'How can you get them out of there?'*

Then, as her foot slipped slightly towards the narrow split of rock, an idea sparked.

After moving so she was standing over the deep crack, the thief snuck a glance at her two companions.

Venic and Alstred were still fighting strongly, but the men were quickly closing in.

It was now or never.

Calling on magic, her skin started to tingle as Valerlanta pictured the rocks vibrating underfoot.

The magic seeped to her fingers, then let go.

Only as a long stream of fire.

The thief nearly fell backwards in surprise, but the magic had the same effect as what she wanted. The flames licked towards into all the small hiding spots in the huge crack, and a swarm of pixies flew out of the bottoms to escape. They swarmed the men, assuming them to be the culprits.

Standing, Valerlanta saw majority of the soldiers were preoccupied with the sudden attack, but some were still keeping the two boys from being able to escape.

For a small moment, the thief let her eyes drift up battlefield to the man sitting upon the horse. He watched her too; with those violence craving eyes that she knew all too well.

Her best enemy, Elfailden, did not look all too happy to see her; so naturally, she smirked, gave a flirty little wave, and watched as pure rage contorted his face. His hand reached for his sword, and she stuck out her tongue.

The thief took this chance to knock her arrow, take aim, and put the forest walker in her sights. She saw his bruised eyes widen, but she did not let him suffer long. The arrow pierced his head, right into the forehead. He fell hard like a rock and did not move.

Good riddance. Forest-Walkers never betrayed their own. Never.

Then, before she could fully raise her next arrow and put Elfailden in her sights for a final time, something else caught notice out of the corner of her eye.

Alstred was being overtaken; something strange for him.

Knocking an arrow, she instead turned her aim towards Alstred, then fired.

The closest to the man to Alstred fell, and the boys took off running. Valerlanta followed from above, watching as some of the soldiers gave chase.

Alstred was slowing, and with wide eyes, the thief realized why; he was injured. The tall man was clutching his side and was slowing with each step.

Slinging her bow over her shoulder, Valerlanta took a knife in hand and jumped from the rock.

The man did not see her coming until she tackled him to the ground and used gravity to let her knife go deep. As they both hit the ground, she rolled to her feet and took her bow and aimed at the already startled men. They dove for cover, and the thief turned and ran while smiling at them for falling for such a simple trick.

By the time the men realized she was only bluffing, enough distance was between them and Alstred for it to be far less of a concern.

She caught up and found the tall blonde only just barely able to stay standing; his feet sliding in the muddy ground while clutching his side and gritting his teeth. It was then she noticed how dark his side had become. Blood stained his soft-armour, and also reddened his hand.

"Alstred...," Valerlanta started, but she had no time to finish because they were running too hard.

Venic slowed to be beside them and kept casting glances back at the advancing army.

They had the head start, but the army had horses. Once the horses got the lead...

"We need a way out." The annoyingly calm voice of Venic suddenly called, breaking her of her daze. "Lead the way! Now!"

And so she pulled away from Alstred and ran, ran as hard as she could and trusted the men behind her to follow.

But where? Where was she running? No, she did not have time to think of that, she just had to run and trust her instincts.

Valerlanta bounded over logs, around the trunks of trees, and across solid rocky ground, but not once did she look back.

They would be there, she knew they would be.

Her heart slammed in her chest, and her breath gushed out to the point where her lungs hurt, but she did not stop.

Shouts could still be heard from the soldiers, but she did not worry.

This was her territory. She would not let these soldiers get the best of her; not here.

"They are gaining on us!" Alstred wheezed.

But not the horses. She made sure of that by leading them into a thick patch of willows and other bushes; however it was slowing the three of them down.

Suddenly her feet came out from under her as the ridge came sooner than expected. Dark dirt appeared under her, and so did the unfortunately steep slant it sat on.

Feet hitting the muddy ground, Valerlanta fell, and let herself slide.

Her vision came as a blur as speed rushed everything. Dirt and rock flew in all directions, and ate at her clothes and exposed skin.

All three slid down the mudslide on the steep cliff, and when she stopped and got up, covered in mud, she hurried over to Alstred and tried to pull him up by his arms.

"Get up!" She urged. He wheezed, but hardly budged until Venic came and forcefully pulled his friend up, and took some of his weight. As Venic was helping Alstred along, Valerlanta lead the way.

There was no way that the men or the horses would dare follow her down that ridge, but just in case she had them cross a rocky riverbed and follow it for a time before she felt it was safe enough to make camp.

By that time, Alstred fell like a log when Venic released him.

"Start on a shelter, I will help Alstred." Valerlanta ordered Venic, hoping that the knight had learnt enough to do so. Venic hurried off wordlessly, and Valerlanta pulled off the material near the blondes wound.

It was bleeding badly, but could be worse.

He did not react as she cleaned it out; though perhaps he had passed out by then.

Sewing it shut as quick as she could, she then crushed the flowers of yarrow and placed it over the wound. Lastly, she bandaged it tightly.

Once done, Venic had finished the shelter, and helped drag Alstred inside.

The large man did not make a sound.

Valerlanta shot Venic a worried glance, but the knight just took off his own cloak and placed it over his friend before sitting down with a heavy sigh.

The thief looked back to Alstred and tried to hide her dread at his condition.

Even with all that happened, Valerlanta was trying very hard to hate Alstred; telling herself that she should be reminding herself over and over again about how he had betrayed her, but instead her mind kept turning back to the memories from long before that. Seeing him, laying there peacefully, for whatever reason caused childhood memories comes to mind. Alstred was far older than Valerlanta, but even so, when they were kids, he took the time to teach her how to have fun. They never saw each other for long, so when they did, they would wrestle nonstop in the forest, and sometimes he would even carry her on his shoulders, making her feel tall as could be.

He betrayed her, but in some ways, long before that, he also saved her. The king of the thieves had taught her how to survive, but Alstred had taught her that surviving was useless if she did not remember to live.

She should hate him, and yet she didn't. Not anymore.

Pulling the bag in front of her, she inspected the items inside.

Her book was ruined. The pages were completely soaked through, causing the ink to run in ugly splotches. There was no saving it.

Tenderly running her hand over the spine, the thief said a silent goodbye to her first steal before reluctantly setting it off to the side.

Everything else in her bag seemed to be faring well, though all her knives had to be taken from the sheath to avoid rusting.

Lastly, there was just the metal puzzle ball.

Out of the comer of her eye she saw Venic look up at her, watching her carefully as she brought the treasure into her hand. It looked fine, and to test it, she flicked a ring and it spun fine.

Would it rust?

Just to be sure, she put it beside the warmth of Alstred's body.

Valerlanta set down her gear, and slowly let her eyes trail to where the swordsman sat. They could not light a fire, so they had only the light warmth of a rush-light. He stared at his shaking hands, his face and unreadable mask but his breath sounding broken.

The swordsman had already turned on his first home, so how did it feel to turn on another? How did it feel to fight those who had first accepted him as a person?

Valerlanta could not even imagine the confusion.

Moving up to him, she sat cross-legged directly in front of him. She did not do anything, just waiting there, and slowly, his eyes slid from his hands to meet her.

His face was a mask, but his eyes were a torrent of emotion.

Since there were some conversations where words failed, they simply sat for a moment, looking into each other. After time, the storm in his eyes settled slightly, and a he forced a half-smile, though it failed and sunk back downwards to a frown.

“What are you doing?” He asked with the slightest hint of amusement playing in his pain

“Bringing you back from whatever dark place you were being dragged to.”

At that he smiled. “You have to be the strangest girl I have ever met.”

"Hmm. Among my father’s guild, strange seems to be the normal; such as with the man who refuses to eat any other meat than what comes from a snake." Valerlanta said, thinking. "So unfortunately, you seem quite normal to me."

His smile grew slightly, and his bloody hands dropped into his lap, seemingly forgotten. He opened his mouth to say something, but then stopped when he noticed the blood showing on the bandages on her palm. "You are bleeding."

Instinctively, Valerlanta pulled her hand back to hide behind her. "It is nothing. I just cut the burn slightly."

"You should treat it properly."

Valerlanta shook her head. "It will be -"

She was cut off when his fingers outstretched, waiting for her. "Give it here. If you don't want to, then let me."

The thief could not help but glare at him. "Why are you suddenly being so nice to me?"

"I could ask you the same question."

She flushed. "I just owe you, is all."

"And now, I do for you too." He urged her to comply by pushing his hand further towards her.

"Come on, then. Do not be a child."

At that, she slapped her hand into his. "I am not a child!"

"Good, then sit calmly and do not complain." He told her, un-tying her wrappings. "You know, one of these days, your pride is going to get you into trouble."

She rolled her eyes in reply, but he did not see as he let the wrappings drop, and pulled her fingers downwards slightly so her palm opened up fully towards him. Her hand looked as painful as it felt. It was still pink with burn, and had some fresh cuts along it from where she had fallen.

"You cannot shoot like that for a while." He added, and he was right; she was not giving it a chance to heal.

"I will try my best." She smirked.

He grinned slightly at that- the corners of his mouth twitching with a bitter smile-before turning her palm towards the candle so he could see it in the dim lighting better. As he looked, she tried to ignore how warm his hands were compared to her own. Warm, and rough, yet gentle.

"What was that plant you mentioned to ward off infection?"

"I have some in the pocket there." She pointed to the bag with her free hand, and he grabbed the mixture of plants.

She winced from the sting as he put it on the wound, even though he did it with great care. After, the swordsman bandaged it up carefully; wrapping the wound with more ease than a person should know. It seemed it did not matter if you were a knight or a forest-walker; wounds were a common part of life.

'How many scars do you have?' She found herself wonder. *'How many do you hide below the skin as well as upon it?'*

Venic tied off the wrappings, and both looked behind Valerlanta as Alstred groaned in pain. He shifted, but did not wake.

"Thank you." Valerlanta said, quietly.

"No." He said with a smile, "Thank *you* for coming back."

Valerlanta winced inwardly as she felt the guilt of knowing how close she had come to not returning at all. Instead, she turned back to the swordsman. "They have horses."

"They do."

"And they know the general direction we are heading in."

Venic glared slightly, as if mad to be reminded. "That is also true."

"So why not use my skills as a thief? It is not quite night. If I go now, I can retrace our steps back to their camp and slow them down."

"It is too dangerous."

"It is who I am!" Valerlanta hissed. "How far do you imagine we will get like this?"

"...On horseback, they could likely outrun us before we have a chance to hide our paths."

"So let me do something about it! Like it or not, it has to be done, and Alstred is injured, and you do not know how to be a thief. I can do this. Is this not why I am here? You said you wanted someone to guide you safely through the forest."

"I wanted a guide, not a body guard."

"Well you got a guide and a thief. I am a thief, so let me do that job. It is something only I can do. While I am gone, someone needs to stay with

Alstred while he rests." She urged him to listen. If there was something she hated, it was feeling as if death was fast on her heels. Even if the knight refused, she would wait till he fell asleep then go anyway. "I know you might still be feeling some regrets, but-"

"Fine, go." He interrupted, startling her.

"What?"

"You want to go, so go. I will not stop you."

The thief blinked in surprise. "Really?"

"Yes, really. It is as you said, you are a thief, so I should not stop you from being one if it will give us an advantage." He looked away from her as he started cleaning the blood and water from his sword; one careful wipe after another. "Go, before I change my mind. Just come back, understand?"

"Huh. Yes, I will come back, I promise." Valerlanta gathered her things hesitantly. It had to be some sort of trick, right? It was only days ago that he was being so untrusting with her, so why would it change now?

Yet, as she pulled her cloak hood far over her head and stepped out into the rain, the swordsman did not stop her. He simply sat in the shelter, cleaning his sword.

"I am really going." She told him, but he did not say anything; seeming to care only about making sure that not a drop of anything remained on his sword.

Suspicious that he might spring some sort of trap if she waited, the thief swiftly left the camp in the distance.

It was mere seconds until complete nightfall, so she had to move quickly. Valerlanta ran through the forest and water soaked her completely through.

When she found the first of the fires and she crouched behind the bushes, the sun fell completely and darkness overtook. Most the men appeared to be inside the tents that spotted the clearing, but some were unfortunate enough to be on guard duty. They huddled close around the fire, seeming miserable in the cold rain.

Silently as she could, the thief neared the men.

Rain thudded all around her, muffling all sound.

Valerlanta took out a knife.

Using the shadows, the thief darted tent to tent, making her way through the small camp.

A man exited one close to her.

Sinking low into the mud, the thief eyed the man. He looked around, a rush light torch in hand.

Light ate at her shadows, nearing her fingertips. It danced over her knife as the thief ducked lower.

The light pulled back as the man left.

The thief was on the move again.

She came across no other obstacle as she found the place she was looking for. It was the thickest of all the tents, and stationed carefully in the middle of the camp. Valerlanta knew the one because she had seen it before.

Another time, long ago, she had snuck in just like this, and was betrayed by those who sent her. As Valerlanta entered the warm tent, the man who nearly beat her to death was there, snoring away.

Rain pattered heavily on the tent.

She neared his bed. Water and mud dripped onto his carpet.

Standing over him, she shifted her knife in her hand. The blade glimmered; droplets falling from it to land upon his blanket.

He looked so peaceful for a man intent on killing.

His face flickered with the candle light; illuminating the scar that stretched over his eye.

She had given him that scar, just as she had several scars herself from the very same night.

The thief could end it now; the thief could end his obsessive search by gifting him with eternal sleep.

The knife hovered closer and her eyes stared at a visible soft spot in his neck.

Then, it pulled back, and her hand snatched the map from his table before she left again into the rain.

As much as Valerlanta had wanted to, she would not murder someone in their bed; even if the person happened to seem to be more monster than man.

Tucking the parchment safely away, the thief once again used shadows as her cover. This time, she neared something else entirely.

Among the several horses was a man trying very hard to hush them. Thunder was rumbling, causing the horses to thrash and nicker in dislike. Best to his ability, the man was keeping them calm by soothing each and every one individually.

"Easy, now!" He called to one that was stomping its feet in worry. It tossed its head against the man's touch as nostrils flared. "Easy, easy!"

The thief felt the whole man's body stiffen as her knife sunk deep. The horse squealed as the man fell.

Valerlanta watched him fall without feeling anything.

Not fear, not regret or pleasure, just simply hollow emptiness.

'You are becoming a monster like your father, Val.' She thought to herself.

The men at the fires had turned to look, but were the light blinded them from their night vision.

Uncaring of them, the thief cut the horses free one by one.

Without warning, lightning flashed and thunder roared. The horses that she had freed bolted across the camp, gaining the attention of the guards. As the thief moved to cut one the last free, the men screamed for attention.

"Ashes." Valerlanta swore.

The final horse tossed its head wildly, making the ropes fly uncontrollably in her hands. Hooves sprang at the thief as she struggled to both dodge, and keep control of the knife.

Men emerged from tents in startling numbers. Some ran after the horses, while others spilt off to near her location.

"Stay still!" She screamed at the horse, her knife sawing through the thick material.

The men pointed in her direction and screamed out in alarm.

Her knife broke free.

Giving the horse one hard slap on its rear; the thief stumbled back as the frightened creature took off in a blur. It charged towards the men, and they had to dive away to get out of its path.

Valerlanta used this distraction as a way to escape.

Running back to the forest, the thief hurried to its darkness just as the form of a man appeared from the commander's tent.

Lights followed her into the forest as her boots slipped against the mud.

Using the coming forces as her compass, she rounded back to the way she came; ignoring the branches that bit at her skin and pulled on her clothes.

The lights gradually disappeared into darkness behind her, and the thief slowed her pace, trying to find her way through the maze of trees.

There were no stars to guide her, no landmarks to recognize. There was only darkness and the branches that seemed to reach out like bony hands and grab her.

Valerlanta realized she was lost.

As she wandered aimlessly, her eyes could not spot anything that could be familiar. All her skills and years of learning were being proven as useless under the blanket of a rainy night.

Then she saw a light.

The glow was small; not nearly big enough to be a torch. It hovered in the forest; flickering in the rain.

It could be a will-of-the-wisp; it could be trying to trick her into getting more lost. Despite the warnings in her head, the thief approached it and found Venic.

As Valerlanta stepped into the light, out of breath and soaked to the bone in water and mud, the knight turned to her and looked her over.

Relief flashed on his face, and despite how cold, wet, and miserable, she was, the thief smiled with accomplishment.

***

By the time the three stopped to make camp again, the pixies were already out; floating about in the strawberry-kissed sky; getting an early start on the bugs before the bats emerged.

Even though the companions waited until the final moments of fleeting sunlight to start on a camp, the three still did not make up as much ground as the thief was hoping to.

Alstred had taken until noon that day to wake up, and when he did, he was in no shape to travel. He did not keep any of the food down they gave him, and his limbs were shaking.

Valerlanta once thought it was impossible for such a big man to look so weak, and yet there he was, pale as can be and struggling with every movement.

If she had looked for them faster, would he even have been hurt? But he deserved it, didn't he? What he was feeling now was only the slightest of pains compared to what she went through, so he should deserve it. And yet she could not convince herself of it.

The silence was deep during their travels that day, and the thief almost found herself missing the constant jabber of the larger knight. His silence worried her. Even as she started on a shelter, he just sat, staring at the spot where a fire would soon be as his head bobbed.

"Alstred, I have to know, is it true that the fake-king made a pond in Hernthorn and filled it with fish?" She asked, careful to keep the tightness in her throat from her voice as she worked.

"Yes, it is." The blonde answered, but quickly diverted the conversation away from him. "Venic knows more about it than I do, though. They purchased from pretty far away, if I remember correctly. Right?"

"King Kohn had the fish brought from overseas." Venic explained, for once ignoring that she had called the king a fake. "The fish were carefully picked, and some are as yellow as the sun itself, and others are white as snow or speckled in between. They were small when they got them, but now some are as long as an arm."

"And the fish live in that pond? The one that was made?" She asked, curiosity getting the better of her. The thief almost glanced back at the two of them, but then diverted her eyes at the last moment, thinking better of it. Seeing Alstred weak like that would only flare more anger in her heart at herself.

"Yes, and now it looks like just like any other pond; and fills with flowering lillys in the spring. The pond is the king's favourite prize, and is very popular among the royals. Often, you can see royals sitting on the benches, watching the fish swim."

Valerlanta did not know if she should be amazed or disgusted by the excessive spend of money.

Once camp was set up and they had spread out their damp and heavy cloaks to dry, they ate what food they had left that had not been ruined.

Alstred was first to fall asleep; dozing off not seconds after she had changed his bandages. Venic went to grab more wood before it was completely dark, and too restless to sleep, the thieves curiosity soon got the better of her as her eyes drifted from the empty fire to where a bag sat waiting.

After all, she had stolen the commanders map and also scared off their horses, so the thief did not really have to be on guard, did she?

Valerlanta let her fingers fidget together in anticipation until, no longer able to take it, she reached in and snatched the puzzle ball from its leather hiding place.

As the cool metal sat in her palm, Valerlanta let her gaze settle back to strange markings on the rings. This puzzle was still eluding Venic, and though he did not allow her to touch it -and somewhere in the back of her mind something was screaming that she should not even dare- she could not stand that it was somehow smarter than she was.

The light of the fire slid across its metallic surface almost frighteningly.

Ignoring such advice from her own mind, Valerlanta lazily flicked one of the rings, and as it spun under her touch, she felt a soft humming from within it.

The thieves unease deepened.

Her hand stung fresh in the memory of the horrible pain it had caused her.

The bright light, the pain, the feeling of her energy being sucked out of her, and the markings on the ball glowing; it was all still so fresh for her.

Her breath caught as she realized with a sinking feeling in her stomach what must be done.

"What are you doing?" Came a voice; Alstred had woken up.

What if that was the only way?

Was it worth the risk?

Hesitantly, she did the one thing she wished to avoid, and let some of the magic seep through her barriers. Breath shaking with fear; she directed the flow to her fingertips.

Instantly the markings of the ball lit up with red glow.

Swearing loudly, Alstred scrambled away as Valerlanta held the ball up in her hands. It was starting to grow warm under her touch, but not nearly as bad as it had before; as if it had almost soaked in all the energy of hers it needed.

Already, she could feel the metal contraption somehow tasting at her energy levels then taking it for its own uses. Even though it felt like to her that she was running long distances, she tried to steady her hands, and brought the ball closer to her eyes.

Just like she remembered, only part of the ruins were glowing; not the whole piece. The markings were just a distraction; the real puzzle was in the glowing parts, which only a magic user could activate; particularly one of elf-kind, with endless reserves of magic.

The scarlet light was filling the whole camp, dancing all over as she turned the ball in her hand.

While Alstred stayed as far away as possible, Venic entered and dropped the firewood.

She knew he was yelling at her, but she could not hear him. It sounded as if a river was rushing past her ears in a constant roar.

Then, as Valerlanta looked into the red, she felt something familiar fluttering her heart. Warmth spread throughout her, and her eyes went wide as the red took over, blinding all from view.

Suddenly she knew the heat was caused by a soft summer's wind that carried the smell of flowers and earth.

The thief opened her eyes, and grassy hills stretched as far as the eye could see; the green blades bending and rising like waves. Bugs flew in every direction, and birds were singing from somewhere in the emerald sea.

A woman was not far from her, gathering herbs. She placed various plants into the basket, and was just about to pick a healthy looking stem of dandelion when something caught her eye and she slowly stood and looked in the direction of Valerlanta.

Without warning, everything went quiet. The birds quit singing, and not a grasshopper chirped.

Hairs rising on her skin, the thief realized the gaze was not on her, then hesitantly turned around and understood.

Not too far away and coming in fast was a dome that flickered with lightening. The blue surface thundered towards them, growing larger with each second.

The woman behind her tried to run, but there was no use. It came faster than any horse, and was growing larger than any mountain.

It easily ate the grasses and the life within.

It came upon them in seconds, and Valerlanta put up her hands to shield herself.

Nothing happened.

Gasping for breath, she tried find the danger, but only saw Venic edging closer peering at the glowing orb. The swordsman looked at the ball, and his eyes went wide, and she could tell he was resisting the temptation to snatch the ball out of her hands to look at it closer. Instead, he looked at her pleadingly. "Valerlanta, I beg you; keep it glowing. Please hold onto it as long as you can."

Dread and suspicion filled her, but she nodded anyways.

Her heart slammed as she realized she was the only one who saw that scene, and somehow she knew it came from the little ball in her hands she was currently feeding energy to.

The warm feeling of the summer breeze was long gone, leaving her with cool mountain air, and the feeling of her energy been pulled away. It felt as if she were hanging over a ledge by only her fingertips and as her limbs started to shiver, she knew she would soon drop off that ledge into whatever waited.

Venic was pushing the dirt smooth as possible at his feet, then scrambled about, digging through the forest floor, his hands searching. "Alstred, find as many small pebbles as you can! Fast!"

As Alstred hurried about looking for more, Venic used what he already had and started carefully setting them down on his cleared patch of ground. Over and over again, he would glance over at the ball in her hands, and then his eyes would snap away as he placed the small rocks. Alstred gave him a pile of more, and Venic started snatching up those as well.

"No, no that way." Alstred directed, pointing at one of the pebbles recently placed on the ground. "It needs to go the other way."

Gritting her teeth together, Valerlanta ignored the tears swimming in her eyes. She was not in pain, but a deep cold was settling into her body. Her limbs were now shaking with the effort just to keep the ball upright, and she found it increasingly difficult to breathe.

In each moment that passed, the ball grew brighter, and her eyelids felt heavier.

"Venic...," She said, though it came out in a whisper, as if it were stealing away her voice too.

"Just a little longer!" He urged. The knight's hands hurried to place the stones in the right locations, and Valerlanta had to keep blinking to keep him in focus. The world was swaying. "Just a few seconds longer!"

"Venic!" Alstred called, looking between the two.

"Stop! You can stop!"

The thief tried, but was not sure if she could. The ball was so warm in her frozen hands; how could she let it go? The red light seemed inciting; bringing her head in to look at it closer, until...

Abruptly the ball was snatched from her hands and tossed away. Venic cursed and shook his hand as if to shake away any magic that might be on it, and Alstred grabbed her shoulders to steady her.

The ball rolled off; the red lights slowly fading, and then dimming to nothing once more.

Her daze remained, and her head wished to only lie on the ground, but arms kept her upright.

"What was that?" Alstred asked, his gaze glancing at the pebbles on the ground.

"Are you well?" Venic asked Valerlanta. She barely managed to nod. "What will help?"

Realizing how sickly she must look, Valerlanta straightened her back and raised her head, though it made her stomach threaten turn. "I am fine, I can take care of myself."

"Of course you can, sweetheart; whatever you say. Now, take this." Alstred wrapped his own cloak around her, and his touch nearly toppled her. Noticing this, Venic stayed beside her, a hand placed on her shoulder as if she might fall over at any moment. Valerlanta did not have the energy to fight him off, so for once she ignored it.

As the thief fought the urge to lie down, her vision blurred and a swaying form of Alstred nodded over to the carefully placed pebbles. "What did we find out? It does not look like anything to me but rocks."

Venic rose to hesitantly pick up the metal ball -as if expecting it to bite- then, when nothing happened, he tossed it in his hand a few times as he walked back over to his diagram.

Frowning at the markings on the forest floor, he took every rock and stick in carefully.

His eyes lifted, met hers, and as she looked into the deep mixture of emotions storming there, she realized it; he did not know.

"I need time to figure it out." He said, confirming her suspicion, and her heart sank.

Valerlanta broke her eyes away from Venic, not wanting him to see her disappointment. Instead, she looked at her hand to where the bandages still were from her last use of the ball. Like always with magic, her fingers and palm were shaking from the use, but already she could sit up straight, and loosing consciousness was no longer a problem. Her earlier suspicions were right; by using magic, she was getting stronger, and for some reason that scared her.

What would it turn her into?

A hand suddenly lurched forward and pointed at the markings as the blonde shot forward.

"Does that not look a little like the constellation of the wounded faun?" He laughed, as if amused.

"Alstred, I hardly think that now is the right time for you to jest about this." Valerlanta clutched the blanket closer around her and watched as Venic crouched and let his hands hover as he traced out each shape.

Stepping back, the swordsman ran a hand through his hair and opened and closed his mouth many times.

"No." He said carefully. "Alstred was right."

Both Alstred and Valerlanta were silent in either shock or doubt, then Alstred was first to break the silence.

"What? How was I right?" The blonde asked, clearly immediately suspicious of anyone praising his intelligence.

Venic shook his head and continued. "Do you see right there? That pebble that continues all the way to here? That is the white stag. See there? From this point to that one? That is the whole of the wolf and the hunter." He sat down and placed his head in his hands as if it could no longer hold himself up any more. His eyes looked over the rocks many times, and then he laughed almost uncontrollably, the light sound filling the night air. "We solved it. We really solved it!"

Valerlanta understood, and her heart raced with excitement

"The stars." She breathed. "That is the answer to the puzzle; the markings mimic the stars."

Without warning, Alstred let out a hoot and threw his hands into the air and danced right where he stood. Both Valerlanta and Venic laughed, and then urged him to sit down before he passed out.

He complied, and all three stared upwards, looking into the vast light-speckled darkness above, and the two men were easily pointing out the different constellations.

"Is that one the dream netter?" Alstred asked her. "It could be that one, right?"

"How should I know?" Valerlanta snorted, and both men looked at her surprised. She felt her cheeks burn with their intense stares. "What?!"

"I thought you would know this." Venic said. "You seem to know everything about life out here."

Valerlanta wrinkled her nose a pointed up. "You see that one right there? That one leads direct north all the time. No matter where you are, if you see that star, you can find the direction you need to go in. What more do I need to know? Besides, how do you two know them?"

Unlike many, Valerlanta had never had much interest in the stars; they always made her feel too small and lost, but the two men beside her were clearly different.

"You never know what knowledge you might need to properly get a woman." Alstred answered ruefully, and Valerlanta rolled her eyes before both looked to Venic.

He shifted uncomfortably.

"I used to go out at night to look at the stars...with my mother." He answered slowly, as if embarrassed.

"Awww." Alstred teased mockingly. "How sweet."

Venic punched Astred in the shoulder.

Valerlanta frowned. "Well. Either way, I am of no use to you two, so I wish you both luck."

"What about that one." Alstred answered.

"No, it is a little off. Wait, what about the fox and the raven?"

Both stared long and hard at the set of stars, then they both agreed. After the two confirmed the stars matched, they announced that the stars were indeed the story of the fox and the raven. It was not just a fox and the raven that the stars showed, but a whole lineup of stars which told one tale; a tale that Valerlanta knew, and made her shutter at its close locked meaning to what they were doing.

It was a sad sort of story, starting with a piece of meat falling from a wagon heading to the king. It had a delicious smell that soon attracted the attention of many animals, but particularly a fox and a raven. The two creatures were soon able to trick the other animals into leaving, so only the two of them remained.

Knowing the raven could easily fly away with the meal, the fox cunningly said "Oh dear, not a raven! Surly it will fly away up onto that hay pile over there where I cannot reach it as soon as I get close!"

And so, overhearing the fox, as soon as the fox got near, the raven swooped over, picked up the meat and flew over to the hay and sat atop it croaking in delight. It just after that when the farmer came out and tried to shoo the bird away. Angered, the raven tried to fight for his perch, and as it did, not only did the meat fall, but so did the pile of hey, falling over into a nearby fire. Much to the dismay of the farmer, the hay caught fire before he could stop it, and spread to his field. Uncaring, the raven turned back to get his food, only to find it in the mouth of the fox as it ran away.

"Woe is me!" The raven squawked from the air. "The fox has caught my meat! Surely it will run into those bushes that are too tangled for me to fly in! I will never get to taste that meat!"

And it was no sooner after he said that when the fox hurried into the bushes that tightly weaved together like knots. Deeper and deeper the fox ran into the bushes, until it came to a cave. Curious, the fox went inside and felt it was very warm.

"This will be a very good place to eat my meat!" The fox decided, settling on a rock; only it was not really a rock. No sooner after he sat on it did it start to shake beneath him. Startled, the fox did the first thing he could think of and dug his claws into the rock top try and keep from toppling off. There was an annoyed screech, and out from what the fox thought were rocks, came the massive head of a dragon.

Yelping in fear, the fox ran from the cave and was chased by the dragon. It smashed the bushes as it followed, nearing closer and closer, then just when the fox was about to be caught, it scurried down a hole, leaving the meat behind in its haste.

Enraged that the fox got away, the dragon took to the air and released his fury on a nearby town, destroying the house of an old lady.

When the fox emerged again, the meat was gone, and it saw the raven flying off again. The fox knew the raven would not believe his lies again, so instead the fox ran into a field of archers practising. Yipping excitedly, the fox waited until the archers turned his way, then ducked into hiding. The archers took notice of the raven, and shot it down.

Before the humans could find it, the fox quickly used his nose and found both the raven and the meat.

"Help me." The raven said, an arrow through his wing, but the fox ignored the bird. Instead, the fox took the meat and went to leave, ignoring the bird's pleas. "Help me! Help me! Help me!"

The fox was only just about to get away when the ravens cries alerted something the fox did not expect; a group of hunters and their dogs.'

The moral of the story was supposed to be about how greed ruins the lives of those around you first, then ultimately comes for yours as well. The constellations told that story, so once the rings were matched up correctly, all three of them guessed that they only had to press the right markings; presumably having to do with the moral of the story. The fox and raven, the farmer, and the old lady; all those ruined by the greed for one item.

All three held a breath before Venic pressed a finger into a marking. It pressed in with a click, and stayed there, making a hissing sound. The swordsman moved his fingers to the next, and it too clicked into place.

"Two more." He whispered, turning the ball over in his hand.

Then the last two clicked into place as one.

There was a pause, and then the rings suddenly broke apart from each other, letting out a blinding light that filled the forest around them in a white glow.

The boys looked away to shield their eyes, and Venic dropped the ball to the ground with a curse, but just when Valerlanta was about to do the same, she noticed a shape there in the light. She blinked several times, but she could still see it; a woman standing in the light in front of them. Her ghostly form looked at them, and the thieves heart started to pound as Valerlanta realized that she somehow felt familiar; as if she had met her sometime before.

Seconds later, the light faded, leaving only a faint glimmer behind. Instead of glowing in all directions like any light should, most of the light was pointed in only one direction; which was towards to only one place she knew.

Alecaven castle; the summer castle of the king.

"We now know where the final place is." Venic said, breaking the stunned silence that had settled between the three of them. The swordsman fearlessly knelt down to pick the ball up from the dirt and held it in his hand before pushing the rings closed. After several clicking of the ball locking back into place, the ball was only a puzzle once again, leaving the darkness to creep back in.

Suddenly the trees seemed much larger, and Valerlanta swallowed hard. "We should leave early as we can. Who knows who might have seen that light?"

"Agreed." Alstred said shivering visibly. "However, it should be known to both of you that I am not carrying that thing any longer! It is far too creepy to be in my hands."

« Chapter 7 »

A ghost was by the tree, glimmering in the rays of sun and distorting by the breeze as if she were no stronger than a web. She was beautiful, with black strands of hair tied tight in braids to show off two clearly pointed ears. Her dress was slimming, and was embroidered carefully to show every detail of the many flowers. Icy blue eyes stared directly into hers, and her lips moved quickly, and yet made no sound.

Valerlanta shook her head, as if to also shake away the sight of the woman who was not in that spot only seconds ago, but when done, the elf was still there, and was still talking with no words to be heard.

Her thin brows pinched together and her mouth widened as if shouting desperately.

'What are you trying to tell me?' Valerlanta wondered, her heart slamming. *'I do not understand.'*

"What is it?" Venic asked, forcing her to tare her eyes away, and when she looked back, the lady was gone, leaving only the swaying leaves and the bending of grasses.

'I am going mad.' She wanted to tell him. *'That puzzle ball has poisoned me into seeing things that are not there, and I think it will only get worse from here.'*

Instead, she shook her head again and shrugged. "It is nothing. I thought I saw something, but it must just have been the wind."

Venic nodded, but eyed the area carefully to be sure.

"How is Alstred?" She asked, eager to change the subject.

"He is faring better than I expected, though I wager he is hiding much of it." Venic ran a hand through his wavy almond strands and glared at the forest, as if it was the one to blame for all of this. "For the amount of blood he has lost, every step should be a struggle."

"He is putting on a good show."

"That he is."

For the last few days, Alstred had been hiking without complaint, and the two allowed it, though quietly helped him from the shadows. Valerlanta attempted to avoid steep climbs, and Venic stopped for more breaks, pretending to be thirsty. Although Alstred was now joking around as normal, he was in too much of a daze to notice their help, otherwise he would have surely had been offended.

"And your hand? How is that?"

Valerlanta flexed her fingers of the hand in question, and felt a dull ache in response. "I have had worse. Come to think of it, I have had worse with *you*...similar to Alstred, I might add." Crossing her arms, she smiled mischievously. "You know, according to the order of how things are going, you should be next."

Venic rolled his eyes. "I think have gotten enough scrapes and bruises to add up to an equal value by now. Can you even see my skin anymore? I fear I am more bruise than myself these days."

She could not help but laugh and it felt good and released a tension in her chest she did not know was building. "You were black and blue from the moment I met you. Actually, I do not know if I would recognize you any other way."

"What are you two going on about?" A voice came from behind them, and both looked back to see Alstred coming towards them. He had her pack on -the only pack they had left since the horse ran off- and would have appeared eager to go, if his face was not so pale.

"Valerlanta here just admitted that she will make sure to push me into the way of the next blade we meet." Venic lamented with a mock sad face.

Valerlanta looked at him in surprise, not expecting such a teasing comment from him of all people. "I did not!"

He nodded at Alstred seriously. "She did."

"Hmmm." Alstred looked between the two, seeming to try and decide who to believe. "Well, a knight rarely lies...but a thief on the other hand...?"

"You are a thief too, Alstred."

"Precisely why I know whose word to trust!"

"Yes, you can *always* trust the word of a spy." She replied sarcastically, and Venic suddenly laughed.

"We have to be the strangest group to ever join together." He announced, laughing to himself. "A forest thief, a spy from another kingdom, and a city pickpocket, all in one group."

Alstred nodded; his face serious. "All we need is a beautiful sword wielder of the female variety, and we will be unstoppable."

"Why a-" Valerlanta stopped herself when she saw the two laughing and nodding at each other with some sort of inside joke. "No wait, I probably do not want to know. Come on then, let's get going."

"She is right; she really would not want to know about *her."* She heard Venic tell Alstred as they followed her.

"Not ever." Alstred laughed, and Valerlanta sent a suspicious glare back at the two of them.

Coughing awkwardly, Venic quickly changed the subject. "So, let us say that we do make it to the final location, and we do get to the riches that are hidden there; what do you both plan on doing with the money once you get it?"

What indeed? The truth was, she had not thought of that at all; as if this -or any of her other steals for that matter- never had anything to do with gaining money. What would she do with that amount?

"I am going to buy an island." Alstred announced, receiving startled glances from the two with him.

"A *whole* island?" Valerlanta said, and Alstred nodded.

"Yes, a whole island."

"What do you plan on doing with that?" Venic asked in an amused tone.

"Well, I will invite all the women I can to come and live there with me, of course. What is an island without a piece of paradise?" He said. Venic laughed, and Alstred called out in surprise as Valerlanta purposely let go of a branch too early, and it swung back and slapped the blonde hard in the chest.

"What about you, Valerlanta? What do you plan on doing with such riches?" Venic asked.

Valerlanta was silent as she tried to think of it. She once had dreams of finding her father somewhere safe to live where they would be untouchable by the outside world, but she knew now that her father would take none of her charity. So, when there is nothing of value to purchase, what do you spend your money on?

"Same thing I always do." Valerlanta answered finally. "I will travel the woods and steal from those who make it sport. Hopefully my father may even let me join his guild after this."

"I should have known." Venic answered with a smile. "But have you ever thought of leaving?"

"Leaving?" Her feet slowed to a near stop. "To where?"

"Anywhere. You already travel more than anyone I know, so why not go somewhere out of the mountains?"

She thought about it then shook her head. "No, this is where I belong."

"Absolutely insane of her, if you ask me." Alstred said teasingly, then quickly changed the subject before he could give Valerlanta another reason to let go of a branch. "What of you, Venic? After all this, you must plan on taking some of the treasure yourself, so what do you plan to do once this is all over?"

Valerlanta felt her interest peek, and she too looked over at Venic. He hesitated in his steps for a moment, his frown deepening.

"I plan on going home." He answered carefully.

"Home?" Valerlanta pressed. "Back to your kingdom? But I thought you said there was nothing for you there?"

His eyes locked with hers, but were somewhat shaky as if he did not know exactly where to look. "I lied. Well, at least to some extent. I have no future waiting for me there, but I still have some business to finish. One more adventure, if I can make it there."

"I see." Valerlanta simply answered, trying to ignore a cold sort of feeling entering her gut.

Seeming to sense her discomfort, Alstred piped in with an offer. "Although you do sometimes hardly seem to know it Val, you are female, so you would be welcome to stay at my island if you would like?"

"You think I would?" Valerlanta shot turning on him and trying to punch him as he dodged away. "You think I would live on your island of women?"

"Well you would not have to worry; I would not touch someone like you." Alstred laughed as he backed away and she gave chase. "You would just be there to work."

"Oh, thank you for the consideration!" Valerlanta snarled, picking up a piece of weathered wood and throwing it hard. It hit the tall blonde square in his back, causing him to loose his footing and topple down a hill. Valerlanta stood at the top with her hands on her hips looking down at him sprawling on the ground, and gave a huff of accomplishment.

"Idiot." Valerlanta said as Venic came up to join her.

"Yes, but he is still *our* idiot." Venic said, looking at her out of the corner of his eye and giving her a small smirk. "Try not to kill him just yet."

Valerlanta raised a brow, watching as Alstred peeled himself off the ground and dusted himself off before shouting something about all the positions he still had available on his island as a worker; even as he clutched his wound.

"I make no promises." Valerlanta said, and Venic nodded.

"I understand." Venic said with one of his rare laughs before descending the hill and continuing on.

Nearing the bottom, Venic all of a sudden lit up and froze, looking around carefully.

They were in a meadow filled with long grasses and flowers, and the sun felt unusually hot after spending so long in the scattered shade of the forest,

"I know this place." He said. "This is close to a road, just over there! We camped here once." He looked east. "Palenwood is just a few hours that way!"

"Yes," Valerlanta said. "But-"

And she was too late. Venic sped up his pace and was suddenly in the lead, near jogging towards the castle.

"Wait!" Valerlanta called, but he was already gone.

Very baffled, both of the left behind looked at each other, and then back at the man nearly out of sight. As if on cue, both raced after the swordsman; trying hard to catch up.

“This was my first campaign as a knight.” Venic explained when she caught up. He was hurrying about a clearing, as if picturing how it used to be. “The Palenwood king chose war, and so I was sent here with an army. I never actually did any fighting, though.”

“Because the king killed himself when he saw he was surrounded.” She knew this part; though she suspected everyone did. Palenwood was the most recent place to find itself inside the boarders of the king; causing the map to grow quickly. The next kingdom over was Buragen, which was part of the reason why they wanted war.

Venic gave her a surprised look. “Yes, that was what happened. He chose that path over his own people, and so it ended up as a peaceful take-over. I was positioned not too far from here, I’ll show you.”

Valerlanta hid her frown by looking back, but unfortunately Alstred caught it. He was only just barely keeping up with their fast pace, but was close enough to see her conflicted expression. He smiled reassuringly at her, but she quickly made her face go blank.

The fake-king and his ventures was not a topic she wanted to talk about. Just thinking about him caused an instant flame of anger in her chest.

He was a man she had never even seen before, and yet there was rarely a day she did not wish him dead. He was not the person his people thought he was, and she was the only person alive who knew that.

"This is where I was; it has perfect cover and views of the castle, which is exactly what we will need." Venic lead them to a high hill that was thick with forest and pointed to the castle laid out far down below them at the bottom of their cliff. It was one of the largest of the walled cities near this forest, and was heavily fortified. Afraid of the creatures of the night, this castle created precautions for creatures both in fable and in real life; which is why the swordsman's next request was enough to make her knees almost collapse.

"I need you to get me in there."

Valerlanta blinked, trying to hope she heard differently. "Pardon…?

* * *

Knelt behind a tree with only her head peaking around at the great castle, Valerlanta was starting to believe this was hopeless.

Sure she could sneak herself in easy enough; after all, the daughter of the best known thief in then land always had connections, but what about the other two? Who in their right mind would help someone with two men dressed as knights?

Maybe if she snuck in and got them some clothes? No, that still might not be good enough. Like the soldiers from the road, the two were far too muscled for peasant life, so they were bound to be searched then their weapons discovered.

Leaning back onto her heels, she tried to sort everything out.

By now, the sun was almost out of the sky, and the blonde knight took to complaining about not having a fire, but she was too busy to even consider his needs. One mistake and this was all for nothing....though she had not the slightest knowledge as to why she even needed this plan. What was so important within the castle walls?

"Well, any ideas?" A voice asked, startling her from her thoughts. Venic was knelt beside her, appearing without her knowing, and looking closely at her with an odd sort of smirk. A mischievous glimmer sparkled in his brown eyes that she found almost entrapping to her own. They were not his usual tired, dim, eyes, they were his real now. They were full of life, full of hope; but most notably full of danger.

Was he finally showing a layer of the real him?

"Uh..." Valerlanta looked away, realizing she had been staring, and made a show of looking on at the castle, though only to hide her tomato red cheeks. "Four, I would think."

"Four?" He asked; amusement on his voice.

She frowned and turned her head farther away from him. "Maybe three. Hard to tell. I really need more time."

"Well, you have all night." The knight said. "I will try to keep our grumpy toddler at bay while you think."

Then he was gone again; off trying to control the man fuming at being compared to a child again.

No killing, none of her father's connections, and two more people then Val was used to. This, yes this, was a challenge.

Abruptly, Valerlanta felt a smile tug at her lips and she bit back a laugh. After all, she had to admit, this was the first time she ever had to steal something *into* a place, and she certainly never stole a person. Did this count as smuggling illegal goods?

'You are a people smuggler now, Val.' She mused to herself. *'My, my. How things have changed.'*

There was movement on the castle, catching her attention.

"Gah..." She sighed irritated as one of the fires lit up on the tower. There was no pause between the changing of the guards.

Three ideas now. Maybe two. Paying a lord to sneak the two in as their own personal guards(and perhaps her a maid), of course depended on the rare chance that a lord she knew would just happen to be entering tomorrow, so, really unless they got lucky, she was down to two. One complicated, one not but more dangerous.

However, no matter the plan, she knew the men needed a change of clothes...and perhaps she would as well. She was not sneaking in at night this time, so she would need some way to blend also. Unfortunately, a female wearing male clothes, a mask, and carrying a bow would attract attention around normal folk.

Three sets of clothes; for two muscled men and a female unwilling to walk maskless. Another puzzle.

Or at least it would have been had a group not arrived at the closed castle gates, only to be turned away for the night.

"Oh." She said aloud, blinking down at the group that solved perhaps both their problems. *'That was simple enough. Why did I know think of it to start?'*

One wagon parked for the night, and the group of fire eaters, bards, and acrobats set to making camp. Well loved, and as such well fed, they walked well, healthy, and most important of all, muscled.

Smiling like a little kid about to pour a bucket of water on a sibling, Valerlanta rose and returned to camp.

Venic took one look at her from where he sat and knew instantly by the grin on her face. "So you have it then?" He asked, sitting forward with interest.

"Have what?" Alstred asked, looking between them both.

Quickly explaining their most convenient situation that they had the chance of taking advantage of, she watched as their eyes lit up in excitement and shift in the direction of their goal.

Then, after Venic decided it was worth the risk, she crept down the steep hillside on her own, wanting to be down and close before the light fully fell.

The two men followed her a fair distance behind -as they refused to let her try without them there to help- and were surprisingly more quiet then Val was expecting. It made her wonder if they had done this before; snuck up on people in the night, and that somehow made the two step lighter than normal.

The thought made her shiver.

Before long all three reached a slight ledge, close enough to see the group, but far enough to not be seen or heard. The group moved around, cleaning their meals, and then most disappeared into the two tents for bed.

"I do not know any of them." Valerlanta whispered from their hiding spot. "Or at least none that I can tell."

Alstred leaned forward over her shoulder and pointed at a form by the wagon. "I believe they came to the castle last fall. I bought a charm from that old lady."

Venic also leaned over, though over her opposite shoulder, making her glower at how close they both were.

Seriously. It was not like the bush beside would make any more noise than her own.

"He is right, I recognize their banner. They came last fall for the king's birth celebration. The king tried to keep their bard to live in as part of his personal entertainment, but he refused."

Valerlanta went to look at Venic, but found his face uncomfortably close as her nose brushed his cheek, so suddenly she pushed them both backwards with her elbows, making them fall.

"So I will go down and lift some clothes, then we will enter later after they do." She said as they got her hint and knelt a little further away.

Venic nodded, but said nothing.

'Is he angry?' Val wondered, trying to see his face in the fading light. *'Why? Because he can not go with me?'*

"Of course." Valerlanta said, then realized the problem all and once and nearly laughed. "Ah, I get it now. You two have yet to see me steal on my own yet! That is why you are both so freaked out."

They both looked at her, as if to say otherwise, but she just sneered at the challenge.

"Just you two watch." She said, looking back on at her prey. "I will show you what the daughter of this lands greatest thief is capable of."

"Yes, well we will be here as backup in case something goes wrong." Venic said anyways, making her roll her eyes.

"Hey." Alstred said, getting her attention. "Be careful down there, understand?"

There was a light tone of hurt in his voice that almost made her change her mind about making him stay.

Alstred was a good thief when he wanted to be, though he was best suited for loud situations such as markets, but still, she would not allow him to go with her this time.

It was still too soon for that, and at least that he understood and never tried to argue.

"I will." She answered.

They waited until the sun was down and the group had settled into sleep or night watch, then she slipped off, through the trees and into the camp.

Feet light as silk glided the forest ground, stepping around obstacles with ease. Her body was crouched, her movement timed slow with the wind, then, reaching where forest met the cleared opening before the castle where the group camped, she waited.

For a moment she felt like a wildcat, crouched and waiting in the darkness for the perfect moment to attack her prey, and the thought made her smile.

From what she could see, there were three up, keeping the fire going and watching for trouble. One was closest to the flames, making her invisible due to fire-blindness, but the other two stood a little further away, increasing their night vision.

She saw no other movement, and as much as she hated it, she knew she had to go. There was only a limited amount of time, so unfortunately she could not watch as long as she normally would.

So, sliding out onto the grass, she knelt lower until she got closer to the road, then went flat onto her stomach. It took more energy this way, but it was much easier to blend.

Her movements were slow, very slow; inching forward in a way that she hoped would be completely unnoticeable. After all, even though the wagon was now almost blocking her approach from the fire-watch, she also had to worry about the tower guards, watching from the high walled castle.

The sweet smelling grasses bent well under her weight, falling almost soundlessly as she pressed, and for that she was glad.

After what seemed like hours, Valerlanta reached the furthest wheel of the wagon, and was about to roll under when her finger brushed against something.

Curious, she slid her hand along it, and found it to be a thread connected to bells. An alarm system of any strangers approaching.

She smiled. '*Very clever.*'

Luckily, there seemed to be only the one, so she slid over, though kept a more careful watch after.

Light from the fire lit up the wagon in flickering motions, but Valerlanta was careful to remain in it the shadows.

Silently as possible she rose back to a crouch, leaned around it to it's opening, and was only just about to reach in when she noticed something.

Another thread became visible just in time. Another bell alarm.

'*Ashes.*' Valerlanta frowned, trying to think of a way to move it. Or at least she would have had a particular smell not greeted her.

It was a new smell to her, warm and comforting, but most importantly, it was coming from one of the tents.

If she was right and that was food, that meant that they kept all their supplies in where they slept, despite the risk of attracting wildlife.

'*Ashes again.*' She thought to herself, suddenly having no doubt that the wagon was empty and nothing but a trap for those like her. To get at the clothes, she would have to enter the tent full of sleepers.

The thief hesitated there in the shadows a moment longer, but then she smirked. Her father would not turn away from something like this, so she would not either. Besides, this was another new for her. Sure she had stolen from the odd sleeper, but from a tent full? Now this was a risk.

She waited until she was sure the three looked elsewhere, and then Valerlanta crept away from the wagon, and towards the smell. Once at the tent, she tugged at the thick fabric only just a crack, and glanced in. A single candle warmed the whole of it, and as expected, there were creates of goods pilled past the sea of sleeping people.

Assuming one wanted to enter this way, they would have to step over them all without waking one, but unfortunately for them, this was not the way she intended to enter. Instead, she rounded the tent and pulled at one of the pegs. It came loose from the ground, so ever so slowly, Val let it release the tension, not allowing so much as a whisper from the fabric. Then, just as slowly, she lifted it, and crawled under.

Inside she was greeted with a surprising amount of warmth, as well as the smell of sweat. From where she was behind the crates, it was almost completely blackened, but she could still hear the rhythmic sounds of laboured breaths from the louder sleepers.

Still, she could smell that pleasant aroma, and curiosity got the better of her. She followed the lining of the tent until she found where plants hung to dry, and here she found one she had never seen before. It looked almost to be some sort of wood, perhaps a layer of bark, but it was not one she knew.

'An import?' She wondered. *'Something brought from over the sea?'*

Just to satisfy her curiosity, she took one, just one, figuring they would not miss only that, and slipped it into her bag. Then, realizing she was about to take the biggest risk, she slipped out around the crates to where the clothes hung by the candle.

None seemed shocked by her movements, so hopefully that meant all eyes were closed, but truthfully there were too many bodies for her to be able to tell.

Still though, trying not to disturb the candle, Valerlanta stepped over to the clothes and piled them into her bag.

As she stuffed the final of the clothes away, a man grunted and rolled over with a raised head.

Val stiffened as his eyes fell upon her, but she dared not move, just kept a calm expression on her face.

Then, as if in his sleepy state he thought she was just one of the group that he just did not recognize, his droopy lids closed once more and his head fell with the sounds of snores.

For a long moment Valerlanta just sat there, stiff as a frightened rabbit, and then she remembered where she was and set back to work. Once the clothes were safely packed away, she grabbed something from her bag and set it where the clothes were.

A gem, one of her steals that she hid from Venic in the hem of her clothes, and worth more than all three sets of the clothes she stole. She hate to leave it, after all, she found it very pretty, but the three needed something to keep the group from creating a scene, and the gem was more than enough to do that.

She did not need it now anyways. It was nothing compared to the treasure she was after now.

Then she scurried back behind the crates, under the tent fabric, and back into the cold air.

Once there she wanted to catch her breath, but forced herself to continue on. Back, to the wagon, across the field, and into the forest she went. She met up with the other two back at the place she left them, then they went up to divide her prize.

* * *

However, just as the group was about to be let through, one of the guards put out an arm, stopping Venic. The man had a rough sort of appearance with uneven lengths of stubble, and scars on his face-perhaps from catching a sickness as a young boy- that extended down his neck to where it disappeared under his messily kept uniform.

Valerlanta felt her heart race; this man just stunk of desperation; and desperation was dangerous.

"You." The man hissed. "What is it you do?"

"I am a fire-eater, sir." Venic said, appearing and sounding surprisingly relaxed despite the current situation. "I am planning on giving a show near the town center before nightfall, and I would be grateful if you would come to watch if you are curious. I can promise you, you will not be disappointed."

The other guard put a hand on the shoulder of the man and muttered something in his ear, but the rough man shook him off and poked Venic roughly in the chest.

Somehow, Venic kept a perfectly calm expression.

"You will prove your skills now." The guard hissed. "Or you will not be having that show before nightfall."

Even as Valerlanta felt her muscles tense, readying herself for a run, Venic nodded easily, reaching into her pack to pull out his gloves. "Well, you see, I did plan on buying the materials for torches while I was in, but if you can find the supplies I would be more than willing."

Unfortunately, the guard complied and came forth with a torch-which he himself also lit.

"To avoid any funny business." He explained, handing Venic the torch. The knight nodded in understanding.

"Of course." Valerlanta expected the knight to look to Alstred and herself to create a distraction, but instead he brought the flames in close, and gave the growing crowd a wink as he whispered quietly to the fire with a cupped hand.

Alstred shot her a nervous look, but Valerlanta ignored it, and because of that she noticed Venic drop something from between his fingers onto the flame.

"It is turning white!" Someone called, and Venic held out the torch as the flames turned from orange to white. Making the crowd laugh, he stole the wineskin from someone's hip and took a swing before giving it back. He pretended to quench his thirst with a large swallow, but clearly left some in as he blew out on the fire and the white flames leapt up over the crowd before returning to their normal size and color.

The crowd cheered, but the guard did not look impressed. His arms were crossed and his expression did not as much as twitch at the show.

Looking between the knight and the guard, Valerlanta knew that if Venic did not do something new soon, the guard would not be impressed.

She stole a quick glance to Alstred, and he gave her a small nod.

She called on the magic.

She pictured fire, she pictured flames, and the magic leapt to action.

She felt a tingling on her hands as the magic worked, but the flames on Venic's torch remained normal as he blew another fiery breath onto the torch.

Out of the corner of her eye, she saw something strange, and looked down.

Frost was making its way from her feet and towards the crowd.

'No!' She tried to mentally correct the fire, but it was not as easy as telling your brain to lift an arm. The frost crawled, and the thief closed her eyes, picturing over and over again what she wanted.

Then opening her eyes again, she put full force into the magic.

Venic again blew on the flames, and a dragon spread its fiery wings from the flames. As the fire creature made its way soaring upwards, Venic managed to play along and pretended to be continue blowing on the flames.

Hand behind her back, Valerlanta spread her fingers wide, and the dragons wings grew as it continued its upward climb.

Some in the crowd screamed and ducked for cover, others gasped and backed away.

Out of breath, Venic pulled his lips away, and Valerlanta stopped the flow of magic with sudden closing of her hand into a fist.

The dragon burned off, and the torch returned to normal size. The flame went into the swordsman's mouth, and when he brought it out again, the flame was out and he raised it out in his hand before taking a deep bow.

The crowd cheered, and Valerlanta was pleased to see the guard's mouth hanging open in shock. Playing the act well, Alstred rushed forward with his boot-which he had somehow taken off without her seeing- and filled it with the money of willing donators.

"H-how?" The guard asked, his hand

Valerlanta came up as Venic looked both ways, as if to first make sure none of the crowd was listening in. "To tell you the truth, it is all show. The white flames is from a type of salt found in the mountain's that I sprinkles on the flames, and the dragon was from yet another ingredient."

Salt? Valerlanta perked up at that. Her salt had those qualities? How didn't she know? Or rather, how did he?

The guard did not seem to trust him. "What possible ingredient causes flames to take shape?"

Venic faltered, and Valerlanta sparked with an idea. Quickly she brought out the mysterious warm smelling bark she found in the camp of performers the night before and pressed it into the knights hand. Without even blinking an eye, he caught on. "This is the one, though please keep it out of sight from the crowd; I have to make my money somehow, you see. This curl of bark comes from a tree far away. You see, there they sprinkle it into the fire and try to tell the future, but most the time it just takes shape as the first thing that comes to your head. Picture love, and it will take the shape of your ideal woman, and so forth. The mind is a powerful thing, and this and flame acts upon it, which is why I started using it for show. It is very, very, expensive though."

The guard took the curled bark and eyed Venic carefully before bringing it to his nose. The warm smell must have been new to him as well, because his eyebrows rose the slightest amount.

"This plant does all that?" He pressed.

"If it is dried in the sun for the correct amount of time, yes, indeed it can."

The guard looked at Venic for a small moment longer, than huffed and gave the bark back and nodded to the gate. "On with you, then."

Venic took another performers bow, and handed the torch back. "Thank you, and I hope you enjoyed the show."

Venic gave her a quick smile, and neared the gate, and was quickly met up by the one-barefooted blonde who was hobbling towards them with a boot clinking with coins.

"Fantastic show!" He called and both men smiled.

As they went under the gate, Valerlanta noticed he still had the bark in-between his fingers and put it out towards her. "Where on earth did you find cinnamon." He whispered, amusement bubbling in his voice.

'Cinnamon?' She snatched the bark and mentally said it a few more times in her head to make the name stick. "Magic?"

He raised a brow at that-his brown eyes twinkling, but then they were inside the castle gates, and all of Palenwood layout in front of them. Palenwood was one of few fully walled cities in the kingdom, and because of that, high numbers of people lived packed into the same spot. Even here at the gate, locals crowded the streets, heading in various directions.

"This way." Venic said, and both the blonde-who was still bootless- and the thief, followed.

"Where did you learn that, anyways?" Alstred asked Venic as they went. "That was more than I was expecting, I can tell you that."

Immediately, the knights cheeks went an uncharacteristic shade of red. "It is not important."

"Oh no, you have to tell us now..." Valerlanta cooed, suddenly interested. "It is only fair."

"Agreed. You went red, that means it is a story worth hearing." Alstred added.

"I-." Venic hesitated, wanting to look anywhere but the two of them. "I might have thought fire-eaters were truly magic, and I might have paid good money for some lessons before I learnt otherwise. It might have also been done to impress a girl who had an interest in magic."

Both companions laughed, but it was Alstred who only nearly fell over due to it.

"You can not mean Usanda!" Alstred said, holding his injury as he laughed, then he laughed even harder as Venic went redder.

"She is a very pretty lady."

"She is insane!" Alstred quipped. "As well as married."

"She was unwed at the time." Venic said, giving absolutely no argument against the fact of the lady being insane, which only caused his friend to laugh harder.

Venic glared and walked a little faster.

The swordsman led them to a place against the shadow of the wall. Generally, the further from the wall you were, the more expensive part of the city you would find yourself in, but this building did not seem too bad. It had a sign hanging in front of it depicting a creature that had the bottom of a seal, and the top of a woman, and though it had no windows, Valerlanta had seen worse buildings in her travels. Inns were generally easy money; there were always people in need of a place to sleep. Even from out here, she could already hear the music and chatter from those inside.

"Welcome to the SaltyLady," Venic said, opening the door. An odd name for somewhere so far from the sea, she thought, but then again perhaps Selkies could be river creatures as well.

Instantly, the smells of smoke, fat-candles, and foods came rushing out to greet them. As they entered, people-probably locals-looked up to see who was there, but then quickly lost interest upon seeing it was no one important. Only a larger man who was missing an arm seemed to care, but Valerlanta still raised her hood further over her head to be sure.

"Welcome, guests." He said, his accent thick; most likely originating from the southern coast. "'re you all lookin' for a place to sleep on this good night? Or is it a table you are after?"

"A bed for three nights, perhaps more if things go as we wish." Venic said easily. "Make it a private room, as well."

The inn-keepers eyes went wide at that. In their current clothes, there was no way they would look like they could afford such a thing, but the inn keeper was good enough not to mention it. "Very well, that will be five gold's, if you please."

At that, Alstred dumped his boot on a near and empty table and greedily started to count. Rolling her eyes, Valerlanta helped; dividing the different types of metals. Once done, Venic pulled out what other coin they needed.

As Venic handed over the coin, Valerlanta caught notice of some greedy eyes looking from various tables. She gave each of them a hard and careful glare before following the innkeeper up the stairs.

Like most inns, the building had a very small private courtyard with a well, and some rooms had windows looking out either into the courtyard or the streets, and others had no windows at all. Everything depended on how much you were willing to spend; some payments did not even come with a bed; just a roof over your head and a spot on the floor between several others.

Their small room did not have any windows, and only had two beds; one a considerable bit larger than the other. The larger of the beds had a plain canopy, while the smaller one was in the corner of the room and was curtained off; making Valerlenta figure the second was for the servant of whoever slept in the nicer of the two.

"This will do fine." Venic assured the inn keeper, and the older man gave the key and scurried off to leave them to look around better.

"There are only two beds." Alstred said, suddenly sounding tired. "I will sleep on the floor."

"No." Valerlanta quickly corrected. "You will sleep on a bed; you need the sleep more than anyone. Besides, I do not plan on sleeping; I will be too busy."

By which, of course she meant was that she could not sleep in a small and dark room like this even if she wanted to.

Alstred gave her a shocked look, and went to say something, perhaps to argue with her, but Venic spoke first after he closed the door behind him. With it closed, the room became completely black except for the light from under the door.

"We need to talk about why we are here before we even think about anything else." Venic said in a whisper, clearly worried about being overheard. "Valerlanta, how well do you think you could gather information here? Do you have sources?"

"Yes I-" Valerlanta started, but was interrupted by Alstred.

"I can help! I can get information just as well as she can, if not better." Alstred said. "I mean no offence, Valerlanta, but I would look far less suspicious."

Far less suspicious than a mask wearing performer? She could understand that as the truth.

"Alstred, we need you well again." Venic said crossly. "You will not leave this room for days. I will bring you want you need, but you have to get your strength back; we will need you if it means going to Alecaven. No one knows those streets better than you, so I cannot risk you getting a fever right now."

There was an awkward silence, and though Valerlanta could not make out the blondes face in this darkness, she knew his pride was hurt.

"Alright." He choked out finally, then cleared his throat and talked to the thief. "Valerlanta, I do not know if it will aid you or not, but Penswith is here."

Valerlanta perked up at that. "He is here? In this city?"

"Yes, he is."

"Who?" Venic asked.

"Someone who was a client of mine." Valerlanta said.

"He decided to sell her out after she stole for him." Alstred explained. "You do not know this, but among thieves, Valerlanta is very well known. She is nearly as sought after as those in her father's guild, so when Penswith was stupid enough to try and get money off of Valerlanta's capture, he ended up as the biggest joke of the land for years."

"I did as was fair." Valerlanta mused, a smile coming to her face.

"Why do I gather that I should feel sorry for him?" Venic said carefully.

"I never hurt him!" Valerlanta said, and both her and the tall blonde laughed.

"Well, the reason why I brought him up is because he might be of help." Alstred said.

"So you can do it?" Venic asked. "I would myself, but some of the king's men are stationed here; I cannot risk being recognized, so the less I leave here, the better."

Valerlanta nodded, forgetting neither of them would be able to see it. "Penswith and some old clients might be of some help, and if not, one of my father's guild members should still be here; though I would prefer not to use him if at all possible. His guild cannot be trusted when faced with that much treasure without him here to control them."

"Good." Venic said, sounding relieved. "Valerlanta, I need you to ask about any rumours regarding anything having to do with Elvish within the city; anything at all. We need to know what the final puzzle piece is, and where to find it."

"Do not worry." Valerlanta assured, reaching for the door. "You are asking a thief to find an item and steal it; that is what I do."

Then she closed the door behind her and when it clicked shut, she took in a deep breath; readying herself.

If she was going to go days without sleep, she had better start asking around right away. First, though, she wanted to take a look around the city for herself.

« Chapter 8 »

Like many rivers crashing into one, the people of Palenwood maneuvered in a rush; meeting in the city center, and forcefully becoming one. They moved mostly seamlessly with one another, until a rock came and disrupted the whole flow by stomping up stream.

At night, Valerlanta had enjoyed the empty streets as she wandered the town, but now more and more people were starting to wake, causing the flow of people to start again.

She ignored the growing crowds while following the waterways of the town just as she had done since arriving the day before.

First she started at the well with the fae spilling water from her eyes. The white stone statue grew out of a carved tree, stretching upward with her one of stone her arms still in the bark behind her, and her body arched forward, looking to the sky with a painful longing.

The water that fell came in a rush of tears from her eyes, and filled the well which was sacred to this town.

In all honesty, the fountain sent shivers up and down her back uncomfortably, but to the people of this land found it more powerful than anything else.

"Fae Water" they called it, and thought it could cure all ailments.

She believed no such thing. Odd as it was, even though she herself held the ability to use magic, she often rolled her eyes at the mention of magic existing elsewhere within the world.

There was a time long ago when she would chase the stories, looking for magic in a hope to be the first thief to steal something of such, but they always came up false tales.

Always.

Just ordinary items with extraordinary stories.

Valerlanta stood in the shadows, watching for a while as a baby was dipped into the cold waters by his parents and cried out in surprise. The water covered the babe to the head, and there was no magic light, no ripple or anything else to tell it was working, and yet there was such a gleam of hope in the parent's eyes that she had to turn away.

As they left, the babe coughed, but the parents continued on, content their newborn would soon be healed.

The water of the well lead downhill, past the houses of the lords and ladies, and into the market, where it met in a grand ring, then left off in many different directions, and in the center of the ring was a grand tree.

Even though Valerlanta had seen it before, even now she found herself gawking at its size. It grew taller and wider than any house in the area, and kept the market shielded with its large leafy branches.

Fae water, the town said, was the cause of it growing so vast, and not to mention the reason why it supposedly shredded golden leaves in the fall. Not real gold, of course, but the locals swear that they glimmer just as brightly. Valerlanta had never been here to see it herself-this being too far north for her likings for so late in the year-but sometime she would like to.

Reaching out, she placed a hand upon the smooth bark, and felt like no more than a butterfly in comparison to the sky-reaching tree towering high above her.

Beautiful. That was the only way to put it.

Although she knew better than to, her adventurous side begged her to try and climb it to where the birds were rustling about in the morning sun above.

Envy struck her as she watched the feathered creatures flutter about; some even landing on the stalls of the shops, looking for crumbs as freely as they wanted as there were none yet to shoo them off.

Unlike most markets, this market was protected within one of the outer walls of the castle, allowing business to go on much later without fear. As such, since the folks could safely walk about at such late hours, those of the market were unfortunately late risers.

It was just as good for her as the birds. This way, she had the morning to herself, free of the market crowds that annoyed her so.

Letting out one more smile at the leafy tree, she rounded it, letting her hand drag along the bark, then was off again.

She still had more places she could look, and people she could ask.

Guards passed her along the way, to which Valerlanta would flinch away and duck her head respectively as any other peasant would, but of course would glare at their backs as they went by. Although the castle guards were not all of noble blood, many still demanded with force to be treated as one.

Nobel or guard, they were all lazy and useless. Any man who did not know where to empty his own chamber pot or how to make his own food could not be very much help in the wild. Dependant on others as a baby was not, in her own opinion, an attractive quality.

The waterway she followed disappeared down under the castle walls of the royals, leaving her frowning. Most castles being built left reminders of those they were most proud of at the time, but so far she had nothing of interest.

Giving up her aimless search, the thief made her way back to the inn she had left the two men at. It was a typical sight for a city; a wood and stone built place with off white walls and a hanging sign telling of the pub inside. Inside, the stench of food, fire, ale, and man sweat came all at once; something else that also seemed to be common.

Calls were being made for wishes of food and drink, and feet were stomped enthusiastically to the beat of a bard. Nearly every table sat full, and even at those that were filled had some people standing around them in places where no chairs would fit.

Nearby, a group laughed particularly loud as some drunken man walked, apparently trying to mimic the walk of a lady, and in result he landed flat as a fallen tree at her feet.

Pausing a moment to blink in awe at the strangeness of these people, Valerlanta quickly stepped over the passed out man that none attempted to assist, and hurried through the sea of loud talking people.

At the far table in the corner at the only place with an empty seat, was Venic.

He looked completely different now, with his bead fully shaven away and his face washed free of any dirt, and as he greeted them with a smile and slid the waiting drinks across the wooden table, Valerlanta made herself blink several times to make sure it was really him. This way; with his shaven face showing his strong defined cheeks and hardened almond eyes; he truly did have an air of a noble around him, even in the clothes of a fire-eater.

He smiled small as she came up and waved to someone at the bar.

"I ordered some pottage for the two of us for when you showed up. It is supposed to be good here; I hope you are hungry." He said, and Valerlanta eyed him with a feel of suspicion.

Valerlanta felt her brows rise as she sat down. It had been a long time since she had purchased food, so best she tried, curiosity sparked within her. When the bowls came; which were wooden carved bowls -and much nicer than her own- the smell and warmth was enough to make her forget her worries.

"Go ahead." Venic urged, motioning with his spoon for her to start.

Gingerly, Valerlanta grabbed the spoon, and let it hover above her bowl. The knight stared from across the table, urging her with his gaze, so Valerlanta took a bite, then another.

Pottage in the woods never tasted this good.

As she dug in eagerly, Venic leaned across the table. "So do you have any leads yet?"

She shook her head. "No. I followed the waterways, but so far I have seen no signs of the elves ever visiting here. Now that it is morning, I will start asking questions."

"Good." He nodded, but there was clearly another reason he had asked her here than just to get some information and to make sure she had eaten. Glancing around, he leaned over the table a little further so his next words would be quieter. His eyes were serious. "Did you sleep at all last night?"

Valerlanta shook her head, and the swordsman did not look pleased.

"We have a room to ourselves."

"It is not that."

"Alstred and I could wait down here for a time."

"It is not that!"

"Then what is it, exactly? What is causing this?"

Letting out an irritated breath, she leaned back in her chair. "Walls."

"Walls?"

"And darkness, and small spaces, and so much more."

"Like a cell." He asked, and she looked up in surprise. "Like the cave we stayed at; and just like a cell."

She opened her mouth but no words came out, her throat clenched and she gave a tiny nod.

He frowned deeper. "We will leave soon. Right after we find what we are looking for, we will be back into the forest again."

Looking only at her pottage, she took the last few spoonful's and pushed the bowl away. "Good. I am going to go search, then."

And she left, knowing full well that he was carefully watching her go.

* * *

The shop she looked for was on the furthest edge from the others, and had thatched work covering holes where the shingles had failed. There was a pathetic attempt at a small garden around the back, but of course the darkness of the tall wall blocked it from getting any sun, so now it was just lifeless dirt.

There was a sign hanging beside the door, and upon it was the picture of red and white stripes, telling that this shop was home to both the surgeon, and the local hair-cutter. Unfortunately for him, work was exceptionally slow for wounds and gouges during times of peace, and most men still attempted at cutting their own hair, so his place was falling apart.

To compensate, Valerlanta noticed an assortment of chimes and charms hanging in the window that he was clearly selling to the more superstitious of the people.

At first she raised her hand to knock, but then she knew he would not answer anyways-and not to mention she did not have the knight babysitting her at the moment- so instead she carefully looked around, then brought out her lock picks.

The inside of the shop was almost the same as the time she was here before, with countless dried, plants hanging from the roof, and many more crates lining the walls, but now there was a strange bed made mostly of metal; perhaps for his injured clients.

The smell was of all things earthy in one; like dug up wet dirt with root, dried leaves, and perhaps a hint of spice or sweet, and Valerlanta breathed it in with a smile.

At least there was one other man who understood the importance of wild cures over the kings alchemists.

Curiously she poked around, eyeing some of the charms, and smelling and trying to identify the strange herbs, while all the while wondering when her host would wake. When that got boring, she went into his kitchen, which was to the back to the house, and made herself a sort of tea of the herbs she knew.

She could tell he still lived alone, despite this being a house intended for a family, and, apparently by some of the plants she had seen, he was still not completely a law abiding man.

It was not as she lit the fire or boiled the water when he came out in a hurry, but instead when she was lounging back in one of his wicker chairs and sipping her hot drink.

"W-who is there?" He burst in with a hurry, a walking stick raised up like a sword, and a wild eyed expression on his face. When he saw just who it was sitting in his chair, the stick lowered, but he backed away two extra-large steps, as if to avoid something poisonous. "You? What are you doing here?"

"I would like your help." Valerlanta said. "And clearly also your tea. It is very good."

"My help? I should call the guards is what I should do! How did you get in here? That was a new lock!" He was mocking bravery, but the thief saw how his sunken eyes quivered, and his hands fidgeted on his weapon. He was still in his nightwear, and she supposed she should be embarrassed, but instead she found herself far more uncomfortable with how thin the man was. He was lacking in just as much muscle as he was fat, and it made her wonder if he really ate at all.

Noticing her gaze, it was him instead who cringed away in embarrassment and grabbed a coat to make himself at least a tad more decent.

"I see business is not as strong as is needs to be." She said as she eyed his tight wrists.

He huffed.

"I should call the guards." He said again. "You should not be in my home."

She felt her eyes roll. "Call the guards? Really, love? With all those kings teas you sell? It's illegal to sell those, you know. Just as illegal as killing any man."

This far from the king, it was near impossible for the nobles here to try a tastes of his tea with proper permission, but not wanting to appear unfashionable, they were often willing to risk buying it in more shady ways.

The man before her paled.

"What is it you need?" He asked.

She leaned forward in her chair, her face becoming serious.

"I need some information."

It was a known fact that Runen was a well-read man, and that was rare, even among nobles.

His face lit up, clearly expecting something worse. "Information? What sort of information? I hope you do not mean on my contact, because those I will not give, no matter what you do."

"Runen, you are making it sound like I burned down your house! Unless I am remembering wrong, it was you who sold me out to a castle guard for a few coins."

"And then I came back home and half my things were stolen!" The man shouted. "Half my things! All gone! Right down to one shoe there and one shoe gone!"

"Half your things for me very nearly being caught." She grinned in a way she hope made him regret ever daring to try and cross her. "I would say that is more than fair. Actually, it was probably much more then you deserved. Your things surprisingly sold for little."

"Of course they did! Who would want one shoe?"

"Everything can be sold." She replied confidently. "But not everything should be. Some things come back to haunt you when you try."

The man swallowed hard then made an act of clearing his throat. "I must say, my curiosity is getting the better of me. What brings you this far north? Has some rich noble you are on the hunt for come this way?"

Valerlanta watched him for a long moment, letting her dark gaze take full effect in the silence.

He looked back uncomfortably, his hand still tight upon his stick. Then, after giving him a warning glance as way of telling him not to try anything, she reached into her bag and removed the ball.

It was wrapped in a dirty cloth, but she could still feel the gentle hum it gave off from under her fingers. She sat it on the table, but did not remove the wrappings or take her hands off it.

"This here is my reasoning for visiting you on this fine day. You see, it is missing its sibling of sorts, and I would really like the family to reunite."

Greed and interest flashed over the thinner man's face, though he tried to hide it. She expected that, though. He thought her rich as a king, not that she did not help to spread such rumors to anger nobles and help her buisness.

“And can I see this object?” He said. “Or am I expected to guess?”

Valerlanta looked him deep in the eye, judging him, but then slid it away, back to safety and away from his hungry eyes. “I can tell you more than enough about it. It is of elf make, and once upon a time it came from a castle high up on a mountain where it sat with a sword, as well as other things. Unfortunately, it is a puzzle, and all good puzzles come with clues.” She leaned forward in the chair, hoping to stress the importance of this matter. “I need that clue, Runen. And you are going to point me in the right direction.”

“And why should I do that?” He dared press, his voice cracking with desperation. “Why would I help someone who helped me fall into this life? Did you know I can barely afford food now? Who in their right mind would run wounded to the door someone who looks half dead themselves? Or would trust them to sell nobles teas? I am ruined! Ruined!"

Annoyance clawed at her chest, but she caged it in. She simply wanted a quick answer, not to give out advice on life!

"Do not blame it all on me, you bug. It was not me who made you stop bathing so that you smell worse than a pig." She spat. He opened his mouth to speak, but she continued anyways. "Nor was it me who was supposed to clean this mess of a house or go out and sell your illegal goods. This was your own doing, so do not start blaming me. However, you will help me."

Now he was clearly shaking and angry tears sat in his eyes. "Why?"

"I can get you a special selection of wounded people; people who do not want word going around that they need fixing, or even that they are in the area. Secret clients who pay well to remain as such. You help me, and I will get your business."

His jaw trembled, his grip shifted, then finally he slumped in surrender against the wall and let the stick fall to the ground as he cradled his head in his hands.

"There is a door, one lined with elf script." He spoke through his fingers. "Rumour says what is down there was a gift to the ruler of this kingdom from his brother who supposedly wed an elf. I have never been down there, I have never been allowed to, so I cannot say what there is, but it is your best clue. I have not seen any other elf script old enough to be true."

She sat there a moment longer, waiting to see if silence could judge if his words were true or not, but when he spoke no more, she rose up and went for the door, but not before leaving her now empty tea on the floor next to a pile of trash.

As she was only just about to step out and leave the poor man in his filth, she gave one final look over her shoulder. "Sell me out again, and I will kill you."

The man said nothing in reply, so Valerlanta exited, but did not head back for the inn; not quite yet. In this part of the city, nobles were less likely to gather, so instead the goods quickly changed from extravagant-and, in her mind, *useless*- items, to practical and inexpensive goods such as baskets and clothes made from donated old rags.

Here, the people clustered about more hesitantly, as if not wanting to be seen on this end of the market longer then needed.

This was where she started her act.

“Good morning!” She said to the first of the targets; a man in near rags, but not quite a beggar. He was sitting on a barrel, selling what appeared to be tangled fishing nets. His hands were picking at the rope when she walked up and startled him.

Truth be told, it was almost noon, but it seemed morning enough for him as well. “Good morning.” He mumbled back. “What are you? Some sort of performer?”

She smiled her best smile, hoping to put him at ease. “That is exactly correct. Nothing too exciting, I am afraid. I just can shoot blindfolded; nothing as exciting as the acrobats or fire-eaters sadly.”

"Hmm." Was all he said, and then went back to picking at his knots. Not willing to give up yet, Valerlanta pressed on.

"Well, as you can probably tell, I am not from here-," She ignored his snort, as if that was clearly obvious. "- but I have stumbled upon a rumor that has me fascinated, and since you look to be a smart man, I thought I might as well start with you."

Now he looked up, but only to glare as if he were looking at a misbehaving child. "You are not talking about the swamp, are you? We have had just about enough of you visitors going down there looking for trouble. That place is haunted, and all you are doing is disturbing the spirits there!"

"Oh dear no. I would not think of it!" Valerlanta gasped, when she had actually already been there several times herself. "It is nothing nearly as dangerous; I am not nearly adventurous enough to venture such places. I just wish to know about a door. You see, I travel with a story-teller, and he just loves his elf stories, which is why I am driven know more; but so far all I have been able to find out is that there is a door, and upon it is elf writing. Not much story in that, but you must know more, do you not?"

He stared at her for a moment, then some sort of light sparkled in his eye; perhaps at the excitement of someone hoping to learn something from a soul as lowly as him, and he nodded.

"Good." Valerlanta knelt on the ground before him and smiled brightly. "Do tell."

« Chapter 9 »

Life in the mountains is always harsh. The sun sets earlier, the water of the rivers always feel of ice, and winters blanket lays over the land heaviest in these spots, and yet people still live in these lands and live well.

Out of all the cities in the land, Palenwood was always the one that Valerlanta felt the most ease in relating to. True they were overly superstitious and held rituals she had no means of understanding, but she could see in their eyes a restlessness growing there; a sort of animal instinct that she knew all too well.

Summer would soon be leaving; leaves would be turning to colors of fire, letting all know that their moments of warmth were coming to an end.

She should be stocking up on food in her hidden storages throughout the forest, thinking about replacing her ruined jacket, and worrying about sleep under winters sharp bite just as she was sure these people were doing now, but for the first time, she had other things to think about.

True, instinct still told her that winters presence was behind her every step; watching to see if this time she would slip up, but she was ignoring it. It was a very strange feeling. Her soul was telling her that there was only a limited amount of time to secure her survival, and she was ignoring it like it was a long-time friend she no longer wanted.

However, as she watched the commoners around her hurrying about their daily tasks, for a moment she could not help but feel their pressure.

She should be drying and salting meats, hanging herbs, and...

Abruptly she was broken from her daze as three soldiers walked by. Instinctively she sunk away, hoping to become smaller, but the men did not even look her way as they strode by.

As they went, she noticed something that sent a chill up her spine. Their armours were all new. In fact, looking around, she suddenly saw what she had been missing before. Old holes were being filled, battlements were being fortified,

This was not a good sign.

Stuffing the rest of her stolen bread into her mouth, she was only about to turn and leave, when suddenly Venic was there beside her, causing her to choke in surprise.

Anger, and perhaps also knowing the fact that he was not armed, made her punch him hard in the shoulder. "Warn someone before you walk up to them! You are like a ghost! One moment you are loud as an ox, and the next no one knows you are there! I could have died!"

Venic cast her a startled look, then much to her surprise he laughed. "This is coming from you of all people? The wildcat of the forest that walks across a field of sticks and does not snap a single one? I dare say, revenge has come to greet you."

This time she had to resist a very strong urge to aim her punch a little higher...perhaps on that pretty little face...just below the bangs but just above...

She was only just about to ask why he was there when a clanging rang out into the air. Both companions looked up with a start, and saw two of the men she saw before training. They did so right in the middle of the street so that people had to walk around them, but Valerlanta had no doubt it was for strategic reasoning's that they were practising here, where all the already fearful commoners could see their deadly abilities.

They circled one another, a playful smile on both their faces but fierce determination in their eyes. They of course wanted to be the winner amongst such an audience, even if they were just using blunt training swords.

Valerlanta watched with growing interest as they lunged in and out at each other like wolves snapping their bites.

Glancing over at Venic, she saw the knight watching with a sort of distant longing on his face. His expression looked suddenly empty, and what was more, she noticed his body twitching with every movement of the men, as if it were he who were one of the opponents.

This was the reason why he risked leaving the inn; he wanted to see the fights.

"You miss it." Valerlanta stated, surprised by the bitterness in her own tone.

That seemed to startle him from his daze, but he continued watching as if bewitched. "With every waking moment." He answered in but a whisper.

This confused her to no end. He was missing the life of those who were at this very moment hunting him down? Was he not enjoying the freedom? Did he not now crave the taste of meats ban from all tables but those the king favoured most?

"Why?" She asked finally. "What is there to miss?"

"Plenty." He said with a sad little smile that faded quickly as it came. "To wield a sword for the king is something all young boys wish for. What meaningless life you had before is gone, and suddenly, with but a few words of the king, you are important in the eyes of all those around you. From then on, walking the halls of the castle, you feel all the spirits of heroes of knights walking with you, because now you are one of their families.

People by the hundreds come for your help and protection, and for once you actually have the power to do it. You are no longer helpless, you no longer act with fears will, you are a knight, and anything is possible."

With his finally words, his hardened shell came back over, once again hiding away his true self. "It is not something you would understand."

No, she did not understand. She could not make sense as to why a man felt he needed a title and a sword to feel like he had the power to do something, but then by his words she was reminded of a time long ago. A time when a fearful little girl put on a leather mask to become someone new, and never took it off again.

"I understand well enough." She answered. "All people miss their home. Even those who enjoy the thrill of gambling with death feel an urge to always return where they feel strongest."

He glanced at her, his gaze still cold as ice, but she still knew he caught on to her meaning.

By then a thick crowd had started emerging around them as people stopped their repetitive lives to see the power of the two men fighting. Many blows were taken by both men, and although the dulled blades were not enough to chop a man, all watching had no doubt it was still enough to brake bones.

Unlike a real fight, these men had the option to not fight to the death; they were fighting until the other was either defeated, or surrendered.

"How is your searching coming?" Venic asked, and Valerlanta winced inwardly.

"I heard about something of interest." She said.

The look on his face was startling. His eyes grew wide, and the brown depths filled with an intensifying hope that almost drown her under the pressure. His whole body tensed with anticipation, and although he tried to hide it with relaxed shoulders, his whole body looked prepared to run a long race in excitement.

Valerlanta opened her mouth to answer, when someone else spoke first.

"You! All of you! You are blocking the road." Screamed a familiar voice. The guard -the one from the gate- was struggling to get through with a group of men. "Move aside! Move aside!"

Without thinking, Valerlanta sunk away into an alleyway, and by the commotion behind her, others were rushing to do the same. She stopped to look back, but a hand grabbed her by the arm just above the elbow and kept her walking.

"The soldiers are all on edge." Venic explained. "Something is making them abnormally tense. Yesterday I saw one nearly beat a kid to death for dropping a basket in front of him. I cannot help but think that they would not overlook a chance to take their aggression out on two people dressed as performers. Especially him. We should get out of sight."

It was right then when something came splashing down no more than two steps ahead of her.

"I-is that...," She asked, dreading the answer.

"Yes." Venic answered bluntly, as if it should be obvious. "That would be the inside contents of a chamber pot."

What!?

"Aw!" Valerlanta recoiled in disgust. "That is just-uck! I know I live in a forest, but even I bloody know to dig a hole! What is wrong with you city people? Right on the street!"

"Well it is our fault, really, for walking in the alley." Venic stated, clearly struggling to keep the corners of his mouth down. "Did you really not ever wonder what the smell was? Really. Just be happy we are here and not in the bigger cities. Here they at least have people to shovel-"

"Is it so hard to dig a hole?" She screamed up at the empty window. "They do it at the inn! It just takes a hole! A stupid hole! Grab a shovel, then make a hole!"

By that time, even the lowest class was looking at her strangely as they passed as if she were the mad beggar, and them the sane thief.

Venic was trying so hard to hold the laughter in, he was near tears. When it finally escaped, once again Valerlanta found herself hearing the light pleasant flutter of laughter she could only expect of someone of higher status.

Cheeks burning like fire, Valerlanta crossed her arms. "I do not see what is funny about walking in another persons-"

But his hand came up to cover her mouth-much to her irritation-and stayed there until he had fully regained his composure.

"Come." He gasped, pulling her with him once again.

As much as Valerlanta wanted to kick him where men should not be kicked and leave him to fall where "business" should not be dropped, she could not help but notice the growing eyes upon them, so instead went willingly.

Once far out of sight of any guards they knew of, they stopped at one of the towns many wells. Unlike other city folk who sometimes had to make a long trip to their water source, this place had the many mountains to thank for countless streams of water that ran both above and below the soil.

While Venic got a drink, and splashed some of the cool liquid on his face, Valerlanta took it upon herself to stand watch.

She stood with her back to the well, and her eyes scanning faces for anyone who would take advantage of two distracted performers.

He too smiled, but quickly after, shadows came across his eyes with that familiar worry. "So, that information you said you have, what do you know?"

Her same hesitation came flooding back. "I can not say for sure. What I know are just rumours from men with but a few coins to get them through the year." She found herself glaring off into the corner and fidgeting with a strand of hair. "Supposedly there is a door within one of the passages of the castle that has elf print all over the side of it."

"That is it?" He asked, and Valerlanta knew instantly he was disappointed. What was more, he did not sound surprised he felt as such.

Anger in his doubt of her sent all the information rushing out.

"I have heard the same from multiple sources; all the guards do rotations though various parts of the castle, and many of them, if you get them drunk enough, will speak of the door. They are told to guard it and keep it secret, but do not know why."

"It could be a trap for thieves." Venic sighed. "The king does something similar. He has two treasure rooms, but only shows and brags to people about the one. Thieves go in the night, and find all the treasure has been replaced with guards. It is a simple trick."

"And what if it is not?" Valerlanta pressed. "What if it is real, and it is there, and we are wasting time wondering? You said so yourself many
times that *'we must hurry'* but where is your need for that now?"

"It is too risky." He sighed. "Besides, it is a castle! How can we storm into a keep with only three people?!"

Valerlanta tilted her head. "How did a thief and a knight outsmart a dragon?"

"By luck." He shot. "And magic."

"Well." She clapped her hands together. "We know we have the one, so why do we not see if the other has decided to stick around with us?"

He looked at her as if she were crazy. "No." He said, but she crossed her arms and glared. "No, absolutely not. There is too much at risk for such a thing! No!"

"Too much to risk? Then just send me if you are so worried!"

"No! I will not risk it."

"What have we been doing, then! What have we been doing this whole time? We have already been risking everything since we started this, so why not send me? What has changed? Am I just some sort of weapon to you?"

"I am not going to talk about this right now! Keep looking for information, and we will come up with a plan then. Going into the castle will only end badly."

She let out an aggravated sigh, wanting to pull out her hair with irritation. "But Venic, I can go-."

He put up a hand to silence her. "No, and that is it. I will not risk it. I will not risk you, or any of us."

Then he was gone, storming off and leaving her feeling very baffled.

* * *

Valerlanta went back in to the inn only once between questioning, and when she did, she found Alstred covered in sweat. Only a single candle was lit in be room, but even in the dim lighting, she could see the beads of perspiration gathering on the man's brow.

Placing a hand on the brow of the man she once wanted dead, she found his skin hot under her touch. Traveling as hard as they had with a wound was not good for a man; it had no chance to heal, and it seemed to have become infected.

'Idiot.' She thought. *'Why didn't you tell us?'*

The thief did not have what she needed to treat fever here, and she could not risk leaving for the plants otherwise she might not be let back in the walls again; she had only one choice; Alstred needed a healer. Which also meant she needed to steal them some more coins.

With a sigh, she sat on the edge of a bed. Was this how adventures were supposed to go? If only she was stronger. If only-

Her eyes fell to her hand.

If only she could heal. If only she was stronger.

She thought of helping Venic with his fire, and her fingers curled in tightly. Why had the frost came? She knew she was thinking of fire, so why frost?

No, there was no way she would risk even trying to heal anyone, even if it was possible. If she did and the wrong magic came, she would only make it worse.

Valerlanta knew there were limits to what she could do. She knew she could work with water, ice and fire, but wind was uncontrollable, as far as she knew. It all, also, took a large amount of concentration to create, but that left no reason in her mind for why the wrong magic sometimes came.

What worried her more was when she called magic, but with nothing particular in mind, and the right thing came to save her. It was like the magic had a mind of its own, and when she was in danger, it would jump forth to protect its host...and yet at the same time, using it was what could kill her.

She just did not understand.

Slowly, she uncurled her fingers and called on magic. She directed the flow to her fingers, and instantly, her fingers lit up with flames like candles. Like with all fire, it needed oxygen to breath, but this flame did not need any wick or wood; because it was her energy levels which worked as fuel.

The small flames brought more light to the room, and as it forced back the shadows, Valerlanta saw a form standing there; the elf woman. She looked drained of all energy, and this time did not try to speak, she simply looked at Valerlanta with sharp desperation in her eyes.

Then the door to the room swung open, and when Valerlanta looked back to the corner, once again the woman was gone.

'I am going mad.' She thought. *'Every day, I am going a little madder.'*

Venic closed the door behind him as she brought her gaze back to her glowing fingers.

"What are you doing?" He asked in a whisper.

"I am trying to figure it out." She cut off the flow of magic, and the flames went out. Then, she directed the flow, and the flames came back, but this time she let it take more form, so her whole hand was covered in the flame. "I want to know why it is that sometimes the wrong thing comes."

The swordsman walked up and crouched in front of her, his eyes wide as he looked at the flame balancing there. "It is amazing, do you not think? What I would not give for just half of your power."

Wrinkling her nose, Valerlanta cut off the flow again, and the room went darker. "When I was younger, it was more of a curse. If I got too scared or angry, sometimes the magic would come on its own and I did not have the power to control it. This magic; it's the reason why my father will not let me join his guild. He thought not letting me in would also keep me from wanting to be around people. He will not say so, but he worries that I will lose control again like I did as a child, and the wrong people will see it happen. This magic; it has done very little to gain my favor."

Venic nodded thoughtfully, then got up to check on Alstred. It was then she noticed the bucket he had brought in. He wrong out a cloth in it, and placed the cloth across the older man's brow. Alstred did not even flinch. "You say, though, that you have more control now? How?"

"Well...when you move your arm, it is an act you do pretty much without thinking. You do not know why it lifts when you want it to, but it does. If I choose to, I can lift my arm part way and hold it there; restricting where it goes. Magic is the same, I can lift it when I want, and restrict its movements." She put her head in her hands. "That is a stupid explanation...."

"I understood it." Venic said smiling at her. "So using that same description, I suppose that sometimes you mean to lift a arm and your foot lifts instead?"

Valerlanta nodded.

"Well," he started unloading some food onto the table beside the bed. Apples, some sort of pies, and even some fish, all came out of his bag. "By that theory, you are a baby learning how to walk. It is a new movement to you, so you have to think hard on moving each foot. After time and practice, your feet will move with ease."

"You are saying that I have to try to walk to be able to run; that the more I use the magic, the easier it will become to use it." She said, and dread filled her, knowing she was right. Her father kept her from using magic in fear that she would lose control and someone would see, but that same reason was why she had no control.

"That is exactly what I am saying; though right now it is just a theory." He paused to look at her, his eyes scanning her face in the darkness. "I might just be guessing as to where these thoughts came from, but Alstred will be fine, Valerlanta. When he wakes, I will tell him that he needs to remain here and meet us in Alecaven when he is well, but I know it will not take long. He is a strong man."

"I am not worried; I just have things to do." She said, jumping up and walking for the door. "Why would I be worried about someone like him?"

And yet, when she left, she quickly put a pause to her questioning, and instead went to the richer side of the city to find some coin.

Immediately after, she gave the healer Runen the first of many customers she planned to send his way.

* * *

Her final questioning went fine.

It was a lady recommended by her last source, and the widowed wife of a castle guard. She was blind now, but did not seem to notice as she had pat the dirt off of the pants of one of her boys with swift efficiency. They were living with her husband's sister now, according to her, since her husband had passed and fever turned her blind.

Unlike the last people Valerlanta had asked, the woman seemed more suspicious of the motive behind the questions. Instead of just quietly answering then taking the money, Valerlanta felt the woman's unease in helping. After all, she had children to look after, but in the end she took the money like the others, and told Valerlanta the same thing she had heard countless times before.

The door, it was true. She knew it was.

Now she had only to convince Venic the same. Letting out a sigh as she walked, Valerlanta wondered about just how she could do that.

She was almost back, when she froze in her steps at the sound of a hollow wail coming from over the wall.

A horn.

Valerlanta felt all blood drain from her face and her heart skip a beat.

The gates were already closed since the sun was almost set, so they could not get in, could they?

As she worried, a group of guards went rushing past towards the gates; urgent expressions on their faces.

'Could that be...?-' Her thoughts trailed off, for she already knew the answer. The thief stared off at the gate as if it were the mouth of a monster about to swallow her whole.

He was already here.

Valerlanta shot a glance to the direction she knew the inn was in and hesitated. Turning back around, she hurried back towards the way she came; towards the castle.

People around her rushed about, everyone clearly already knowing the news of possible enemies at the gate, but even though she kept her head down, none of them were the knight she did not want to see.

He was not there, in the swarms of people. At least not yet.

Once out, the sun was down. She crouched in the shadows of a building, and looked up at the castle walls. She was at the very same spot she once visited before, where the water disapeared under the wall.

'I need to go now.' She told herself. *'While they are all distracted.'*

Finding a thick stick that she suspected was from an old broom, Valerlanta pulled out a long rope, and, after a long breath in, tied the two together.

It was now or never. She had no time to see if it would work.

Hurrying into the open, Valerlanta swung the rope in circles over her head. The circle got wider and wider, and then finally it slipped from her hand, and clattered against the stone above. Valerlanta flinched, expecting a large sound, but there was none with all the commotion and she pulled on the rope until it went tight.

The weather smoothed stone was slippery underfoot, but quickly she got her footing and started her climb.

Below, she did not hear anyone try to follow.

One hand in front of the other, she climbed her way, all the while willing with all her heart that by chance, none would notice a soul person climbing the wall on such a dark night.

Suddenly everything but her own breath and slamming heart became silent, as if the world had hushed to watch.

Finally the top was just ahead of her, and she reached out her hand.

Her fingers gripped the top. Pulling herself up with an outbreath of air, she was ready to climb up fully when she heard movement and instinctively dropped again.

A solider was approaching; she heard the clanking of his boots as he neared where she hung by only fingers.

'Do not notice the rope or fingers.' She urged him. *'Just walk by!'*

Already her fingers were trying to slide from the slippery rock. Her eyes glanced at the rope, but knew her anchor would surly clatter if she dared grab it.

Valerlanta held her breath.

The guard was right in front of her now. He paused; she could hear the heavy breathing of an older man.

Then he walked on, his steps disappearing down the wall.

Knowing she would not have much time, Valerlanta heaved herself back over the wall, and upon it. The thief cast the man's back a quick glance as he walked away, then she threw the rope back down from where she came.

She had no choice now.

On the wall, she was positioned carefully close to a tower. No fires were lit inside, but she figured they must all go to the same place.

Keeping low but swift as she could, Valerlanta went to the tower door. It was waiting for her open, but before she ducked in side, she quickly listened.

Hearing no approaching visitors, she jumped in.

Inside was black as any night she had ever been in. Instantly her heart hammered and her breathing quickened as she let her eye trail to the staircase. Light crept up the stone steps, lightening the heavy feel of the black around her.

She stepped towards it, and as she did, she heard a peculiar huffing sound. It was only seconds after that when something came at her.

Her body instinctively dove away, rolling across the round room and narrowly missing the bone crushing hit of whatever swiped at her.

Her back pressed against the cold stone wall, and her eyes strained to see her attacker.

Then, with large paws the size of her head stepping forward, a bear came within the light pouring from the open door. It's head was bobbing up and down, heavily breathing as it judged the threat of its intruder. Scars ruined it's fur, causing a splash of pity to drop in with her fear.

"Everything will be fine." She softly cooed at the much larger creature. Her feet slowly shuffled away, but not once did she dare turning her back to it; she knew much better than that.

The bear huffed, cheeks flaring, and large clawed paws stomping at the ground. It was blind in one eye, but Valerlanta knew she would still be little match for it.

She resisted the urge to look away, but still knew the stairs were close now. All she needed was to keep up her small steps against the wall. "I know, I know." She told it. "I disrupted your sleep, but fear not, I am on my way. I will not harm you, though I know your owner has, am I right? Poor thing. A creature like you deserves to be free to be wild, not hurt for the show of it." She broke her gaze to look at the stairs she was almost at. "Perhaps once I am done here I can-"

She was cut short as the bear charged. With a yelp, Valerlanta dove away and rolled down the stairs. Digging her feet and hands into the walls, she was able to stop her decline, but her head throbbed from the hard stone.

Above, she heard the heavy breathing and rattling chain of the bear that could not follow.

"Fine!" She hissed up the stairs. "Stupid giant gopher!"

Rising up, she patted down her clothes and gave an unsatisfied huff of her own, then started down the stairs the proper way; with her feet.

The steps spiraled down, almost in complete darkness except for the occasional light of a torch, creeping it's glow around the circling stone as it danced eerily.

Sucking in a breath, Valerlanta followed it.

The light led her down, then as soon as she reached it, another light awaited her further down, then another.

Down and down it went, and she went as fast as she dared in risk of getting dizzy. On this narrow of a staircase she would have nowhere to hide.

She passed one doorway, flinching as it came near, but it was not the one she wanted, so continued down without seeing everyone. It seems all were either in bed, or wishing to see the current excitement at the gate.

When the next doorway came into view, Valerlanta pressed her back against the cold stone and slowly glanced around the doorframe. No one.

Before her stood a large field with the royal gardens in the center. On the air, she smelt horse stables that must be near, as smoke.

Keeping low, Valerlanta darted to the cover of a wagon.

Now she could see a guard in the distance, probably guarding the gate, as well as many on the walls above. They would be patrolling everywhere...everywhere, that is, except perhaps the royal garden.

Which was across an open area from her...

She could not wait; there was no time for that.

Getting on her belly, she crawled slow and stopped often, trying to keep her overall movement to a minimum.

Then, when the bushes came up around her, she rose up to a crouch and hurried through, being careful to keep her head down.

Ahead was the main doors, but she did not head for those, instead she headed off to the left, to a much smaller door hidden by careful stonework.

This time, she saw no one, so darted across as quick as her legs would carry her.

Inside was still warm with the smell of fresh meals on the air, but there was no one around. The cooking fire was down the embers, and the plates were carefully stacked into corners.

For a brief moment, her heart skipped a beat, thinking that by some chance this could be a trap like Venic suspected, but then she shook the idea away. Not even she knew she was coming at this moment, so how could they.

With that thought she slipped into the doorway, and out of the kitchen, and nothing happened.

She did, however, hear an awful amount of giggling coming from a doorway on her side, and saw a broom leaning against the door in waiting.

An amused smirk came to the lips of Valerlanta as she continued.

At the end of the hall, she found a small servants staircase, just as was described to her.

It was good that she made it this far, but if her source was right, then she had a bit longer of a walk.

Down the stair case, past the columns where the whisper of ghosts frightened lone men to death, to the door...and that was where her hints ended. All the they knew about the door in the castles underground was its elvish writings, the rest was a mystery.

Valerlanta found herself smiling despite all her worry.

The next staircase was even more narrow then the last, leaving no room for more than a person, and was completely dark in some points, leaving Valerlanta to tentatively feel her way down.

Exit found, Valerlanta peeked inside just as before.

The view made her eyes widen.

There were dozens of columns, many more, all carved with a talent she had never seen. Each stonework was different; but each told a tale. The one closest to her showed a commoner bravely taking up a fallen knights sword and battling a fierce dragon. The story spun all the way around the column, until the end on the opposite side.

'This was not just any hall,' she silently realized with a caught breath. *'This is their recordings of their past, carved in stone to last the centuries.'*

Valerlanta had never cared about castles and those who lived there before, but suddenly she felt an urge to circle, every pillar; as if each one was a puzzle waiting to be solved.

However, this was something she would have to come back to do, and not just because of her pressed time.

There were soldiers here. Just as expected.

She could see at least three wandering ahead, passing between the columns as casually as if on a stroll. They had grown calm in their safety down below here, but that was a double edged sword. They would not be expecting her, but they would be eager for the chance of some excitement.

Instantly Valerlanta sunk to a lower height to rid of her obviously noticeable human outline, and peeked in. After waiting until all three were either out of sight or looking away, she crept forward from pillar to pillar any time she had the chance.

While one bent down to pick up his water, another turned his back only just and closed his eyes with a yawn.

With only seconds to lose, the thief shot behind the yawning man before either could look back.

The door. If you could call it that.

It actually had long lost the actual doors of it, and was now just a frame with a silvery shine.

Valerlanta had no time to admire the writing across the thick wooden surface as she ducked inside, and almost ran right into a thin cord in her haste. At the last moment she was able to bounce over it, narrowly escaping setting off the bells it would have rattled at her touch.

Letting out a breath, she continued on inside.

Before long she came to a small set of stairs, then beyond that, a large opening. Inside was more tables of things than she was ever expecting.

Upon the wooden surfaces, there were golden cups, weapons, baskets, books, and other treasures.

'A clever trick.' Valerlanta realized. *'If you hide one item of value with hundreds of others, only a person knowing what they were looking for could find the right one.'*

She felt pressure of time running out clench at her chest, but she forced her pace to slow as she walked up the first table.

There were a few elf scripted objects here, but somehow they felt off. It was just too easy.

And she had few doubts that if she grabbed the wrong object, something terrible could happen.

'A room full of goods, only one item matters.' Valerlanta thought to herself as she tried her best to soak them all in. *'Most would reach for the most expensive item, other thinking smart would reach for the least. Neither of those would be it.'*

A broom? Of course not.

A jewelled dagger? Too obvious!

Suddenly she stopped and went to reach out, but stopped her hand mid-way, and let it hover over a specific object.

'Neither expensive, nor the other, nor useful, nor useless.' She swallowed hard and touched the box.

Then, with one final intake of breath, she pulled.

The item came free.

Her whole body tensed, waiting.

Nothing happened.

Hesitantly she again looked at the item in her hands.

It was a small wooden box with a horse carved on the top. Items rattled inside, but a small lock kept it closed.

A lock for a toy box.

Curiosity ate at her, but she instead slipped it away into her bag and took one last look over the other items.

She only had one chance at this.

The thief hesitated only for a few counts longer, then raised her shoulders confidently then left.

After she was only just about to exit, a commotion came from the stair case. All the guards in the room immediately straightened and edged towards the door.

Scrambling out, Valerlanta only just made it behind a pillar as a series of soldiers marched in.

They were the king's men, one glance at their uniforms was enough to tell that, but the person with them was enough to make her heart skip a beat.

Askyel Lochsell.

The black market leader lead the group of men down the columns as if in charge. No, he really was in charge.

He sent three men into the room, and Valerlanta pressed her back against the cold stone.

Her hand brushed her dagger longingly, but she bit back her ache for revenge. Not now. Not when he is protected by so many.

"It is gone!" One of the guards said as he returned. "We could not find it in there! Someone has taken it!"

Her heart slammed with excitement. 'I have the right item.'

"We should lock down the city." The raspy voice of a younger man barked. If she had to guess, she would say that the voice belonged to the young nobleman who was now in charge of the city. "We will search every home, and burn down those who do not comply!"

'What a lovely boy.' She thought to herself sarcastically.

"No." Askyel soothed, with obvious amusement playing lightly on his voice. "There is no need for that."

"Why not?" The boy screeched in protest. "You said so yourself it is important. If a commoner has it, we must get it quickly before their filth stains it!"

Askyel laughed, and she heard him pacing, as if looking around at the designs on the columns. "There is no need for that, because if it were me, I would have used the distraction of the kings army in order to get in to the castle."

Valerlanta tensed.

"Why does that matter?" The brat asked in clear annoyance.

"It matters because,-" he snickered. "I have little doubt she is still in this very castle."

The boy gasped, but before the guards could have any time to comprehend what he was saying, Valerlanta shot from her hiding spot and into the open.

"Hey!" A voice shouting in warning.

The two guards at the stairs made a grab for her, but Valerlanta ducked under their arms and sped past.

"After her!" She heard the boy squeak.

She took the stairs two at a time, pushing as fast as she could possibly climb.

Suddenly something grabbed her ankle and she slammed against the hard stone steps.

The hand started pulling her back, down towards where the men were waiting. Valerlanta scrambled her hands to find anything to hold onto, and kicked with her free leg.

The man grunted in pain and annoyance, but kept pulling.

Then finally a kick landed square on his face and knocked him off balance. He let go and fell backwards, and took the man behind him with him.

Before any had a chance to recover on the narrow staircase, Valerlanta continued her climb.

Up, up, up she went. The constant circles making her head spin.

She came to the floor, but this time did not wait to see if anyone was there. She simply shot through with a speed she hoped would take anyone waiting by surprise.

When no one grabbed her she quickly ascended the next rounding staircase. This time however the spiraling mass was full of sounds of movement, but she had no time to think.

By some manner of luck, she did not meet anyone as she span up. He could hear people both above and below at going up through the staircase but ran into non-directly.

She shot out onto the same wall where she came up from but had no way of returning to the street.

Panicked, she rushed along the wall looking for a new down but instead came to a dead-end in the means of men armed with arrows.

She spun back the way she came, only to find the doorway was blocked.

She was trapped.

She spun looking for any possible way, but saw none.

Down below the wall, for no more than a second she thought she saw movement, but when she looked closer, she saw nothing.

No one could save her. Not from this.

"Give up." A familiar voice ordered, and the thief did not have to turn around to know Jerstain Elfailden was on the wall with her. "There is nowhere for you to run."

She had only seconds to react. Before she knew it the guards would be right on her, so she had to think of something fast.

With a sly smile she removed her pack and turned to face her enemy.

"Aww, do I have what you want?" She taunted, swinging the bag in her hand.

The man grinned wickedly. "My dear, you are in no position to compromise. You are surrounded. You have nowhere to go."

Valerlanta raised a brow, stopped swinging, and let the pack slide from her hand. It flew over the edge, and down below the wall into the darkness. "Oops." She smirked, then they were upon her.

Valerlanta managed to get her knives out, one in either hand, but there was simply too many of them. She slashed, stabbed, and even dropped a few men, but it was not enough.

A hard blow hit her on the back of the head, tumbling her over, and jumbling her thoughts.

She tried to get back up but the world whirled and she stumbled again.

Hands twisted her arms behind her back and kicked out her knees so she knelt at her enemy. She thrashed in their hold, but they held her strong.

"I caught you this time." He sang, laughing as she struggled to get free.

Any thoughts she had of finding the time to concentrate enough to use magic ended as the leaders boot started slamming into her.

« Chapter 10 »

Nothing was as crisp and clear as it should be as if she had stepped into a foggy dream. Although she was awake, certain moments were simply skipped over...or perhaps she had forgotten about them only right after they happened. The thief had no idea what was real anymore.

Everything hurt. Even a light in her eyes or twitch of a limb was enough to cause her to pause her breath in shock of the pain.

Valerlanta was in trouble, and she knew it just as well as anyone who saw her, but she was too drunk on pain to even think about doing anything about it.

She was brought to a cell what seemed like seconds ago...though was more likely hours. Her nose told her it smelt like urine and blood, but her body told her she did not have the strength to move away from it. Although she did not want to think what she might be laying on, the cold stone was a relief against her sore skin.

Moving seemed impossible.

As a key rattled into a lock and the door creaked open Valerlanta went to sit up, but her hands were tied tightly behind her, and the whole world painfully swayed as she tried. Her body gave up, and she found herself against the cold stone once more.

"Oh no, do not get up for me, my dear. I will not be here long." Elfailden said, kneeling beside her and looking down at her as if she were a mere bug he had successfully squashed. She attempted to keep track of him, but his movements seemed choppy, as if he were moving too fast for her eyes to see.

"After how many times I have nearly caught you only for you to wriggle away the rat you are, this is more than you deserve." He smiled. "You should be thanking me, really. It was because I made you such a..." he pinched up some strands of bloody hair, then dropped them again as if touching something filthy, "...sticky mess that the men did not want to touch you. Maybe that will change, though. You will have plenty of time to get cleaned up between here and Alecaven."

She stifled a gasp, but he noticed her cringe.

"That is just precious! Did you think I would let you heal up here? My dear girl, my blind uncle could break out of this miserable excuse for a dungeon in little under a day! No..." He leaned in so that she could smell the stench of garlic on his breath, and see the full extent of hate burning in his eye. "No, you are not staying here, in fact, I am not even going to have you killed. Is that not so very nice of me? Instead, you have a nice dark hole waiting for you to rot in."

And that was the moment Valerlanta felt true terror come over her like a cold blanket. It both choked the breath out of her in shallow gasps, and sent her heart slamming in her chest.

Her nightmare of her childhood was escaping into the real world again.

"I will see you dead!" She rasped, but Jerstain Elfailden ignored her words.

"Do not lose hope, though." He continued as if she had said nothing at all. "Somehow, the hole cuts lives shorter than they should. Perhaps because of the complete darkness...maybe humans need sun as much as grass does. Do you know you cannot even see your hand in front of your very face? And some are so narrow of a circle that it forces you to always stand?" He talked eagerly, and her stomach clenched more with every word.

It was too much; every word of it made her heart slam to the point she thought it would surly escape from her chest.

He edged in closer. "Do you wish to know the best part, though? The very best part is that the only way out is if someone lower a rope to get you! All around you is solid rock. No digging, no climbing, no escape. Just darkness."

But she already knew that, and that knowledge was eating away at all the courage she had carefully built up over the years. It was as if her walls of protection were suddenly hit by a fierce wave, and now only pebbles remained; useless pebbles being swept along with the current of terror.

Her whole body trembled.

Jerstain Elfailden laughed darkly, and in a last desperate moment of fire, Valerlanta curled her foot up, and kicked at him as hard as he could. With fast hands, he caught her attack easily and pushed her foot away.

His expression was blanketed with rage, and in a blur, the man was back on his feet, punishing her with painful kicks again. She tried to make herself into a ball, curling away as far as possible, but it did little to help. Each hit was felt right through her body, but she whenever their eyes met, she forced herself to glare; to poor out every feeling of hatred she had in the force of the only defence she had left; her stare.

Then he was gone again, slamming the door behind him and leaving to catch her raspy breath in the lonely cell. The darkness of the corners seemed to creep in upon her, grabbing hold with a cold grasp and squeezing out what little hope she had.

* * *

After some time, Valerlanta was collected from her cell by two men.

The whole way, they tightly gripped her arms which remained tied back, even though everyone knew she had little chance of escaping. She could not even walk right, so the men half dragged her along with them.

She went willingly, vaguely thinking she should try to think of getting away, but her mind refused to venture any farther then that so the thought simply repeated again and again in her head.

Reaching outside, the light was piercingly bright. Wincing, Valerlanta tried to look away to shield her eyes, but the light was a sharp knife into her temples that made her head spin. Her feet stumbled out from under her, but the two men held her as she gagged.

"Do not dare get sick on me!" The man on her right shouted in a panic into her ear. "If you do, I swear I will cut your stomach right out of you!"

She could not even find the energy to reply, but she had gotten control of her stomach again, so they dragged her forward.

"He almost killed this one." The other said with a tone of annoyance. "Why not get it over with? She is too much of a bother now."

"It is not our position to ask." The right one replied. "But I think he wants her alive to win over the kings favour. Why else would he keep the mask on?"

Mask? So she did still have that on then. It was a relief to know. but she had not even thought about it before now, which was a strange thing considering it was something she never stopped worrying over on a normal day.

Something was very wrong with her.

Once out, she was brought to where the men waited and her hands were retied in front of her and a leading one was attached to a saddle. Her two guards were gone, leaving her to stand swaying back and forth.

She could see now that it was just after sunrise, so there were few people around apart from those soldiers readying to leave. There were still some, however, who lingered close, looking on at her with interest, pity, or disgust.

Unable to look any more, she lowered her eyes to her feet.

'Away.' Her mind told her. *'I need to get away.'*

Instead, Valerlanta fell to her knees and nearly whimpered while holding her own head as if to squeeze out her confusion.

What was she going to do?

At that time, Jerstain Elfailden had arrived. He came up shouting directions, then stopped as his boots appeared in front of her. She did not have to look up to know he was watching her with a warped sense of glee. She could feel her eyes hot upon her.

Despite how it hurt, she glared up at him through squinting eyes, and he looked down with matched amusement.

With a snort, he turned and climbed up on his horse. He shouted a few more commands before they started out, she was pulled along with them like a pack horse.

The pace was slow and relaxed only just enough to let Valerlanta hear the laughs and rude remarks of the people they passed.

Only once she glanced up to see, and that glance was all she needed. A man from her fathers guild was there, shaking his head and looking at her with an intense pity as if she were already dead.

No one would try to save her.

Then the castle gate came, then the farms, then the forest. Never before has the leaves appeared so bitterly painful to her; as if she were in a cage surrounded by freedom strong enough that she could smell, feel, and see the magnificence of it, but she was still trapped from it.

At some points, her body would simply give out from under her, leaving her to be dragged along by her arms. No one stopped for her, no one tried to get her up, but in some strange way she was glad. She was so tired.

She would fade in and out of sleep, or perhaps it was something else, and very slowly, like the creeping of a spider, with it came nightmares.

Suddenly she did not know if she was standing or being dragged, because the world was flashing between. One moment she was there behind the wagon, the next in terrifying darkness. Best she tried to fight it, a sort of comforting warmth came over her eyes, and she fell into it willingly.

Everything was dark. It closed in around her making it hard to breathe; suffocating her. Sometimes she confronted her fear and felt her way around the round cell, but other times she could not help but wonder what lay in the shadows around her.

A monster?

A ghost?

Then the blinding light came from above, and like always it seemed so beautiful she wanted to cry. However, after the food and water was dropped in, it closed up and whatever feeling of hope she had went with it.

The light would fade, and then it was gone.

They said this was charity; that she should be thankful her father let her live, but she could not feel the same.

After her nanny had died in the hole, she had no one to care for her.

The dark became thicker, and the walls crept in closer.

She was in the mouth of a terrible monster, and best she tried to scream for attention, her calls only blended with those being slowly killed above.

Then the world faded again, and she was back with a gasp.

Unfortunately, she was heading to the same doom; the very reason why she could not bear to even sleep indoors. Her greatest nightmare.

The ground scrapped against her skin painfully, but even that was better than trying to face her current situation.

When they stopped, someone tried to tried to give her water, but it was kicked out of her hands by another, much to the amusement of those watching. Many chuckled around her.

"What are you doing?" Someone snarled. "We have orders to keep her alive.

"Well." The man who kicked her water smiled at her in a way that sent a chill up her spine. "Do not worry your head, boys. I just want a little kiss before the boss gets back from doing his business."

And with that, he edged closer, and she glared back but did not shuffle away.

He came closer until she felt his breath, and she let him.

At the last moment she punched him hard as she could in the ear, then with a burst of speed, wrapped her ropes around his neck and held from behind.

He tried to pull up and away from her, but it only tightened the rope against his airway. Men came and tried to pull them apart, but she held tight with a sort of savage anger she did not know she had left.

When they finally were able to pry her lose, the man was unconscious or dead, and Jerstain Elfailden was back watching her with crossed arms.

He raised a brow, and she smiled sweetly.

"My hands slipped." She mused.

He ignored her, and knelt before her, with his sword spinning in his hands. "Since you seem a little more...alive, I suppose now is as good of a time as any to begin."

Begin what?

He leaned forward, tilting his sword so that she could see her foggy imaged in its shiny surface. Was that really her? She looked like a monster. "Where are they hiding?"

Her lips pulled into a smile, though the tug hurt with dried cuts she did not even know she had. "They?"

The disgust in his eyes was so strong, one would assume he was looking on at a pile of maggots. It was enough to even make her tired heart slam in anger.

"You know bloody well who I speak of." He hissed. "Those two, the runaway knights, where are they? Where did they take it?"

So they did not get the bag she threw over the wall.

"I am not certain I know who you mean, commander."

No, she would not tell him that, if those boys were smart, they would be escaping further north where no one would find them. Valerlanta could see the commander nearing his breaking point, and by the sounds of shifting my way around her, she guessed the loyal soldiers were not enjoying her either.

"Quit playing around or I will remove your lips with my knife if that is what it takes to get the information I need!" He said in a snake hiss warning.

Her smile grew larger and more mischievous as she gave a confused shrug. "Oh commander, I am not sure my lips will do much talking removed from my face, commander."

Oh how she loved seeing his fists clench. The sword came uncomfortably close and nicked at the edges of her mask. There was a sort of dark urge there, she could see his desire to cut if off of her face visibly in his eyes, but without the mask, she was just a girl, and no one would believe who she was.

"Last chance." He whispered.

She looked deep into his eyes and kept her sly grin. "There is no one else."

Then came more pain.

* * *

It hurt to move even her fingers; she figured even they were broken. Her ribs too, she knew they were broken from every breath she took. Every other part of her, she had no energy to move to test the extent of her injuries.

Days ago, she was a free spirit on the path for treasure, and now she was a prisoner lying bruised and battered in the dirt.

Her eyes looked on longingly at the forest she could not reach, and her ears listened carefully to birds she could not see.

The morning sun was competing with the coming of dark clouds, but it was strong enough only just enough to cast golden rays through green leaves. Beams danced with the swaying of the wind, and somehow, she felt as if she were falling into that light.

The sun itself seemed to grow brighter, and slowly, with every blink, the forest was swallowed up into the bright rays.

'No.' Valerlanta thought in a panic as the light consumed her too. *'I am not ready! I do not want to die like this!'*

White took over her world, and took her with it.

The light did not fade, it was everywhere around her, and suddenly she was standing within it. The thief turned around, looking this way and that, trying to find her way back, but no matter where she went there was just white. Nothing but white.

"No!" She screamed into the fog. "No! Not yet! I am not ready!"

The thief thrashed against the white, trusting that soon, just beyond it, she would feel an exit.

"I do not want this! I do not want this end!" Her voice became choked with tears, and then all at once she stilled, with her whole body tensing.

Someone was there, right in front of her and looking on with thin brows tensed with a sad expression.

"You are not dead, not yet." The voice said; her voice as gentle as a song birds call. Perfect lips pressed in a thin line as she looked her over, than relaxed again. "You have gone through so much because of him."

The thief looked down at herself, and saw what the woman saw; bruises splotched over any skin not covered, and blood stained any skin that was.

"I am not done fighting." Valerlanta urged. "Once I get free, Jerstain Elfaiden will not stop me. I will put everything I have into fighting him."

"It is not him I am speaking of." The woman said with a small, sad, smile. She pushed some silky black strands of hair behind a pointed ear, and let the hand fall along with the length of it, then stilled, right below the shoulder; as if she were trying to gather strength from within the thin hairs. "The man you must face calls himself a king."

"Khon." Valerlanta said confidently.

"Yes." She confirmed. "The man who has fought his way with blood since he was young, and, if he has his way, will turn rivers red as he takes down those who face him."

"What? What are you talking about?" Valerlanta asked, then it hit her. "The treasure we are searching for..."

"It pure, gathered, magic." The woman confirmed looking into the distance as if seeing her past there. "It was my mistake. My husband wished for a land without magic, but it could not be taken away, not fully, so instead it was gathered into one place, and that which could not be put there was sent into the blood of a royal family. I am sorry, child, you are of my blood, though distantly so, and yet it is my cause which may bring your destruction."

Valerlanta looked at her feet and fought to breath. "So why are you here, then? Why have you been trying to connect to me?"

"Even without the key, the king will find a way down into the chamber." She explained. "He has to be stopped before then. My husband had the puzzles created in case anyone in his line ever sought to bring magic back to the world, but not like this. He would not have wanted this!" She took in a sharp breath and paused, as if she were fighting away tears. "You are of my bloodline, and so you are the only one I can help guide to the truth. You are the only one I can guide to stop him. You may die during it, but you still must try!"

"Why?" Valerlanta took a hesitant step away, and glared on at her ancestor. "Why do I have to do anything? The fake-king may be cruel, and his past and plot may be those of evil, but he has not been so greedy to cause his people to hate him. Past kings have taxed the poor more and done worse too, so why should I care what he does? It will not affect me! His boarders may grow and kingdoms may fall, but as I hide in the forest, life will just go on for me!"

The thief expected anger, but what she did not expect was the look of pity which washed over the elves face. "You cannot always run from your fears, someday, they will be faster than you are."

"I am not running! I am surviving! There is a difference."

"So, your goal, is to let yourself survive and hide away while kingdoms are brought down? You are so sure you will not lose sleep over the children killed for you choice?"

"It is not my choice!" Valerlanta swept a hand, as if drawing an invisible barrier between them. "I am one person; defeating the king was never a choice to begin with. It is a suicide, and only that! Now let me go!"

"Sweet child, you do not know what such a great power will-"

"I do not, and I no longer care to know! Now let me go!" Nothing happened, and the elf opened her mouth to say more, but the thief spoke first. "No! No more words! No more visits! I just want back to what is real! If you want to keep your husband's ideals alive, then do it yourself, because I will have no part of it! I am a thief, just that; a thief! I am not a warrior, not your hero, I am just a thief! Now leave me alone, and never come back."

The woman clearly hesitated, but no longer argued. Now tears visibly clouded her bright eyes as she looked on at Valerlanta; possibly hoping to see another way of convincing her within the injured girls green eyes.

"Let me go." Valerlanta hissed again. "We are done here; there is nothing more you can say."

Eyes locked onto each other, a tear slipped down the perfect cheek of the elf woman. Then, her arms wrapped around herself, hugging her own small form, and she walking backwards, fading into the white with each stepped. She stepped slow, as if in each step she had the hope that the thief would change her mind, but that never happened.

The elf faded away completely, and as she did, Valerlanta fell to the ground and cried out as her skin once again throbbed.

The pain was coming back, and the white was once more being splotched with green leaves.

Soon, the white was gone completely, and she realized she was back to where she lay; her face in the dirt on the road which lead to her greatest of all nightmares.

The light of the morning sun was gone; hiding behind clouds and setting the forest in darkness.

'Not yet.' She reminded herself. *'You cannot give up yet; not when there is still one last hope.'*

Her mind was still a fog, but she figured she had only just enough clarity to call on one small thing. Anything too strong and the men would see and cut her down, so instead the thief asked for a type of magic she had never successfully used before.

She directed it into her fingers, and waited, her body curling her body into a ball as she hid her fingers best she could as they started glowing a faint white.

Within the glow, within the magic, without warning her bones were forcibly snapped back together. Valerlanta pressed her knees closer to her chest and a hiss came out of her clenched teeth in replacement for the scream her body so badly wanted.

The pain of having bone forcibly mended back together was horrible, but not near as horrible as the thought of staying laying there.

She pushed more magic into it and all breath was swept from her lungs. Her hiss became a soundless scream.

Then it was over. The white faded to nothing, and she flexed her fingers. They bent willingly, with little to no pain. What was once broken now felt only like a bruise.

She did it; for the first time ever she had healed herself.

Hope filled her to the brim. Perhaps, if she were careful enough, she could keep healing what lay hidden under the skin, while keeping the bruises above intact. The thief could keep up the act of being near death, and maybe, if she was careful, if she was lucky, it could lead to her escape right before they reached the castle. This magic took a lot of energy and gave more pain than the injury it was healing, but Valerlanta had little doubt that if cutting off an arm would be what it took to get away, she would do it willingly.

All she wanted was to escape into those leaves that was oh so close, but for now, though, all she could do was barely keep her eyes open as half her face lay in the dirt.

Rain started to fall. Droplets splashed against her sore skin. Half aware, she asked for more, and the rain complied; pouring down upon her and the waking men.

The water soaked her through and brought mud into the forest floor, but all she could think about was how nice it the cold felt upon her sore skin.

"Commander! Commander! Kynbin has been murdered!" Someone called, and Valerlanta found the strength to lift her head to look over her shoulder. A man was running to the commander, and was babbling about how his throat had been cut. "It must have happened in the night, but no one saw who it was!"

Valerlanta forced herself to sit up, though she swayed back and forth.

Indeed not too far away was a person who had not yet got up for the morning, though it was already almost time to leave.

Her heart leapt.

He was here.

« Chapter 11 »

The first solider died without so much of a whimper; leaving the others only to find out he was cut open when they went to wake him up.

He was murdered, that much was certain, but by who?

Immediately they were put on edge, and almost just as quickly, gazes started shifting to the tied-up thief. Even with the rope still tight on her wrists, suspicion poisoned their common sense.

Even the commander was doubtful. Valerlanta would feel his gaze upon her sharp like daggers as he sat afar, watching her intently. He did not want to lose his catch, so his insanity was slowly causing an invisible net to tighten around her. She could not even flinch without him noticing and coming over to pry open her hands and mouth to make sure she did not have anything.

Quickly after the murder, he ordered a larger night shift and forced the men to sleep in torchlight, however, despite all their efforts, another one did not wake by next light, and with yet another death, their worry grew.

She supposed to some extent she should be happy for that, as their fear was giving her time to heal...but at the same time she worried. Although she tried not to notice, she could see the hate growing in the depth of their eyes with their fear. If this kept up, they were going to kill her.

And yet she had to wait.

'Just a little more time.' She told herself. *'Just a little more.'*

She still played along as the weak defenseless woman who stumbled and passed out in pain, and although it still mostly true, she did add to it more than needed. She pretended to pass out multiple times a day, and it worked.

'I will not go back.' She told herself again and again to keep anger in the place of despair. *'I will escape. I will not go back...-'*

Night after night, one more solider would die, but it was the days that were causing her heart to pound, for that was when they drew closer to her greatest fear.

"You see?" Jerstian said one afternoon as he grabbed her by the chin and forced her to look at the thinning trees that would soon become plains of grass.

"Soon your witchcraft will do you no good. You do not have time anymore. Within a few days, you will be starting to rot! Always clinging to the hope you will get out, always eating what food is tossed your way, but rotting away in the dark without you even knowing about it. Does it scare you, my dear? Well?"

She did not say anything, but instead pulled her jaw away from his hand and glared.

He laughed, kicking her back into the dirt. "So pitiful! Like a caged rabbit about to be slaughtered!" Still laughing to himself, he walked away, and as soon as his back turned, Valerlanta felt the heavy glances of the men around her.

She could not help but notice how separated they all sat from each other now, as if little groups were safer. Although fear was driving them apart, it was also drawing more and more eyes to her.

'Just wait.' She told them in her mind. *'It will happen soon.'*

Later that night, it seemed like enough was enough, and their brave commander rolled over a stump of a log, and sat across from her and simply watched. Like cat ready to pounce, his entire body was tensed up while watching his prey.

Valerlanta could not help but shift uncomfortably under his gaze, but also noticed the hopeful glances of the men around him.

'Smart.' She realized. *'You are going to sit there to prove to your men who it was causing the murders.'*

Rolling her eyes dramatically, the thief simply curled up on the dirt with a large yawn and closed her eyes. Her brave watchmen snorted with disapproval, but this time seemed determined not to let her win by invoking his anger.

Neither of them slept, and although she did her best to pretend at moments, eventually her eyes would flutter open and lock gazes with her enemy.

Even as the moon reached the highest point in the sky, their silent war went on.

When eyelids started to droop and heads nod, the other would shift and even just the slightest amount of sound was enough to startle the other back into awareness. Neither would let the other relax, not that night.

As boredom struck, Valerlanta grabbed a sharp stone nearby, but did not try to cut her ropes, but instead smiled sweetly as if to tempt him near. He reacted as expected, by stomping over, ripping it from her hand, and throwing it far into the darkness.

She kept this up until he growled in anger and jumped over and started sweeping or plucking anything sharp out of reach. It was when he crawled about that she carefully slid a sharp rock high up her pant leg to hide behind her knee. After, he checked her hands, and did find one last rock, which he also threw away and huffed in accomplishment.

She almost giggled, making her realize she was more tired than she thought.

The sun started to peek as light streaks across the sky, then that became swirls of pinks and oranges causing the sleeping men began to shuffle.

Before long, they were all awake, more or less, and the first meal of the day was being prepared. At that time, when the tantalizing smell of whatever it was they were cooking came wafting over, that the commander smiled victoriously and rose from his stool.

As Jerstian got up and left to go and approach his men, Valerlanta grabbed the sharp rock from her pant leg that she had hidden when he was busy removing the those from her hands.

She started to saw at the fibres.

"You see?" He told his men enthusiastically. "I sat up with the witch the whole night, watching her every move. Not once did she so much as lift a finger to try for a spell under my careful eye! It would have been more than impossible for her to sneak out of her bounds, since I slept not even a blink of a moment."

His men cheered, though she did not quite understand why. Did they think they broke some sort of curse upon them?

"Now," he clapped his hands together, as if to close away the past where it belongs. "Since you are all awake and well, let us eat and drink! Morning it might be, but I feel we deserve a celebration! Our travel home will be a light one, as we will have much less drink to carry."

Now the men roared, but she tried to ignore it and instead concentrated on pulling the stone across the rope again and again. It was starting to fray, but she was not even part way through.

'Hurry.' She told herself, though the back of her mind told her she could not be that obvious.

Ale was brought out, and the last of the sleeping men were being shaken awake to join the festivities. At the same time, food was passed out and enjoyed, and some fearless enough from the events of last night even threw some her way. It splattered on her clothes and face, and although they laughed, she held her head high.

'Keep sawing.' She told herself. *'Just keep sawing.'*

The men were getting plenty drunk as intended, but then a shout came out over the air that sent everyone still.

"He is dead! Falan is dead!" The terrified voice screamed. "He is dead! Dead! His throat was slashed! He is dead!"

Presumably the caller was one of those waking the sleeping men, causing a stunned silence over everyone.

Even the steady hands of Valerlanta stilled for a moment and she swallowed hard.

"S-She did it!" Someone squeaked. "It must have been her!"

That shocked the men back into reality. Some grabbed weapons out, others backed away. Valerlanta continued sawing.

"No!" Screamed another. "It cannot have been! She was watched the whole night!"

"It had to have been one of us!"

"No it was her!" A man with thick brows came towards her, pointing accusingly. "Kill the witch!

"There was guards stationed around us! It was someone from the inside!"

"Ulaquin got up in the night!"

"No, Yalenden was arguing with Falen last night! I saw."

A single push became many, and a shout became a roar from the many men as they started to turn on each other. Jerstian and his others in command tried to break it up, but it was to no avail. Liquor, fear, and lack of sleep was proving to be the most of deadly poisons.

And of course, madness was infectious, and their leader had long since strayed into the deep end of that.

Desperation threatened to close her throat, and suddenly she gave up caring about being discrete. Hurry. She had to hurry!

The frays of fibre were starting to build up.

Someone screamed in pain, and the thief looked up just in time to see a man fall with blood at his chest. The attacker roared, brandishing his bloody weapon.

'No!' Valerlanta swallowed hard. *'Not yet, please not yet.'*

But it was too late, and the sight of blood sent all the men crazed. Suddenly fists were flying, weapons were striking allies dead, and she was not yet through the rope.

Out of the corner of her eye she saw movement approaching, it was almost upon her as she bent over her work protectively. Then a man fell dead beside her, and her rescuer was the leader of the men responsible for her capture.

He cut the lead from where it was tied high in the tree, wrapped it around his arm, and roughly pulled her up with him.

"I will not let you escape." He hissed, his eyes wide and angry. "You will get where you belong, even if it is just me who gets you there."

However, her makeshift knife cut through and she glared defiantly. "No."

Bringing the rock up, she sliced it across his face. As he pulled back, she hurried in a running stumble before she could see if it did any real damage.

She was in tremendous pain, but she was not sure she had ever ran so hard. Warriors killing other warriors blurred by. In the chaos, some tried to dive for her, but she somehow managed to jump out of the way and continue.

Her chest burned like fire. Her bruised limbs made her want to cry out in pain. Her heart leapt as her feet left the road and touched the forest floor.

Leaves hit her face, filling her with immeasurable joy.

But it was at that time her unsteady footing caused her to stumble on a root and land hard on her back.

The air was pushed out of her, and tears brimmed her eyes from the pain of her surly broken ribs. By determination alone, she rolled over on to her stomach to rise up, but Jerstain was on her before she had a chance.

Snarling like a wolf, he tried to pull her arms behind her back and force her flat against the forest floor, but she managed to wiggle one hand out of his grip and punched at his only good eye.

He recoiled and she crawled away, but her foot was grabbed, pulling her back.

Flipping around, she kicked at him hard and managed to get away once more, only to feel his crushing grip pulling her back again.

"You will not escape!" He screamed. "You are mine!"

He was trying to pull her back under his weight again, but she was fighting like a cornered wildcat and kept managing to wiggle away. He managed to twist her hand up underneath her and she shouted in pain and reached out for something, anything.

Her fingers searched the forest floor desperately.

His elbow smashed her in the head, trying to stop her struggle.

Her fingertips brushed something, and without time to think, she brought it up at her attacker. Though it broke in her hand, the branch sunk deep and the commander screamed in pain.

Using the only advantage she had, Valerlanta took his own blade from his belt and sprang upon him. Letting out everything, she stabbed and stabbed.

At first he struggled, at first he screamed, but then he stopped. She kept going.

Then, as unwilling tears streamed down her face and mixed along with the blood, she rose up and kicked him as hard as she could before turning to escape.

Unfortunately, she was not alone.

The man, the one from before who accused her of being a witch, was blocking her path. She knew by his expression that he had seen what she had done to his leader.

His lip curled up at her. A wound was darkening his right shoulder, but he did not seem to notice. He strode forward, and Valerlanta grabbed the commander's sword and awkwardly brandished it between the two. It was then the man smiled, and raised his own sword tauntingly.

Valerlanta swallowed hard, her hands positioning then re-positioning on the sword to try and guess the right way.

He swiped her hard from the side, and she brought up the sword to block it. Her opponent's blade bounce off the blade, but the sword almost fell from her hands.

She barely had time to lift it again when the other sword came down again, then again.

Her feet were being forced backward, and each time she brought up her sword, she found she was only just in time. The thief had no time to think of counter attacking. He was too fast; too strong! It seemed just as she had a moment enough to recover from the shock of one blow, another would nearly knock her off her feet.

Suddenly her foot stumbled backwards on a root. She swung out to balance herself and stayed standing, but that was when his blade hit.

It smacked hard on the weapon she had, catapulting it out of her hand and out of reach. Valerlanta watched it land with a gasp.

The man sneered.

He re-balanced his sword in his hands, and then approached.

Back hitting a tree, Valerlanta realized she had nowhere to go. Behind her was the feuding army, ahead was her attacker.

Her heart slammed in her chest, but she forced a brave face. If she was to die, it would not be as a coward.

The silvery blade raised between them, and Valerlanta cringed.

Then in a blur of green, a sword came out and met her attackers. Once, twice, then again.

The thick brow man's eyes went wide, but the other swordsman was too skilled. As their blades danced off one another, Venic suddenly changed stance, and his blade lunged forward and into his enemy. Just to be sure, he pulled it out of the stunned man, and made sure he would not rise again with one last swipe.

Her savior, breathing hard, gave her a quick glance, then nodded her onward and left. Letting out a relieved breath, wordlessly she followed.

She heard them chasing not long after they started their run into the forest. Their furious screams echoed around her like ghosts on the haunt.

Like never before, she temporarily put aside her hiding skills and simply ran, not caring how many branches she broke or prints she made.

She would not go back! They would not catch her again!

Abruptly as she jumped over a log, the forest floor came out from under her and she rolled down a rocky cliff. It was not a far drop, but she could not help but lay at the bottom and grit her teeth in pain.

Her eyes watered and tears fell as her everything around her swayed.

After a few breaths the pain calmed enough to sit up, and Valerlanta staggered to her feet and gingerly stepped over to a tree for support. The rough bark was somehow comforting; as if she craved to hold something solid.

What adrenalin she had masking her pain before was steadily failing, and it was enough to make a step cause a soft whimper and turn her stomach.

Venic hurried to her, looking on with a concerned eyes. "Can you continue?"

She stilled her raspy breathing long enough to glare at him. "That is my cloak."

He grinned. "I found it left in a forest by some careless person. I think it looks better on me then it would on them anyhow."

She opened her mouth to say something, but froze when she heard a light sound on the air. Bird speech.

At about the same time, they froze as they heard men reaching the cliff above.

"We need to go!" Venic hissed. "Can you move?"

Taking a deep breath, she squeezed her eyes shut, if only for a moment.

'What are you doing, Vall?' She thought bitterly to herself. *'You are not like this; you are not a scared defenseless child, so stop running and think! You are better than this! He is waiting, so move!'*

After one more shaky breath, she took a step, then another, then more and more after that. She used the trees for balance as Venic followed close, walking backwards with his sword drawn.

'You should be ashamed of yourself.' She hissed to no one but herself. *'Absolutely pathetic! You are beyond this now! Beyond fear! A small hole is nothing compared to a dragon! So pick up your feet and move!'*

Her self-pep-talk did help; filling her with a sort of horrible anger at herself that made any step she did not take feel like the worst possible thing.

She had no doubt that the men were still behind, but now she was making every step count. Even though her knees wobbled, she forced them to step carefully and lead her around anything that might snap or bend over from her weight.

Changing her path, she turned from where she was walking downhill, and instead walked horizontal from it, making her way back towards Palenwood. Venic followed wordlessly.

If she did not pass out before then.

Inclines that were normally no matter for her, suddenly were stealing her breath and aching her surly broken ribs. She knew she was more injured then she was letting herself think, and although to continue could mean further injury, she could not stop.

Birds sang in the forest around her, enticing her like a lullaby into just laying down to rest, just for a moment.

"Not yet." She told them, though it came out as a hushed whisper.

As trees passed by, her vision kept blurring no matter how many times she blinked. The sun started dipping away when she finally fell to her knees at a stream and drank her fill, she wondered how she would get up again. Drinking caused her to come up coughing, but the cool liquid made her feel better.

Dizzily, Valerlanta looked around her, trying to place herself. Everything seemed different right now. Even the mountains looked strange.

A heavy sigh escaped her, but she ignored it and took another drink while Venic watched her with something she could not stand; pity. As if to spite him, she forced herself back up again and staggered to a tree to lean on. There, she put her hands in her mouth and whistled.

A reply came shortly. It was close, but not close enough. He was moving her; leading her away.

"You need to stop." Her rescuer interrupted, startling her. She did not look at him, though. She could not see that expression again.

"I do not have a choice." She answered bluntly, and gingerly took her next steps forward before he could do something stupid, like offer to carry her. Valerlanta was not sure she could handle him asking that.

One step, then the other.

He followed her along the river to where the waters branched off with a little mill running just off of it. The door was closed, but Venic kicked it in easily and ushered her inside.

There was two men working inside, turning the seeds to flour, but upon seeing the two burst in, they wordlessly put their hands up in surrender and hustled past out the door. Venic let them go, and brought her over to where the largest wheel turned using the current of the waters.

Once there, he held both her shoulders tightly, as if afraid she might just collapse at any moment, which was a high possibility. He looked her over, and a swam of emotions washed over his face, until finding only one; anger. At first she thought it might be directed at her, and then unexpectedly she was pulled into a hug.

She blinked in surprise as his arms tightened around her and she was brought against his chest. It felt warm, it felt safe and warm, and she did not know what to do, so she just stood there, wide-eyed and confused.

Then he released her and grabbed her by her chin to inspect her face from the dim lighting coming from the door. How many bruises did he see, she wondered. How many injures did she have and did not even notice through the pain of the others?

He then simply dropped her chin and reached over his shoulder to bring out her bow. He wordlessly and gently put it over hers, then turned away.

Taking some of the flour bags, he puffed the powder into the air. The clouds burst into the air, turning his clothes white, but he did not seem to care.

She watched him, trying to understand through her fog of confusion.

And that was when she realized it.

He was ensuring enough flour was floating in the air for her to finish the job.

He was going to fake their deaths and take some of them with it.

The voices were coming, nearing closer and closer, and Venic looked to the opening into the water, then back at her. No, not just shouts, horses. Horses that were helping them gain ground.

She bit her lip, looking back towards the door. They needed a way to slow them down; to stop them from following.

A shadow showed at the door.

Using what energy she had left, she called on the magic, and as she did, Venic tackled her into the icy cold waters.

But she was not too late.

Right before hitting the water, flames leapt off her finger tips, and that was all that was needed. The amount of flour in the air ignited, causing an explosion.

Even as she was underwater, she felt the heat, and saw various debris hitting around her as the current pulled her onward and deeper.

She surfaced.

The cold of it made her gasp and her whole body tried to tense, but she forced it to relax best she could to keep from going under.

It was cold, and yet it's very touch burned.

Her feet kicked and arms pushed, but every so often a rough current forced her under and she did not have the strength to resist. It pulled into its icy depths again, and this time she could not rise. Something came around her, pulling her back up.

She came out gasping for air, while Venic held on with one arm, and tried to swim with the other. Rocks came out of nowhere, bruising her already pained body, and the cruel waters swept them along even when Venic dug his heals hard into where their feet had the chance of touching.

He swam with the current, trying to reach the edge.

She tried to help or swim on her own, but he refused to let go, as if not trusting her to not go under.

When he reached the shore, the waters tried to continue to push them along, but he grabbed hold to a root. With a grunt, he pulled her over and pushed her up onto land, then pulled himself up as well.

Her feet still dangled in the water, but just for a moment she had to lay there, half in and half out, while catching her breath. The air came out harsh and shaky, but it seemed like every part of her was trembling, so it did not surprise her.

Venic seemed to feel the same way, and simply collapsed beside her, eyes closed. "Well, I would wager that gained us some ground over them."

Despite everything, she laughed painfully. "Yes, I would say we did."

She paused for a moment, taking everything in. Leaves rustled in the wind above her, waving back and forth.

It took every ounce of her strength to keep from weeping with joy.

"You should not be here. You and Alstred should be far away with the treasures. Why? Why are you here?" She asked finally while she felt she still could.

He shifted uncomfortably. "Well... it is that child of ours, you know, the one older than us with blonde hair? Well the whole time you were gone he kept looking at me with these huge eyes; I kid you not when I say they would put an owl to shame. So I did not have a choice, really."

A smile found her lips. "I see. Well you are still an idiot."

After she heard his breath steady beside her, there was a rustle as he sat up. "Can you still move?" He asked.

"Yes." She sighed, though in reality she doubted she could. Opening her eyes even seemed like a chore. She just wanted to lay and dry in the sun. "I could use a hand up, though."

Without a word of complaint, he grabbed her forearm, and helped her to her feet then waited until she steadied.

"Thank you." She said, but he ignored it.

"Who did you talk to?" He asked instead. "When you whistled?"

She looked at him, wondering if he knew how much he should fear the title she was about to say. "My father."

His eyes narrowed slightly, calculating, but she ignored him and stumbled on. She did not know how she had the strength, she simply did. That was the strange thing about the human body, even when it said that it was done, you could normally find a little more if you wanted it hard enough.

However, she had used that left strength long ago.

The world went dark.

« Chapter 12 »

Valerlanta figured she must have passed out, possibly for only a few moments time, but she was too tired and sore to care. Even lifting a hand against the glaring sun seemed like too much work, so she simply turned her head further into the dirt.

She knew Venic was there beside her, she could feel him turning over her pant leg to see the bruises she had there, than him let out sigh of a breath.

She knew what she was supposed to be doing, she knew she should move, but she suddenly had no will to try. Eyes half closed, she let the world blur around her.

So tired...

At the sign of movement, her eyes finally fluttered open and focused on a little orange butterfly as it settled on a flower and fanned it's delicate wings. It had a tarnish on the one side, but it was still gorgeous to the thieves eyes. Such thin wings carrying it about with the grace of a leaf in a gentle wind...

Letting out a grunt of pain as she tried to shift her arm, Valerlanta watched as the butterfly fluttered off, thinking of what her father once said. He had told her that those butterflies were a sign of change to come; and that following it would lead you to your fate.

Slowly, she got up to follow it.

"Hey, what are you doing?" A startled Venic asked. "Stop, you need to rest!" She did not know why she stumbled after it, but a part of her said it was just a good thing to be moving.

Venic appeared in front of her, blocking her path. "It will be the death of you if you continue." He snarled. "You need to stop!" In a daze, she simply stumbled around him. He blocked her way again, but again she stepped around.

"Val!" He called, but she continued.

More than once she had to lean against a tree for support, and when she would Venic would try and talk her into stopping, but each time the butterfly flew on, urging her onward.

It led her pass a large bed of moss she was tempted to lay on, through a meadow that made her feel exposed, then onto a ridge.

It was there that the butterfly got away from her. It fluttered on-wards, down the valley, past all the horses, past all the men, and then disappeared somewhere among the tents.

With a hard swallow, the thief watched the butterfly go, and then stumbled back away like a deer spying a hungry wolf, and yet she could not tare her eyes from it fully.

An army, large enough to start a war.

Hundreds of men, maybe more, stood out on the break in the trees before her.

They were practicing their skills such as the bow on hay stacks, readying strange equipment such as a log with handles on it, and many more sat about fires talking and laughing with eerily ease.

From here, she could see the marking of the white gryphon on the tents and armour, and for once, it forgot to fill her chest with heat, and instead sent a chill up her spine.

So many men…

More than enough to start a war...perhaps even enough to win.

Without warning, a hand was clamped over her mouth and she was pulled backwards into the thicker brush. She struggled weakly, but was easily over powered.

As soon as they were a safe distance away, the blonde thief wiggled free and looked on the swordsman with a glare that he easily ignored.

"What are you thinking?" He snarled. "I come all this way to rescue you, and you nearly prance on into another army to capture you? What is wrong with you?"

Valerlanta opened her mouth, but completely forgot what she was going to say. Then Venic started blurring over and coming back in waves.

Scrambling her hands over to a tree, she held onto it for support and focused on breathing and trying to overcome the warmth spreading over her eyes.

When she looked at the blurred vision of Venic again and he slowly became clear, he was not alone. In fact, a rather sharp looking knife lay across his throat, making the knights face pale.

The attacker was taller than Venic, but hardly. However, what he did not have in height, he easily made up for in fearsome appearance.

Greying red hair, tall, earthy clothes, and fierce blood-lusting eyes…

"Father." Valerlanta near stuttered, her eyes wide and her heart slamming, as if, even at her age, she was still but a child that had been caught snatching up some extra sweets.

Venic blinked in surprise, while her father looked on at her with a cold and angry expression. It was like his eyes were glowing with rage, and oddly, it scared her more than any dragon.

"You wretched excuse for a daughter…I do not even know where to begin." He snarled, and she shrunk back as his deep booming voice loomed high above her. "Well, I suppose I do have some idea. Are you an idiot? Did I drop you as a child and forget? Or did it grow with your age?"

Valerlanta opened her mouth to say something, but his sharp glare indicated that his question did not actually need to be answered, so she slammed it closed again.

"First you say you are coming back, and then I have to go looking for you because you never do! I search a castle, find the army that took you, help you escape, and how do you thank me? You run off again with this pathetic excuse for a man. Is that what you wanted? To leave your father behind?"

Valerlanta shook her head, froze stiff as she saw the blade turn over from the flat side, to the edge. Venic winced and arched his head back, but apparently had enough instinct to know he was better off not saying anything.

"Do not kill him." She ordered.

A brow rose in interest, and the thief guild leader seemed almost tempted to disobey. "And why should I not kill him? He is a knight, though that I am sure you know. Even without his armour he has the stench of those blue bloods. And did you notice how straightly cut his hair is? He probably had someone do even that for him. The whole lot are useless as children, and have the temper of spoiled brats."

He would do it, she knew he would. He has many times before, and so has she, but she would not allow it this time.

Valerlanta locked eyes with her father, her expression as serious as her tone. "I still owe him. I will not let anyone to kill him. Even you, father."

He looked at her a moment longer, his face a mask of calm waters, but his eyes fierce like a storming sea, than released the startled knight.

Instantly Venic put his hand to his sword, but stopped when Valerlanta grabbed his arm. He glared, but reluctantly released his weapon.

As her father walked passed, she reserved a light smack across the back of her head, causing her to turn her dagger like daggers to a new prey while he continued. "In dept to a knight? I hope you have learned what a terrible mistake that is. Now come on then; let me see if I can fix this mess you put us in."

He started walking away, and in the first time in her life, she felt little urge to follow. Her feet felt rooted to the ground, and her eyes ever so slowly broke from her father and drifted west, to where Palenwood castle, and the forest in between, waited.

Venic was there beside her, standing quietly with his face still drained of color, and his hand rubbing the skin on his neck where the knife had been. There was not so much as a scrape, but her father had clearly made his point

Venic knew now the risk that came with crossing paths with the darkest shadow in the woods.

Just ahead, her father noticed her hesitation, but continued anyways. "I will not wait for you." He said bluntly.

Valerlanta forced her eyes from her westward dreams, and followed. Her throat clenched as she went.

Venic hissed for her to wait, but when she did not, he hesitantly followed, but at a great distance.

Her father led them far away from the men, his steps light as a feather and his eyes always searching.

With his sharp eyes, he never missed a thing; be it a slightly bent blade of grass, or a faded print of a boot. When he found them, as usual, she could see his mind calculating; working out who would dare enter his forest. If it was someone he did not want, his eyes would flash would anger, and he would wander on again with her stumbling after.

As she watched him work, she suddenly realized that was her before, searching and killing strangers...now it simply seemed unnecessary to her. She did not want him to see it, but this forest was not the only thing that haunted her every thought, now there was another thing she craved more than ever; even when it led to markings from rope around her wrists.

After the sweet and dangerous taste of adventure had tempted her, nothing felt as meaningful. All she could think about was two men with a ball of puzzles.

When she could hardly stand and her legs were walking her like a drunkard, wordlessly Venic grabbed her arm and pulled it around her shoulders. The strain hurt, but at least now she could stand. She looked at him to argue, but thought better of it and shot her gaze away and silently allowed the help.

Ahead, her father tilted his head back and saw her being assisted, but his cold expression was unreadable.

Eventually, her father felt it safe enough to stop, and by that time she was shivering and covered in sweat with eyes strained and knees weak. He set the camp up and readied the fire, but did not light it; he would wait for the cover of night for that.

So camp ready, he sat crossed-legged by the unlit fire, and she stood with Venic at the edge of the camp, both of them hesitant to stand any nearer.

"Come then." Her father said, waving her over. "Let me take a look at what damage has been done."

Venic looked at her, but her feet did not move.

"I am going to keep going." She said finally.

The guild leader sighed and waved her over again. "Come here, child."

"I am going to finish this." She repeated again. "I am not done, father. Not yet."

"There are people who must be warned about that army, Val. Plans that must be made..."

"I am-"

"-leaving, yes, yes I know." He tilted his head at her, and although his eyes were masked by his hood, she could still see his lips pull up into that wolf like smile everyone so feared. "Of course you are, you are my daughter after all. One scent of riches and off you go....but not now. Now," He raised his strips of cloth that would serve as bandages. "For now, you need rest and mending. And I would like a good story while I work. I think you probably have an interesting one by now, would you not agree?"

He looked on at her expectantly, and she knew those fierce and wild eyes he used to control everyone would be watching. Though to her, they always looked a little lonely instead of scary.

Reluctantly, Valerlanta sighed in defeat and stumbled away from Venic and collapsed in front of the only family she had.

He went to work immediately, his murder drenched hands soft as feathers as he patched her wounds. As he did, she told him everything.

She was not surprised to find out that his favourite part in the tale did not involve a dragon, but instead three companions who foolishly disturbed a next of pixies and were forced to run. He laughed like a little boy all throughout that part.

At some point during the story, Venic hesitantly came to sit closer and listen into the story he already knew, though he kept glancing at her father out of the corner of his eye.

Every so often, her father would return the gaze, showing the terrifying cage of pent up bloodlust, but then he would break it again, giving the knight only a taste of what horrors only two eyes could hold. Then the guild leader would laugh again, as if he had not a care in the world.

As time went on, Valerlanta felt the tension in her shoulders loosen, and her eyelids grow heavy.

Her father started telling his own story of how he managed to steal a nobles horse and replace it for a one eared donkey, but she never heard the end of it. His deep voice soothed her like a lullaby, and before she knew it, she fell asleep at his side.

***

When she woke, she found herself oddly warm. Immediately suspicious, she shot up, and greatly regretted it with the pain that shot through her. Her fever had broken, but the pain remained.

She was covered in her father's cloak, and beside her was his pack, knives, and everything else but his bow. He even left all the plants she would need for her wounds, already prepared to use.

"Father!" She hissed as her throat tightened, and Venic was startled awake with a sputter. He jumped up from where he was asleep, sitting against a tree, and grabbed for his weapon. She ignored him and staggered to her feet and angrily looked around to see if her father was still near. She found only a small sign of his prints, and they had left long ago. "You idiot! You cannot do this! I will not take your things and leave you in the woods with nothing! It is my fault, my burden! You-"

But her words to no one faded from her mouth when she saw an arrow made out of three sticks sitting upon the ground, facing west. Three rocks sat at the end of it in a line.

Her eyes blurred with tears, and with a frustrated sigh, she turned away from the message started stuffing the things into his pack. "Idiot father." She hissed.

Venic came to join her, but did not seem to quite understand as well as her. He opened his mouth to say something, while she was already pulling on the pack on.

"Just who was that man?" Venic asked suddenly, finally breaking the silence that was so unnatural for him. "He never made a sound. Not once."

Valerlanta paused and could not help but give a small smile. "Simply be glad that nature makes the harshest of men uncaring of sides. If he ever chose one, I would hate to see those sent to stop him."

Venic only frowned deeper at that. Then, with a sigh, he crossed his arms at the symbols again.

"Alstred will come to meet us in Alecaven in a few days' time. He has the ball with him." His eyes hesitantly looked north, and Valerlanta felt the corner of her mouth twitch with amusement. 'That way?' His gaze asked, and Valerlanta rolled her eyes and started west.

"Last night, when father was looking for prints, he was looking for a specific pair."

Valerlanta explained, though she herself was only just realizing it. "A pair that belongs to one person heading west. They assumed we were heading towards Alecaven, which means they know that is the final location. We are heading the right direction."

Venic only grunted unhappily in reply, possibly angered to have been beaten again.

Their pace was perhaps faster than it should be, but she dared not slow. Not with a whole army heading the same way.

She had time to gain ground, though.

Without even a moment of consideration, her feet turned north.

There a valley to the west, and it would take those heading that way at least a full day to find a way around. She knew another way, a way that would give her at least a half day ahead of the army.

Just like her father, she tried to always be full of surprises.

« Chapter 13 »

Staring at her hand, her eyes looked at the creases and wondered how much evil such small hands could be capable of.

'She is not real.' She told herself in her head. *'She was just invented by my mind from stress.'*

Closing her fingers, she shook off the feeling and focused on her leg. The white glow came to her fingers, and she pressed it onto her leg. Just like with before, the pain doubled as the wounds there were forcibly mended. Bones were smoothed over, muscled stitched as one again, and her skin burned as bruised and battered skin was replaced with new.

When she was done, a patch of perfect skin the same size of her hand was there; completely healed among the bruises.

Her hand moved to the next spot, eager to get rid of her limp so she could travel faster, but this time it shook as she moved it.

She still had not regained her full strength, but even if she had, she had little doubt that this magic would still drain a vast amount of energy. It was as if this was nature's way of keeping control; it was a magic she could not master otherwise she could eventually make even the dead walk again. The dead and dying had to remain as such, so that also meant that she would remain shaking like this until she was better.

Pressing her hand onto the next part, she winced as the magic began to work.

She finished just in time to pull down her pant-leg before Venic walked into the small clearing. She did not mind if he saw the magic, but she was done with seeing his concerned expression when he saw what wounds were left.

"Good, you are awake." He said, walking towards her and holding out a skin of freshly filled water. Valerlanta took it and drank it gratefully.

"Thanks." She said when she was done, and he nodded as he took it back.

"Ready to get going?" He asked, and Valerlanta hesitated.

Eyes drifting to the forest, she looked there, considering them, then got up.

"If you need more time-" Venic started, noticing her hesitation, but she interrupted him.

"I am fine, let's get going." Putting her hand on her knee, she leaned forward and pushed off it, taking every ounce of energy to get herself up.

She had no way of knowing if it was due to magic or wounds.

"You know, if it's just for a while, I can carry you on my back."

Valerlanta put all her weight on her wobbly legs, and sent him a measured stare. "Not a chance. I might be injured, but I am still a thief, and you are still a knight."

"A *fake* knight, if you care to remember." He countered with a smile, his eyes sparkling. "To be a knight, you would have to have first been a squire, and that I was not. I do understand that accepting help from a knight would bring endless shame onto your delicate pride, but what about a spy simply pretending to be a knight? a criminal helping a criminal? Even I cannot see the harm in that."

Despite her strict attempt to keep a straight face, her lips pulled into a small smile. "I will not let you carry me."

"Fine, but will you let me help you? I know you are incapable from seeing your own condition, but trust me when I say you should not stress yourself more than needed. By now, with all that has happened, I would say we are more than friends enough for me to help with that, but if that is not enough, than how about you let me repay you for not letting me get lost and starve every day?"

The thief looked away, then slowly, so slowly, let her gaze lead back to him, and ignored the burning feeling coming to her cheeks. "I suppose we are friends enough for at least that."

Before she could change her mind, he stepped forward and reached for her arm. She flinched back at his touch, but he was too quick. He swiftly swept her arm around his shoulders and took half her weight onto him. The stretch on her ribs made her gasp and brought water to her eyes, but she forced herself to let in several even breaths, and it passed.

The thief would not admit it, but moving was much easier with his help. He kept her weak legs from tripping on every root they passed, and guided her up steep inclines that all seemed as daunting as the tallest mountains to her.

"This brings back memories." Venic mused, and Valerlanta too found herself thinking of far back when they first met and an arrow led to a very similar situation to the one they were currently facing. She was so determined back then....Valerlanta wished greed was still a strong enough motivator to keep her going.

"It is funny," He continued. "how both injuries were of your own cause."

She looked at him with eyes wide in surprise. "Are you lecturing me?"

He looked away, as if something in the distance had suddenly caught his interest. "Well, your father does not seem to be doing much of it, in fact, for some insane reason he seems to encourage you and that blasted pride of yours, so someone has to clue you into how things work."

"Well, fear not, learning for me takes a lot of beating, but I think it is starting to stick."

"Good, I am getting tired of rescuing you."

Valerlanta gave him a sideways glance. "Excuse me? I saved you from the dragon."

"Only after I saved you first. Do you forget that I jumped in front of you to face the monster with a sword? Just a bloody sword. It was like a tiny stick compared to it."

"I took an arrow for you."

"And I kept that arrow from letting you bleed to death."

"I helped you and Alstred get out of danger in the forest near Palenwood."

He grinned at her. "And I just did the same for you. I dare say, we have a habit of keeping things even between us."

She raised a brow. "That does mean that you should be next."

"Yes, I suppose then I should be thankful that with as you are right now, you have no chance of keeping up with me. Especially after I trip you."

Valerlanta looked at him, and despite all her worries, despite all her pain, she laughed. Laughing somehow felt good, even if it hurt her ribs to do so.

He laughed too, but raised a brow when her smile suddenly faded and she looked away to the ground.

The elf was fake-just a imagined figure from whatever madness was growing within her-she had already convinced herself of that much, but even if the power the king was going for was fake, did she still want to continue?

"Was it so bad? What he did?" Venic asked; his voice even but hinted with concern.

Valerlanta shook her head. "I am fine. I am just tired."

He looked at her closely, but nodded and said nothing more, clearly not believing her, but deciding to let it go.

They traveled onwards, him helping her every step of the way. They traveled far from the road, far from any people, then headed west in down ways Valerlanta knew would have no chance of coming across people.

It was near nightfall when they finally stopped, and by that time Valerlanta was too tired to even think. She had planned on healing what injuries were left on her legs before bed, but instead she just made the fire and sat there, staring into it and not even caring about food or shelter.

Venic, at least, seemed to care more than her, so sat beside her and put some dried meat in her vision. With effort, her eyes focused on it, and after what seemed like seconds, she finally realized in her clouded mind that she was supposed to eat it. Valerlanta took it, and ate it in small nibbles, ignoring the pain it brought to her jaw. "Thank you."

The fake-knight nodded and simply say beside her, watching the dancing of the flames. Somewhere in the distance, an owl called to the fading sun.

Luckily for the both of them, keeping watch was no longer necessary, as those chasing would have assumed they died in the windmill, so they instead just sat, side-by-side, and though it was silent between them, it was not at all uncomfortable.

When the meat was done and there was nothing else she could do to keep herself busy, the fire became almost hypnotizing. The heat of it warmed her body, and the flames danced about, soothing her head forward into bobs of near sleep. It seemed to be begging her to try sleeping near its heat; even if just for a moment.

Before she knew what was happening, her head fell against something warm. Part of her told herself that she should try to lift her head; that she could be near the fire even, but she was asleep before she could even try.

And for whatever reason, the person she was leaning on the shoulder of did not try to shove her off.

* * *

Waking the next morning, Valerlanta found herself covered with a cloak. Confused, she sat up and blinked, her eyes getting used to the bright sun as she looked down at the cloak.

It was her cloak that Venic had been using.

She struggled to remember the night before, but it was all blur. Then, as she picked up the fabric and rolled it up for traveling, she vaguely, with the slightest amount, recalled the final memories before sleep. A warmth under her head...

Shaking it from her mind she glanced around.

Venic was nowhere to be seen.

Placing her hand on her leg, she healed it. The amount of energy doing it took was the same, but she was getting better at it; faster even. By the time Venic returned, both her legs had healed fast enough to at least encourage her legs to hold her up without shooting pain.

They started traveling again, and though Venic helped her when she needed it, she was able to travel mostly using her own strengths.

They traveled the whole day, then days after. Along the way, Valerlanta continued her healing in secret, until the castle was one day ahead and all that was left was the bruises which were hiding her hard work.

Venic was lying near the fire under the night sky, and though there was no extreme need for a watch, she could not bring herself to sleep, so simply stared off towards where the castle was.

She could not see it, but like a bad dream, she knew it was there waiting.

Bringing up her knees, she wrapped her arms around them and frowned.

She did not have much time to decide all the details. Come tomorrow, she would get Venic settled, then disappear. He might look for her at first, but he would never find her, and after he gave up, he could decide his own path.

Valerlanta wanted no more to do with this.

"Something wrong?" Venic asked, the sound of fabric shifting coming as he rolled to look at her.

"I have not been back there since..." She said quietly. "I have not been there since my father found me. I have always had this fear that somehow, someone would recognize me, so I just never went back."

"Hmm." Venic sat up and shifted closer to her. "If they did recognize you-if someone saw through the mask and somehow noticed something about you that they recognized as part of a bloodline they once knew- what do you worry would happen?"

She glanced at him, judging his expression from what she could see in the flickering firelight. "You would not believe me anyways."

He huffed. "Perhaps, but then again, you are surprisingly honest for a thief. In fact, I find myself trusting your words more and more each day!"

"Fine." Valerlanta shifted towards him, accepting the challenge. She looked him in the eyes, wanting to see every emotion that crossed his face. "I would be taken to the king, and, more likely than not, I would be tied up and would be bled out very carefully so not a drop would be wasted. They would kill me slow to keep the blood fresh so that the king could easily absorb what magic may be left there."

His brow rose up, and his lips twitched, clearly trying to see if she was joking or not.

How easy it would be to tell him that every word she just said was a lie? He could laugh, she could laugh, and maybe, just maybe, something in the laughter would help her believe it was not true too.

Instead, she leaned back and smirked at him. "See? I told you that you would not believe me. I do not blame you, though, even I know it sounds mad. I used to often wonder if I made it up to keep from going mad."

'Little help it did.' She thought. *'Seeing a woman invisible to everyone but me certainly does not define sane.'*

He stared at her then shook his head. "That is mad."

"Is it?" She poked at the flames with a stick, sending sparks flying into the air. "Just think about it without the mind of a knight; just try. Think it through with me; in one night for whatever reason, every royal but one was killed. Then, for good measure, they also killed anyone old enough there who could remember what happened. Why?"

He shook his head. "Because they were rebels! They kept the youngest of children alive because they were innocent. The king survived because he hid."

"This was not a rebel against the crown." She shot. "They killed everyone; the cleaners, the cooks, and everyone to the last stable boy."

"They got caught up in the battle; it happens. All it takes is one person to do an act, and as if they all share the same mind, the whole mob follow suits."

"Have you ever done it? Killed a young boy because someone else did first." She asked, her words sharp as her arrows she carried. "But you know, I went there; I went to the place where the rebels supposedly came from; that very same place we traveled through with Alstred, and there I met someone. She was an old lady, she was dying and said she was done running and wanted to die in the village she was born in. The lady told me of a boy; the boy who lead the revolution. He was a violent kid who was always picking fights, but when the village was attacked by soldiers, he was first to fight back. The village realized they were wrong about him, and with his aid, they rustled up an army and, with the help of people on the inside, they overtook the castle. However, no one came home. Every adult that could oppose them was dead, but not a single rebel came home."

"The king killed them and drove them out. He was not able to sleep, and that saved him when everyone else was being killed in their beds. He used his magic, and got away."

"No." Valerlanta said flatly. "He let the rebels do all of the dirty work, and as they did, he drank the blood of those who were killed. After, of course, he wanted to test them out to see if they worked, so he did it on the rebels."

"That is insane. You do not-"

"I was there, Venic!" She screamed, jumping to her feet. "I was there; I was trapped, and I would have been a part of it if they had not killed everyone who knew whose blood I have! That woman, the one at the village, she knew that rebel was the fake-king. She ran off with her daughter and survived because of it, and never told anyone what she knew in order to protect her daughter! It is not just in my head, Venic! It is real!"

He stood up too, and put his hands in the air, telling her to calm herself. "Easy, Valerlanta, I do not mean any offense, but you said so yourself; it sounds-"

"Mad?" She finished for him. "Yes. Well maybe I finally hoped I had found someone who would believe me."

Whirling about, she stomped into the dark of the night, ignoring the calls from Venic behind her.

Once she had finally tripped over enough roots, once she had finally been whipped by enough branches, she collapsed back against a tree and looked up at the sky.

She shivered from the wind, but just stood there, feeling like just another star lost in the black of the night.

***

The next morning, Venic pressed his finger into the dirt, making an indent into the dirt there.

Carefully, he places rock after rock, and built up walls with the thinnest of sticks.

For the smallest of moments. the thief watched through the fresh green leaves and let her eyes search across his wavy strands of brown hair, strong chin, slightly long nose, then lastly, his almond eyes.

Could she really convince herself to hate him enough to leave him? Could she really tell herself that she no longer cared if he died?

Shaking off the thoughts, she brushed through the leaves and entered the camp. He looked up as she came close, and gave a small half smile as greeting, but then swiftly looked back to his work.

'Are you mad at me?' She wondered, kneeling beside him and looking over his work. 'You would be if you knew even half of how horrible of a person I am.'

"What are you doing?" She asked instead, pretending to have interest in his sticks, dirt, and rocks. This attention was the closest she could come at a peace offering, and he willingly took the bait.

"It is a map of everything I remember about the castle and the city." He said without looking up. "These are the castle walls, and here, in the field to the south east of it, is where the celebrations will be held."

"Celebrations?" Valerlanta asked, wrinkling her nose, and she finally got him to glace up at her, though the look he gave was only one of surprise.

"It happens every year; they are the last games before winter, so naturally they are the largest." Venic looked back down and pointed at the blank spot of dirt. "The nobles will not let anything spoil their fun; even if they have word of war, they will still party. They think they are untouchable, so things will continue on as if nothing were wrong.

Every year there is knightly games, right here, and afterwards, the favored knights-most often the winners- are accepted into the castle for one night only so they can feast like the nobles do. That is our chance."

Valerlanta fought back the dread filling in her chest. "Chance?"

"To get inside!" He pressed. "If I do well at the games, I can be invited to the dinner and bring you and Alstred along. After a quick slip away without anyone noticing, we will be in and can figure it out from there. Once we are inside the castle walls, it will be nothing to get into the castle itself. Doors might be locked, but if you can get through a window, then you can open a door for us. It is simply, and, most importantly, it is quiet. The ruins of the old castle are here, in the inner courtyard, and is the most likely place for the treasure to hide. Everything of the old has been torn down and built on except for that one spot. It will be our goal."

"I see." Valerlanta said, trying to sound enthusiastic, but instead her words came out flat.

"What is it?" Venic asked, noticing her tone. "Do you not like the plan?"

'Not even a little.' She thought to herself. 'What I wish is that your plan involved throwing away the treasures and leaving that castle far behind.'

Valerlanta got up and turned away, leaving him to his planning. She pretended to take interest in something as far away as possible. "It is nothing; the plan should work."

"You do not seem convinced it will." He said flatly. "Why?"

Valerlanta turned back and forced a small smile. "No reason, I am just tired is all."

His eyes grew several shades colder as he ran a hand through his wavy hair. He glared up at her. "No, that is not it. You have been tired before, and that has never stopped you."

Crossing her arms, she let her eyes slowly slide down to her feet. She thought of the biggest scar she had; which stretched down her back. "I think I am going mad." She near whispered.

"What?"

Shaking her head. "No, never mind, it is nothing. It is just a healthy mix of magic and fear playing tricks on my mind."

He did not say anything; she hesitantly looked at him, and saw he was standing now, his eyes carefully searching her own.

The swordsman opened his mouth to speak but she did first, blurting words out before he had the chance to try.

"We should get going." She said, grabbing what little things they had and heading for her biggest nightmare.

Venic followed, and much of the time she could feel his eyes on her; his concern hot on her back.

She ignored it, and also tried not to notice the forest thin then, finally, leave completely. Fields of gold and green lay out before them in rolling hills, and just beyond them was the castle.

Sucking in a breath, the thief continued her pace.

The two companions were walking in a vast emptiness, filled only with sky and grasses that swayed in the wind like waves. They walked across the fields to continue avoiding the roads- and the soldiers upon them- when possible, and as they did, Valerlanta wondered if she had ever seen the sky look so large. It stretched over everything, making even the furthest of points visible.

"When this is all over-" Venic started suddenly, breaking the long silence between them. "-We can still be like this; you know. We can still be friends; still have adventures."

More than likely, he noticed the hesitation in her step and was trying to help, but instead he just made her feet feel heavy like rocks.

Glancing back, Valerlanta smirked. "You are really up for another adventure? After all this?"

He thought about it then smiled at her. "Well, perhaps after just a few moments of rest."

Valerlanta looked at him, and then gradually, her smile became genuine. "Very well, one more adventure then, after this."

"Good."

They walked a while longer, silence again threatening to take over, then Valerlanta turned back, making up her mind.

"Venic, if you want that plan to work, there are things we are going to need, things I cannot easily steal."

Venic eyed her. "Is that not why I have a thief around?"

"Or," Her lips twitched with a smile "Instead how about we give an old friend a visit?"

« Chapter 14 »

Venic led the way through the city, his footsteps confident as if he had been here hundreds of times before; which he just might have been for all she knew. Somehow he was able to walk normally so that someone looking would not be concerned, and yet he was also cautious, looking carefully for any guards with a casual turn of his head.

Reaching their target location, they exchanged glances, and that simple gaze seemed like it told enough, so Venic nodded, bent down low, and intertwined his fingers. Valerlanta put her foot in his hands. Upon her touch, he immediately brought his hands up, lifting her upwards where she grabbed hold of the roof above and pulled herself over.

Staying low, she scanned around the building, then leaned back over to see down at Venic and pointed east, then tapped beside her eye and pointed just a little far off from the same direction with two fingers.

Venic nodded again, and hurried off.

As he disappeared into the dark of the night, Valerlanta took in a deep breath and felt herself smile as she looked back to her target location.

After waiting a total of ten slow counts, the thief crawled on her belly up the rough roof. Once near the top, slowly peeked over and saw a man down below. He walked around with a sword clearly at his hip, and was stomping around with scanning eyes.

Valerlanta waited until the man had turned to march the away, then she scurried down the other side of the roof.

When she reached the edge, she jumped.

Instead of finding herself on the ground, she hit softly against the side of a building, with her hands gripping above her. Quick as she could, she stepped up the wall with her feet until she was able to pull herself up onto the stables roof.

High above on the connecting building was the window she needed; too high for her to reach just standing. Her gaze found the walls jutted out from the rest of the wall for square mock towers.

Below, she could hear the sound of horses complaining of her presence, but before the guard could turn back again, Valerlanta hurried over the opposite side of roof, and pressed herself low against the wood tiles.

In the quiet night air, she could easily hear the soft leather boots of the guard tapping the ground with each step.

Valerlanta cocked her head to one side, listening closer as she heard the man near, then pause.

Her heart started to slam at being able to hear him, but not see him. Even though she knew she was fast enough, part of her still wondered; did he somehow know she was there? Was that why he stopped?

But then, the steps continued, fading off again, and she let out a breath.

Getting up again, she rushed across the tiles, picked up speed, and then leapt towards one of the walls to the tower. Her foot touched, pushed off, hit another wall on the opposite side, then as she was propelled upwards to the other wall; her hand instead grasped the aimed-for windowsill. Using the nearest wall to walk her feet up, she peeked inside the window.

Just as thought, no movement came from inside the room, but it was not open either; she needed to unlock it.

Easy enough, but she did not have much time before that guard circled back.

Despite using her feet on the wall to help keep her up, her hand hooked onto the windowsill was still starting to shake with the exertion. Ignoring that, Valerlanta reached and grabbed a knife with her free hand, and hoisted herself a little higher until she could slide the blade in between the window and the wall, and she felt the blade glide smoothly through to the other side. Then, all she had to do is bring it up, and instantly she felt the blade of the knife hit the wooden latch. Just a little farther and it slid up.

Still using the knife, she pried it open by pushing on the handle of the knife, and the window swung outwards.

Wasting no time, the thief crawled inside and softly closed the window back behind her.

Outside she saw the guard come into view, but he made no indication of noticing her.

Smiling she turned back to the dark room.

From the light of the window, she saw various baskets, crates, and barrels piled up against every wall, but what made the eyes of the thief light up was a small pile of black powder sitting on the table.

She told herself she should continue on, that there was no time for this, but she could not help but pinch up a little bit of the powder between her fingers. It fell back to the table through her fingers, landing in the pile once again.

So this was the magic powder? It seemed little more than sand now.

Flicking the rest of the powder from her finger back into the pile, Valerlanta went to the door and almost walked right into a string strung at ankle level, leading off to somewhere in the room. Her foot was nearly right against it as the silvery light from the window became enough to make the string show.

Carefully, the thief stepped over it, then quickly inspected the door to be sure that there was no other surprises intended for someone about to open it, or so it seemed.

Slow as can be, Valerlanta opened the door just a crack.

The hallway was equally dark, but down the way a light came from under a door, and soft voices could be heard as a whisper.

Seeing as all the protection was directed to the supplies and other items, the rest of the way was simple enough. Just gentle but swift steps down the hall, through two doors, and she was almost there; but she could not enter here. Instead she entered a near room with just enough dust for her to know it was empty, and then opened a window and peeked out. A gaurd was directly below, just where she wanted him.

Crawling out the window, she was again greeted by the chill of the night air. Luckily, the tips of her toes found a wooden beam only just enough to stand on, and so she pressed herself against the outer wall, and edged her way over. With much less effort, she was at the other window and open it wide.

Once inside, the thief found herself surrounded by the clothes of the wardrobe that smelt of furs and dust. The room she needed let in a golden glow into the one she was in from an open door.

Peeking into the room, she saw the very man she was looking for sitting at a desk, as usual. Face lit up by the candles siting on his desk, she saw he looked calm and relaxed as he scratched what information he needed upon a note.

It seemed to her that that was where this man always seemed to be, as if taking the illegal route was almost more work than the honest one.

Grabbing her bow, she knocked an arrow and emerged into the light.

The black-market king glanced up, and paled. His eyebrows rose, and even though the quill dropped from his hand and left a large ink mark on whatever he was writing, he still gave a shaky smile.

"Valerlanta! Now this is a surprise! I had heard only just recently of your death in an explosion." Askyel Lochsell said in mock calmness, but there was a slight tone of worry rattling his voice.

"Yes, well, I am sorry to disappoint you, but, as you can see, I am very much alive." She smirked, though she could fear anger flaming in her chest like a swarm of bees looking for an exit. She kept her arrow up, and moved closer to properly see the fear in his eyes. "You moved and tightened your security, I see. Now this might be a guess, but I believe that your security is not yet tight enough."

The man stilled, and she saw his throat flex as he swallowed hard.

"I will get to the point." Valerlanta said, letting some of her dark feelings drip upon her voice. "You did the worst thing you could have, and made me your enemy. I would like nothing more than to put this arrow through your head right now, but that would be too fast of a death for you." She tilted her head, eyeing him over. "No, I think I would rather shoot you right through the leg and then help you pull it out. That way, you will be able to watch the blood leaving you too fast for you to stop it, but slow enough for you to feel every moment of death creeping in on you."

"Now, now," The man cooed as if talking to a child, "there is no need for that, I am sure we can come to some sort of agreement."

"Agreement? Unless I am mistaken, you tried to kill me!"

Now he smiled again, his lips curling up in an almost charming fashion. Almost. "It was a necessary action. I need what you have, and I very well knew that there was no thief good enough to take it from you. The only way you were going to hand it over is if you were dead. I have to admit, though, it was quite a surprise to see it in your hands; that was very unexpected."

Valerlanta felt her brows narrow. "What do you mean?"

"What I mean is," He shifted forward and rested his elbows on the table so his chin could sit upon his interlocked fingers. He peered at her with challenging eyes. "You were never the one we intended to let find that trail. We knew that knight was going to get away, and we knew what area it would likely happen in, we thought that territory belonged to someone else..."

Valerlanta dropped her hands slightly, but realized she was doing it and quickly brought it back to proper tension.

It was true; the location she found the ball in was not her area to rule. That place belonged to the person she had been visiting before she came across the trail.

"My father," She realized, "it was him you were after."

"Yes, so you can imagine my surprise when it was you who appeared here with the ball, though we imagined that many things would be different. As an example, this situation in your fathers care, I can imagine him right out interrogating the knight for information, then quickly killing him before coming down the mountain."

"Then you would kill him; you would have killed my father."

"Yes, that was the plan. I have to say, no one thought it possible that you two might actually join forces. You two have caused us an increasing amount of trouble."

"Until now." Valerlanta said, and the man raised a brow.

"What do you mean?"

"What I mean is, that there is no longer an 'us' in the factor of those coming after the knight and I; after tonight, there is just the king, not you."

The man's expression darkened, and his gaze wavered, and muscles tensed. Then in a flash, he was moving.

The arrow shot from her bow, and hit right into the wooden board he quickly lifted from his desk.

Discarding the makeshift shield, Askyel spun away from the desk and ran for the door behind him and was hit square face-first with the hard smack of the wooden end of a shovel.

The black market king hit the ground hard onto his back, and lay there stunned and blinking for several seconds, until everything, including the huge blonde standing over him, came into focus. Blood dripped from his nose, and a red mark was already showing across his face.

"Now, now, Lochsell." Valerlanta mockingly soothed as she knocked another arrow and approached. "Do you think I would really let you get away so easy? You forget who it is you are dealing with."

Still lying down, the king of all things illegal regarded her carefully. "So that is it then? You and your friend here are just going to kill me, and that is that? You think that my men will simply just allow you to slip from their minds?"

"Oh no, nothing of that sort." Valerlanta said teasingly. "Not yet, anyways."

"You see, my small pathetic friend," Venic knelt down and brought his sword to the other man's neck. Askyel glared, only making Venic smile all the more. "You are going to work for us."

At that moment, his eyes grew more wide then they had been than any of the moments where his life was at risk. "Pardon?"

"You heard me."

Askyel looked back to Valerlanta. "Surely you jest."

"No, not even in the slightest amount. This is your one and only chance to redeem yourself. If you disagree, you will have nowhere in this kingdom where you can hide from me, nor enough men to protect you. However, your life is not the only benefit."

The man raised a brow. "Is that so?"

"It is." Valerlanta released the tension on her bow and smiled with a tilted head. "You know of the scouts from Buragen, so I will not even ask, but there is something I saw that you did not; the army that is no more than a few days away from here." Askyel froze, so Valerlanta continued. "There is an army superior than any your king has, and that is a fact that I saw with my own two eyes. So, that known, it is right now that you can choose if you want to be on the winning side, or the losing one."

Despite her words, there was a sort of doubt on the man's face. "Our king has magic; and even if those who are attacking do as well, as soon as they crossed our boarder, they would have lost their ability. No one can take on the king; no one."

Valerlanta felt her smile falter, and she knelt down near the man. "I am going to tell you a secret our king does not want anyone to know; that he is not true to the blood of the throne, and yet he has magic. Strange, that is true, but it is because of this that he has grown intoxicated by the love of his own power. He is weak in his thoughts of his own invisible powers, that he is missing one important factor." Valerlanta raised her hand and focused all her thoughts into her hand. Almost instantly, a white flame licked across her fingers, adding a ghostly light across the whole room. "I can take on the king. When Buragen sees this, they will no doubt take my side. This kingdom will fall, and if you are with him, so will you. It is all up to you; it is your choice."

All blood that was left in his face drained away, leaving him as white as the glow in her hand. He watched her hand as if it was a snake about to strike, and for the first time ever, she saw him shutter in fear.

Venic pushed the sword tip a little harder against the man's chin. "Make the right choice, friend, or do you want to take on a kingdom, the biggest thief guild in the kingdom, and someone of true royal blood all, all on your own?"

She could see Askyell calculating the possibilities, and then he swallowed hard and pushed the sword tip away from his neck so he could raise himself a little higher. Venic allowed it, but loomed over the other man like a bear to a rabbit.

The black market kings jaw tightened then relaxed. "What do you need?"

* * *

By the time they had arrived, the very air of the market seemed to be vibrating with excitement. Crowds huddled tightly around the cramped wooden stalls as everyone tried to catch even a glimpse of the expensive goods. After all, this was not just an average market for common folk, it was for those well off enough to afford the right to be here, and the rare goods sang off that fact with ease. Bright fabrics, fur trimmings, spices, and even strange pets brought from other lands were all proudly put on display for the onlookers, much to the glee of the greedy-eyed customers with their coin fattened money pouches.

It seemed everyone in the city had their minds on the coming games, and this location was no exception. Decoration banners and flags were being strung where possible for the coming events, and all put up by men on wobbly ladders balancing carelessly upon the uneven cobble stones.

Laughter was never far to be heard on the air, and those many of those passing pointed at the decorations and gained a skip in their step as they continued on.

Compared to the perfectly cleaned roads of the market, the place where Valerlanta was standing now seemed like one of the largest of contrasts.

In the alleys, one cared if there was animal droppings or if dogs fought over rotting scraps, so places like this haunted the sparkling clean act of those who lived here like a much darker shadow. While they pretended that places like this did not exist, many carried perfume balls on a chain to push off the smell the places caused.

An act; their entire lives were a giant play pretending to live somewhere better than they did.

It almost rekindled an old sort of hatred in her chest, but then a passing stray dog brushed her leg as it passed, bringing Valerlanta back into the moment.

Peeking further around the alley, the thief looked just in time to see two men drop off what she was hoping for, before they turned and disappeared into the sea of people.

Right where specified was a simple but large crate; but there was also more than she was expecting; two things to be exact. Two fine horses were waiting attached to a small cart. They were not a rich knights horse breed to say the least, they were simply a sort of mix breed draft horse of some kind, but they would do perfectly well.

Perhaps a little too perfectly.

She could not help but wonder which of the men would suddenly turn on her as she approached the cart. Perhaps all of them would; she could picture Askyel going through that much trouble to stroke his own ego.

Would they turn from their daily chores and face her with weapons revealed from the folds of their clothes?

'No.' Valerlanta shook her head sharply. *'Their clothes are not nearly large enough for that, Val. They could not hide more than a small knife!'*

Turning back, she saw both Venic and Alstred approaching.

Alstred saw her and the bruises still on her face, and his expression became a torrent of emotions. Suddenly his pace quickened, and he grabbed her by her shoulders, and she let him.

"What were you thinking?" He asked, shaking her. "Why did you go alone? Why did you not wait for us?"

Before she could answer, a hand came up onto the shoulder of Alstred. "What is done is done, Alstred. Just let her go for now."

Alstred stayed staring for a moment longer; angry eyes looking down into hers, then he let out a breath and his one hand moved to ruffle her hair until her hat was on the ground and her hair was scattered all over her face. It was a strange sort of revenge, but it was enough to make him smile after looking at her.

"Never again." He warned as she sighed with irritation and worked to sort her hair back as it was.

She nodded.

"Good, then let us get to work, shall we?" Alstred left to make his way through the crowd and towards the cart. He was to go around one way, and her the other, so that the three of them would have a full triangle of observation on the cart, then they would decide on what to do.

Now it was only her and Venic left in the alley.

She turned to face him, and he looked at her with a rather grim expression that was enough to cause a momentary ripple in her confidence.

"Everything will be fine." Valerlanta reminded him. "Alstred and I are more than used to this game, so we know what to look for when it comes to traps."

Alstred had showed up just that morning, and they were quick to put him to use.

He let out a breath and ran a hand through his hair. "I am too far back, I am the furthest position from the crate."

"We did not have any clothes to fit you, and as you are now, you would stand out far too much. It is better if you stay here where no one will notice you. Alstred will be doing the work, so all you and I have to do is stand and watch."

He did not seem convinced. He looked at her with his lips pressed into a thin line, and his eyes darting over her face, looking for something.

She supposed that she should not be too surprised by his reaction to the plan; after all, he did not know that she had been healing herself. He had no idea that movements were now becoming easy to her.

In truth, part of her thought Venic was lucky for being able to stay in his clothes. The pants she wore were rough on her skin, but what was worse was the tight wrappings on her chest that with movement caused her to realize she was still sore in some places. As but a single breath cause a flicker of memory of how the pain began, she found herself wishing for her old clothes.

At least with her hair in a quick knotted bun, and tucked it into the hat she pulled on, none would question her gender, so ignoring the pain did have some benefits. Of course, anyone in her father's guild would recognize her mask, but no one else should pay attention. Even from where she stood, she could see a small handful of people wearing masks to cover ugly scars or marks left from sickness. It was an odd sort of custom made so that people might be more likely to care for her personality rather than their appearance, and it worked greatly in her favour.

Finally, letting out a sigh, Venic nodded her off, so the thief smiled and swiftly disappeared into the crowd and to her location.

As Valerlanta peered under the brim of her stolen hat while pretending to be interested in a barrel of fish, she carefully eyed the people around her, but still saw nothing that worried her, not that it mattered. Even if there was an obvious danger, did they have any other choice but to try?

As if to answer her quiet question, a small group of young men in rather worn clothes approached the cart and eyed it with an unnerving amount of interest that sent a chill up her spine.

Heart starting to slam, Valerlanta let her eyes dart to where Alstred was waiting, but his eyes were only for the three men. Even from where she was across the market, she could see his muscled arms tense and his brow narrow as he looked on at the three.

'Just wait,' She begged the tall blonde with her mind. *'Just wait a little longer.'*

The boys approached the crate, and casually glanced inside, and Valerlanta held her breath as they did.

Nothing happened.

No men snuck upon them with weapons; which to her could only mean one thing; Askyel really did want to help her.

And that help he gave was about to go to the wrong people.

A few seconds, that was all they would have before the three would have the cart and the only way to get it back would be by creating a scene. She had to think of something, fast.

The youths glanced around for the carts owners, and Valerlanta diverted her eyes as they looked her direction.

However, when she looked back, a man in bright red clothes was blocking her sight. He stood with tense legs, as if trying to make himself look taller than he was, and his arms were folded across his chest. A thick brown brow rose at her as he scrutinized her from head to toe.

"Your face is not one that I can say that I know." He said, his voice slippery as a fish.

"No, it would not be, I am a traveler here." Valerlanta said, trying to sound pleasant, though she really wanted to push the man aside to get a better view. Instead she settled for side-stepping so she could see over his shoulder.

Alstred was now shooting forward through the crowd. He ducked and dodged the bodies attached. Despite his best efforts to go fast, it was like trying to walk upstream.

"Perhaps, it might be because your face is one that you want to hide?" The man said, also stepping to the side so he could again block her view. He eyed her mask and she saw his jaw tense.

"No, it is nothing of the sort! I apologize if that is the message it gives but-" She again stepped for a view. "-unfortunately my reasoning's for wearing this mask are much less exciting. I got some ghastly burns as a child is all, and people are far more comfortable with looking at the unknown than looking at something that looks painful. Now if you do excuse me, I have a task I was sent here to fulfill..."

She went to step around him, but he grabbed her tightly by the arm with a quick hand.

"This here is my market. It is my job to inspect anyone suspected of selling faulty goods, as well as to keep out trouble makers and thieves. You would not be either of those two, would you?" He hissed, spit spraying from his clenched teeth and onto her mask.

Calmly, Valerlanta reached up an wiped the liquid away, without once breaking her gaze with the man. "Let go, sir. I do not appreciate you ruining such a beautiful day with your accusatory tone."

Then she twisted out of his grip and dove into the crowd of people before he could catch hold of her again. As she weaved through the tangled knots of arms, treading deeper and deeper into the heart of the crowd in order to keep distance between her and the strange man, Alstred was nearing the men.

'Wait, Alstred, wait!' She glanced at one of the banners being stretched out by a rope high above, and wondered if she could make it in time. If she could knock the ladder, the man upon it would fall, drawing attention in the general area of the cart. For any thief, such wandering eyes of a crowd would be a deterrent enough to back off from a steal.

If Alstred waited long enough for her to try.

She was almost at the ladder near the cart now.

As one of the three youths was testing he reigns of the cart, Alstred tapped on the shoulder of an old shopper he passed and muttered a gruff. "Excuse me?"

With both arms full of wood, the man turned towards the blonde, and hit one of the young thieves right in the back of the head.

Reigns still in hand, the boy stumbled with a shout of surprise and outrage, and turned back to face the older man.

"That hurt!"

"Oh, I apologize!" The old man said with wide eyes. "What was it that you needed?"

"Needed? What are you going on about, old man? Are you crazy?" The youth pointed at the elderly man threateningly, and as he did, Alstred ducked under his arm, and effortlessly snatched away the reigns and sprang up onto the wagon.

For a second, Alstred sat there, as if panicking as he realized he should have thought a little further.

"Uh. Go horses?" Alstred shouted, whipping the reigns.

Snorting in excitement and not caring if it was the right command or not, one of the horses pawed forward, much to the surprise of the three men. The other horse also gave in, and the wagon lurched into movement.

"Hey!" The closest youth to Valerlanta called, turning back to grab hold of the cart, but before he could she dove on him and pulled his hood over his eyes, ignoring as he thrashed.

The cart was starting to pick up speed now, and the end of it rushed past her in a clop of horse hooves.

"Ashes!" Valerlanta swore, sticking out her leg and pushing her captor sideways over it so he landed hard on the ground, and she escaped after the cart.

Another boy tried to jump on the cart as it rattled over the cobblestones, leaving Alstred both trying to drive, and also kick the attacker off.

Grabbing hold of his kicking foot, the boy tried to pull the larger man off, while in turn also using his large leg to climb in.

His bottom slid across the bench, and as he reached the edge of the seat, Alstred temporarily discarded the reigns to fall at his feet so he could reach behind him and let his fingertips brush the crate.

Grasping the lid, he brought it up in both hands, and smashed it into the man's face.

The boy lost his hold and fell backwards, causing the thief to smile ruefully as he watched him roll across the ground.

Gasping in surprise over the sudden body, Valerlanta was forced to jump over the rolling boy as she attempted to keep pace with the near running horses.

"Alstred!" She called as she was being left behind. "Alstred, stop!"

Clearly not hearing what she was saying, he looked back and smiled at her, although his glee was short lived as a sharp scream reminded him of a more pressing issue.

Valerlanta saw a woman dive to the side in order to avoid the speeding cart, and several more people parted with shouts of surprise.

She saw him bend forward in the seat, fumbling for the reigns until his fingers finally closed around them, and he pulled them back like she had seen riders sometimes do.

Instead of stopping, the horses only snorted in annoyance and pulled forward, waiting for a vocal command.

"Stop, stop, stop!" Valerlanta screamed at the horses as they nearly ran down a man with a walking stick.

Squeaking in terror, Alstred gave up trying to make them stop, and instead tried to steer the thundering horses through the crowds of people, leaving her breathing hard to chase him.

"Alstred!" Hearing the name over the screams, Valerlanta looked to see Venic also struggling to keep up while snaking through the crowd, though he was having better luck in keeping up. "Stop, you fool! Stop the cart!"

"How?!" Alstred screeched back then his mouth fell open as a low hanging flag came towards him. Ducking just in time, the cart by fine, but the man adjusting the sign fell off the barrel he was using for height. Sign coming down towards her, Valerlanta dove and rolled, and kept running as the sign came down behind her.

'What can we do?!' She wondered, looking at Venic for guidance, but he was already acting.

Picking up speed, Venic bolted up a staircase, and when he reached the top stone, he sprang into the air towards the cart. Then he disappeared from view, and for a long moment she thought he missed and landed on the hard road, but then his brown head of hair popped up in the back beside the crate.

"Hey, stop there!" A solider called, appearing on her left as both the cart-and the masked thief-sped past.

"I am bloody well trying!" Alstred screamed in answer, then suddenly the reigns were snatched from his hands as Venic came up beside him and pulled back on the reigns.

"Whoa." He called confidently. "Whoa there, easy now."

The horses slowed to a trot, and Venic continued the tight hold on the reigns until they gradually stopped completely. "Whoa there, whoa."

As she caught up, the horses shuttered, but did stay, whooshes of air coming from their nostrils.

"I-Idiot." Valerlanta breathed, punching the blonde in the leg as she collapsed against the cart.

The blonde only grunted in reply, his whole body slumped forward, and hand on his chest as if to calm his heart.

Venic was leaning back in his seat; the knight let his head fall back so his face was too the sky. He too was breathing hard, his chest rising and falling in quick gushes of air, while she was downright gasping.

"'I am going to stand and watch. Everything will be fine.' Is that not what you said?" Venic asked, and much to her surprise, he let out a soft chuckle. He rolled his head over to look down at her and a smile came to his lips. "Just as I suspected, staying out of trouble is impossible for you two."

"It was not me this time!" She pointed out as Alstred shot back up and crossed his arms over his chest.

"Oh come now, this was hardly my fault! These things are terrifying and impossible to control! I suspect they are part demon! My uncle had horses like that once and-" The blonde was interrupted as Valerlanta reached up and pulled him right out of the cart. He fell into the dirt with a squeak of surprise.

"No excuses!" She shot, motioning to her flat chest. "Do you have any idea how hard it is to run like this?"

However, that only caused him to giggle and opened his mouth to probably let out an insult, but she gave him no time before diving on him, elbow first.

As they fought, Venic got down from the cart, pulled her away from pulling the blondes ear, and pressed the reigns back into her hands while brushing past her.

"Children! Calm yourselves." Was all he said, his words heavy with amusement.

As he walked around the cart, the solider trying to keep up from before finally reached them.

"What did you think you were doing? People could have been killed!" The solider snarled at Alstred and Valerlanta before Venic stepped between them, drawing his cloak far around his clothes. "Ah sorry! A small group of men tried to steal our master's cart, and the boy here is not so bright, and panicked! This is exactly why our master says the boy will never be good for anything; completely useless he is!" Venic shook his head with a sad smile

"He is always wasting our masters hard earned coins simply by failing to follow a simple task; like keeping an eye on a cart, should be easy enough, but no! Instead he gets distracted by shiny goods, and nearly has the whole cart stolen! Then, to make matters worse, he near tramples the whole crowd! If this keeps up, I am certain my master's heart will fail. Which is why, I must beg you to please let us go unnoticed just this one time? You do look like an understanding fellow, after all."

The solider ran a hand through his hair and sighed as heavy as the horses were. He looked back at Alstred with strict eyes. "Fine, but do not let it happen again, understand?"

Venic nodded eagerly and bowed several times at the hip. "Thank you, thank you so much."

The man left and Venic glanced back at them, his mouth suddenly pinched into a thin line as if to keep from smiling. Despite this effort, he started to chuckle.

Valerlanta and Alstred glanced at each other, and in seconds, all three were laughing so hard that they had to lean against the cart to keep standing.

"Alstred, you idiot!" Valerlanta breathed through gasps of breath.

He shrugged innocently.

"Why is there even horses?" Venic asked, quickly gaining his composure again.

"An extra gift?" Valerlanta suggested with a smirk. "Perhaps a way of saying that he is serious?"

"Or he is trying to win someone over. Most likely me, because of my handsome looks. Poor boy does not know that men are not in my tastes list."

Venic and Valerlanta exchanged glances, and then both rolled their eyes.

"Right; that must be it." Venic said, words dripping with sarcasm. "Well, either way, we should get moving. A crowd has started to gather to see what we will do next."

Valerlanta glanced at the horses then shook her head. "I think I will walk."

Venic nodded and hopped in the cart himself, but Alstred remained where he was, as if stuck firmly to the spot. The swordsman raised a brow at him; an amused twitch tugging at the corners of her mouth.

"No." Alstred told them in response to his wordless question. "I think I will walk with Valerlanta this time."

« Chapter 15 »

After the last whistle escaped her lips, Valerlanta let her hands fall at her sides, and her eyes linger on the site before her.

She heard the reply, and took in all the information carefully.

Her father would comply to her requests.

When the last note sounded, Valerlanta was left with the near silence of the morning.

Behind her was the quiet fields and farmlands, and before her was the song of birds welcoming the morning. Standing at the very edge, her feet were only a single step from entering her world of green again, she could easily enter and disappear until she wanted to be found, but instead she spun back around and made her way down the dirt road.

When she returned to the farm, she nodded at the quiet farmer as he was making his way out to work his fields, and the man waved in a small greeting.

He was still letting them pay to sleep in his barn, and since they had arrived, Valerlanta could not help but notice that no one visited the man, nor did he leave to visit anyone. He lived with only the lonely silence, which she would not find strange if he did not have a barn and fairly large house. His farm was clearly once a rich one, but some event must have changed that.

The farm was still when Valerlanta neared to the barn, so instead of potentially waking the two men, she made her way over to the fence that divided the farmers land from the one next to it. Sun danced across the sea of farms, and even Valerlanta had to admit there was some beauty to it. Although she preferred the green of leaves and the scent of moss, there was also something to be said for a place so open that the ground seemed to meet with the sky.

Noise came behind her, and she looked back briefly to see Venic emerge. He saw her, and nodded before walking over to the rain-barrel to wash his face.

She looked back over the scene, and after some time, Venic joined her. They both stood, watching the last of the sunrise.

"You know," Venic started, but he was not looking her way. Instead, his eyes were fixed on the sky. "After this is over, if you are fine with another adventure...-" he trailed off to run a hand through his hair. "What I mean to say is that I could use some help-or I would like the company if you did decide to come along-"He looked at her, and she saw his brows were creased as if frustrated, but his eyes glimmered with worry of her reaction. "With me. Maybe even Alstred if he agrees."

Valerlanta blinked in surprise, but before she could even think about an answer, Alstred joined them outside, and Venic turned away from her, his expression clouded over.

"Well, shall we get ready?" Alstred asked, chipper as always. He had already trimmed down his beard, and his hair was brushed out, causing his appearance to already look almost entirely changed from the hairy and dirty man she knew. Even his hair had some sort of charcoal mixture brushed into it; making his hair considerably darker. Now all he had to do was get changed.

Venic nodded, and disappeared into the barn without looking at her.

Alstred lingered before following, raising his brow at Valerlanta. "You stay out here. No peeking, young lady."

"Like I would!" Valerlanta snarled, picking up a rock and tossing it at him as he ducked inside the barn with a laugh.

Hands on her hip, Valerlanta let out an exasperated sigh, and shook her eyes as she let her eyes look back to the city that they would soon be heading to.

The sun had returned fully, and by the time the set once again, the three would hopefully be in the castle finishing this. No doubt, the king would have heard that both Venic and Valerlanta had surely died in the flour-mill explosion; and as he had his men looking for their bodies-and the treasure-in the river, the three would complete everything right under his nose.

"What do you think?" Alstred asked as both him and Venic emerged again, both in the plated armour of knights. Valerlanta looked on at them with an odd sense of disappointment. The armour fitted them both perfectly; and would easily blend them into the world she would never know.

Valerlanta put on a thoughtful expression and walked around them in a circle. They stood willingly, both with amused expressions.

When she came to a stop, she nodded in approval. "It worked! You do indeed look like my favorite kind of target practise!"

Venic laughed, but Astred dove at her. She moved to escape, but his long arms snatched her up. One arm went around her neck, while his other hand pinched a good chunk of her cheek.

"Now see here!" He snarled playfully as she attempted to swat him away. "We went through all this work, and all you can think of is target practice? Is that the best compliment you have for a dashing man, such as myself?"

Thinking of nothing else to do against the armour-clad man, she brought her fist back, and smacked him right in the nose. The huge man recoiled with a whimper, rubbing his nose and going on about how mean she could be, while Valerlanta and Venic prepared to leave.

When done, the two men went to town upon their new horses, with Valerlanta following at a distance, wearing the guise of a knight's apprentice.

They approached the castle, and crowds grew thicker. Along the way there was the thick smell of exotic spices, performers lulling people into hushed tones to hear tales of valiant heroes, and even music from instruments she had never seen before.

One of the instruments had a loud crying sound that occurred when the man squeezed what appeared to be a sack of some sort with hollow sticks coming from it. Valerlanta had no idea what to call it, but whatever it was, it made her heart pound with excitement.

When the crowds neared their thickest and the sounds of voices came as a steady roar like crashing waves, Valerlanta saw her first knights. Some were barely the age of 15, hardly even men in her opinion, but others rode through the area with carefully polished armour, and heads raised proudly. People jumped out of their wake, and some women even swooned and attempted to give favours of various items to those who passed.

One passed on a shire horse fairly close to Valerlanta, and she suddenly felt small as the towering knight passed by.

The horse snorted at her as it went, as if in dislike, and Valerlanta glared back with similar feeling.

After successfully snaking through the thickest groups of people, the two boys made it to a rather flamboyantly dressed man with a ruffled collar and pointed boots. He was speaking to a servant, and shooed him off with a squeaky voice as the men approached.

While the man carefully scrutinized the two men, Valerlanta casually went not far off to a crudely made wooden fence where she could pretend to watch the games shoulder-to-shoulder with other people, but really she was listening in.

Out in the field some young knights-to-be were starting off the day with some jousts. As she watched, she felt her breath catch involuntarily as she saw a lance shatter on the other boy, throwing him off his horse. The crowd cheered wildly, and the boy gingerly picked himself off the ground.

"And who might you two be?" The herald squeaked from behind her.

"Knights traveling from afar under the crest of Isalden." Venic replied confidently. "We are here to grace the tournament with our talents."

Valerlanta rolled her eyes at that, but the man seemed interested, and even more so after the coinage was probably being placed in front of him.

It was her coinage, unfortunately, and the last of it too. Though perhaps after today, she would have more than enough coin again.

Her gaze fell hungrily upon the fat purse of the well-dressed man beside her.

"Where I am from those competing pay a fine to do so; that is the same case here, am I right?" Venic cooed, and Valerlanta could almost hear the dark haired knight grinning.

"Oh yes, of course!" The herald lied smoothly. "And by what name can I have you announced as?"

"I am Kellun Hendranill, and this man beside me Ulaknen Janif. We both ride under the same crest."

"Right, right. Everything is settled then! Would you two sirs like to join me to watch the games after some cool spirits? I have a shaded tent away from these...common folk."

The two men agreed, and much to Valerlanta's dismay, they withdrew to a place in which she could not follow; a tent with guards carefully positioned outside to ward off commoners and other folk.

As they disappeared inside, Valerlanta frowned deeply and could only watch as the tent opening folded closed behind Alstred; shielding both men from view.

Nothing else to do, Valerlanta broke her gaze from the fabric barrier between her and her companions, and reluctantly looked back to the games. Two new boys were dueling now; both charging at each other from either side of the fence with lances drawn high.

As she stood there, a similarly hooded man came up behind her, and looked over her shoulder with mock interest.

"Enjoying the games?" The familiar voice purred, and Valerlanta glanced back without surprise to see Askyel himself there. Although he preferred to dirty his hands through the use of others, Valerlanta knew that a player of a game could not help but want to see the outcome themselves.

"Mostly fair enough, and yourself?"

"I more so come for the goods, myself. During a tournament like this, you can purchase more goods from overseas than any other time."

"Fascinating."

He leaned in a little closer, so she could feel his warm breath on her ear. "I see that the armour fit fine enough?"

"Perfectly, so far. I trust they will stay that way?"

"Of course. I may sell things of illegal value, but I am still a businessman. My reputation directly influences my volume of returning customers; so it would do me harm to fail to stand up properly in a time such as this."

She glanced back, and eyed him suspiciously, and could not help but notice how his lips twitched in the working of a near smile. Instead, his eyes broke from hers, and settled on the large castle that rose up like a mountain. "Soon my assistant will come to take you to my storehouse just off of the market; and the news she carries is terribly important. So important, in fact, that it cannot be said here among so many ears. Do go there with her, thief Valerlanta. Your life, and the lives of many others, just might depend on it."

Before she could even utter a word of question, he was gone, disappearing as quickly as he came.

Crowds again cheered, and a boy was carried away on a stretcher.

While the area was being cleaned up, the crowd shifted its attention to a different form of entertainment.

Two men were facing off in full armour, circling each other with swords.

And Venic was one of them.

His opponent attacked, and Venic used his shield to take a blow, and as momentum curved the opponent's blade upwards, and Venic pushed it away with his shield and used the second of opening to bring his sword into the man's side. The opponent stumbled at the sudden hit, and it was all over. Venic knocked the man over with several smashes of his sword, then suddenly seemed to realize he was winning. He went to strike, then faked a stumble and fell onto his back. His opponent sprang up, and took advantage of Venic's fall by bringing a sword to his neck.

Venic stayed down and was disqualified.

'He pretended to lose.' Valerlanta realized. *'We only had them fight for the chance to get into the castle, but something must have been said in the tent to make Venic realize it was not worth it.'*

Her thoughts fell short at that as she watched as Venic exited the ring, and the next two to duel entered.

"Did you see that?" A man whispered to his female companion from somewhere behind her. "I do not believe I have ever seen someone with such talent."

"I agree." The woman said. "I think it will be him I shall cheer for in the next round."

There was a gasp through the crowd and Valerlanta glanced back in time to see a man bring down a blade on an unarmed opponent who was kneeling on the ground.

The blade came down on the armour at the base of the fallen man's neck, and the he crumpled before letting out spine tingling screams.

The larger man put up his arms, and despite the yells of the injured opponent, the crowd roared with excitement.

Valerlanta frowned.

She did not like the looks of that giant of a man. He won this match, so he was going to move onto the grand melee-a full out battle until there was only one man standing- and he could be a threat to Alstred and Venic.

Although, perhaps not...

If she snuck into his tent, she might be able to...-

"Excuse me?" A voice came from behind her, startling the thief from her thoughts. Looking back, Valerlanta saw a woman standing there that seemed somehow familiar. The pretty woman wore a worn out cloak, but it was not going to fool Valerlanta. One look at her perfect and pale skin was enough for Valerlanta to know that this woman was no commoner. Her icy blue eyes locked on the thieves with an unnerving amount of confidence.

Askyel's assistant.

What was her name again? Ah yes, Sellclie was it?

"We need to talk." The woman said. "In private, if you would."

"Why?" Valerlanta pressed. "What cannot be said in the safety of a crowd?"

The woman did not even flinch at the thief's hesitation to follow her. Instead, she kept that cold expression and casually brushed a black strand of hair back behind her ear.

"It is too important to risk being heard by the ears of others." The assistant replied easily. "I was told to tell you, and only you. I swear that no harm will come to you but I need to deliver this message. I can promise you this, he would not have sent me if he did not think that it was very important."

Valerlanta let her eyes narrow into a glare. She trusted this woman just as little as she trusted Askyel himself, and yet, a glimmer of curiosity was slowly eating away her suspicion.

"Where?" Was all she asked.

"This way, please." Then the woman turned away, and left without her even saying she would follow. Valerlanta watched her go, and then let her eyes drift around her hesitantly one last time before she followed.

The woman led her down the road, away from the crowd. Her steps were confident and fast, as if she had walked this way hundreds of times before, though she probably had.

They turned onto a road behind the market, and then she glanced around before opening the door to a building and holding it open for the thief.

Valerlanta glanced all over, but saw no signs of a trap. Yet, at least.

"You first." Valerlanta said, nodding towards the door.

Rolling her eyes, the assistant entered, and Valerlanta followed. The thief glanced around inside, but the room was empty except for crates of what Valerlanta could only see as fabric.

"Close the door behind you, please."

Valerlanta raised a brow, reluctant to shut her closest exit.

"I promise you that we are quite alone in here, so please, close the door."

'Like your promise means anything to me.' Valerlanta thought, but she did close the door, and the wooden latch clicked shut behind her.

With it shut, the only light came from the cracks in the crudely made door. As her eyes adjusted to the change, she saw golden light seeped in from the edges of the wood, causing dust to be seen floating lightly in the beams. The assistant was still there, thankfully, and regarded Valerlanta with a harsh gaze, as if judging her entire character.

Then, as if deciding it was not her choice, she let out a long sigh, and brought something from the folds of her skirt and handed it to the thief. It was a rolled up piece of parchment, from the looks of it, and old too, if the tattered edges were any indication.

Valerlanta glanced at the assistant in warning one last time before she undid the cloth holding the parchment shut, and unrolled it it see.

The insides were breathtaking. Colors were painted upon the one single page that Val had scarcely seen in the entire forest. Within the box holding the first letter was a huge tree with an opening in the middle. On one side was a man with a crown-a king, and on the other side from within the tree was a woman with pointed ears.

An elf.

It was the story; the story from her book!

Her eyes quickly skimmed across to the other letters, but of course she could not read it.

Putting on an unimpressed face, Valerlanta lowered the parchment.

The assistant was waiting patiently, her face unreadable.

"What does it say?" Valerlanta said finally, and could not help but notice a twitch of a smile on the assistance lips, as if this was some sort of victory for the assistant.

"It says what it is that the king is truly after." She answered plainly, as if it should be obvious.

"I see, and Askyel thought he should tell me? Why?"

"Master Lochsell thinks there is something in you worth staking his money on. For some reason that I do not know, he thinks that you will someday be worth the money of having on his side." Her lip curled slightly at that, but was quickly smoothed out as she put on her blank face again. Jealousy, perhaps? For what, though? "However, that is not the issue here. The issue here is that Askyel got his hands on that parchment through some certain sources, and he cannot have it on him any longer, nor anyone connected to him. Particularly if it does happen that you should fail."

"Why?" Valerlanta pressed. "What does it say?"

The black haired woman sucked in a breath, and said; "It explains that the treasure to be gained from those keys you collected does not lead to treasure any treasure that can be held in your hands at all; the treasure is power. Pure, collected, power, trapped within the very tree the elves once used as a portal to and from their world. To answer as to why; Askyel cannot have that with him is because if the king should gain that power, nothing will be able to stop him. Askyel can have no ties to you; particularly with the arrival of the king today."

Valerlanta felt her stomach sink and she grasped backward onto the table behind her to keep from falling. Standing very still, Valerlanta let the information sink in. *'The elf, she was real. She was real, and the king is coming here.'*

She should have known.

When the king married the elf, all power was sucked away from the kingdom except for those who have royal blood. However, that could all be changed if the king found the source of those powers. If that happened, he could give a whole army their powers, and just as said in the pact with the elf; as his boarders grows so will the spell that drains all powers. Kingdoms that are dependent on their magic for defense and daily life will suddenly become defenseless as the king takes over.

Nothing will stop him.

Nothing.

She felt as if her chest and throat were constricting all the air from her body as if the king's dark shadow was behind her, slowly enclosing her in a cold grip.

"The task that I was sent here to complete is now finished, so I will be on my way." The woman briskly crossed the room, and then the door closed behind her, leaving Valerlanta alone in the darkness as she gasped for breath.

'Does Venic know?' She wondered. *'Is that why he never destroyed the puzzles? Because he wanted the power? Or did he too believe in the treasure?'*

Her mind swam, and she found herself sinking to the ground. Settling on the cold ground she looked at the parchment and felt a shutter go through her body.

'The king is coming here.' Her mind sang over and over again. *'The king is coming himself. You should run, Val. You should leave now.'*

~

When Valerlanta finally gathered the bravery to move, it felt like she was walking in a state of drunkenness. She stumbled through the crowds, watching as the blurred faces of various people swept by her as her feet carried her aimlessly.

She heard only the odd word of those passing, and most of what she heard made her knees feel so weak she was sure she would stumble.

"The king is here!" They called. "The king has arrived."

She bumped into something, and realized she was back at the fence where people were watching the games. Her fingers grasped the smooth worn wood, glad to be holding something solid.

'The king is here. The king has arrived!' Her mind said over and over, causing her stomach to threaten to turn.

Bringing up a hand, she placed it across her forehead and squeezed her eyes shut, hoping to make the world darker; a little less overwhelming.

As she moved her fingers to rub a temple, her fingers felt something and her eyes flickered open again.

Her mask.

"I am not her anymore." She uttered under her breath, as if that alone would make it true.

The sword fighting was over, and now knights with horses and lances were taking turns to see who could catch the most hanging rings in one ride.

What was she going to do?

Without warning, a hand gripped her arm in a tight grip.

Spinning around, Valerlanta saw Venic reaching through the crowd to grab her. "I have been calling you!" He said, and then his lips pressed in a thin line as he looked her over. "You are pale, what happened? Are you well?"

She had to tell him-she had to tell him the full extent of the power he was searching for-and although she knew that, Valerlanta shook her head. "Not here." Then looked around and said. "Where is Alstred? Is he not with you?"

"He went to go find us some food; he will meet us back at the farm. Come, will talk back there."

They went right away, quickly making their way through the crowds of people and back to the countryside. Along the way, Venic continued to send her little glances. The worry on her face must have been more clear than she had thought.

Alstred caught up with them on the way; his arms full of food he clearly stole, but she did not pay him any heed.

'It will be ok.' She told herself. *'We are almost back.'*

A scream echoed throughout the quiet air, causing Valerlanta to jump in surprise.

It came again, and both were able to pinpoint the sound; it was coming from the same direction as the farm.

Exchanging glances, the three companions hesitated, and then Venic spurred on his horse, and the horse galloped up the road.

"Wait!" Valerlanta called, trying to follow fast as she could on foot, but soon the horse was far ahead.

When they reached the farm, they saw what the commotion was about in a matter of seconds.

A woman stood at the edge of the farm, her arms hugging herself and her body bent at the knees as if to curl into herself and make herself as small as possible.

Her wide eyes were locked on something bloody steps away from her.

The farmer was dead.

Venic's horse was at the barn without a rider.

"Venic!" Valerlanta called, running over to the hay pile that hid her bow. Pulling out an arrow, the thief quickly knocked it, and rushed to find the knight. "Stay here and cover my back." She shouted to Alstred as she went.

Valerlanta followed her bow inside the barn, quickly looking around for any sign of danger. Hay was scattered in all directions, and all the large animals the barn had held were gone, but there was no movement to alarm her.

Venic was standing near the back, his whole body leaning on a beam as if he was no longer able to support himself.

One more careful glance around the barn, then Valerlanta lowered her bow and walked up to the knight.

What she saw made her stomach turn.

Their hiding spot, the spot in the rafters, had a ladder perched against it.

The three treasures were gone.

« Chapter 16 »

Quickly leaving the barn to avoid becoming suspects, the three stood at the base a large tree, watching from afar as a group steadily grew larger and larger at the farm.

Men on horses were arriving for the city too, so the three companions would probably have to leave soon to avoid being seen.

Temporarily freed from the cart, the two horses ate happily from the long grasses and Venic stood beside one, absentmindedly stroking its side as he stared in the distance. His eyes were glazed over, as it he were not seeing the scene at all, but instead seeing his own troubles placed before him.

Everything was silent, as if even the birds were surprised by the sudden death.

"What are we going to do?" She asked, finally breaking the silence. Her voice sounded small, so hopeless.

"What can we do?" Venic said, anger heavy on his voice. "It is over, we lost."

Even Alstred did not seem to have an argument to that, he just sat against the tree looking lost, but Valerlanta shook her head.

"No, we cannot stop here, we cannot!"

"What else can we do?" Venic shot. "Go against a whole army? For what? Your precious treasure? Does it mean so much to you that you would even risk the lives of your friends to gain it? Or do we not really mean that little to you to even be called that?"

Anger splashed over the worry inside her chest, and before she could stop herself she said. "Oh yes, very well spoken for a man working for the king! So when were you planning to kill us? Before, or after? I know everything, you know! You were hired by the king to pretend like you were on the run, but really at the last moment you were told to turn on us, and as such become a hero, am I right? Crowds would swoon at your very feet, and everyone would chant your name; is that what you were picturing? Well how about this, did you know that the king was going to betray you too? As soon as you delivered him his treasure, he was going to kill you. Instead of you, he would be called a hero if he did that, and no one would suspect a thing! You were just his puppet!"

Venic was silent through her whole outburst, and even after she finished, he stood there, looking at her with an emotionless gaze.

"I knew." He said finally. "I knew what he was planning to do. I found out only just before I left."

Valerlanta blinked in surprise at that. "What?"

"You were right, I was going to betray you; my lifestyle was depending on it. I was going to kill you-or rather your father as it was supposed to be- and become a hero." He smiled bitterly. "However, the king had different plans. I was suspicious of him from the start, so I paid off a maid to do some spying on the king, and I found out. I still went though; instead of going into hiding, I wanted to take the kings treasure right from under him. I wanted to make him regret betraying me."

"It was revenge." Valerlanta realized.

"It was revenge." He confirmed. "I was still going to kill you, otherwise you would have caused a problem in the end, however..." His eyes looked to the castle. "I changed my mind. Not that it matters now."

"It does matter. If we do not at least try, thousands of people will die."

Now both Alstred and Venic looked at her with the same amount of shock.

Alstred gingerly got up, using the tree for support as he apparently pulled on his still injured muscles. "What are you talking about, Val?"

The shadow of the tree suddenly felt longer as she readied to tell them.

Hesitantly, Valerlanta brought out the parchment and tried to hand it to Venic, but he seemed reluctant to grab it, as if dreading what was inside. He simply looked into her eyes, as if not believing that she was still capable of hiding things from him.

Her hand was still outstretched, the parchment waiting there, so instead Alstred snatched it.

She watched his eyes go wide as he read what she could not, then his hands fell down at his sides, his face paling. That made Venic grab it as well, and though there was surprise there, he made little other reaction. "How long have you had this? When did you find out?!"

"I-I. When I disappeared today, it was because Askyel's assistant came to collect me. She gave me this, and told me everything." He looked at her as if not fully believing her. "I am not lying! Why would I hold this back? If I knew, I would have sunk them all at the bottom of the sea! Or buried them all in the forest where no on would find them! Instead..." She trailed off when she saw the look Alstred was giving the swordsman. The tall man was staring, and with every growing second, more and more rage settled on his face.

Suddenly, Alstred burst forward and roughly grabbed Venic just under his neck by his cloak; forcing him to look up at him. "You knew? You knew this whole time that there was no treasure? Are you saying that you lead us this whole time for your idiotic revenge?"

Venic successfully kept a blank face. "Yes."

Valerlanta felt her eyes widen and her legs feel weak.

Alstred could not cage his rage any more. Within a blink of an eye, a fist smashed into the swordsman cheek; knocking him back several steps.

Venic touched the spot, but made no attempt to fight back. His eyes shifted from the blonde to the thief; and Valerlanta stepped away from him; taking everything in. "Why?" She murmured, then rage overtook her for a moment, and a scream jumped into her voice. "Why did you make us believe a lie this whole time? I thought we were friends!"

Something flashed in the swordsman eyes, and his mouth opened to say something, but was silenced as once again a fist met his face; and this time knocked him off his feet. Venic simply took it and stared up at Alstred; not even bothering to get up.

"Speak! Tell us what important reason you could have for this?" Alstred snarled. He moved as if to attack Venic again, but Valerlanta jumped forward and grabbed his arm, stopping him.

"Alstred, stop!" She snarled, struggling against his huge muscled arm. "This will not help!"

"How could you do this to the only friends you have?" Alstred yelled, ignoring the thief and trying to shake her off. "After all the three of us have been through together?"

Still Venic said nothing, and simply allowed the two to think of him as horribly as they wished to. His eyes found hers again, and Valerlanta found it hard to breathe.

"I have to go." Valerlanta said finally. "All that will happen, it is because of my actions, and I have to make it right.

'I should have listened to her, I should have destroyed them!'

"No!" Alstred snarled at her. "He is right, this is done, and if the world burns because of it, the king and his pet here will be the cause; no one else."

"It can not be done, I will not let it! I am stronger than that." She shot, releasing Alstred and grabbing her things from the cart. "You two will only slow me down. I will sneak into the castle and end this myself."

"It will only lead to your death!" Venic finally spoke up; climbing back to his feet. "If you go, you will die in that castle! You can not beat the king;

not anymore. We lost that chance. It is done; it is over, so give up!"

"Never." Valerlanta said. "I am done doing that. I will never run again."

"Then you are an idiot!" Venic called. "If you do not turn around and leave right now, then you are the biggest idiot I have ever met. Go home, Valerlanta. I asked for a guide the forest, and you did that. You are not a hero; you are weak. You are nothing more than a thief with a few lucky tricks. The king will kill you in a blink of his eye."

Valerlanta said nothing, and so Venic gave up.

"I will not stay to watch you commit suicide." He snarled at her, his gaze filled with more rage than she had ever seen from him. Then he was gone; stomping off with the horse trailing behind him.

After all they had been through, he did not say goodbye, he did not even offer a wave, he just simply left and did not look back. The thief tried to appear like she approved of his choice, but really it just made her feel numb.

She looked at Alstred next, but he ignored her gaze.

"Do not look at me, now." He lectured, clearly forcing happiness into his voice, though it was still tight with fear. "What kind of person would I be if I let my little sister go into danger alone?"

"You are not my brother..."

"I am close as you will get!" He ruffled her hair, and she cringed away with a glare. "Now, there is no point in arguing, you know I am more stubborn than you are. Even if you leave without me, I will chase after you like a lonely puppy, so not a word about it!"

She wanted to tell him no, she wanted to convince him to follow Venic away from her, but instead she simply felt relieved that not everything would be left up to her, that she would have help.

Pretending not to care either way, the thief closed her eyes and nodded.

Both headed for the nearest inn; their hoods up high as they hurried down the streets. The people they passed were bouncing with excitement of the current celebrations, but to Valerlanta it felt like she was watching some sort of play. That happy world the people were living in seemed like a detached one from her own.

Horses now cared for in the stables, Alstred sat at the darkest part of the inn where light was less likely to make visible what they hid beneath their hoods, and she sat across from him; eyes trailing to the empty seat beside her.

Three seats, only two companions.

"We do not need him. " Alstred told her, as if reading her thoughts. His eyes also lingered on the chair, as if Venic were really there, but was invisible as a ghost.

"I am not worried." Valerlanta snorted, crossing her arms and pulling her eyes away from the chair. "If he does not want to be here, that is fine with me. He is just a coward, is all."

Alstred raised a brow, and the corner of his mouth attempted to pull up into a smile, but the tall blonde said no more on the topic as he took a slow drink of his ale.

He somehow looked older at that moment, as if what they were about to face aged him. For the first time ever, he looked the age he actually was.

His brow was pinched in pain or thought, bringing lines across his face that she had never noticed before then.

"So, what is the plan, then?" Alstred asked, his eyes quickly flickering around for anyone attempting to listen, but everyone else was leaning into their small tables while immersed in conversation.

"I can get us inside, and then all we would have to do is find the area." She leaned forward on her stool to talk hushed across the table. "The guild told me the army is not far away now; they might even be here by morning. All we have to do is be in the castle walls by the time they get here, then all of the castles attention will be on the army. The guild also said they would help so long as the danger to them does not get too costly."

"Val." Alstred started, clearly choosing his words carefully. "I trust you as much as anyone could, but curiosity is gnawing at me, and I must know; how is it that you know how to get in the castle?"

Valerlanta felt herself shrink as her posture failed, and her fingertip picked at the letterings someone carved upon the rough table. She had no way of reading it, and few people in this room would, but somehow she knew it was a declaration of love. "That is because we will be going in the very same way I escaped from once; through a passage in the dungeon. We will need a little bit of help, though. I would imagine that the exit will be caged shut now."

Alstred was frowning deeply at her, his eyes serious as all the pieces of her past started coming together for him. He ignored her attempt at a change of conversation, and continued instead "Why were you in the castle to start?"

Her finger stilled her nail right at the tip of a crudely carved heart.

Part of her wanted to push off the conversation as quickly as possible, but how could she expect to face the place of her nightmares if she could not even talk about it?

"I was a prisoner there; if you can call it that. My crime was being born from a mother that the father was not married to, so we were both left to rot." Her throat clenched and she swallowed hard to ease some of the tension. "There is no way I will forget the way out; I was there too long for that. I had almost forgotten to walk and was near blind from the constant darkness. The only reason I escaped is because of the king himself, and one woman who took pity on me." Her heart was quickening in memory, as the inn suddenly faded away, and all she could see was the cold stone walls surrounding her. Suddenly, she felt the need for fresh air; to be away from the walls that seemed to be closing in on her. "It was horrible, what he did. He had all the royals murdered in their sleep; most by their own servants, or so I was told. Then, as he ordered everyone else in the castle of adult age murdered as well, he drank the blood of the royals. He was not born with magic, but he did manage to steal it.

As that was happening, the lady who fed the prisoners knew who I was-but more importantly who my parents were- so pulled me out of the pit with a rope and pointed me in the right direction. I actually did not want to go. By that point, knew nothing else and I was so scared of the light that I panicked. She was killed, and I almost was, but I got out, and my new father found me." Her voice softened and an odd sort of chill came over her. Despite all her pain, despite her blurred vision, she smiled bitterly at the table.

"I suppose it is fate, after all, I am the last. It is funny, is it not? The one the royals never wanted is the one who has to save their kingdom. They are so ungrateful, and yet, in the end, it was their hatred that saved me. I survived, and they did not, only because they did not want me."

"You know." Alstred said evenly. "You know you have royal blood."

She took in a raspy breath of air. "I know. I have always known. My blood is royal, but blood is just the liquid in my body, nothing more. I am not, and nor will I ever be. I am a daughter of the woods, not a royal."

'I am scared.' She wished she could tell him. *'I am scared of him and even more so of that place, but I still have to go make things right.'*

Alstred was quiet for a long moment, and she took that time to try and get control of herself. Then a warm hand grabbed hers, and she looked back to see serious eyes finding hers. "It is not you who will fight, but *'us.'* You are not alone, Val. What kind of man would I be if I let you run off to save the kingdom with your skills alone? We would be doomed! Do not fear, I will take on all the important things, you just have to be there."

Somehow, she was able to laugh, and it broke the tension growing in her chest like a bird escaping from a cage.

As thanks, she pulled her hand away and kicked his shin from under the table. "You think you could get far without me? Ha! Do you really think all that heavy muscle helps you so much in battle?"

Alstred smirked and flexed his unhurt arm so that the big bulge of muscle popped up. "The ladies seem to think so."

As Valerlanta rolled he eyes, the inn keeper came and dropped off the food Alstred asked for. The aging man set it carefully between them, and said, “I hope you enjoy."

"We will." Valerlanta ensured.

He went to leave, but as he turned, Alstred suddenly grabbed him by the elbow.

"Do you have kids here?" Alstred asked bluntly to the inn keeper, surprising Valerlanta. She sat forward in her chair, her eyes pleading him to be silent.

The inn keeper puffed up his chest in warning, but hesitantly nodded. "Indeed I do. Why do you ask, young sir?"

With a frighteningly serious expression Alstred looked at the man carefully in the eye. "There is a storm coming, and kind men would be particularly wise to close early and seek shelter away from the storms reach."

The inn keeper paused; carefully reading Alstred’s expression, then nodded, said a curt 'thanks,' then hurried off.

"Why did you do that? What if he spreads the word before we can act?" Valerlanta asked.

Alstred shrugged. "Perhaps I have a soft spot for families."

Valerlanta frowned; thinking of the woman Alstred had married, but never had a chance to have children with. It was the future he nearly had, but never did.

She ate fast, then pushed her plate away and stood up. "I have some visits to make before nightfall, you best get some sleep."

Alstred nodded, and so she left, exiting into the fading sun.

A few hours; that was all she had until she had to act.

She could only hope that she had even the slightest of chances of this work becoming worth it.

* * *

"You are more than welcome to use the door, Valerlanta." The black market king said smoothly with one of his winning smiles.

"There would be little fun in that." She answered. "And besides, we both know we do not trust each other that much as of yet."

Her eyes settled on a particularly strange cat-shaped statue beside him on a windowsill, and the black market leader carefully slid it out of her reach.

"Too true, and yet, here you are, and to ask for my help yet again no doubt?"

"If only that was it." She tilted her head at him, eyeing every inch of his face. "You told him. You told the king where to find us."

Now he turned to fully face her, his brow rising quizzically as if shocked she would even ask. "Of course I did! When the king asks you a question, you do not refuse, you tell him straight out as quickly as possible to get his hot breath off your neck! My business is one that will not work under the harsh eyes of that man. One word from him and all those noblemen who purchase my goods will suddenly turn on me for the name of justice.

So what now, then? Am I to face the consequences by the hands of yourself and your large friend?"

Valerlanta shrugged and walked over to his desk, her hand running across the smooth wood that was polished more than any desk she had the luxury of seeing. Then, on a whim, she sat in the chair and was pleasantly surprised by how comfortable it was.

Askyel watched carefully as she leaned her elbow on one of the arm rests and regarded him with her head leaning on her hand.

She tried to appear cruel, and perhaps a little offended, but in reality she was not at all surprised by his actions; after all, if it were her in the same position, she would probably have done the same to him. It was the game they played in, nothing less and nothing more, and yet she had to pretend like she believed otherwise.

"I will figure out what to do about that later. Perhaps I may even have my father cut all ties with your...'company'. I told him I am working with you, so I would imagine when he hears what you did, he will not be too pleased. My father's guild always gives the same amount of respect they are presented with, after all."

His throat tensed at that, and it quickly became clear to her that his business was more important to him than his fear of anything she could do to him. He tried to smooth out his expressions, as if to make it appear like this was simply one of his business transactions. "So if it is not my head that you want, what is it you need? More horses? Or perhaps some better weapons?"

Valerlanta smiled, taking a quill and twirling it between her fingers tauntingly. "What I would like is the use of some of that exploding powder of yours."

That shocked him. He grew stiff with surprise, and clearly did not know how to respond to that request. "That is what you want? Why?"

"I need to get through iron. It will be thick, and of good quality, but I need to get onto the other side of it. I trust that you have the power to help me."

His eyes lit up, sparkling with sudden excitement as he caught onto her plan. The king of the black markets smiled darkly. "You know a passage into the castle."

Valerlanta nodded. "I know a passage into the castle."

Now he regarded her in a totally different light, as if his curiosity had melted away all his fear. Within his eyes, she could almost see his mind working out everything at incredible speeds. "What do you plan on doing when you get in, may I ask?"

She carefully ignored the question. "Do you have what I need?"

"Indeed i do, though I am afraid that to use it, there is more care needed than one would think. You will need the help of someone I trust."

"Fair enough." Again the quill spun between her fingertips. "I am still curious as to your motives for helping me, however. You are not a man to choose sides."

"Oh, but I do choose sides!" He answered with a devilish grin. "I am always on the side that will win, however, this is the one time that the future is fogged to me, so I cannot help but want to see it end. Can you defeat the king? I would like to know. The odds are against you, but then, they always are and yet you always win. You can call me a man watching a show, if you would like, but I cannot help but admit it; I am curious as to what the outcome will be when the greatest of odds are facing you."

"That is simple." She shot. "I will fight, I will win, and the fake king will fall."

"Good, then I have quite the show to enjoy. I do hope you know who I have my money on."

"I can make a good guess."

His hand reached across the table, and the fingers opened on the wood in front of her, leaving a rusted key behind. Then, before he pulled back, he snatched the quill from her fingers, and also moved his extras to the far edge of the table, out of her reach. "Then be sure not to waste my efforts."

« Chapter 17 »

As the light was slowly fading from the sky, two hooded figures hurried towards the castle with a horse and cart being pulled behind them.

'Quiet' was not a word that could describe that night, not with the many parties that could be found throughout the city.

Over-top of the 'clip clopping' of the hooves on the cobblestone, there was a constant roar of people, like the hum of bees circling a hive. Occasionally, they heard a close voice or laugh on the air, but for the most part, the two easily evaded the excitement that comes with tournament nights.

Even with the busy night, the two assumed that were more than less alone on this route, so when the smaller form heard a whisper that sounded like it was almost directly beside her, she nearly jumped off the ground from fear.

"Hurry!" The light voice said, causing Valerlanta to whip to the side, and find the place beside her empty. Eyes searching around, she tried to pierce the darkness, but saw no movement of anyone that could have been near.

"What is it?" Alstred asked, stopping with the horse to also look around.

"Did you not hear that?"

"Hear what?"

"The voice! It was right here, right beside me!" Even in the dark, she could see the brows of her companion raise.

'The elf queen; it was her!' Sucking in a breath, felt a sudden flood of relief and went to continue on, when once again she stiffened and carefully looked around the darkness of the town. The moon was bright enough in the sky to light up the darkened street with easy, but it still cruelly left plenty of shadows to lurk in, but then it was again.

It was no more than a swish of sound like the flutter of a birds wings, but it was enough to cause the thief to still in her step.

The taller hooded figure quickly followed suit, his hand slowly reaching into the depths of his cloak for a weapon.

Eyes straining to pierce the surrounding darkness, Valerlanta whirled after another flutter of sounds, and this time caught notice of a form she recognized.

"Father, stop this or i will put an arrow in the head of the next man I see." She told the darkness, and just as a living shadow would, he put her hand on her shoulder without her even knowing he was there.

Alstred swore and jumped away, much to the amusement of the others shadows in the surrounding darkness, who chuckled as quietly as a mouse squeaks.

Instead of being surprised herself, Valerlanta turned and wrapped her arms around him. He smelt like pin needles, moss, and everything else she knew and loved. His warm arms wrapped around her, but before she could allow herself to get comfortable, she pulled back into reality and pretended like nothing happened.

"Now then, little bird, this is your call; tell us what to do." Came his voice and Valerlanta felt a surge of pride, and also fear.

This was what she always wanted, was it not? To become part of her father's guild? To join up with him if only it was once?

And yet she only felt numb.

"Send some men ahead to scout; they cannot be seen. You know where it is we are going."

And her father did not question that, just whistled and wove a hand forward like a chop into the air, and some of the shadows moved, shooting forward silently like black cats on a hunt.

Then the king of the cats also did the same movement behind him, creating a full circle of thieves around them. There would be no surprises now, not without a fair amount of warning.

"Come, time to go." She said, and Alstred started moving again, with the horse snorting in agreement behind him.

As they went, Valerlanta took one last look behind her, as if expecting one last member of their group to appear behind them. He never did, of course, so instead the thief broke her eyes away from the empty street, and let her eyes look only forward.

They moved swiftly, and though she could not say it, the thief felt relief in the fact there was the blonde beside her, and her father close behind instead of having to do this all alone.

When we get in the walls, we will have to split ways." Valerlanta whispered to her father.

"Alstred and I have somewhere else to go, and you two will have to move like rabbits in order to get the treasure out before the battle locks you in."

"Hmmm. For the most part, that will work." He said, surprising her.

"What do you mean for the most part?"

What was she missing? She thought this part was simple!

"Well, yes my guild will steal, and yes my men will leave with those stolen goods quick as can be, but I will not go with them fully. I will stay in the city, waiting for my daughter. Someone will have to sneak you out after that secret mission that you dare not tell even your own father the details of, after all."

Valerlanta felt her throat tighten, but this time it was not with fear. "That is foolish."

"So is my daughter."

Irritation as well as love swelled in her chest. "Well, just do well not to be seen, and if I am not back by midday, do not wait for me."

Her father raised a challenging brow like he always tended to to when being told what to do, and Valerlanta nearly stopped as she was filled with a flash of anger.

"Do not wait!" She said again. "And do not dare try to come after me."

"Hmm." Was all he said, and Valerlanta sighed heavily in frustration.

Looking back over their surroundings, Valerlanta found they were almost there. One more corner now, and they would be there; at the place where her new father once found her.

She did not meet him just then, after all, she had already long since passed out from blood loss, and instead she met him in the forest.

She could still remember it; opening her eyes, and seeing the first light she had seen in a long time. The coming of the morning sun lit through the gaps of leaves, and hurt enough to look at to make her eyes weep, but was also incredibly beautiful. The leaves swayed in a warm wind, and a wonderful earthy smell filled her nose with every breath. When she tore her eyes away, he was there, sitting patiently beside her with a smile on his face...

Valerlanta stopped to grab some items and set them on the ground before she carefully struck her knife across her flint stone. The sparks licked the torch, and within moments, the dark alley was filled with warm light.

She was almost hesitant to pick it up, knowing that with what they were about to do, there would be no turning back. Still, her fingers wrapped around it anyways, and as she picked it up, eerie shadows were cast upon the buildings around them.

Nodding to her father, they rounded the final building.

Waiting beside a wagon was the castle wall. The castle had gotten overconfident in these days of peace, so the guards only passed this area a few times a night.

With a trickling sound was part of the drainage for the moat blocked by an iron gate. Due to an underground spring that spilled out from the tall mountain the castle was on, unlike most moats, this castle had free moving water, leading to several creeks winding through the castle grounds, and out through gates like these.

However, this gate was different. Although it looked the same, and if you were to look through you would indeed get a glimpse of the other side of the wall, it was what was IN the wall which was of most importance.

Valerlanta stepped towards the gate, about to move down from the path into the rounded waterway where her father had found her so very long ago, when a hair-raising hawk call broke the silence of the night.

Valerlanta whipped around in time to see solider spilling out from inside and under the cart, blocking their path to the wall. Instantly as they emerged, arrows rained from the shadows and upon the solider. They raised their shields, but some were too slow and fell dead. Alstred took out his weapon, but Valerlanta only removed her knife.

Despite the raining of arrows, the guards edged forward, pinched together into a human wall. They neared, and in response, several guild members burst from hiding to position themselves between the solders, and the leader they would gladly die for.

The solders came upon the guild members.

The arrows had to stop to avoid hitting their own.

The soldiers attacked.

Within moments, several guild members were dead, and within the panic, several more soon followed. Thief guild members were not supposed to be seen; they were supposed to lurk in the shadows and escape when things got tight; not fight head on with armoured men.

With a roar, Alstred simply flung some of the guild member's aside in order to take their place in the fighting. Confused by suddenly finding themselves on the ground, the thieves jumped up again to join.

Valerlanta took her advantage and slid down the stone bricks and into the waterway. Water seeped into her boots, and three enemies followed her. The first attacked with a high swing of a sword towards her head, and Valerlanta rolled under it. Springing back up, she ran up the waterways edge, and pushed off it while twisting in the air.

Landing on the confused solider, both of them fell, but only Valerlanta came up again with a bloody knife. The other two advanced, and Valerlanta had nowhere to go except backwards, and that was the one way she could not go.

She repositioned her grip on the torch

The soldiers neared closer.

With all the strength she had, she threw the torch. It spun in the air, above the startled solders.

It landed against the gate.

The explosion happened, and both her and the solders went flying back. Her head smacked back against stone on her landing, and there was a familiar ringing in her ears as she stumbled up.

In the unexpected blast, the thieves suddenly had the advantage. The thieves attacked the shocked soldiers, and all those above were taken care of.

That only left the two getting up from the waters in front of her.

Valerlanta lost her knife in the blast, but she had plenty more where that came from. Taking out a spare, she repositioned herself, ready for a fight.

They glared at her as they got up; the one had blood dripping down his face, making him look ominous.

With no warning, silvery sheen flew through the air and lodged itself within the furthest guard. Despite the knife in his shoulder, her remained standing, looking at the blade in shock.

Before the other had the chance to react, her father was behind him and slid his knife across his throat.

The last solider raised a sword, but his eyes went wide as he realized what her father had done; he had severed a muscle on his sword arm.

Like a blur, her father spun, his foot smacking the solider in the wrist and sending his sword flying.

The solider fell too, leaving her father to look around the area with an almost disappointed look on his face. "Pity. Is that all of them?"

Valerlanta smiled. "For now. Thanks for that."

He raised a brow, as if what she said was the most confusing thing she had ever said. "Of course! You are my daughter. Besides, this is the most fun I have had in years!"

Knowing her father, she doubted that last part. This was just a normal day for him.

Laughing anyways, she rolled her eyes and approached the wall.

True to what she asked for, Askyel did indeed blow the iron wall away; with a good portion of the wall.

Yes, she would have to ask for some of this powder once all this was done; she was very quickly growing to like it when it was not her it was being used against.

Oh the places she could get into with it... b

Inside the wall, Valerlanta squinted into the darkness, and there, between the castle grounds and outside world, was a narrow opening; only just wide enough for someone to squeeze through. Valerlanta went through first, and was quickly followed by a lineup of thieves.

A few held torches, lighting up the small tunnel, and just as Valerlanta thought, no one waited for them here. How could they know? As far as she told anyone; she was planning on getting in through the castle grounds; not through a secret passage no one knew about.

"Go ahead; be on the lookout for traps." She told the men, and they wordlessly did as she asked; knowing better than to question the authority of the daughter of their leader. They disappeared into the tunnel ahead, and Valerlanta and the others followed from behind.

"That Askyell betrayed us again." Alstred said and Valerlanta smirked,

"No, he didn't."

"What? Then how could of-"

"His assistant did."

Alstred gave her a surprised look. "The assistant?"

"When I met her earlier, I could tell that she did not look impressed to be having to deal with me. Then, when Venic and I went back to question Askyel, it seemed like he was protecting someone."

Alstred's eyes went wide with understanding. "She has been the one betraying us? Why?"

"To protect him. I suspect they care for each other a lot more than they are letting on."

Alstred smiled ruefully. "I will have spread that around when this is done. Sometimes shame is a very effective weapon for revenge. Who knows, maybe it will even bring them together."

Valerlanta smiled at Alstred's childish tactics, but it quickly faltered with her steps as she saw bones partially in the water of the tunnel.

"What is it?" Alstred asked, following her gaze.

"She helped me escape." Valerlanta said with a hard swallow. With all the rats and water, there was nothing recognizable about the woman anymore, but her face was still fresh in the thieves mind; covered in scars with a crocked smile.

She was the one who used to feed Valerlanta; and also the reason she was still alive. For whatever the reason, she took pity on Valerlanta, and helped get her out of the pit. When the men came to kill everyone, she fought like a wildcat; using even her nails as weapons to gouge eyes. It was because of her fighting that she was able to get them into a storage room and block the door. They were both injured, but she was much worse than Valerlanta. She opened the passage way, and begged Valerlanta to keep going when she fell and quickly died.

And here she was; still so close to freedom.

A warm hand was put on her shoulder and gently lead her away.

"We can come back for her another time." Her father said gently. "We will give her a real grave when we do."

Valerlanta nodded, but each step after that seemed like a step from the past.

She was wobbly on legs she had never used; and felt blood dripping from the gash on her back. The woman lead her onward; finding the strength to help little Valerlanta when she fell, even though the woman was death.

'I never learned her name.' Valerlanta realized.

She stopped again, but this time not because of the harsh memories, but because this was where the memories started. It was true that Valerlanta did not remember much from that age, but escaping; she remembered every moment of it. After all, it was the first time she had ever been out of her cell.

"It is somewhere here." She told her father, and he called his men back, and they all started searching the wall for clues.

"What is this place for?" A raspy voice asked. "Why a tunnel here?"

It was one of her father's men.

"I would imagine the rich once came down for interrogations and private executions." Her father explained. "This must be an escape for them in case this ever happened. Most castles have passages like these; though commonly only the servant's, looking for a quick way to get chores done, ever come to find them."

Valerlanta let her hand run over the smooth stone, feeling for any differences.

"i found it!" Alstred found, pulling out a long stone. Reaching into where it was, he found a rope; luckily kept dry in its sealed hiding spot.

Her father motioned to two men, and they started to pull on the rope. Within the wall was the sound of grinding metal, and the wall before them started to lift.

Inside was a storehouse filled with extra hey for the cells, as well as items for cleaning.

"Torches out." Her father told the men, and they complied; quick to snuff out the lights. Darkness crept over the room, and within the shadows, thieves moved for the door. A small stream of light came as the door was partially opened and a thief peeked out.

In a burst of movement, the thieves exited into the cellblock.

Inside there was no more than a gargle of surprise, then silence.

Valerlanta and Alstred with the remaining men followed, and as she entered, her feet froze.

The room was dark, after all, these were prisoners, so they would deserve no light, but her father and men quickly changed that as they entered with torches held behind them burning brightly.

"Get them out of here." Her father told the men, pointing at various cells. "If we are late, the guards will waste time trying to round them up. Point them in the right direction out the tunnel."

The men leapt to work, hurrying to various metal cells, and as they moved about the room, the darkness she had been staring at intently was lit up. With the light, a latched door on a floor came into view; and she knew what would be inside it.

There would be darkness.

There would be silence.

There would be cold.

Shivering overtook her as her eyes were transfixed on the item of her past. Suddenly her lungs tightened and her breaths came out in short gasps; she was suffocating in fear.

Somehow she was able to tare her eyes away, and though her back was to the cell, she could still feel it causing her heart to pound.

She wanted to go; to be away from here as soon as possible, but instead she put on a brave face.

"We need to go." She told Alstred as he came up beside her. "I need to go now."

He wordlessly nodded, and before anyone would say otherwise, she pushed her way through her father's men and up the stairs.

Bricks loomed over her and seemed to constrict over her, as if to swallow her up into the darkness. Her feet pounded the stairs, but the door always seemed to be just ahead, just out of reach.

Then she burst free, into the fresh air of a courtyard.

Where she was, people could easily see her, but as she stood with her hands on her knees gasping for breath, she decided not to care.

"Are you well?" Her father's voice whispered, gently grabbing her shoulders and guided her into the shadows of the castle.

She nodded. "I am."

"Then there is no time we can spare." He said. "My men have already scouted ahead; so there should be a clear path for you most of the way. Stick with Alstred, and come back fast. I will be waiting for you when you return. I do not know what you have planned, Valerlanta, but be strong. When you are, there is nothing that can stop you." His eyes grazed over her mask. "You are not weak, you never have been. Not even before you put that on. Now go, Go!"

He spun her around and shooed her forward, then waved his hands to urge her forward.

She took one last look at her father before he went to steal, and he took one last look at her before she went to what would surely be her death. Then, they both broke their gazes and did not look back.

"What took so long?" Alstred asked as they ran along the garden, side-stepping the bodies of guards laying in their path.

She still felt the chill of the past clawing at her heart, but she told him. "I lost myself for a moment, but I am fine now."

He frowned at her, but before he could say more, men came pouring out into the courtyard. One in the lead had the weapons of a guild thief, and Valerlanta knew instantly that someone had failed. Now, tipped off by the intruders, they filled the courtyard with well-trained speed.

"Stop where you are and throw down your arms in surrender!" Someone in the crowd yelled.

However, they had not even the slightest urge to comply.

"Go!" Alstred shouted, rushing towards a staircase onto the wall. She saw why, the wall had a door open into the tower; if they would make it there, they might be able to make it into the castle.

He took the lead, and Valerlanta was right behind as she knocked an arrow and fired it.

Upon seeing it, the men dove out if the way. The arrow missed hitting anyone, but they reached the stone stairs because of it.

Feet hurrying up the steps, they both ducked as arrows clattered against the wall.

"Stop!" The same man called. "Stop or you WILL be killed."

Reaching the top, they were just about to hurry into the open door when a man stepped out with a bow raised.

Both companions stopped.

A whistling sound came from above.

"In the air!" A solider called.

Valerlanta was only just able to turn her head in time to see an object flying towards them before she had to jump sideways, and Alstred down the stairs.

The doorway they were once standing in was smashed to rubble, some of which followed her in her decent.

Her back hit something soft, and then she fell through and landed on rock

Opening her eyes, she saw she was in an empty pen of a stable. There was a hole in the very old thatched roof that she fell in through, and light pebbles from the attack still rolled in after her.

No time to lose, she sprang to her feet with a hiss of pain, and raced through the stables. Horse snickered in surprise as she rushed by, but she was quickly gone as she vaulted out of an open window and was back out in the courtyard.

She had no way to get back to Alstred; the men were blocking her only path. They were scrambling now, some running to the walls to fight the attacking army, while others tried to figure out which of the two of them they should chase.

Alstred waited by the door for no more than a second, just enough time to see she was alive, then disappeared inside with men following at his heels.

They noticed her now too, but before they could act on it she saw an open window on the second floor of the castle. Running for it, she burst forward and walked up the wall as far as gravity would allow, then reached forward and gripped the window and swung herself inside.

She doubted any solider would be able to mirror her in their armour; they would be more likely to follow Alstred now.

She was in the bedroom of some noble; that much was clear. Clothes scattered the floor, and a chamber pot stood ready next to a canopy bed.

Luckily, no one was in sight, so she slipped into the hall while being careful not to squeak the door.

In the hall, the thief found herself in a world completely opposite from her own. Rich carpets softened and warmed the floor, and elaborate tapestries and framed paintings covered the walls. Everything was carefully decorated, even a door frame she saw with creeping stone vines and a wooden bench under a window that made it look like one was sitting upon the back of a resting unicorn.

Upon the air was the warm smell of herbs, similar in scent to what she sometimes saw nobles carrying with them in a small metal perfume ball. The only thing that seemed familiar to her at all was the light smell of smoke from a fireplace.

Although she refused to admit it to herself, part of her admired the careful dedication to detail.

Stepping out of her hiding place, she looked in both directions, trying to decide which way she should go.

Both sides of the hall looked the same to her, and neither had any clues as to which direction she was going.

Frowning, she went to take the path directly to her right, and was brushed with surprise as the voice came once more.

"This way!" A voice whispered from behind, startling the thief to a stop.

The hallway was dark, and with no one insight.

Valerlanta hesitated.

"Who is there?" She whispered.

"Hurry!" The voice only said, seeming as if hiding in one of the doorways ahead.

After taking one last look towards the hallway of her other choice, she decided to follow the voice, and did so at a brisk pace.

Doorways sped by, but Valerlanta had no time to use the care of a thief; she simply had to run and hope no one came out of a door and saw her pass.

"Over here!" The voice came as she neared another corner, and Valerlanta responded with a quick turn which lead her to a lesser decorated wing that had no windows to light her way.

She kept running.

"Down the stairs." It said, and Valerlanta complied, taking the stairs as quickly as she dared.

"There is a guard ahead! Hide in the shadow of the statue till he passes!"

Ducking next to the stone version of the king, the thief silent brought up her hood, and crouched lower so that her cloak completely melted her human form into the shadows as much as was possible.

Valerlanta heard the man before she saw him; the slight steps and a low whispering voice.

When he came into view, she saw the man was not alone. He had a woman holding onto his free arm, while the other held the lantern to light up the hall as they stepped.

The flickering golden glow filled the area where she hid.

Hand finding the metal of a knife, the thief knew the man would have no chance to both shake off the woman and grab his sword before her blade found him.

The woman's eyes flickered across the face of the statue, then they had passed, giggling off down the hall as their light was slowly replaced with shadow.

"Now!" The voice hissed, but the thief was already moving.

"Left!" Said the voice.

"Right." Said the voice.

Then finally the voice simply said "stop," and the thief found herself at a large set of double doors. A faint roar came from the other side that the thief recognized as voices.

"What now?" She asked the stranger, but this time, no reply came.

Slowly as can be, Valerlanta clicked the door open, and slowly slid it open towards her. No one was directly on the other side, but she heard a large group of people nearby.

A cool breeze tickled her skin, and the air smelt fresh with flowers.

The secondary courtyard? Was that where she was?

She had no time to find a better path.

She opened the door only enough to slip through, then darted for the nearest hedge.

No alarms were raised, and no arrows licked by.

She found herself a place where hedge was at her back as well as her front, then crawled on her stomach through an area where the leaves and rough twisting trunks left a gap.

The group was still a good few paces away, but were easy to see with their blazing torchlight. Even from where she was, Valerlanta could smell the mouth-watering scents of the food carefully placed on the tables.

Licking her lips, the thief broke her gaze away from the full tables, and let them instead slide across the faces of those surrounding them.

People dressed in tight and elaborate clothing surrounded the tables, all talking and laughing while apparently waiting for an invitation to eat. Banners for the tournament covered every inch of the garden, and there was even a bear on a chain. Music played from somewhere the thief could not see, and some even danced in tune.

There was an army outside their walls attacking their people, and yet these nobles were so confident in their king that they refused to call off the party.

It was enough to make her sick to her stomach.

Even a large group of soldiers- which she assumed would all be on the walls to fend off the army by now- stood in a group on the far side of the hedge filled garden.

They stood stiffly, as if nervous, and whispered conversation to each other through the sides of their mouths as if they did not want to be caught speaking. Armour covered their bodies, some with mail, and others with plates as well, but all wore the mark of the kingdom.

Following where majority their gazes lingered, she saw the fake-king.

In the flickering torchlight, the man looked just as frightening as she had ever imagined. He wore armour himself, but his shone like silver and was decorated with swirling gold trims. He looked older than she had pictured, with wrinkles around his eyes and grey in his hair, but the fierceness in his features made up for it.

The sight of him was enough to inflame the disgust, and turn it to rage into her belly.

Somehow, his controlling look only aided her anger. Even now, it looked as if he might turn dragon and devour the woman in front of him in a single bite, and the woman seemed to know that.

She kept making nervous glances to the king, while fidgeting with the object in her hands.

The thief felt her eyes go wide.

Askyel's assistant.

The thief reached for her bow, then stilled when she saw what it was that the assistant had; the puzzle ball.

"Well?" The king asked impatiently as Valerlanta shifted closer to hear what they were saying. "What have you found?"

"I-It is not reacting to anything I enter." The assistant answered. Setting away the ball onto a table, she instead brought up the key. "The men have to be missing a clue somewhere. There has to be a key hole! It would only make sense that this is what we need."

"My men have searched every inch of this place!" One of the soldiers shot, probably the leader. His chest puffed up, clearly not enjoying the fact that someone dared doubt his men.

Valerlanta slipped forward until she came out the other side of the hedge. Then, using the darkness and the garden, she crept forward and hid behind a smooth stone, which was more than likely the ruin of the ancient castle. It was cold, but she pressed herself further against it as she slowly rolled her head over slightly, so her eye peeked over the top.

"Then look again!"

"Why? To find nothing again? Do not use us as a way to get out of the fact that you have no idea what you are doing."

"No idea?" The woman huffed. "No idea?! I am the only one left who knows even a small amount of this language. Besides, you would have nothing if not for me. Who do you think trailed them back to their farm so you could get the objects? Because of me, those trouble causing miscreants are probably blown to pieces right now."

"Enough!" The king said before his solider could say more. "Arguing like children will get me nowhere."

Sliding her back across the rock, the thief peeked around and saw the ball only just a reach away.

Then bells started and everyone looked in the direction of the main city gates.

"They breached the first wall!" A man screamed from the tower. "They are in the city!"

Now the nobles were finally looking nervous. Some screamed lightly with fear, while others huddled close and whispered worriedly to their armed guards.

Using it to her advantage, Valerlanta reached around the stone pillar and let her hand find the puzzle-ball. The cool metal touched her fingertips, and she grabbed and pulled.

She had it! She had the ball!

Stepping back, she went to disappear; to slip into the shadows and go; when the body of he fake-king stiffened and whipped around with a hand raised.

Immediately upon facing her, a rage of flames leapt into the air and hurtled towards her.

Magic came to her without asking.

A wall of ice sprang from the moisture in the air, blocking the flames just in time for her to still feel the heat.

The fire stopped, her ice melted, and both thief and king stared at each other with wide eyes.

Magic; he had seen her use magic!

He knew what she was now! He knew!

Gasping, the thief turned and ran; springing over one of the ruins and stumbling over the short hedges.

"After him!" The fake-king screamed, clearly not seeing her face as well as she had seen his. "Someone bring me his head!"

She narrowly avoided the advances of two men-both armed nobles attempting to dive for her-by some quick steps, and then nearly stumbled as she saw the face of one of the guards standing there among the crowd of stunned onlookers.

He seemed to go by in slow motion, her eyes taking in ever strand of hair, every inch of his strong jaw.

Her breath sucked in, and she knew she was doomed.

As she pulled open the door, Valerlanta heard people coming after her, but did not look back.

There was no time for that.

Bursting down the hall she found herself in a high ceilinged room that let even the top floor look down through intricately detailed balconies, each with a thick curtain to close off the room in privacy when needed. A fountain stood as the centrepiece to the room, but Valerlanta did not pause to look.

Feet speeding up, she ran at the nearest wall and walked up as far as gravity would allow until she was forced to grab the thick drapes hanging down the wall, and used it to pull herself the rest of the way. The fabric groaned with the tension, but within seconds she was over the railing, and crouched low.

She heard the feet and the words of the confused men, and then they went off in several directions.

Catching her breath, the thief let her eyes fall onto the metal ball still clutched tightly in her hand. She should be thrilled that it was there-clutched in her fingers-but instead she could only think of one thing; Venic was there.

Venic was with the king.

Running a shaky hand through her hair, she squeezed her eyes shut and tried to slow her racing mind.

What was going on?

As she sat there, a tingling feeling spread over her skin and across her eyes. Her vision blurred, then faded to black.

Heart pounding, she touched her eyes and started to panic.

Then, from the darkness, came an image of a woman. The image was foggy, but Valerlanta could see she had silky hair and a perfect figure.

"It will not be forever." The woman's silky voice said, it's sound hauntingly familiar. "If the kingdom ever needs it, these items here can be used to turn things back to as they were." She took one of the items into a delicate hand, and even from the blur, the thief could tell it was the sword. "Your sword is one of the items, and it will come with us to our new castle. The other two will be placed elsewhere in other castles who have kings that would never give the other the power without great need."

"Or if the kingdoms are overtaken."

"If it ever comes to that, only someone with your bloodline can use magic, and only someone with magic can unlock the vault. If the case may come where the need is dire, the items will be the key to;"

The image faded away, as if she was not strong enough to continue talking, and maybe she was not.

Either way, Valerlanta understood.

She had to get into the vault; and there was only one way to do that.

Grabbing her bow, she looked at the carved wood, and ran her fingers over the smooth texture. As she did, she pictured the forests, and when she breathed in, she tried to smell pine needles and damp soil.

Then, she went to go get captured.

It did not take her long to find soldiers; and as she came around the corner and found them, she was forced to dive into a doorway for cover.

"Wait!" She called around the corner. "Tell the fake-king I can open the vault. He will not get in if I am dead!"

She heard murmuring, but no one came to flush her out

Was it working?

"Come out." A voice said. "Come out slow and you will not be killed."

Swallowing hard, she readied herself by shaking out her hands.

It was either now or never.

Getting up, she rounded the corner and was not shot, was not cut down, she was just stared at.

Archers pointed arrows at her through tense bows, but she was not shot down.

Instead a man- the one who she recognized as the leader-walked towards her with a rope swinging from his hand.

Raising a brow, Valerlanta willingly put her wrists out.

« Chapter 18 »

Back in the garden, back in front of the king, Valerlanta swallowed her fear and glared right into the eyes of the man looking to make an army of magic users. He stared back, then a twitch of a smile pulled up at his lips as he gestured to someone behind him.

Alstred was there, tied up with a knife to his throat. Blood was already streaming from a shallow cut in his neck, and bruises covered his body, but none of his wounds looked deadly. Despite all the danger, the blonde smiled slightly when he caught her gaze. His eyes sparkled, as if glad to see her.

"Who are you?" The king asked, as he strode towards her. His eyes looked her over as well-muscled arms folded behind him.

"A thief from the forest." Valerlanta said with a smile, and received a warning squeeze on her shoulder from the man holding her. Luckily, his anger hid the movement of her pulling a knife from his belt. She tucked it far up her sleeve.

"Answer properly to your king!" The guard hissed in her ear.

"Ohh...." Valerlanta tilted her head as if she had just heard something silly. "He is not my king. In fact, he is not anyone's king."

She saw the muscles on the man in front of her tense, but he managed to keep a straight face.

"And what do you mean by that?" His deep voice asked calmly.

"What I mean is that I know exactly who you are; and a royal is not one of the words I could use."

The others in the garden laughed as If she were insane, but there was one who did not. Khon stared on at her, and she caught a glimpse of hidden anger shown only by a slight twitch under his right eye.

She was getting to him.

"I can do magic because it is in my blood to do so." Valerlanta called out, and that made the crowds silence. "It is in my blood like it is supposed to be; not stolen like it was for yours!"

Some of the guards whispered to each other, most were silent. They wanted to see what the king would do to someone who spoke so freely.

Without so much as a flinch, king Kohn raised a hand, and the knife on the throat of Alstred pressed deeper.

Blood dripped down his neck and the blonde flinched.

"You will not get what you want without me!" Valerlanta yelled. "And if he dies, nothing is exactly what you will get."

This time, a small smile pulled up the one side of the kings lips. Victory sparkled in his eyes, and Valerlanta realized how much she hated him.

His hand dropped, and the knife obediently loosened only so slightly.

"You think you can open the puzzle...?" The king said, a mocking tone on his voice.

"I know I can." Valerlanta said. "I have done it before; it is how I knew where to come."

Her eyes searched the crowd, but she did not see the face she was looking for. Venic was not among them.

"Very well, then show us!" The king gestured to the people around him. "Show us all what you can do, then."

Her arms were freed, and the puzzle-ball was once again placed into her hands. It hummed with life, ready to do what it was made for.

Valerlanta took in a breath, and was only just about to do as she was supposed to when something caught her eye on the ground. On the huge stone circle on the ground was three simply juniper berries.

A smile neared her lips.

Clicking the puzzle into place, she entered the code. Instantly, the ball split in her hands and the glow pointed directly into the center of the circle. Stepping over it so that the line of light was pointing exactly downwards, the thief put out her hand.

"I will be needing that key now."

The king said nothing. His eyes glared on at her, clearly not impressed that she had made a fool out of him. He was underestimating her, and it was a good thing.

She would already be dead otherwise.

He looked on at her for a time longer, then nodded to someone and the key was pressed into her hand.

Valerlanta locked eyes with Alstred.

His expression begged her not to do it; to just let them both die.

The key entered the light of the ball, and got stuck there. The magic held it in as if it were inside a keyhole, so, Valerlanta turned it.

The ground rumbled, and people cried out. Everyone near backed away as the light from the ball seemed to be soaked into the circle. As if it were suddenly a liquid, the light followed the engraved swirls and markings upon the stonework, until the whole display was alight right under her feet.

Without warning, the light within the ball went out, but the glow remained under her feet; as if all the energy had been transferred.

Suddenly the stonework under her feet began to shake and creak. Startled, Valerlanta stepped back just as a crack appeared in the stone. It grew; splitting the circle in two as the stone was somehow being pulled away under the ground.

Hurrying off the moving circle, the thief watched as the last of the circle disappeared, leaving a huge hole in the ground. Peeking over with several other people, Valerlanta saw the hole went further underground than she could see. A covered staircase with carefully crafted pillars circled around the outside of it.

Where did it lead to?

She wanted to know.

The king showed up near the stairs and glanced down. He had several guards with him, otherwise Valerlanta would have just pushed him right where he wanted to go. The thief doubted either of them could create a magic that would save them from that sort of fall.

Greed glimmered in the old man's eyes.

"Hang them." He said as if that were the simplest thing in the world, and then started his way down the stairs, followed by many soldiers.

Those who remained turned on Valerlanta; readying to grab her. The thief eyed the one holding her bow, but then ripped her eyes away to the one trying to pull Alstred to his feet.

Grabbing the knife they did not see her steal from her guard, she let it fly from her fingers. It struck the man holding Alstred in the shoulder.

Taking the advantage, Alstred jumped over his ropes on his wrists so his hands were in front of him, and stole the man's sword and cut him down.

With a roar, Alstred charged at the other men.

Luckily for Valerlanta, one of the first he cut down was the one with her bow. She scooped it and her quiver up and also started taking down man after man.

"Go!" Alstred called to her.

She looked at him in surprise. "Are you mad?"

Alstred cut down another man; using his size and strength against the other men. "There is no time for this! If you do not go now, it will be too late. Everyone will be dead. I owe you this, please go! Go!"

Valerlanta hesitated then reluctantly nodded. Pulling her bow over her shoulder, she broke from the fighting, ran to the pit, ignored the stairs, and jumped.

Her clothes rippled in the wind and her stomach leapt.

Hitting the railing of the staircase, she whirled around and pushed off again, aiming for the railing on the next side.

Before she hit the third, she saw the king and his men blur by.

They tried to hit her with arrows as she went, but she was falling too fast.

No one tried to follow her using her way down.

Feet hitting the bottom, Valerlanta landed in a kneel then shot forward through the open door.

When she did, she found herself on a balcony overlooking a forest.

The room was larger than any she had seen. Lush emerald trees flowed for miles, and moss and vines climbed up the blanketed she stood on. Somewhere, she heard water trickling, and somewhere within the thick canopy of leaves, birds were singing.

Awe swelled her heart.

It was a world under a world.

At least finding where to go would be easy.

Looming over every other tree in the forest was the largest of them all. Even from here, it looked taller than any castle tower she had ever seen. It brushed with the roof, hiding whatever light source was feeding these plants.

Hurrying down the stairs, the thief disappeared in the green stilled.

Not long after, the king appeared.

Instead of the amazement she had felt, when his eyes looked over the green expanses, only greed glimmered there. Just as he had hoped, he pointed at the largest of the trees.

She waited until the group stepped down the stairs, then disappeared on their journey towards the tree. It was only when her area had grown quiet again that she stepped out of the trees and nearly stepped right into the man standing there.

Clearly, even she made mistakes.

"Well, what do we have here?" The man hissed and two of his friends joined him. "If it is not our little so called Royal. Why not show us some magic, princess?"

"I would-," Valerlanta said, backing up. "-but I am trying very hard to save my energy to kill your fake-king."

His face contorted with rage at that. Him and the others lifted their swords, and Valerlanta knocked an arrow.

"Do you think you can shoot us all before we can get to you?" The man asked.

"Yes." Valerlanta answered. "Yes, I do."

Before she had a chance to prove it, Venic burst from the trees and his blade drove clean through the back of one of the men. Her arrows easily took down the other two. At such a close distance, there was no way of the them surviving the hits.

Breathing hard, Venic stepped forward. "I hate running."

"Hello to you too."

"You got my message?"

The thief nodded her head, then looked over the man who was in completely new Alecaven armour. She thought of how, despite everything, Venic refused to talk back about the king. "As soon as you knew we lost, you went back to his side?"

"Yes he answered." Looking uncomfortable. "But also no. I think he found my return amusing so accepted me back without any questions."

"So you have the life back that you wanted."

Pain flashed across his eyes. "Valerlanta, you should not be here. Go, go now!"

"Why? Just so you can try and kill the king and take the power for yourself?" Valerlanta felt her eyes narrow, then rushed past him. "I do not have time for this!"

"I am not going to let you go alone!" He followed her, his sword at the ready. "Believe it or not, I am on your side."

"Then I suggest you should be ready for a fight." She glanced back at him, her eyes looking into his, as if hoping to find the strength she needed there. "Even if I have to go through you to do it, I am going to kill Khon and destroy this place or die trying."

"You will not die. I will not let you." Venic told her. Something like anger flashed on his eyes. "I still need your help to get out of this place."

Valerlanta at that she gave him the a gift of the smallest of smiles, then picked up her pace.

Her feet sprang over log and brush as if she were born doing do.

Leaves blurred by and branches scraped past her face.

'I am almost there.' The thief thought in her mind, though she doubted the elf queen could hear her. 'You had better not have lead me here for nothing.'

Of course, she got no answer.

Venic somehow was able to keep up with her as she picked her way through.

The forest opened up, and Valerlanta found herself at the base of a monster of a tree. It was easily three times the height of the one in

Palenwood, and easily the same wide. Not even with ten people hand-in-hand could you circle the trunk.

Roots spread across the ground like a tangle of giant snakes, and directly above was a healthy green canopy large enough to house thousands upon thousands of birds.

"Amazing." Venic answered.

Valerlanta could only stare.

There was no sign of the army yet, but it was hardly surprising. With so many men, it would take much longer to traverse through the thick brush.

"We need to get to higher ground." Venic suggested. "These roots...we can use them as cover. You go up the highest vantage point and take them out with your bow. I will hide further down right there, so I can flank them when they get close. It is our only chance."

"The king will use magic on us." Valerlanta warned. "Stay far away from him. I will handle him if I can. Once we start fighting, most the army will likely take cover. They will not know how to fight me."

Venic nodded. She went to turn away, but suddenly he grabbed her by the elbow, turning her back to him. He looked into her eyes, seeming to search for something there, then just as quickly, he released her and urged her onward. "Go, now, quickly. Before they get here and see."

Valerlanta hesitated, looking his face over carefully, then broke away before she could change her mind. Now was not the time for such thoughts.

Walking upon roots easily taller than any horse, the thief zig-zagged her way further and further up until she jumped down into a tangle of roots. She could not help wondering if this was how an ant felt at the base of a normal tree.

Pulling up her hood to better blend into the shadows, she peeked over the mossy wood.

So far there was nothing.

Stealing a glance to where she knew Venic hid, she saw him waiting; his hands nervously flexing and tightening on his sword. He we keeling down and pressed against a root; invisible to anyone coming the same way they did.

"Any tips would be great." She whispered to the elf-queen. "Any at all."

Of course she got no response. Perhaps it was because even the queen knew Valerlanta was a hopeless wager now. It was two people against an army; in the queens position, Valerlanta would give up too.

Valerlanta let out a shuttering breath, and flexed her fingers on her bow.

Then they came.

Through the break in the trees, Valerlanta saw the first man.

Slowly, the thief grabbed an arrow and knocked it into place.

Somewhere behind her, a bird tweeted cheerfully; unaware of the coming blood.

Shaft sliding along her fingertip, she pulled back and, slowly as could be, she leaned over the giant root.

Her fingers itched to release.

The target fully stepped out of the brush, and others followed. She had to wait; wait until they were somewhere where it would be too late to run for cover.

The man came closer.

The arrow flew.

Her hand shot and knocked and fired another arrow as her eyes watched the target fall. The second hit the one directly beside him.

The men lifted their shields and neared closer.

In a swipe of steel, Venic burst from his hiding spot and took down a man. The others turned to face him in surprise, giving Valerlanta the chance to let more arrows fly.

Men fell, but not enough.

They had to kill as many as they could before-

A ball of fire soared towards her.

In a gasp, the thief jumped from her perch. She felt the heat of the fire as she rolled down the hard roots.

Debris came down as she rolled right onto her feet.

The king was there, surrounded by his people.

Another ball of fire hurtled towards her, and the thief narrowly avoided it by ducking into the cover of roots.

Burning branches and leaves went every way.

He was using the surrounding trees to help fuel his attack.

As she emerged again, an soldier appeared right over top to attack her.

Kicking him in the stomach, she forced him back.

He recovered, his arms flexed.

Her arrow flew, and seconds later he fell.

If she was counting correctly, then she only had three left.

The thief had to act now.

Bodies littered the surrounded ground. Hopefully it would be enough. If the thief failed to defeat the king, perhaps-with this many men dead-Venic would have a chance.

Pulling her bow over her shoulder, the thief called on magic.

The air seemed to ripple around her, and goose-bumps rose on her skin as the magic tingled across it. The sounds of war faded to silence.

Men charged at her from many sides.

Valerlanta slammed her hand into the ground.

The ground rolled in waves under her touch, and from the dirt shot roots. The lengths shot forward and were unstoppable. They ran clean through some men, and knocked over others.

Then they met fire and wilted and curled to a stop.

She had cleared a path between herself and the king.

The men who had seen what occurred now backed off in hesitant steps back.

Valerlanta glared at the king, and he stared right back; confidence glittering in his eyes.

She wanted to change that.

Once more pushing her magic into the soil, the roots shot for the king. If they reached him, they would cut holes into his body.

The thief looked at him carefully, wanting to see when fear showed there.

Instead, all she saw was his lips curl into a smile.

His hand lifted.

White fire exploded.

The blast splintered the roots and burnt them to dust, and it kept on coming.

Men screamed and ran.

Valerlanta stepped away and felt her back hit the roots.

Heat waved across her skin and grew hotter as the flames burst closer.

Without a moment to lose, she slammed her hand into a rock at her side. It changed form; shooting forward to shield her in a half-dome of stone.

The heat hit and she pressed herself against the rock as the heat waved over the edges of her shield.

Then her shield broke.

Tossed backwards, the thief hit the roots of the tree and tumbled away. Her shield of rocks went with her, and pelted both the thief and the dirt around her.

Luckily, she was thrown to the dirt, and the rest of the flames flew over.

It stopped, and the thief grunted as she moved. Some of her skin ached with burns and bruises.

She gingerly stood up again.

The king was still there, smirking at her even as he stood near the burnt skeletons of his own men that he burnt alive. What men he had left now edged away.

The battlefield was only big enough for two, now.

Ignoring her new pains, the thief emerged from her covered hideout, and approached the king.

"Do you know what the problem is? Do you know the answer to this riddle is?" The king asked, eyeing her with amusement as she neared. "How is it that you can hardly compete with me? The answer is in your blood, and now it is in mine. The secret is that you have the magic of only one person-yourself-and I have the magic of over ten more. You cannot win against me."

Valerlanta stretched out her arms which now ached as if the fire were still upon them. "Yes I can."

He laughed. He dared laugh right at her, as if she were simply a jester of his court. "Child, you know I am stronger than you."

"Perhaps." She smiled. "But I do not know how to give up, unfortunately for you."

The flames came again, but this time Valerlanta was ready.

Before the blast could reach her, the thief pulled moisture out of the air and when she put her palms out in front of her, the skin pressed against a wall of ice. The flames ate at it, but she kept feeding into it. No matter how much the king melted away, she replaced it.

Her arms started to shake, but she continued.

Then the flames stopped.

Hands sliding down the ice, the thief gasped for breath.

The king was distorted through the king ice; he paced back and forth; his image changing with each step.

"You cannot keep it up." The king said. "Look how pale you are already! Magic has already started taking its toll, and I have not even started yet! Give up. Maybe, if you are good enough, I will even allow you to join me."

Sliding her bow off her shoulder, she took it in hand and eyed at him down an arrow. Her tensed arm shook with tired muscles, but the thief ignored it as she stepped around the ice to get a better view of him. It was true; the older man did not even look fazed even though he had been using far more magic than the thief. "Not a chance."

"Very well, then. Your body will do will to help fertilize the soil here."

The soil moved, and the thief ran.

Using her trick against her, the king put magic into the soil and sent it after her.

Valerlanta ran along the roots; jumping off as the magic came to get her.

Rolling across the soil, she let an arrow fly. Instantly, a root jumped to block it, and the arrow sunk into the wood.

The thief kept running, the roots chasing her.

Magic tingling across her fingertips, the thief let another arrow go. It sprung forward, carried by a hurricane force of wind and gained speed with every moment it flew.

Again the king was able to block the arrow, but this time it was imbedded in the root halfway through. The point of the arrow was inches from his eye.

Noticing this, his smile faded and he shot her a level glare.

He was clearly not having fun anymore, so to help him make up his mind, the thief gave him a smirk.

The heat came instantly.

Eyes wide, the thief watched as her ice shield came up to save her.

This time when it faded, the thief was barely staying on her feet.

If this kept up, even if the king did not kill her, the use of magic would.

Leaning against her shield, she eyed the king.

Something vibrated under her feet.

Eyes wide, the thief jumped away, just in time to avoid a group of roots.

They turned towards her, and Valerlanta ran.

The thief hurtled behind a rock and crawled backward as the roots struck the dirt only a finger space from her toes.

One arrow left-barely enough energy for magic-and a growing doubt that she would be able to trick him again. Any plan she went through with; he would not fall for again.

Trying to catch her breath, the thief peeked over the rock.

The king was not there.

Panic skipping her heart, Valerlanta leaned fully around the rock, and was thrown into the air. The rock she was using for protection slammed into her.

Rolling across the ground the thief came to a stop on her stomach. She just barely found the strength to lift her head.

Everything hurt.

Warm blood dripped from her brow and over her mask into her eye.

The king looked at her as if she were a bug he had just squashed underfoot.

"Oh, do not get up on my account!" The king said as she tried to bring an arm forward. "I am pretty knowledgeable on making people hurt, and I imagine you are hurt pretty bad right now. About three bones broken, if I am not mistaken. The two you might be able to ignore, but the broken arm? I imagine that using that bow of yours will not be as easy now."

Bow. Where was her bow?

The thief tried to rise, but all she could manage was to roll onto her side before pain took her breath away.

She saw her bow not too far away-just at the base of a tree-but to the thief now, it seemed like an impossible distance to get to.

King Khon took the ball from one of the men, and approached the tree. He was not going to kill her, and with growing horror, Valerlanta realized why. He wanted to keep her alive so he could drain her blood for her magic.

The king was joined by several people; more of his army coming from the direction of the stairs.

That could only mean one thing.

Regret ate at her heart.

Alstred. There was no way the tall blonde would have let them pass if he was still alive.

Gasping with sudden anger, the thief used her good arm and gingerly pushed herself off the ground. Every movement hurt as the thief staggered to her feet. Just standing took the greatest of efforts.

Her knees shook and threatened to collapse.

'Alstred.'

She started towards the fake-king. The regally dressed man worked his way up to the tree until he was at the trunk.

Ball in hand, he turned the key opposite from how it had been before, then around in a circle one last time.

Instantly, a light came from the direction on the stairs and entered the clearing. The glow was traveling through the roots of the forest; causing the snaky spirals to glow eerily as it neared its goal. As it reached the mother of all trees, the glow took over the tree and made every vein show a clear white. The complex knot work of veins all around the tree showed vividly, and when it did, the ground started to rumble.

The magic that was once in the ball-the magic that opened the first door- it was now being used to open something else entirely.

The very trunk of the tree started to pull apart down the very middle. The ground was shaking violently as the split grew, causing Valerlanta to collapse to her knees several times.

No one cared to notice her as she pathetically crawled her way upward. She caught a glimpse of Venic, and he pointed at the king and spun his finger around in a circle.

She nodded.

As she climbed, the split in the tree grew, and as it did, it reviled a beautiful woman with elf pointed ears. A soft white glow held her in the air, also causing her black hair to float around. Her eyes were closed, as if she were only sleeping.

It was the elf queen; the one that had been visiting Valerlanta in her mind.

The king let the ball drop from his hand and did not care as it bounced down and away in the roots.

Next, the king reached to his hip, his hand reaching for the dragon-sword.

Valerlanta knew what would come next.

She pushed herself harder, but someone got there first.

Using his uniform to blend with the other men, Venic was able to get up close to the king. He charged at the king from the side and brought his sword down.

The king only was just able to block the attack by pushing it off with the thick of a root. Venic cut through it, and immediately went for a second strike; lunging the sword forward.

Again he was deflected.

The king smiled.

A burst of flames came forth; engulfing Venic in the light.

Valerlanta attacked from the kings other side, and dug her knife in deep. The king whirled on her, and she too was thrown backward. In last seconds before she was hit, Valerlanta was able to bring up her ice-shield to take most of the hit. The left over force slammed into her, and as she was tossed in the air like a rag doll.

As it hit, she noticed something. The touch of magic tingled on her skin, and felt familiar.

Then the ground came.

"Was that really worth it?" The king asked as the thief attempted to roll off her stomach.

"Well, I am a thief." She flipped over, showing she had something in hand.

The sword.

She had used stabbing the king as a distraction to cut it from his belt. Him blasting her back made him not notice the change.

The thief smiled.

His eyes went wide then contorted with rage. She rolled and a burst of flames hit where she had been only moments ago. The blast sent rock and wind in all directions.

The force of the impact hit her like a punch to the gut.

As it sucked all air from her chest, she realized something.

If only she had found it out earlier.

A solider came and ripped the sword from her hands and kicked her as she made a pathetic attempt to reach for it.

Pain, there was so much pain.

As the man walked away, the thief opened her eyes and found herself looking at her bow.

Somehow, she was able to make herself reach out and take it into her hand, and then once again, stand up.

The last arrow came into her hand.

Tension went to her bow, and her broken arm burned in pain.

The arrow flew, and the man carrying the sword fell forward.

"Was that really necessary?" The king asked. "I have more men, and now you are out of arrows."

Valerlanta limped to the sword and picked it up. It shook in her grip.

She pulled it from the sheath, and turned to the king.

The other men with the king had no doubt had word with those who watched the fight, because now even they backed off hesitantly. All were watching the masked thief approach the king.

"Why are you even trying?" The king asked, watching her and letting her bring the sword closer; most likely so that he would not have to go down and get it himself. "Why even bother? You are losing. In fact, by all eyes, you have already lost. No one would blame you now if you chose to lay down and wait for death."

Valerlanta smiled at him. "I am not dead yet."

"You might as well be." Raising his hand, a burst of white fire came towards the thief. She felt the heat of it and knew this hit would kill her. Putting up her hand, she tried something that would more than likely kill her. Instead of shielding herself against the magic, she opened herself to it.

Flames covered her-surrounded her-but she did not get burnt. Instead, the flames danced happily around her as her skin shimmered with the protective coating the fire gave her. Moving forward in the flames with her hand forward, she neared the king.

Eyes wide with horror, the regally dressed king backed away from the filthy thief. "How?"

Limping pathetically, Valerlanta came up until they were facing each other and completely eye to eye.

"It was never your magic to wield." Valerlanta said, and then slammed her palm against his chest. The reaction was instant; the king screamed as a white like swirled out from where she touched, and snaked around her hand before plunging within her bruised and bloodied skin. Forcibly, the magic was ripped from his body.

It was leaving quickly; eagerly searching for the blood it was supposed to be paired with all along.

She could feel the energy of it enter her body like a wave of warm water.

When it was done, when the king had no more magic left to give, he crumbled to his knees. His hands rose up, and he stared at the palms and flexed his fingers.

No magic came.

"No." He said. "No, no, no! It was mine! It was mine!"

"It was never yours; you just stole it." Valerlanta said. "Trust me, I am a thief, I know these things."

Screaming in rage, the king dove at her, and both rolled down the roots. They separated and to their feet. The king reached for a knife on his belt, but found the sheath empty.

Now she had both sword and knife in hand. "You really are a slow learner."

"Kill her!" The king said, turning to his men. "Kill her!"

A man stepped closer; a man with short hair and a high-ranking looking uniform, but did not near Valerlanta. His unsure eyes danced between the two of them. After all, from the day of being born, all in the kingdom were told that only those with magic could truly be royalty.

No one else moved.

Howling in anger, the king slammed his fist into one of his own men, and stole the sword there. New weapon in hand, the fake-king charged at Valerlanta.

Bringing up her sword, Valerlanta deflected the blade and swept in with her knife. The blade ate at his shoulder.

Screaming, the king swept another blow.

He was stronger than her with the sword, and they both knew it.

Valerlanta readied to use magic, when suddenly the king stopped. Hands still in the air, the man looked down and saw a silvery tip peeking from his chest. Dark red started spreading over the folds of his expensive silks.

The man who did it stepped back, showing the face of the high-ranking man.

Fake-King Khon staggered.

The sword of his highest ranking soldier remained in his body. Screaming, he was able to give strength again to the sword over his head.

The weapon came down at her.

Valerlanta moved faster. Her sword dove deep.

He gasped and wavered.

Giving the sword one final push, it went deeper. His eyes glazed over.

He fell backwards and hit the ground hard. Two swords stuck through his body.

Her whole body swayed as the thief looked on in disbelief.

The fake-king was dead.

Remembering, she looked around for Venic, and saw him approaching the elf queen. His sword was in his hand, and was dripping with blood; his blood. Horrible crusty black burns covered majority of his body.

"Venic, stop!" Valerlanta called.

Ignoring her, the spy looked up at the elf face and simply stared, his sword clenched tightly in his hand.

The spy wanted power; more than anything, he wanted power.

"Venic!" Valerlanta screamed in horror. Her hand shot up, ready to call on magic and strike her last friend down. "Get away from there! I will not let you!"

He looked down at her, his eyes swimming with emotion.

Instead, he tossed something in from his other hand.

The puzzle-ball landed at the queen's feet, and with a bright white light, the opening started to seal. Ever so slowly, the queen was once more covered in bark, taking the only way to opening it again with her.

Venic waited until it was completely closed, watching all his hopes for revenge disappear.

Then he fell.

Body rolling down the roots, his sword was tossed from his hand.

Valerlanta hurried towards him.

The swordsman came to a stop near the bottom, and somehow again staggered to his feet. His head bobbed, his face hidden by his hair.

He neared, and collapsed in her arms. They both fell to their knees.

His head was limp against her shoulder.

She felt warm blood and burnt skin against her fingers.

"We did it." He rasped.

"We did." She answered.

His arms encircled her, and his fingers gathered up her clothes and held tight; as if scared she would disappear. She held him back, tears welling in her eyes.

Then he fell.

The swordsman collapsed side-ways, and when she helped guide him down onto his back, he did not move.

Nor did he move when she crawled forward and held his jaw in both her hands and gently stroked his burn covered face.

"Wake up!" She urged. "Wake up!"

He did not move.

"The army is almost through the wall." The general said softly, clearly not wanting to disturb her, but having no choice. "We have to act now."

All the other men neared closer, suddenly waiting for orders from the thief they had very recently tried to kill.

Valerlanta did not look at them; she only had eyes for the fallen knight.

"Announce our surrender." She whispered, and a murmur of shock rippled through the crowd. "Do it now; we cannot wait. Go quickly before more people die without need."

She heard movement as people went to do as she said, but some stayed, waiting.

"What of you, miss?"

"Go with them."

"I cannot do that."

"Go."

"I will not. I refuse." Came the furious voice of the general. "All this time I have been serving the wrong soul, and I must atone for that. I can do nothing other than protect you; so, I ask again, what of you?"

Her fingertips moved from the swordsman chin and rested on his strong chest. "If I survive, carry me out. Take me to the dungeon, and a man waiting there will see to the rest."

"If you survive? What do-" He was cut short as her hands started to glow.

She put everything into it; she put every ounce of energy and magic into Venic.

Warmth turned to icy cold on her limbs.

Energy turned to an overwhelming urge to sleep.

Bloody wounds sealed and blackened flesh became new again before her very eyes.

Her teeth clenched with the effort.

Then, the magic stopped, and her hands that were once on burn and blood was now on perfect skin. Her body swayed, but she urged herself to stay awake.

She watched his face intently.

A finger twitched.

Eyes opened.

Valerlanta smiled and tears started flowing down her face. "Venic."

"H-How?" His hands rose up, clutching her shoulders as if not believing she was real. Then suddenly, she was pulled against him and he was holding her tightly.

The world was fading in and out but she did not care.

Happy tears kept coming.

Then, in his arms, she saw something. It was no more than a faint glimmer in dirt and root, but the shine of it caught her eye.

"Treasure." Valerlanta murmured bitterly.

Then the warm hands of darkness carried her away.

« Chapter 19 »

The thief could feel herself being carried.

She could feel warmth on her skin as something wrapped tightly around her, and heard the splash of footsteps in shallow waters.

There were voices; faint and few.

A cold wind.

Then her eyes opened and she saw sky of a rising sun as a cart started moving.

Looking around, the thief saw many of her father's men, as well as the general of the dead king who had promised to help her. Her father was not in the cart, but she suspected he would be close; somewhere in the shadows watching over the escape.

Venic was beside her, his sword in his hands. He was alive; and had bare patches of skin where wounds were.

At her feet lay Alstred.

His face was pale, and his eyes closed.

Slowly, Valerlanta attempted to sit up. Her limbs shook as violently as grasses in the winds of a storm, and pain from her broken and bruised bones took her breath away. Venic grabbed her elbow, helping her up until they were sitting shoulder to shoulder.

He looked relieved, but she did not see his face for long. Her head rest against his warm shoulder, her eyes staring at the blonde.

"Is he dead?" was all she could manage to ask.

"He is on the near edge." Venic replied. "He was a one man army, but now he has to decide on if he wants to visit his wife in the afterlife. There is nothing we can do to help him now."

Valerlanta let her eyes squeeze shut, fighting away all the tears that wanted to form there. "I can-."

"No." Venic shot firmly. "You cannot. Even I can see that using any more magic would kill you."

Valerlanta stilled with defeat. Even she knew that magic would be impossible; but it felt horrible knowing that she had the power to help, but was too weak to try. "If he passes, he should be buried next to his wife."

"We will head there first." Her Venic said.

Good. Alstred deserved no less.

Shaky hand reaching up, her fingers found the ties of her mask and let the leather pull free. Her bare face felt naked without the worn strip of leather, but she did not need it now.

By tomorrow, whispers of the sole-surviving noble of the surrendered kingdom would be the most common of news, and her mask would no doubt be one of the largest of details. The new king would no doubt look for her, and the mask would be one of the first things they would want to find.

She let her hand -and the mask with it- fall at her side. Her eyes stared at it for a long moment, and then she was startled as fingers worked their way around hers. Two hands held onto the person she once was in a final goodbye.

"You could have stayed." She told him. "You could have just surrendered to the new king, and there would have been a high chance of you keeping your position."

"I could have." Venic agreed. "I could have, but I chose not to."

"You are an idiot." Valerlanta shot.

He chuckled, but suddenly lost is; as if he was too pained for such happiness.

"And what-." Venic took in a breath, as if having trouble with what he was about to say. "What will we do if...if Alstred meets with his wife?"

Valerlanta let her eyes find the blonde, thought of what he, and also she, wanted. She thought of all the pain she went through, but also the bonds she made and the amazing sights she saw.

Before she could answer, the military leader who was helping her escape shifted closer and held out something towards her in two hands.

The dragon sword.

"I grabbed this before we left." The man said, his eyes deadly serious. "As well as the royal seal ring. Both are rightfully yours and no one else's."

Her shaky hand lifted, and found the white leather of the grip. "Adventures are unfortunately addicting." She answered, taking it from the man.

He smiled, and from beside her, Venic laughed, a soft but pain filled chuckle.

"Yes, they are." The swordsman agreed.

The wagon rolled on, heading quickly though the last of the dark of night. Not far from them, cheers rose up as the army received word of the sudden surrender.

Acknowledgments

The Purest Blood would not exist if not for the help and support from all my friends and family.

Thank you to my online pen-pal Victoria Smith for being there with me from the very start and for being my first beta-reader. I also have to thank my family for always being there to cheer me on!

A special thanks to all my beta-readers, and also my sister for her extra help.

And finally, a special thanks to Meghan Wood for finding all my little typos and mistakes.

Thank you everyone!

I hope you enjoy Valentina's adventure!

Chey

Made in the USA
Charleston, SC
18 May 2016